Whitewater Opera
DEATH COMES TO THE ALLAGASH

by

JACK O'MARA

Whitewater Opera: Death Comes to the Allagash
©2011 Jack O'Mara

ISBN: 978-1-936447-48-0

Designed and Printed by
Maine Authors Publishing
558 Main Street, Rockland, Maine 04841
www.maineauthorspublishing.com

This novel is dedicated to those currently in harms way in Iraq and Afghanistan. They are the real warriors who wear the mantle of leadership on a daily basis and provide us with the basic freedoms we so often take for granted—including the right to say what's on our mind.

Author's Note

Stories are like teeth in England—everyone has at least one and most people have several. *Whitewater Opera* is not so much about the alpha males in life who innocently lead us into peril. Rather, it is about those for whom the mantle of leadership and courage is often thrown upon their shoulders whether they want it there or not. The led become the leaders . . . or often die trying. This book is about them and their daily courage, not just to survive, but *to prevail,* as Faulkner would say.

The names and characters in this tale are fictional. Any resemblance to people you might know is sheer coincidence. The names of the actual locations have been changed to protect the trout. Anywhere in the Maine wilderness you may find the same beauty, the same challenges, and the same potential opportunities for the leaders and for the led.

PROLOGUE

A solitary green-eyed deerfly buzzed noisily above the flaring black nostrils. It then dove quickly toward its target—the lower jowl, now dripping with saliva.

The massive black bear seemed oblivious to the insect's bite. It, too, was eager for a desperately needed meal before the June sun heated the forest floor and made both the large and small predator seek comfort in the shade. The bear's senses were heightened almost to a frenzy. It had been weeks since it had had an opportunity for a real meal. Beechnuts, rotten from the winter snows, and young alder shoots were hardly adequate for a 500-pound black bear. The putrefying afterbirths, which the bear had inhaled in several quick greedy swallows, left it still hungry for one of the young fawns or even the mother, weakened by the recent multiple birth.

The bear, too, was in a weakened state and would need another easy meal. Months of rest in its winter cave had barely healed the injury to its hindquarter, which was severely damaged by a hunter's bullet the prior fall. *Brute*, as it had been aptly dubbed by the many hunters who had sought it as the ultimate trophy bear, now limped awkwardly down the beech ridge, sniffing as it went. In his prime, Brute could outrun and take down a young bull moose. Now, small squirrels and voles were a challenge. But a young fawn or a doe compromised by a multiple birth—that would be a meal worth pursuing, and one badly needed by a bear still hunting for his first spring kill.

Brute worked the air. His thick black nostrils flared repeatedly as he sought to confirm a direction. Toward the lake? Toward the swamp?

Toward the cedar ridge? In the distance, Brute could hear a sound he did not like.

Two SUVs all but raced down the last vestiges of the *Golden Road,* an ironically named pothole-filled logging road, which barely justified the reckless speed of the confident drivers.

"We're almost there; I can smell the water. Those trout better be nervous because I'm hungry already," Butch announced with his usual certitude. The passengers in the back seat of the Jeep were far less confident. They were more concerned about surviving the ride, let alone the adventure they were all about to face in the Maine wilderness. Little did they know how justified their fears might be.

Brute hid his hulking black frame just out of view in the alder thicket as first one and then another Jeep whizzed by. The trail of pale yellow dust and pine pollen stirred up by the intruders filled the roadway. It seeped into the alder thicket and into the crevices of the bear's huge black nostrils; it confused the bear in his important, almost desperate search for food. When he was certain that there were no more human sounds, he crept cautiously toward the edge of the road. There were too many immediate smells and too few distinct ones. He could smell the humans. He could smell their food. He could smell the Jeeps' exhausts. However, he could no longer smell the doe or the fawns. He worked the air again and again. It was no use. The smell was gone. He could not find any trail across the road. Reluctantly, Brute returned to the ridge he had just descended, now just content to find a few errant beechnuts or a brown-nosed vole ready to be his lunch.

Eagle Eye

Oh my God! she exclaimed to herself. *This is amazing!* In fact, it was more beautiful than she had ever imagined. As far as she could see in any direction, the lake was a motionless sheet of blue spun silk. One minute it was a translucent mirror. The next it was a soft, barely perceptible blue. The shifts in color were almost indiscernible to those who didn't pay attention to such things, but Ellen noticed everything. She liked to notice everything. After all, she was an artist or liked to think of herself as an artist. The subtle, almost miraculous shifts in color fascinated her. First, they were almost a rumor of blue, then gray—insinuating rather than announcing their hues. The lake was a dreamlike, seamless calm she had not expected or ever seen before. Little did she know she might never see it again.

Ellen Jensen wondered if her brothers or dad had ever noticed how beautiful it was to be on a lake in Maine—the exquisite colors, the delicate fragrances, the bird songs that were rarely heard or noticed in suburbia. If so, they'd never shared their impressions with her. They always came back from their *guy trips* smelling of dead fish and farts, shouting about the moose they saw or laughing about something stupid that dad had said or done. It wasn't fair that girls didn't get to go. Her dad had always invited her, but Ellen knew her brothers too well. Even though she had loved them all, she knew what they'd be like on a five-day fishing trip. Ellen's mother knew, too. "Honey, we'll do some *girl things*. We'll have fun, just like the boys." Sadly, Ellen's mom was already seriously ill, and as much as she tried to do those girl things with Ellen, it was already too much for her to handle.

Eventually, her dad couldn't leave either, and the boys were soon old enough to go on their own. Ellen often thought they went fishing just to get a break from their mom's ever-worsening health. After her mother died, her father rarely talked of fishing, rarely even went out for a walk. He had his baseball games to watch and beer on hand to help him cope with the poor pitching of the Red Sox once again, but as the announcers would often say of the players, dad's "head was not in the game."

Ellen's mom and dad had had their first date at Fenway Park. It was something in the family blood, perhaps. They loved their Sox…and they deeply loved each other. They loved being together. Win or lose. But her mom's death was the ultimate loss for both Ellen and her dad.

For a moment, Ellen had forgotten the lake and its delicate mirror finish. She had forgotten her newfound friends. She paddled her faded green kayak—a cheap lawn-sale special—in a slow, totally mindless fashion, drifting back into a past she often tried to forget.

"Holy shit! Look at that eagle! Grab your cameras, quick!" shouted Butch from the lead canoe.

Ellen snapped out of her trance and looked up. Flying only fifty feet directly above her head was the most beautiful bald eagle she had ever seen. In fact, it was the only bald eagle she had ever seen, but that made it all the more spectacular. Its wingspread was massive. It must have been seven feet from tip to tip. Ellen was amazed that it looked just like the eagles in the magazines and in the Audubon drawings she'd studied many times. Its gold curved beak and white head were so pronounced that even she could have yelled to everyone, "It's a bald eagle!" She wished she had. She wished that she had noticed first. For someone who noticed lots of things, she was rarely the one to shout out about something so cool. She'd get her turn soon, she hoped.

The eagle quickly passed astern of her, gliding upward in the ever-warming morning air and barely moving a single feather to coast along the edge of the thermals. The seven-year-old female had a hungry mouth to feed back in its nest just south of the dam. It scanned the surface of the lake looking for a wounded salmon or togue that had been foul-hooked or injured in a battle with a fisherman earlier in the morning. Injured fish tended to swim near the surface, often rolling with their bellies upward. The light reflecting off their silver or cream-colored sides would announce to the eagle that a free meal was at hand. Neither the mother eagle nor her fledgling in the great gray nest below the dam cared that the fish was an easy and unchallenging meal. Another meal was another day the young eaglet and her mother might survive.

Ellen, Butch, and the others gazed in amazement as the eagle made her dive. The great brown wings were working now, outstretched to the fullest and cupped to catch the air in a backward braking motion. Razor-sharp talons reached out and down, raking just below the water's surface. The salmon must have shuddered at the quick, sharp jab of the embedding claws, but the massive brown and white form barely slowed in its swoop over the water. For one brief moment, the eagle seemed to juggle its catch as the salmon gave a last desperate flip of its once powerful tail. Then the eagle again soared directly overhead to make its way back toward the dam.

Because her now stationary kayak had drifted toward the northern shore, Ellen quickly rotated her shoulders and her paddle to the south to follow the eagle's path. Although she was generally a well-coordinated person and prided herself on her athletic ability, the movement of her upper torso was unfortunately followed by too much rotation of her lower half as well. The enthusiasm of the moment and her previous daydreaming had caught her off guard. Her kayak had what the person at the lawn sale called good *secondary stability*. As long as a paddler was moving forward, the kayak was very stable, and as Ellen had wrongly concluded, she'd always be moving forward. *That's what the thing is for, right?* she'd thought when she bought it.

The combination of her overextended arms and weight shift caused the kayak to roll hard to starboard. A seasoned paddler would have corrected the shift in a second, and Ellen herself would soon learn to make such subtle corrections. However, the grace that day belonged to the eagle. Ellen rolled the kayak beyond the point of secondary stability.

Even as the knowledge of her imminent dunking raced fast-forward in Ellen's brain, the sheer panic of having a wet head and ruined hair initiated a remarkable physical reaction. Much like the mother who jumps a fence to rescue her child from an angry dog, Ellen, too, displayed an otherwise inexplicable set of reflexes. Instinctively, she thrust down with her left hand on the paddle, which caught the hull amidships. Similarly, she pulled up quickly with her right hand. The leverage from the paddle and the lift from her high-necked life jacket pulled her torso up and out of the water before her head or even her face had gone under. Her kayak rolled back up with a smiling Ellen clinging cheerfully to the gunnel.

The rest of the group cheered in amazement. Not a single curl or eyelash was wet. Her Mary Kay dealer would have been proud. Not even a Technicolor tear for an otherwise embarrassed paddler. Ellen treaded water in both triumph and shock. It wasn't how she wanted to start her trip, but it was so funny—at least for her compatriots. In the lead canoe, Butch and Angelo roared with laughter. At one point, Butch thought he would splash Ellen with his paddle to spoil her Cover Girl look and her victory, but even Butch was too proud of Ellen's accomplishment to ruin the moment.

Sean Padraig O'Casey, as always, had his camera at the ready and busily snapped shots for posterity. O'Casey couldn't help noticing just how attractive Ellen looked at this moment. Her big smile and auburn curls stood out in remarkable contrast to the now wet life jacket, which framed her face as she bobbed above the surface. The broad smile never faded, even as she blushed with embarrassment. She laughed, and they laughed. She smiled, and they smiled. It was a triumph of sorts that they all shared.

Everyone knew of Ellen's difficult childhood, of her mom's death and her dad's alcoholism. She was perhaps the most popular and even-tempered member of the group. Although she rarely talked about her past, the others knew. For someone who could easily have been accused of being a "pretty girl" who did not like to have a hair out of place, Ellen did not flaunt her good looks. And now she just laughed, both *with* her friends and *at* herself. They all laughed. In fact, they roared. It was one of the funniest things any of them could remember.

Finally, the laughter subsided. It was clear that Ellen was getting cold in the early June waters of Nellios Lake. Both O'Casey and Butch shouted instructions to her as she struggled to get back into her kayak. Given its complete lack of flotation and the possibility that the cheap kayak could actually sink, they all decided that she should simply swim the fifty feet to shore while O'Casey towed the kayak to shallow water, where it could be safely bailed out.

Ellen was glad that she had brought lots of extra clothes. Right then, she was even more happy that the waterproof duffle bag she'd recently bought at L.L. Bean's and stowed in the bow had kept her clothes warm and dry. She worked her way very deliberately up the shore and into a nearby thicket to get into her dry clothes and take a quick pee. She would have gone in the water, but she was already mortified about having capsized and was afraid that someone might guess she was urinating in the water. Besides, peeing in her water-soaked jeans would have been almost unthinkable. She'd never be able to wear them again. She was shy in many ways, and modest, too. Even if the entire camping gang were women, she would not have changed on the shore, and she would certainly never take a pee in front of anyone, ever.

A simple task like changing clothes or getting a little bathroom privacy was not as easy as she thought it would be. The alders and small cedar trees grew fairly thick by the shore. As determined as she was to gain complete privacy, she was equally reluctant, almost terrified, to get so far from the water's edge that she couldn't find her way back. The fear of getting lost in the Maine woods, and particularly her lifelong fear of bears, terrified her beyond words. Caution won out just slightly over modesty. Ellen found what she thought was a secluded thicket on the nearby ridge. She quickly removed her pants, relieved herself, and changed into her dry clothes.

From his seat in another kayak, Jason Foxworthy looked back, straining his eyes for a quick glimpse of the onshore activities. He smiled briefly as the combined efforts of the sun and a puff of morning breeze parted the alder canopy. The soft light only served to make Ellen's delicate white skin and thin legs even more statuesque as she dressed. Though she lacked the classic beauty of Tiffany, who was paddling ahead in the first canoe, Ellen had a quiet beauty and class that was never more elegant than in that soft morning light…though Jason hardly cared about elegance as he stared briefly before anyone noticed his voyeuristic glance.

"Smooth move, huh!" yelled Ellen as she emerged at the water's edge and began to wring out her dripping jeans and sweatshirt.

"Welcome to Maine!" shouted Butch. He and O'Casey were the only ones from Maine. Actually, O'Casey was not *from* Maine, even though he'd lived there much of his life and went to high school there. Butch constantly reminded him that if your grandparents weren't buried somewhere on the back forty and your parents didn't go to the local grammar school, you really were from *away*. O'Casey hated that term and the fact that he would never really be "from Maine." In fact, he was rarely mistaken for a Mainer although he could do a better Down East accent than almost anyone and could make anyone chuckle over his classic Maine stories.

Granville "Butch" Chapman III loved the fact that he was from Maine. He loved everything about the state. He loved his family heritage, the fact that his father and grandfather before him had been first selectmen in Peckham's Notch, a rumor of a town just north of Cornville. While it took him years to get used to his Christian name, *Granville*, he loved the nickname Butch. It fit his stocky, muscular frame, he thought. Although he was only five feet nine, his bulging biceps and pecs made him appear larger and more formidable. Somehow, too, he thought his name gave him a rugged, masculine edge. He always loved the sound of that name, especially when the girls used to call out the cheer for him at nighttime high school football games. "Give me a B. U. T. C. H.! Give me a B. U. T. C. H.!" he recalled with great fondness. While school was hard, football was easy; and it was football that got him out of high school and into college. In some ways, college was easier for him than high school. He knew he might never have graduated from high school if he were not so good in football. Principal Hoffman loved him. Butch made the school look good, and Mr. Hoffman helped make Butch look good. Almost everyone but the principal's wife called Hoffman "The Penguin" because, as the kids said, he had a fat ass and waddled…like a penguin. Still, Butch liked the guy and knew that without his help, he never would have made it out of chemistry, let alone into South Memphis State, his alma mater.

He knew Memphis wasn't a great school. He'd always hoped to play at a high-profile Division One school. While it wasn't exactly D One, it was pretty high-profile, and he'd even been scouted by the pros, which was both his own dream and his dad's. But it was tougher than he ever expected playing college ball. Being a five-foot-nine-inch, 220-pound linebacker at a Maine high school was something special. He wasn't really tall enough for college ball, but he was a brick. No one could stop him. He had every quarterback in the state for breakfast. At Memphis, getting blocked by a six-foot-eight-inch, 300-pound tackle with a bad attitude from Florida Southern was a different matter altogether. Colliding with that human freight train cost Butch a knee. With a third and final ACL tear, Granville Chapman III would never become a professional football player or college *All American* as he and his father had dreamed, but he would become a teacher and coach as his mother had hoped.

He came home to Maine, and briefly, even back to Peckham's Notch as a history teacher and freshman football coach. But even his biggest advocate, Principal Melvin Hoffman, couldn't stop the rumblings in the community that young Butch Chapman was far too "interested" in a senior cheerleader who liked cold beer and hot young men. So at twenty-five Butch was glad to leave the rumors, and, sadly, the young lady. Getting a solid reference from Mr. Hoffman was no problem. Nor was it difficult to get a coaching position in southern Maine. Butch wasn't much of a teacher, but he was one hell of a coach, and that's what they were really looking for at Welton Academy. In five short years, Butch became the Class B Coach of the Year. Four years later, he became Welton's principal.

Butch smiled as his mind wandered back in time. His canoe paddle glided smoothly and slowly as he thought about his early days as a teacher and coach. Those were good years. Unlike Ellen, Butch could paddle for hours and never have to pay attention to what he was doing. The Maine woods and the lakes and streams were an extension of who he was, just as football was almost instinctive. He didn't need complicated defenses to stop a quarterback. Butch seemed to operate on the lowest portion of his brain stem—all reflex action. He was not a deep or profound thinker. He didn't have to be. He had been given an innate, primate-like intelligence. Howard Gardner might call it *natural intelligence*, which allowed Butch to operate at an almost unconscious level. This was not a bad thing or even a demeaning attribute. He could be kind, generous, and even sensitive when he needed to be, but Butch functioned best at the reflex level.

He lived at that level now, just gliding along, leading a party of friends deep into the Maine wilderness. He paddled and glided, thinking of rolling brook trout hitting a number 16 caddis dry fly. By comparison, the other former football player on the trip, Jason Foxworthy, was still thinking about the sun reflecting on the creamy white thighs he had spotted through the alders as Ellen was pulling up her panties.

The canoe glided along under the strong but unconscious J stroke Butch applied as the stern man. He just loved the outdoors and especially enjoyed his designation as a Master Maine Guide. Butch loved the "master" part. He had actually worked hard to become both a guide and later a *master* guide. He was at peace in the woods, the streams, and on the lakes. While he enjoyed making money on the side as a hunting and fishing guide, what he loved best was just what he was doing right then, leading a party of friends into *his* world. While they all shared a common bond—all were principals out on summer break—they all came from radically different worlds.

But they had chosen to come to *his* world now. His alone. While O'Casey might have shared a different view of that opinion, having done a great deal of canoeing and fishing himself, Butch had the confidence that only a master guide can have …or at least that was how Butch viewed the matter. Tonight, there would be little fireside talk about the things they often discussed at conferences, like student assessments, guided reading groups, and standards-based education. God, did Butch hate that crap. No, tonight they'd be talking his language. They'd be talking about the Maine woods and about shooting the rapids below Nellios Dam, better known as "The Cut." Butch hadn't told them about the rapids or what it would be like, but he knew they'd make it and then love to brag about the terror and the fun. He couldn't wait. However, had he known what was in store for them, he would not have been nearly as anxious to get there or as confident that he could bring the group into and out of the wilderness…alive.

Kashunk, kashunk, came the sound of Angelo Capelletti's paddle as it started to scrape against the hull of the canoe. It was a fifteen-foot L.L. Bean Penobscot "guides' choice" canoe and the love of Butch's life. "For Christ's sake, Angelo!" shouted Butch as he awoke from his daydreams. "Remember what I showed you. If you keep your hips square and your elbows away from your body, then your paddle won't scrape against the hull. If we were fishing for salmon or brookies right now, they'd be diving for the bottom and you'd be hungry tonight."

While it was true that Angelo had rarely looked as though he were hungry, he had lost a great deal of weight lately and was no longer the "chubby cherub," as Butch liked to call him. Instead, his face had developed a gaunt, rather sickly hue. Butch had been surprised at how hollow his cheeks looked and how his eyes had lost their characteristic sparkle. Butch had purposely insisted that Angelo join them on the trip. "The wilderness will do wonders for you, Angelo. It does for me," he had told his friend.

And perhaps that would be true, Angelo thought as he tried to perfect his stroke. He wasn't bothered by Butch's harangue. He had known Butch for many years. He knew Butch almost too well. He knew the cockiness, the "I'm a Master Maine Guide" routine, and even the occasional smugness that some people saw in Granville Chapman III, but he tolerated it all. Angelo liked Granville Butch Chapman almost from the beginning, and for good reason. While Butch was not a great administrator from an intellectual standpoint, he had the one attribute that Angelo admired most in a principal: he loved kids. In part, that was because he was still a kid himself. Earlier in his career, his interests had been juvenile, almost sophomoric—sports, beer, and occasionally, an eye for pretty women. In many ways, Butch had never grown up and didn't really want to. That juvenile vision of life made him a fun person to be around, but it had also cost him a marriage. Somewhat reluctantly, Butch learned to balance a youthful attitude with professional responsibility.

As far as his students were concerned, Butch was a great principal. They always came first. He was fun when it was appropriate to have fun, but he could be almost brutal to kids when he was serious. He could make the toughest kid in the school cry in five minutes when he needed to do so. He had a look that could kill, but he had a jar full of candy, a warm heart, and a willingness to forget the transgressions of the day before. He would often goof around with the kids, juggling or playing Frisbee. He was the only one in the entire school who could do thirty handstand pushups while leaning upside down against the wall. That single act of strength and masculinity bought him more respect from his blue-collar alternative ed. kids than from all the psychology 101 courses he could have taken in college, had he ever been able to pass them.

Angelo couldn't do a single handstand pushup and had never even tried to, but he had great admiration for Granville Chapman nonetheless. He would always be indebted to Granville for the unwavering support he had shown for Angelo shortly after he was hired as a music teacher at Welton Academy. Almost everyone from Superintendent of Schools, John Reardon, to the parents quickly became impressed with Angelo's passions for music and for teaching. Unfortunately, support for Angelo was not unanimous. A new school board chair, Katarina Parokeet, disliked the superintendent and all his hires. Parokeet was a nasty little woman who rarely liked anyone. Fewer people liked her. As the author James Dickey once described a similar person, "She was a pleasant superficial human being, but with the rage of a weak queen."

Parokeet hounded Reardon to death. Eventually, he quit in disgust. Parokeet then hired a druid with a thin gray beard and coal-black eyes, a guy by the name of Steadman to do her bidding. Mr. Steadman did not like Granville Chapman, and he especially did not like Angelo. Parokeet's son Kenny learned the lessons of hate and intolerance quickly from his mother. By high school he had honed that intolerance to a dagger-like sharpness. Kenny, like his mother, saw Angelo's gentleness through a homophobic lens. Only the strong support from Granville Chapman, the music boosters, and a take-no-prisoners attorney had allowed Angelo to survive Kenny's accusations of *flirtation* by Angelo. They all knew Angelo; most supported him strongly. It hurt to hear some staff say they were not surprised that Angelo was *gay,* as though it were a crime worthy of dismissal. However, the more common belief in Angelo's innocence was based upon how well everyone knew Angelo and how well everyone knew Kenny. He was a lazy, nasty, ruthless punk.

Angelo struggled over the painful memories and struggled over the near loss of his job. He was a great teacher and a fine person. Everyone knew it. The teachers knew it. The students knew it. Even Kenny Parokeet knew it and resented it. The superintendent and board chair tried to go for Angelo's throat and almost got there. Almost.

Angelo knew he had to leave Welton Academy, much as Granville had left Peckham's Notch. Rumors and small towns are not fun, whether the rumors are based on truth or on lies, as was the case with Angelo. His good friend, mentor, and boss, Granville Butch Chapman, had convinced him to take a job as an elementary principal in Newton, New Hampshire, only forty miles from Angelo's hometown of Manchester. It was a move he never would have made on his own, but it was one he was glad he had made. He owed much to his good friend and mentor.

And now, Angelo sat proudly in the bow of the sleek green canoe, thinking how lucky he was to have such a friend.

"For Christ's sake, will you pay attention to your paddling!" yelled Butch, half seriously and half in jest. Once again, Angelo smiled and then started to laugh a hearty, self-deprecating laugh. He turned with his broad, almost cherubic grin and said, "Sorry about that, Chief."

Angelo used to call his friend "Chief" whenever there was a group of teachers around. It was a lighthearted show of respect. Today, Angelo thought the nickname fit Granville's demeanor just fine, especially here. He *was* their Chief today, their leader. He was taking this tribe of educators into the Maine woods "to learn about life," as he had promised one night at the Black Rose Pub in Boston.

Few, if any, of the paddlers were thinking right now of the impromptu party that had brought them all together this day. Each would have had a different memory of that night in the pub, a different story of how they had all agreed to come to Maine, and a different understanding of what they would experience. None of the seven principals could have imagined or foreseen what they would encounter and how the trip would affect each of them...forever. If they had, most would have turned around immediately in terror and dread.

FAWNED MEDICINE!

The first mile of paddling was easy. There was little wind, and although the black flies were finally starting to find the necks and legs of this moving picnic, it was not the feasting black flies that were getting the attention. Only O'Casey and the Chief were in good physical shape. O'Casey could probably paddle for hours without stopping. The Chief could paddle for days. The longer and tougher the trip, the tougher Butch got and the better he liked it.

That was certainly not the case for the others. Although Angelo was a rather clumsy paddler, he enjoyed being the bow stroke in the lead canoe. He was pleased that, while his hands hurt, his arms did not. What he did not fully understand was that Butch had as strong a stroke as one might find in the Maine woods. He had competed in many canoe races and had won both single and doubles competitions. His J stroke was strong enough to move the fully loaded canoe forward at a brisk pace with or without Angelo in the bow.

O'Casey, in the next canoe, had a stroke almost as strong as the Chief's, but he had almost twice as much gear on board. Somehow, the two coolers mostly full of beer and ice, had ended up in his canoe. He was not exactly sure how that had happened. Hell, it was Jason Foxworthy's beer, anyway. O'Casey liked beer, particularly a good ale or stout, but he'd never dream of bringing two cases of beer fifty miles into the Maine woods for a fishing trip. A single bottle of Irish whiskey would be more than enough for a whole week, and it could easily fit inside his bedroll. In fact, O'Casey had packed a bottle "for medicinal purposes," as the Irishman was wont to say. But lugging what O'Casey referred to as a portable frat party in his canoe had seemed just about insane. Unfortunately, Foxworthy had whined about his lack of canoeing experience versus O'Casey's many years in the wilderness. *Fine, you drunk,* O'Casey had thought but never said. *Leave your f-in' beer at home and paddle your own canoe. Or better yet, stay home. We didn't even invite you. You forced your way into this trip in the first place.*

Unfortunately, O'Casey didn't want to look like a whiner himself, because he hated whiners and had spent an entire lifetime sucking it up when things got tough. So once again, he sucked it up and leaned into his paddle just a bit more.

However, his bow mate, Maria, also felt the heavy load. In fact, she *was* that heavy load, or part of it, and she knew it. She was also embarrassed that she was not doing a good job, quite literally, of carrying her own weight. And like O'Casey, Maria Consuelo Lopez y Gonzales was far more likely to suck it up and pull someone else's load rather than whine. She actually had a sign in her principal's office that said, "No whining spoken here." Maria could be very tough when she needed to be. Having grown up a poor Mexican American near Waco, or, as she called it, *Wacko,* Texas, she had learned as a little girl how to fight for her very survival. For a while, she was beaten up almost every day at the *gringo* school. It was only when she literally fought back and gave the playground bully a fat lip that she finally gained some respect and some distance from the teasing and bullying.

Still, it was her nature to get along. Her cheerful disposition and positive attitude were hallmarks of who she was. However, she was even better known, loved, and respected for her beautiful voice. Almost every day, a student or teacher would beg her to sing in their classroom. Her superintendent would often, quite literally, put her on the spot at a board meeting or school concert. Once during a tour of her school with the governor, her superintendent turned to Maria and said, "Serenade us." Fortunately, she could always see it coming and had so many songs in her head that singing was a joy and not a chore. It was her confidence builder. While she was insecure about so many things—her weight in particular—singing on command was a "positive pressure." It taught her how to handle other pressures and stresses. She was the ultimate survivor.

Now, even as her hands began to blister and her shoulders ached, Maria paddled along Nellios Lake, smiling with great joy despite the pain. She was enjoying her first morning in Maine doing something she'd dreamed about for a long, long time.

In the remaining canoe, there were few smiles. Jason Foxworthy struggled to learn the J stroke and struggled just to stay a good distance behind the others. He should probably not have been the stern stroke, but he had quickly seen both Butch and O'Casey assume the stern position. It was the alpha male position, and he would settle for nothing less. He was almost as big as Butch, and certainly as strong as O'Casey. He was not going to play second fiddle to anyone.

He would certainly not have allowed Tiffany Goodrich to take the stern, although Tiffany could probably have done a better job. While she was not at all an outdoor person, she was a superb athlete. She had been one of the finest high school swimmers and tennis players in all of Connecticut. She was all-state in both sports, but had been heavily recruited in tennis. She had been the captain of her tennis team at Connecticut College and, when she was younger, had often dreamed of turning pro. The NESCAC finals taught her there were lots of other good tennis players in New England. Her college had gotten smoked by both Middlebury and Bowdoin College in the finals. Tiffany had not won a single match. While she was stoic about the losses, her mother went wild, causing a scene, much to Tiffany's complete embarrassment, by accusing the line judge of being bought off by the other schools. Tiffany, on hearing this, was surprised that her mother had not actually tried something like that herself.

Still, paddling a canoe on a lake in Maine was a nice reprieve from her mother and not a very a difficult task for Tiffany. Her shoulders and hands were up to the task. She was not sure that her head, however, was really up to it. No one was quite sure why Tiffany was even there. Because Jason had all but forced himself on the group, it seemed the collective hope was that Tiffany might just occupy Jason so that he would not ruin the trip—a fear that O'Casey had expressed to Butch on several occasions.

Tiffany and Maria were almost the antithesis of each other. Tiffany was tall, athletic, stunning in appearance. Some felt her beauty brought with it a hint of vanity. Whether she actually *was* vain, no one was yet sure—in part because only Jason knew her well, and his interest in her was hardly professional in nature.

By contrast, Maria was short, stocky, unathletic, and remarkably humble, given her amazing voice. Maria had a great sense of humor, but much of it was self-deprecating. She had been so frequently laughed at and teased, she had gotten used to laughing at herself. Still, her good humor and great laugh made her a wonderful person to have at a party— or on a camping trip. Maria had been invited because she happened to be at the pub when the "plot was hatched," as they later described it.

Tiffany had sort of stumbled her way aboard, literally as the accidental tourist, because she and Jason were principals in the same district. Although Jason and Tiffany had never dated, it was not because Jason didn't want that to happen. It was certainly his plan to get into her pants on this trip, several times, he hoped, if all went well. Right now, Jason was far more focused on what he thought was Tiffany's weak paddling than on her always-foxy appearance. His own arms were aching. His poor paddling and lack of a strong J stroke force him to switch sides every three or four strokes. He was just looking for an excuse to stop or at least slow down. Fortunately, his timing was good.

While Butch Chapman might miss a succession of social clues from his peers, he almost never missed anything in nature. He suddenly stopped paddling and held his hand up. He then put two fingers up to his mouth as a signal for everyone to be quiet. Almost immediately, everyone looked toward Butch. Only Jason kept paddling and muttering to himself.

Finally, Tiffany became annoyed with her stern mate's self-absorbed garble. "Shhhh!" she hissed as she lifted her two fingers to her lips. She felt like a librarian trying to quiet a third grader with a perpetual "kick me" sign on his back. "Quiet!" she whispered with a scowl, although she had not yet figured out why Butch wanted everyone to be so still. She looked over at the Chief, who was still almost a hundred feet ahead of them in the lead canoe. Butch again put his fingers to his lips for continued silence. Then he motioned toward the shore.

"Oh my God," Ellen whispered again to herself.

There on the shore less than fifty feet away were two young fawns and their young mother. The fawns were a bit wobble-legged in their mottled coats of tawny brown-and-white camouflage. Although mothers rarely like to move their fawns during the daytime, black flies will occasionally drive even a cautious doe and her fawn from a swamp thicket. To see twin fawns this young was so rare that even Butch had never witnessed such a scene.

The doe seemed a bit confused as she walked along the shore with her new offspring. This was her first time as a mother. Still, thousands of years of instinct had taken over with the birth of the twins, as first one and then a second slid their way into the world. She had quickly rolled over, slowly stood up, and methodically licked the afterbirth from one angelic face and then the other. Next, she carefully licked the entire body of each of the tiny creatures that had just come from her still-quivering loins. She nudged the fragile, spindle-legged fawns repeatedly. First one, then the other staggered to their feet. Again, a marvelous delicate instinct seemed to take over as the fawns nudged and cajoled the anxious mother to help them locate the teats full of rich colostrum waiting to be drained.

Three-year-old does usually do not produce twins, and often are not successful in bringing both through the spring alive. The young mother was skittish. She seemed to know that having a second fawn more than doubled the likelihood that one or both would be discovered by coyotes or a bear looking for an easy meal for their own spring litters. Just as the salmon had become a morning meal for the bald eagle and her fledgling, death becomes part of the life cycle deep in the Maine woods.

The weary doe had cautiously, almost reluctantly, led her fawns to the shore for a drink. She had not noticed the contingent of campers watching her because she had not glanced out over the lake. Instinctively, she knew there was nothing to harm her in the water. Had the wind shifted and blown off the water, she would quickly have smelled the canoeists— some more easily than others. However, her nose had constantly worked the air coming from the alder thicket and cedar ridge behind her; she seemed more comfortable and less cautious now. She had her back to the water and bent down to lick each of her fawns in turn. Her ears were almost always up, and at one point her tail went up as well. The white *flag* soon dropped as the nervous doe returned to the scrupulous cleaning of her tiny charges.

Maria had never seen anything so beautiful in her life. This is what she wanted. This was why she was here, "to soak up nature," as she had explained to a friend before the trip. But she had never imagined it would be so beautiful. Her face just beamed as she studied the delicate movement of the doe as she waded a few feet into the water and began to drink.

Ellen noticed the water dancing with the subtle colors of cream and brown, dappled slowly across the surface like Matisse working on a Maine canvas. The cautious doe would take a sip and look toward the shore, never losing sight of the now playful fawns. Their tawny brown and yellow spots often made the fawns almost invisible against the overhanging alder leaves.

The alder, maple, and poplar leaves had burst forth several weeks before and were now the size of mouse ears. Butch had reminded the group several times that this was a good sign. He said the leaf size was a good indicator that the warmer days were having their annual effect, days that not only caused the leaves to grow, but also made the nymphs hatch into may- and caddis flies. Butch smiled every time he said this because he loved to fish over a mayfly or caddis hatch. As he had told Jason one time, fishing over a really great hatch was better than sex, because it could mean hours and hours of near perfect bliss. He could never last more than ten minutes in bed, but he had fished from sunup till sundown many times. Better than sex? "No doubt," Butch would say to anyone who asked.

Although Jason Foxworthy couldn't imagine a great day of fishing being better than the worst sex in his life, he had told Butch, as he tried to wheedle his way into the trip, that he really enjoyed fishing. He knew that's what Butch had wanted to hear. When Butch couldn't be on a stream or tying the flies he'd be using to catch trout or salmon, he would talk fishing with anyone who listened.

Jason always listened because he truly liked Butch, but he listened more intently at the Black Rose Pub because he had heard Ellen was going and she'd said something about Tiffany Goodrich. Jason figured that anywhere Tiffany might be on a hot day with little clothing was a place he would want to be. If that were by a pool in Fort Lauderdale or even at a Holiday Inn, it would be fine for Jason. The lake was nice, and a little adventure to talk about over a beer sounded like fun, but it wasn't why Jason was there. Not by a long shot! This nature crap was overrated anyway, Jason had always felt. Shoot a bear or a moose? Sure. Kill a few small trout? Nah. He was stalking Tiffany. She would be his trophy pure and simple.

O'Casey slowly raised his camera again. The shots he was getting of the fawns were better than anything he'd ever dreamed of taking.

Actually, he had just checked again to make sure that all his settings were correct. He had gone to shutter priority on his Nikon D70. He had just gotten the new digital to replace his old Nikon FTN. Film was great, but with his 8-gig memory card, he could shoot almost 2,000 shots in RAW format. "That'd be a lot of film to bring," O'Casey thought as he focused and fired away. Besides, the 6 megapixel digital system would allow him to produce 11⊠ x 14⊠ prints with little loss in quality. If some of these shots came out as he hoped, he would certainly go poster size. Hell, he'd give a print to everyone here, probably even Jason. This was great, he thought. His autofocus 150–400mm telephoto zoom was giving him amazing shots. He had gently slipped into a prone position so he could rest his camera on the gunnel of the canoe. He silently prayed that Maria would be more prudent with her body movements than Ellen had been with the eagle incident. *Please, Maria! Please DON'T move.* O'Casey was more concerned about losing his great shots than losing his new camera. Even his beloved lens, which he had just spent a small fortune for, could be replaced. Someone might spend fifty years in the woods and never see twin fawns at a distance of only t meters. He was able to fill a frame with either of them at this distance.

Each member of the group, with the exception of Jason, sat mesmerized by the scene before them. The fawns were prancing now— bouncing around like young Nubian goats when they first discover their legs. They had been tentative, leaning against each other as their mother sipped and looked, sipped and listened. At one point, O'Casey's camera sounds caused the doe's flag, her elegant white tail, to go up in alarm. O'Casey froze. Everyone else seemed to understand, too, and responded with absolute silence.

The doe again sniffed the air and looked around cautiously. She listened to the night-black ravens talking as they headed for a tall witch pine in the distance. Because she was nursing heavily, the doe needed more water than she would drink at almost any other time in her life, so she tried to ignore her energetic fawns and dropped her head to drink again.

Phew, thought O'Casey.

Ellen sighed with relief as she studied the scene with perhaps more scrutiny than she had ever given to a moment like this before. Although she didn't consider herself a serious artist, almost everyone else did. She was trying to take mental snapshots, not just of the fawns and the doe, but also the texture of the foliage, the subtle changes that were occurring as the reflection of the shoreline danced in the water before them. She had no way of knowing that a much more skilled artist, famed Mainer Jake Day, had come to this very spot more than sixty years before to study the same flora and fauna, including spring fawns, before creating the original sketches that would become the Disney classic, *Bambi*.

Jason Foxworthy had long since tired of the *nature crap*, as he often derided such experiences. Sure, these fawns were pretty cool, but he was ready to move on. Although he liked to hunt, he only rarely hunted deer. Too boring. The last time he was this close to a deer, it was in suburban New Jersey. He had almost hit one. He was driving fast, but the deer, fortunately, moved faster. Jason had had at least a six-pack that night and barely saw the small buck. "Shit. The deer would have spattered my Beemer," he had told a friend. A dead deer was hardly worth a bruised BMW he reflected.

Foxworthy fidgeted as his boredom grew. *God, it's hot*, he thought. The six-pack cooler called his name. The sun was now high in the late morning sky, and although it was only 10:30, it seemed much later, much hotter, much thirstier than that. Slowly and silently Jason found the cooler's small blue handle and slid it forward as he had done so many times. The Coors was even colder than he had hoped. He could just taste its cool, frothy essence. Wrapping one large hand around the icy can, Jason grasped the tab with his thumb and forefingers. He couldn't wait for that first magical sip.

PUUUUSCH! The noise of the beer gushing from the Coors can startled everyone, even Jason. It was as though a rock had been thrown at a beautiful Eliot Porter photograph they had all been studying, fracturing both the protective glass and the delicate image. The sound shattered the silence. The obnoxious hiss seemed to echo off the walls of the cedar ridge, booming back across the lake, screaming, "I am an asshole."

In an instant, the doe looked toward the lake and the canoeists for the first time. She froze for a second and seemed amazed by the audience that had been studying her and the fawns. Immediately, her long white tail went skyward. Her dilating nostrils struggled to identify the smells as the adrenaline coursed through her veins. Her thin muscular neck snapped back toward her infant offspring. They, too, seemed to sense, almost smell, the terror the doe now felt. In one quick leap, she was on the edge of the alders. In another, she was among them. She turned briefly to assure herself that her fawns were at her side. Then they disappeared, too, as they sensed and perhaps smelled the panic in their mother's quivering legs. The mouse-eared alders rustled ever so slightly in the breeze, and newly hatching caddis flies sought comfort on the gold-green leaves. The deer, now quite invisible, panted heavily in the relative safety of the cedar thicket.

"You shithead!" O'Casey shouted as he turned in genuine anger on Jason Foxworthy. Had the camera and the prizes it contained not been so special, he might have thrown it at the jerk. Had they been on land, he would certainly have done more than just yell at the *imbecile* as he had always viewed Jason.

Even Tiffany had thoroughly enjoyed the moments with the fawns and was now embarrassed that such a wonderful interlude had been ruined by her canoe partner. She turned toward the stern. "Nice move, Bucko," she said with a contempt that was obvious to everyone, even Foxworthy.

"What? What?" implored Jason, as though his actions had been as natural as the doe's. "Shit. It was getting hot and we'd watched all those freakin' deers for at least five minutes. I bet O'Casey's probably got fifty pictures of them already. Let's get rolling. My legs are cramping up in this damn canoe."

Dickhead! O'Casey thought. *What a freakin' loser.*

A good guide can usually feel when a battle is about to break out within his tribe and finds a way to refocus the warring parties. "Come on everyone. Let's get going. We're not that far from the dam," said Butch ,once again assuming the role of the Chief. "We'll be there in twenty minutes. Hard paddle! Let's go."

He knew it would be closer to forty minutes, but most of the group wouldn't care. Only Jason might complain about the extra time, and Butch knew that as long as Foxworthy could stay busy with his cooler, he'd probably be all right.

The dam gradually loomed into sight and shifted from a small spot on the distant shore to a goal that could be focused on, paddled toward, and ultimately reached. Ellen arrived first. Though far from an accomplished kayaker, as her modified wet exit had shown, she could move the kayak at a fairly brisk pace. She was hoping that the fields, the dam, and the caretaker's house on the hill might make an interesting composition for a future painting. She was a serious student of Andrew Wyeth's art. She loved how Wyeth could take a simple rustic setting and turn it into a masterpiece. *Imagine. Observe. Reflect. Compose*, Ellen ordered her subconscious.

She also snapped quick pictures with a small digital camera. Unlike O'Casey, she had no real knowledge of photography and no real interest in capturing the nuances of the scene. She would do that with the canvas and with her imagination. Right now, she was capturing proportion and perspective. At least that was what she told herself.

Ellen was glad that she had hurried to be the first at the dam. She would certainly lose any creative instincts as soon as Jason Foxworthy arrived. She was also afraid that he and O'Casey might get into a fight, which she had always thought was just a matter of time. So she rushed to make mental notes and grab a few photos as the rest of the crew gradually approached.

O'Casey's canoe moved slowly toward the shore. By this time, Maria had to rest. She had tried hard to help O'Casey paddle the overloaded canoe, but she knew that she was part of that overloading, or at least that was how she viewed herself. She had always been self-conscious about her weight. She also really liked Sean Padraig O'Casey as a friend and didn't want him to have to paddle the canoe completely by himself. Her hands were blistered from paddling. Her shoulders ached and, although she would only have told Ellen this, her butt ached, too. After Ellen had capsized, Maria was so afraid of a similar plight that she hadn't shifted her weight at all. Her cheeks and upper thighs were already "asleep" because of the confining, uncomfortable metal thwart seats.

O'Casey could read Maria's fatigue. He could read people almost as well as he could read streams. He could see Maria's pain in each stroke. As the paddle would get even with her opposite shoulder, her stroke would begin to fade. It lacked energy and effort, not because Maria wasn't trying, but because she was exhausted and in pain. "Take a break. Really. I've got it covered," O'Casey would say every few minutes.

At first she resisted, but eventually Maria did have to rest. She was glad Butch had suggested that she and O'Casey pair up. Although she found Butch to be more physically attractive—quite cute, she thought—

she found O'Casey to be a great paddling partner and was glad to be taking one of those breaks now.

Angelo Capelletti and Butch Chapman were close behind. Butch had carefully placed his canoe between O'Casey's and Jason Foxworthy's. Butch knew how wild O'Casey would be after Jason had startled the doe by opening his second beer of the day. Foxworthy had obviously forgotten that all the beers had been thrown about as they were tossed from one car into another, then into the canoe, and later into Jason's cooler. No one else worried about shaken beer because no one but Jason would give a thought to beer before 5:00 P.M.

Jason already had a *breakfast beer at 6:00A.M.* and had been drooling for a second by 10:00. He was actually wearing half the beer that had spooked the doe and her fawns, but that didn't embarrass Jason. He and his brothers had a legendary reputation for drinking beer. Today, it showed both in his behavior and in his body. The once powerful running back on Butch Chapman's college football team looked much older and slower than the guy they used to call "Flash." In fact, Jason was anything but a flash now as he struggled to finish his third beer and paddle toward the dam at the same time.

Embarrassed by her *sometimes friend*, Jason Foxworthy, Tiffany alternately paddled and shook her head as their canoe made its approached to the shore.

One by one, the canoes pulled up at the small sandy beach just above the dam. The log booms that had once held back thousands of logs now sat idle, collecting insect larvae and creating a natural breakwater by the dam. It was also a reminder for all who knew the long and storied history of loggers and logging in this part of the Maine wilderness. *The Cut* or man-made stream below the dam had played an important part in the "logging wars" of the nineteenth century. Danger, mystery, and conflict were always silent partners in this region ...and would certainly be on this trip as well.

SUNSHINE AND WAR STORIES

Everyone rested briefly on the inviting shoreline by the beached canoes.

Tiffany stretched out in the sun, half in exhaustion and half in exhilaration as the noontime sun warmed every part of her fatigued body. The Long Island blonde's hair was no longer neatly coiffured. Instead it was a relaxed tangle—almost wild, yet surprisingly becoming, as though revealing a side of Tiffany that neither she nor the tribe had ever seen before. Tiffany discovered a pleasant exhaustion from her first jaunt in a fully loaded canoe. She tilted her face in worshipful deference to the warming June sun she loved, closed her eyes, and bathed in a momentary joy and freedom she found remarkably liberating and pure.

Maria and Ellen chatted quietly as they soaked in the beauty of the lake behind them and the Cut before them. They could hear the waters of the dam spillway crashing on the rocks at the base of the eddy, but they were more focused on the sensory experiences of a warm, early-summer sun, a light breeze blowing down the lake, and the rich, sweet smells of cedar, pine, and spruce that filled the air. For them, this natural extravaganza, this sense of being fully alive, sang out to their inner spirits. The vitality of the Maine woods filled their beings. For Ellen, the artist, it was almost epiphaneic. For Maria, celebrating a common bond and happy moment with almost anyone, female or male, was a unique and treasured moment. This wonderful, cheerful woman had surprisingly few close friends, though she would have been happy with even one.

As the women drank in the visual nectar of the river valley, they could hardly imagine the history behind the area where they now sat …

including the pain, the cursing, the blood, and the too-frequent death that had given the Cut legendary status. The woodsmen who had worked here, the granite cutters, and the log drivers who had labored here surely must have felt the warmth of the June sun and drunk in the sweet smells of the cedar and pine as well.

However, for Maria and Ellen, this was intoxication worth celebrating by a Wordsworth or, better yet, a Thoreau. In fact, it was Thoreau's journey to this very spot over a hundred and fifty years before and chronicled *The Maine Woods* that had helped to inspire Ellen to become first an English teacher, and later, an artist. Ironically, this was her first real trip to a wilderness she had only experienced vicariously in books or through the stories of her father and brothers. Now, she understood. She could feel, hear, smell, and all but taste the Maine her imagination had told her existed.

"How will I ever capture this in my paintings?" she pondered with Maria.

"Just soak it into your pores. Drink it in. That's what I'm doing," answered Maria. "I'm so glad you let me join you. I can't imagine having missed this, now that I know how wonderful it is. I've never done anything like this before. Never. I saw Butch wearing his hunting knife this morning and cutting some rope for tie-downs, and I thought, in the barrio where I grew up, a knife like that had only one purpose … and it wasn't a good one."

Ellen and Maria became fast friends on the grassy bank in that noontime sun. They shared in the joy of the moment, in the common love they had for the simplicity of nature, in the clarity of the water, in the delicate sounds and smells—all heightened by their mutual interest in the uniqueness of an experience they were sharing for the first time.

Meanwhile, Angelo, forever the good sport and willing audience, sat patiently as Jason held court. Neither had moved from the embankment by the dam where they had first beached their canoes. For Angelo, it was a welcome opportunity to rest and relax. His health had declined significantly in the past year, though few would notice. He was thoroughly exhausted from the grueling paddle down the lake, and somewhat surprised by how unprepared he felt, physically, for the trip.

For Jason, it was once again story time, his favorite passion. Actually, his favorite passions were drinking and sex, in that order. However, he was perhaps better known for his stories. While they were often crude and frequently serious distortions of the truth, "Jason stories" were almost always funny, as long as the person listening was not the subject. Even his students loved to hear his stories, several of which were so off-color that they got Jason into trouble with parents, other teachers, and even his superintendent.

However, the stories never stopped. They were central to Jason Foxworthy's most positive and endearing attribute, and in a person like Jason, who had many shortcomings, it was important to make the most of an attribute almost everyone enjoyed. While there was much that Angelo did not admire about Jason, he was too tired not to listen and too respectful to walk away as Jason blabbed on. The more Jason drank, the more he talked. He had just cracked another Coors. He chatted away as Angelo dutifully listened—sometimes smiling, sometimes laughing, and sometimes drifting into faraway places and thoughts.

Everyone seemed to enjoy the reprieve from paddling and their quiet R and R on the sunny bank—everyone, that is, but O'Casey. Once he had helped Maria from the canoe because her legs were numb from the two-hour paddle, O'Casey had quickly swapped his paddle and camera for his other real love, his fly rod. Like Granville Butch Chapman, O'Casey loved to fly fish. Although Butch was a better fisherman than O'Casey from a technical perspective, Sean Padraig O'Casey had almost a transcendent, metaphysical love for fly-fishing that Butch Chapman lacked. He had learned from Butch that a hot June sun could bring out midday caddis hatches and big trout just below the dam. O'Casey was tying on a golden cream caddis fly before Tiffany and Jason had even set foot on the lakeshore. By now, he was oblivious to the rest of the group enjoying the sun on the knoll behind him.

Having already recharged his battery with a two-minute rest and a handful of homemade beef jerky, Butch stretched noisily and began to plan the rest of the day. The Chief was always moving, always anxious to do something, always planning for the tribe. He could not turn the guide switch off. He loved guiding. He loved turning people on to his world. He was actually more comfortable here than he was as a principal. In fact, if he could have afforded it, he would long since have retired to follow his passion full time. *Three more years,* he thought. *Three more years of budgets, buses, and babysitting, and I'm gone. No more Welton Academy, no more board, no more meetings, no more bullshit.*

Butch felt the warm sun on his face. He smiled briefly now that the tribe had arrived safely after the easiest part of the trip, but he knew he had some important work ahead. His mind was already working now as the Maine Guide, the leader, not as the principal of Welton Academy or the drinking buddy who had put this trip together. He needed to reassume his role as the Chief. He was "off to reconnoiter," as he phrased it. "Why don't you guys just hang out for a while? I'm going do a little checking to see what we have for stacks on the river."

What the heck are stacks? Maria wondered. It sounded serious, but she had tremendous confidence in Butch and knew that his "reconnoitering," or whatever it was that Butch had said, would help everyone. She also loved it when Butch called them *guys*, but not because it had a masculine connotation. Butch was sexist, but in a well-meaning, "aw-shucks" kind of way. When Butch said *guys*, which he said to everyone, he meant team, tribe, gang—all terms Maria could relate to in a very positive way. *Belonging.* That's what it felt like. It was an emotion, a connection she had rarely experienced—not in her youth or even now as a professional educator. She was glad she was here, glad Butch was leading, and glad she had been chosen to be "one of the guys."

"You guys better save your strength because we're going to have to hump all the gear but the canoes down the portage road to the end of the Cut. That's almost a mile portage, so we'll earn our money big time. If you guys were really good, we'd shoot the Cut with everything in the canoes, but if we dumped the beer, Jason would freak. If we dumped the dry clothes, Ellen would pee her pants—again.

"Hey, I *resemble* that remark," Ellen smiled. She loved Butch Chapman's sense of humor, even when it was at her expense.

Jason Foxworthy, who had never been accused of being quick, was just beginning to realize that he'd been insulted, though in a playful way that Butch could do all too well.

"The last time we were here, the dam keeper hauled our stuff down on his tractor," Butch continued.

"Then let's go get him," Jason piped up as he drifted into the conversation. "I don't want to have to haul all this shit." He seemed oblivious to the fact that much of the shit, including two large coolers of beer, was his. "I'm toast. I just want to hang out here for a while."

"Unless you've got the keys to the dam keeper's tractor, we're hauling gear," replied Butch. "Blair Besmond, the old dam keeper, isn't here anymore. What a shame. He was one funny bastard. Everybody and their brother used to try to beg him or bribe him to haul their gear, but we were the only ones he'd help out. All it took was a pint, a 'please,' and a couple of fresh whitefish. God, he loved whitefish."

"What the heck are whitefish?" asked Ellen.

"Whitefish are kind of a cross between a trout and a sucker," said Butch. "Ask O'Casey. He was catching some big ones a couple of years ago at the dam and was throwing them back. Blair, the dam keeper, came out of his house and started yelling at O'Casey. 'Hey, shithead! Yeah, you! What the fuck do you think you're doing?'"

Butch grinned at Ellen, a bit embarrassed at dropping F bombs, and continued with his story. "O'Casey had no idea who this guy was, why he was yelling, or what he had done to piss the old guy off. But the old guy kept it up. 'Stop throwing those whitefish back in the river! They're only the best-tasting fish God ever made. You've caught some of the biggest whitefish I've ever seen here. I can't seem to catch 'em. Can you get one for me?' About two minutes later, O'Casey pulled in a beauty as if the dam keeper had willed the fish to hit O'Casey's caddis fly."

Butch went on as everyone sat spellbound on the bank. "Then the dam keeper smiled at O'Casey and said, 'Thanks! I love these fish. Sometimes I make a *chowdah* with 'em. The meat is sweet and *tendah*. Better'n trout and not real strong like the salmon. Some ol' wicked freakin' good! If I only had a little whiskey to wash it down with, I'd be all set.'

"That was my contribution," chuckled Butch proudly. "I had a half pint of Jack Daniels in my pack so I gave it to ol' Blair. You would've thought it was Christmas. Five minutes later, he had the old John Deere cranked up and hauled all our gear down the Cut road to the lake. He drank and sang to himself the whole ride down. Go figure. Most people looked at him as a grumpy old fart, but he was great to us. I wish he were here now. I heard he had a heart attack and died, but I'm not sure that's true."

"Unfortunately, Jason, we're going to be hauling lots of gear, so rest up, and go easy on the beer. As I was saying, Blair's gone now. The cheap bastards who run the dam never replaced him when he got sick. They show up about twice a month to check on the gates and dump water. It gets pretty amazing around here when that happens. The Cut turns into white water all over the place. But Blair doesn't open the spillways anymore now that they can do that electronically from Bangor. He's gone for good—and so is our taxi! Sorry, Jason. Well, I'm off," said Butch. "I'll be back in about a half hour. Have fun and don't party too hard."

He headed off with a determined stride to check the condition of the rapids. While the headwaters just below the dam looked tame, they often caught novice canoeists off guard. Butch did not like to be caught off guard, ever. That was the purpose of his reconnoitering trek. At low water, Aggamog Cut could be a class one or two rapid, a quick-moving but easily navigated stream 100 feet across at most. It was often canoed by Boy Scout troops during July low water.

However, early in the spring, after a very hard rain, or if three or more gates were fully opened at the dam, the river could rise with almost no notice to a class three or even a class four level. More than one fisherman or canoeist has been washed to a watery death in Maine after such a dam release. The power company is supposed to blow an alarm when they're about to release water. The alarm doesn't travel very far into the woods or down the canyon, but the water sure does. Even a partial dam release can result in haystacks, or white-water waves three to four feet high. Such rapids can be fun for a hotshot paddler, but they can be brutal, even lethal, for a novice. Unfortunately, the tribe was full of novice paddlers.

Although Butch had never actually canoed the Cut during spring runoff, he and O'Casey had fished it several times before. Butch was having fun checking out the river and knew everyone else needed and would enjoy the free time. While each member of the group found a way to celebrate the leisure of a sparkling June day in Maine, Butch explored the Cut and the challenges that would soon come.

"When the Chief's away, the tribe will play" seemed to be the motto of the group as each member sought to make something of the free time they'd been given. It would have been difficult to decide who enjoyed this break time the most. The midday sun seemed somehow to legitimize Jason's fourth beer and then his fifth. Even Angelo, perhaps the straightest member of the group from a drinking standpoint, was enticed to grab a "brewski," as Jason called them. The cold beer went well with the Italian sandwiches the group had grabbed at a convenience store along with the bug dope, toilet paper, and other final necessities they had picked up around dawn before heading into the *Big Woods*, as the Allagash region is often called.

In a strange way, Angelo enjoyed this time with Jason Foxworthy. As obnoxious as Jason could be, he could also be exceptionally funny. He was in rare form on this day. As he quickly finished beer number four and popped open number five, Foxworthy held court. Angelo Capelletti alternatively laughed and shook his head in amazement as Jason told story after story about this student and that.

"You wouldn't believe it," Jason went on with a particularly crude tale. "Here he is, banging this girl behind the World Book Encyclopedias, when old Miss Brewster, with her great st-st-stutter, comes around the library stacks and says, 'Sssh! Sssh! You're making too much noise back here.' She then sees two kids going at it and realizes what's going on. She can hardly get the words out because she's in freakin' shock. Then she yells, 'St-St-St-Stanley Wasenewski, you stop that at once! This is m-m-my library. Not a motel. Go to Principal Jackson's office right n-n-now!'

"She then saw who the girl was and said, 'Oh my God! Helen. H-H-Helen Gamble. Your m-m-mother ...!' "

"Poor Miss Brewster almost died," Jason went on. "She was stuttering and stammering; she could hardly talk. Here's Stanley Wasenewski zipping up his fly. And here is Miss B. She's just caught Stanley screwing Helen Gamble. Helen's mother, Alice, was the freakin' school board chair. Can you believe that! That's how I got my job. Alice Gamble was so pissed and so embarrassed that she wanted to fire everyone. She couldn't fire poor Miss B. because she had tenure and a bad heart. So she fired poor Mr. Jackson, the principal at Morton High. Later, she fired Bill Berger, the assistant principal. That poor bastard wasn't even there that day. He had taken the debate team to the state finals. But, Alice Gamble wanted *everyone's* head. What she really wanted was Stanley's dick chopped up into little pieces and fed to the sharks, but all she could do was expel him since the sex was *very* consensual.

"Poor Mr. Jackson and Mr. Berger," Foxworthy went on. "They'd been at Morton forever. They were there when Christ was in high school," Jason grinned. "They were two of the straightest old guys in the world. Nineteen-fifties types. It wasn't their fault that Alice Gamble's daughter was a freakin' nympho. Somehow, Alice convinced everyone that her daughter had been drugged and was really the victim. Yeah, right. Victim, my ass! She was the victim of some bad Ecstasy that she had just sold to Stanley. "But that's how I got my job," said Jason. "I was the only administrator left. I was the A.D. They needed someone to hold the fort. I was the new guy, and besides, foxy ol' Helen Gamble thought I was hot. Thank God I didn't chase her, although I sure was tempted. Boy, did she look good in a pair of gym shorts, particularly when she'd intentionally skip wearing panties just to tease the guys during the girls' sit-up contest. Anyway, shortly after the library fiasco, Helen told her mom to hire me as the interim principal, and I've been there ever since."

Angelo laughed, in part because he could picture old Miss Brewster stammering in shock, and in part because everyone laughed at Jason's stories. They were one small part truth, one large part Jason.

It was because Jason was such a pistol and such a good liar that Tiffany had been attracted to him at all. There was no strong bond between them, no real romantic link, although Jason would have liked that. There was simply mutual self-interest. Jason had a great sense of humor and was quite good-looking—once upon a time, a real pretty boy. "A bit fat, but good-looking," Tiffany had told a friend once. Actually, Tiffany was most interested in the *timing* of the trip. It would be a perfect excuse to miss her mother's *opening* the Hamptons cottage. The weeklong celebration welcomed in summertime and was always held the first week after school got out. It was considered the de rigueur social event of June. Tiffany hated seeing her mother drunk and holding court with her rich friends. Invariably, one of her friends would end up naked in the swimming pool, or, more often than not, trashed and in bed with someone else's husband or…wife. Tiffany had learned to despise that event. Her mother used to parade her around like a trophy, showing her off like a prize she'd won. "You need your best outfit, dear. Judge Adams will be here, and he's on the board of Daddy's new company. Good impression. Good impression."

Tiffany loathed the event, the pretense, and the empty social behavior that had been so much a part of her life. But somehow, it always seemed impossible to say no to her mother. *No* was a word her mother refused to accept. The trip had been a perfect excuse to avoid the forced pilgrimage to the Hamptons. Tiffany knew the canoe trip would be a hoot, or at least she hoped it would. Even though she didn't really like nature and had never, ever camped before, she did like everyone on the trip, especially

Ellen and Butch.

The trip had been the talk of the New England Principals Conference. Everyone had heard about the plans and everyone wanted in. Tiffany was disappointed that she had not been invited personally, but also knew that there was no reason she should have been. She had known both Butch and Ellen for a number of years, but had not been at the Black Rose the night the trip idea had been hatched. It sounded a bit like a frat party to her, one part sun and one part fun, when Jason had first told her about it. Although she rarely liked to encourage Jason to think that he might ever get to first base with her, the night he had told her about the party, she had sent him every body language message she could. "Get me invited to the trip, and I am yours." It didn't matter that *she* was not serious about that sexual message. While Jason Foxworthy could miss a subtle but well-directed insult, he couldn't and didn't miss the body language and what he felt was the ultimate reward in this Maine adventure. Jason figured he'd just get Tiffany drunk and hop in the sack, "or sleeping bag, rather," he had often chuckled to himself.

"Sure, I can get you an invitation!" Jason promised. "Butch and I are like this," he said, crossing his fingers as any good fifth grader would. "I know they weren't planning to let anyone else in as part of the trip. They wanted to keep it an even number, but we're best buddies, so I guess that means you're in," Jason assured her.

In reality, he purposely waited until just a few weeks before the trip to announce to Butch that he'd invited Tiffany. Butch rarely got angry, but he was ripped that Jason had invited someone on *his* trip. *Who the hell does Jason think he is? He's lucky he got invited*, Butch had thought. However, he genuinely liked Tiffany, and knew Ellen did as well. So Tiffany back-doored her way into the group, and Butch had no way of knowing what a good decision that would be for the entire tribe.

In fact, Jason himself had not been part of the original group at the pub that night, and had certainly not been part of the original plan. As Butch recalled, it had all started when he and O'Casey decided to extend the conference happy hour at the Hynes Convention Center and move it to their favorite watering hole so they could talk fishing—*far from the maddening crowd*, as English teacher O'Casey put it. Angelo joined them and later, Maria and Ellen. When Butch and O'Casey talked about their last fishing trip to the Cut, everyone sat spellbound. They were drawn by the lure of the Maine wilderness and by the vivid images the two fishermen created before them.

Imagination can magically fill in details to personalize someone else's adventures. Ellen, Maria, and Angelo were soon customizing the adventure that Butch and O'Casey were sharing with them. Ellen could imagine herself sitting on the rocks sketching the pine trees that stood majestically along the banks of the river. Maria could imagine sitting by the campfire singing songs, laughing, and bonding with the others. Angelo simply admired and almost adored his friend Butch. He just found the Chief to be a rugged, handsome adventurer—a throwback to the past, to the woodsmen who had tamed the frontier and created legends for themselves.

Each sat mesmerized as O'Casey and Butch traded images. The fish got bigger, the current faster, and the scenery more spectacular. As one beer turned into three and three turned into five, the stories of the Maine woods captured the hearts and the imaginations of the listeners. They were also getting drunk. Somehow, alcohol can be a great bonding substance when properly applied. One healthy dose of imagination and one beer. A dash of vivid imagery and another beer. Soon the five were best friends, each captivated by thoughts of the Maine wilderness and what it might mean for them.

"So, when do we go?" asked Ellen with a beer-induced giggle.

"Yeah," said Maria. "It's not fair that you guys have all the fun. What about us?"

"Would you really like to go?" Butch asked. "I've never done a co-ed trip before. I've done a lot of guy trips and several husband and wife trips, but I've never just taken a gang of principals before."

"Well, we're you're gang, honey!" said Ellen in a way that showed she was both half in the bag and getting more familiar with Butch than she probably meant to convey. Her grin, however, was so infectious and her request so much an expression of what everyone was thinking that momentum just took over.

"Let's do it!" Butch shouted with an excitement and energy he had never felt in planning previous trips. "Are you guys up for it?"

Each of his drinking companions immediately chimed in, talking over each other with enthusiasm. The tribe had formed. The Chief had been elected. The trip was on. At least that was Butch Chapman's recollection of the events. It was only later that evening, well after Ellen and Maria had faded and gone to bed that Jason Foxworthy even showed up. He'd heard from friends that the happy hour had moved to the Black Rose. Jason knew that would be fun. Any late night of drinking was fun for ol' Foxy, as Butch often called him. And shortly after Jason had joined them at the pub, O'Casey had left.

Sean Padraig O'Casey and Jason Foxworthy were much like oil and water. O'Casey saw Foxworthy as a drunk and a lightweight. As O'Casey had once described him, "I've had sixth graders with more brains, and I've had second graders with more common sense." Butch knew how lucky Jason had been to get his job as a principal. He was clueless about being a principal, but, according to Butch, smart enough to have hired the best assistant principal in Massachusetts. Someone had to know how to do what needed to be done. "Otherwise," Butch had told Angelo once, "his high school would have been in the toilet by now and he'd be selling shoes."

O'Casey was usually not so critical of others, but he was a passionate educator who had little respect for people who got into education for the wrong reasons. He had heard from friends in the profession that Jason Foxworthy spent more time planning the staff football pool than he did dealing with his students. By contrast, O'Casey had tremendous admiration and respect for Butch and for how much he cared about kids. Butch knew every student, every parent, and half the grandparents. While he didn't know much about curriculum or even care to know, he did know his kids—and for O'Casey that was the bottom line. The trip sounded like fun and O'Casey was in. Had he ever thought that Jason Foxworthy was about to wheedle his way onto the trip, O'Casey would have stayed at the pub to discourage him.

By the end of the evening, not only was Jason a part of the trip, but everyone at the conference had heard about the impending jaunt "up to the Maine woods." Everyone wanted to be part of it, but Butch had managed to shut it down even as others pestered him for the rest of the conference.

He was not so lucky with regard to Tiffany. Jason had purposely waited until late May to tell him about Tiffany. "She's already bought her camping gear. Hell, I think she bought out L.L. Bean's," Jason argued. "We can't say 'No' now. I saw Ellen the other day and she said she'd be willing to take the kayak she just bought so that Tiffany can ride in my canoe." Jason had said it as though his 1970 Sears Roebuck aluminum canoe had just come off the production line in Old Town rather than out of his backyard, where it had been stored for years. Jason's arguments echoed of the third-string linebacker begging to go in. "Can I, can I? Oh, please coach," Jason seemed to say. Butch relented. Jason was in. Tiffany was in.

…And here they all were. Tiffany was still sunning herself. Maria and Ellen were having a wonderful time talking and enjoying the day. Angelo had fallen asleep after one too many of Jason's stories, and the storyteller had grabbed one last beer and gone for a walk.

FISH ON!

O'Casey's instincts about the possibility of a caddis fly hatch were right on the money. Often, by early to mid June, they'd started to hatch and skitter about the surface of the water late in the day. However, it was a very warm day for this early in the summer. In reality, it was still late spring, but as all teachers and kids know, once school lets out, it's summer regardless of the calendar. The cream-and-amber-colored caddis flies were everywhere … and so were the fish. O'Casey worked with precision. His Orvis five-weight graphite rod seemed to be an extension of his hand and wrist. Ten, two. Ten, two. Cast! Ten, two. Ten, two. Cast! O'Casey had learned that cadence as a nine-year-old. *Ten o'clock back to two o'clock. Imagine the clock. Imagine the clock.* Those were the words his grandfather had taught him. He would pass those lessons on to his own grandson … or granddaughter, O'Casey had thought to himself—that is, if I ever had one.

But for now, he was concentrating on the fish. Casting above a rising brook trout was his greatest joy. O'Casey loved to catch fish. However, his real love was in the presentation, in fooling the fish into hitting. Catching the fish was simply the icing on the cake. For Sean Padraig O'Casey, casting over rising trout was the most poetic thing he could imagine. He saw it as a ballet of sorts, a dance on a natural scale. The line's silky flow forward and backward and then forward again had an intrinsic grace and beauty that he carried with him all winter. Here on the river, with a June caddis hatch, O'Casey felt a harmony, a poetic sense of self that eluded him much of the year. Now he was home … on the river. He was at peace.

Suddenly the caddis fly disappeared. O'Casey's fifty-year-old eyes missed the roll of the big brook trout and the slurp as the large male sucked in the fly. The barbless #14 hook had barely pierced the wary trout's upper lip when O'Casey saw the leader pull forward ever so slightly. Bam! He set the hook with an instinctive reaction that even his grandfather hadn't been able to teach him. "If you miss setting that hook, you'll miss all the big fish," his grandfather would tell him. Still, it took years for that wrist strike to become instinctive.

"You've got a big one!" cheered Ellen.

"Who's gonna win?" shouted Maria as the two women focused on the battle.

The big brookie had been hooked before, several times in fact, and had only lost once. Fortunately, that year a fly fisherman with a strong catch-and-release ethic had let the male brook trout go. Now it was much bigger, stronger, and more formidable as an opponent. It dove for cover in the deep hole at the base of the dam.

Zzzzziz! Zzzzziz! The reel sang as the brookie ran toward the bottom. The rod tip arched in an almost perfect U, its composite linear graphite backbone doing exactly what it was designed to do. O'Casey had the rod up high with the reel almost at shoulder level. He stripped in what line he could, but would let it quickly zip through his fingers when the brookie made its runs. *Get the fish on the reel*, he thought. But he still had too much fly line loose in his fingers.

Zzzzziz! Then again, *zzzzziz, zzzzziz, zzzzziz!* the reel hummed and buzzed as the brookie dove for the bottom again. Much more powerful now than it had been when it was caught and released, the brook trout shook its huge head in terror and anger.

O'Casey could feel the headshakes and then the surges as the brookie would dive for the bottom, rest in the current to catch its strength, and dive again. The runs were shorter now. The brook trout was tiring. O'Casey knew this was a fine trout, perhaps the biggest one he had ever hooked. He was determined not to lose the fish. However, he knew that if he let the fish get too tired, it might not recover. Releasing a trophy fish only to find it belly-up and bloated a day later would spoil any joy or sense of victory such a catch might otherwise have. For O'Casey, there was a cerebral, ethical side to fly-fishing. He didn't want to lose the fish, yet he also didn't want to kill the fish. Applying leverage with his rod butt, he used his left wrist to turn the brookie's head.

It worked. The big male turned his head and then his massive body downstream. O'Casey then quickly stripped in line as the impressive trout came toward the surface and swam in his direction.

Angelo was awake now, thanks to the shouts from Ellen and Maria. He joined the cheering section as the trio hollered encouraging words to the fisherman. O'Casey smiled broadly and looked momentarily to see if the Chief was among the group, but he wasn't. O'Casey and Butch had an unwritten, unspoken competition going when it came to fly-fishing. Both knew that Butch was the master. He could cast farther and smoother. He was far better at fly tying and at matching the hatch. However, when it came to results, the two men were pretty close indeed. On rare occasions, O'Casey actually out fished the Chief. The pupil outdid the master. Given how hard Butch played his roles of *Master* Maine Guide and *the Chief,* O'Casey relished the thought of having Granville Butch Chapman eat just a small portion of crow. *A little healthy competition can be good for even the best of friends,* thought the big Irishman.

Unfortunately, O'Casey had gotten a bit careless as he imagined himself hoisting the trophy trout up for the crowd. The big brookie had reenergized. Rather than pulling against the leverage of the powerful graphite rod, it was now running with the current straight toward O'Casey and the rapids below where he stood. In all sports, momentum is everything. O'Casey had all the momentum when the brookie had run for the deep hole. The strength of the rod and his adroit line play had tired the fish to the point of exhaustion. Still, the wary fish had grown to be a six-pound trophy fish because it had strength, speed, and stamina that had broken many a leader before. Only one fisherman had conquered it. That Master Maine Guide had released it to fight another day, and today was that day. The enormous male fought with a renewed energy that made it a worthy opponent for the best of fishermen.

The big brookie quickly surged past the fisherman and out into the strongest part of the current. For an instant, O'Casey had been able to strip in enough slack to turn the broad head of the brookie toward him once again. Doing so brought the entire flank of the fish across the current and right to the surface, exposing a large muscular body that was as broad as a football at the dorsal fin level. When the onlookers saw the fish turn, they gasped at its size. Even O'Casey, who knew he had a lunker on, had no idea the trout was so large or he would never have tried to turn it.

What a stupid move! he now thought. He quickly stripped in line again to pull the fish back toward him and away from the sluice of rapids that led to white water and freedom for the fish. Just as he was about to regain the momentum and finesse the monster into the shallows to his left, the trout shook his head again to throw the fly. O'Casey backed off just enough to avoid ripping the fly out of its bent, char-like jaw.

Sensing that bit of slack, the trout jumped completely out of the water, exposing a crimson belly and a magnificent spotted body almost two feet in length. It was a trophy trout worthy of the skills of the best taxidermist one could find. In an instant, O'Casey knew he had just seen his dream trout—the perfect fish in color, in size, in temperament. Seeing it leap, he once again had to give the fish some slack to prevent the three-pound tippet from snapping in midjump. The leap was just enough to put the trout into the middle of the rapids with its body at an angle to the current. This made the six-pound fish feel like a ten-pounder on the line.

There was no chance that O'Casey could run downstream to stay even with the fish. A large boulder stood in his way and the steep bank meant he couldn't go up and around the boulder.

Zzzzziz! Zzzzziz, zzzzziz!

The powerful fish could no longer be held in check. The squaretail, as Maine brook trout are often called, was now well into the buff-colored backing. O'Casey could only follow the fish by watching the end of the neon yellow fly line two pools below him. For a brief moment, the fish rested in that small, deep pool. With the respite, O'Casey gave some thought to swimming toward the fish himself as a way to save his trophy. However, as he applied some pressure to keep the fish within the eddy, the squaretail sensed that the battle had been rejoined. With a thrust of its massive six-inch tail, the magnificent fish made a final leap and threw the caddis fly free of its lip for good. That one instant seemed to last several seconds. It was just enough time for everyone to see its huge crimson flank and jagged jaw, just enough time to appreciate the strength, the beauty, the perfection of the trout in its finest moment.

In the next instant, the fish was gone. O'Casey could hear himself panting even over the roar of the rapids before him. He could feel the rush of adrenaline and the pounding of his heart. The afternoon sun sparkled like a million slate-colored crystals off the churning water where the fish had made its final leap. O'Casey stood transfixed, oblivious to everything else. His breath began to slow. His hands stopped shaking.

"Nice fish! Nice try!"

O'Casey looked up to see Butch now standing with the gang. The Chief was genuinely proud of his protégé's efforts, though he had seen O'Casey's mistake from the edge of the trail. It had happened just as O'Casey had responded to the crowd, just as he had looked up to see if Butch was watching with the group. In fact, Butch *was* watching, but not on the bank where O'Casey had looked. The Chief knew that by letting the fish run directly downstream, the big brookie would find its way into the middle of the current and the outcome would be exactly what it was. Butch would have worked the fish immediately toward the shore, forcing it into the shallows where it could be released.

In fact, that's exactly what he had done with that very fish sometime before. Butch was that other fisherman, the one who had caught the big male when it was a four-pounder and not quite so wise or so strong. Although he could not know it, Butch was the one fisherman who had successfully caught and released that trophy trout. It was smarter now and stronger. It had learned something about fishermen. Neither Butch nor the trout would get a chance to test their skills against the other again, but had you asked the Chief that day, at that time, he would certainly have said, "Yeah, I would have owned that bad boy. That brookie would have been all mine."

Fortunately, O'Casey could not read Granville Chapman's mind. Had he done so, his general sense of frustration might have quickly turned to anger. Instead, as Sean Padraig O'Casey worked his way along the shore back to the group, he replayed the tape he would have forever lodged in his mind of a fish that would only get bigger and more beautiful in his memory and in his heart. While it was, in one way, a sad experience, in another sense, it was almost the perfect contest between fish and fisherman. "The fish won," O'Casey was finally able to chuckle to himself. Then he thought, *Hell, I fooled* him. *That was my fly. My caddis.*

Aside from the Chief, the other onlookers were far more congratulatory of O'Casey and his prowess as an angler. Maria, Angelo, and Ellen seemed in awe of what they witnessed.

"Man, that was just amazing!" said Angelo. "I never really wanted to fish before. Now I can see why you and Butch talk so much about fly-fishing."

Both Ellen and Maria were struck by the sense of poetry, the simple elegance as they had watched O'Casey casting for trout. From their angle on the hill, with the sun backlighting his casts, it seemed like a magical event. However, the magic suddenly turned into sheer combat once the monster trout was on the line. "I wish I'd had my video camera going," said Maria.

"*You* do? I'd pay a hundred bucks just to watch that video even once," said O'Casey. "I guess I'll have to settle for the one that's running through my brain right now."

"Nice job, Paddy!" said Butch.

"Thanks, Chief." It was the first time that Sean Padraig O'Casey had ever called his friend *Chief*. He knew that others, especially Angelo, used the term often, and the women had quickly picked up the nickname. Given their subtle and sometimes not-so-subtle rivalry, O'Casey had always felt that the nickname was an extra star that Butch did not need. He already had *Master* affixed to his Maine Guide title. His football-player frame and natural good looks did not require another boost to an already significant ego. However, O'Casey had been stunned when Butch had said, "Nice job, Paddy!" Usually, Butch called him *O'Casey* like everyone else. Only his very best friends, almost all of them micks from his hometown of Boston, used the nickname Paddy, the diminutive for Padraig, which was Irish for Patrick.

Although Butch didn't know the etymology of the name, he knew that calling O'Casey by his favorite nickname was paying him the ultimate compliment. O'Casey had picked up the nuance in a way that none of the others had even understood. In effect, Butch Chapman had told O'Casey, "You did a great job with the fish. I'm proud of you." It was the first time O'Casey could recall Butch ever calling him Paddy. It may also have been the first real compliment of sorts Butch had ever paid to his fishing buddy. It was about as sensitive and as personal a moment as the two fishermen had ever had. Sean Padraig O'Casey turned slowly to see the Chief with a big grin on his face. O'Casey returned the smile.

Butch clapped his hands. He had that familiar take-charge look of the Maine Guide on his face. The Chief had returned to motivate the tribe.

"Let's go, gang. Time to hump the gear. I want to be at the head of Wilson Lake by five so we can get camp all set before it gets dark.... Where the heck is Jason?"

"I don't know. It wasn't my turn to watch him," said Tiffany, who had rejoined the group shortly after O'Casey had hooked the fish.

"Hey, Angelo! Where's Jason?" said Butch. "The last time I looked, you guys were sharing a beer, and he was telling you a bunch of his war stories from Moron High School."

Everyone laughed at Butch calling it Moron High. They all knew that was the hometown slang for James Morton High School—a school with a less than stellar reputation. Jason's friends often teased him with the accusation that Moron High was an appropriate fit for him. He secretly hated that dig, even though he knew there was a modicum of truth to it. Who else would have hired a social studies teacher/football coach who had flunked three separate college English courses?

"I don't know where he is," said an embarrassed Angelo Capelletti. "I fell asleep. I'm probably the only person in the world who can pass out after one beer."

"You passed out from boredom," said Tiffany as she came to Angelo's defense. "You're just lucky you're not his canoe mate. At one point this morning, I was ready to jump overboard and drown myself. Then after his Bozo move with the fawns, I was almost ready to drown *him*."

"Hey, Chief," Angelo pondered, "do you think he might have passed out in this hot sun? He's probably already had four or five beers."

"Oh, man," said Butch. "If that freakin' Foxworthy has passed out, I'll be really pissed. The only thing that could be worse is if he got himself lost. Other than Alaska, this is probably one of the worst states for someone to get lost in. The next big town you'll run into due north of here is Quebec, and that's a ten-day hike and one country away. None of you wants to get lost here. Not ever! Sometimes hunters come across human bones that are I.D.'d as a person lost twenty years ago. That's *if* they find the bones. The bears like to crunch on old bones to sharpen their teeth. Damn it! He had better not get lost. I'll find him and kick his ass."

The tribe could sense the Chief's concern, and, to a lesser degree, his not-quite-hidden disdain for Jason Foxworthy. As much as Tiffany really wanted to find Jason, she was struck by the thought of a bear gnawing on human bones. It sent a shiver to the base of her spine. It was a strange and primitive feeling—one that made her feel absolutely terrified, but very much alive at the same time.

Everyone was surprised by the change in tone and language the Chief had used. For someone who rarely got flustered in the woods, he did sound genuinely concerned. Only Ellen had given any thought to getting lost in the woods—when she'd gone to change her clothes and take a pee. Instinctively, she had known that in a heartbeat she could be lost and might, in a panic, run *away from* rather than toward the lake. That's why she had traded a little modesty for the proximity of being able to see the lake.

She was also truly terrified of bears, after a scary experience while visiting the zoo as a child. Still, she was determined not to let that memory or her childhood nightmares of that event even briefly enter her mind on this trip. *Butch would never let that happen*, she kept telling herself. Had she known just how much Jason had been ogling her naked thighs that day as they literally glowed in the morning sun, Ellen might have opted for being lost in the woods or chased by a bear.

Rrrh! Rrrh. Chuppah. Chup. Chup. Chup. A strange metallic-sounding monster coughed and sputtered, interrupting the group's thoughts of Jason's possible plight. First, it seemed like an odd kind of distant thunder, then perhaps a fire warden's helicopter. But as it grew louder, it took on an antique motor quality.

"What the heck is that?" asked Maria with a puzzled, almost fearful look on her face. Talk of getting lost had raised her adrenaline level immediately. As someone who'd grown up in the barrios of west Texas and the tenements of Lawrence, Massachusetts, Maria saw the woods as a foreign, almost hostile territory. However, she also had a love for nature and animals. This trip, in many ways, was an effort to conquer some of her fears.

The sound grew louder still. It had everyone's attention. Briefly, they even forgot the fact that Jason Foxworthy was missing. They should never have worried. He was missing no longer. The strange chugging noise became a tractor—a classic 1946 John Deere Series 88—and it was moving in a slow, almost primitive mechanical dance. This would not have been a commercial the John Deere Company would ever wish to run.

"You stupid asshole!" yelled Butch, outraged. "You stole the freakin' dam keeper's tractor?"

"He ain't gonna need it," Jason retorted as he throttled back the faded eighteen-horse John Deere and steered toward his thoroughly stunned colleagues.

There sat Jason Foxworthy, driving with one hand, a Budweiser in the other, and a grin half the width of the enormous rear tires. He almost forgot where the brake was as he reached the crest of the hill and had to turn the wheel sharply to avoid hitting the gang.

"You're freakin' crazy, Jason! You'll get us all arrested," protested Tiffany, half in anger and half in amazed admiration.

"I told you I wasn't gonna carry all that shit down the road," said Jason. "Me and Mr. John Deere are good friends now. He didn't like it much when I hot-wired him, but he's a-coughin' and a-singin' now."

Jason Foxworthy was in hog heaven. It had been years since he had been this proud. He'd tell all the seniors on the football team next fall. He'd tell everyone back at next year's Principals' Conference. He assumed he would be telling almost anyone at any bar who would listen about this moment in time. He was wrong about that, but for this one moment, he was literally the King of the Hill. These were his fifteen minutes of fame.

"Grab your gear, gang. This train is departing on track number nine and heading for points south. Al-l-l aboard!"

He was in rare form now. His smile was like that of a nine-year-old at Christmas time. He was not a braggart right now. He was not a drunk, not a thief, not a scofflaw. He was a happy nine-year-old showing off a toy to his friends. He was a kid again. And he soon brought out the kid in all of them, including O'Casey, who pretty much despised him. But now, even O'Casey saw the humor and roared with laughter.

"Al-l-l aboard!" Jason shouted again, now that he had everyone's attention and approval. It was only then that they noticed the old hay wagon Jason had hitched to the tractor. The wagon's low wooden profile as a tethered extension of the smoking, lurching engine made it easy to imagine a turn-of-the-century train hauling logs or loggers from the dam here in the north woods.

"You heard the engineer," shouted Butch, as he good-naturedly reinforced Jason's metaphor. "Let's load up our personal gear before this thing dies or Jason falls off."

Everyone joined the fray, and it was Chaos Central as beer and backpacks, sleeping bags and sandwich bags were thrown on board the hay wagon.

"Let's toast to our trip!" shouted Jason, still grinning broadly.

Dangling from the emergency brake lever was a six-pack of Bud hanging by the one empty plastic O-ring of the pack. The entire crew shook their heads in amazement, but not disbelief. This was a true Foxworthy moment, one that could be told and retold for years. If Butch was the trip's chief, Jason had now assumed the role of cruise director. He quickly snapped off one beer after another and tossed them back to the others, who had wiggled in amidst the gear like a group of teenagers ready for a hayride. The jostling of the tractor and the long toss to the back of the hay wagon made the beers all the more explosive. *Puuuushhh! Pusssh! Buushhhhhhhh!* Beer after beer sprayed and splattered. By beer number three, everyone had joined in with self-induced showers.

"Yee-hah!" crowed Butch as he wiped the first beer from his face.

Tiffany quickly grabbed a beer that was still rolling along the wagon floorboards. "Hey, O'Casey! Enjoy your shower!" she said as she pulled the tab and tilted the can in the direction of O'Casey's face. *Puuuushhh!* went the beer as the spray showered both O'Casey and Ellen, who sat next to him.

"Hey, Tiffany!" yelled Maria as she got caught up in the playful spirit. Tiffany instinctively turned her head, and Maria showed both her prowess and her good humor in close-quarter combat—and pulled the beer tab. Tiffany no longer looked like a former debutante. Her face was covered in foam and froth and her hair was wet and straggly. For a moment, everyone held their breath.

"Yee-hah!" she cried, echoing Butch Chapman's response and surprising them all. "Party on!"

"Let's make a toast," said Angelo with a sincerity that seemed to rise above the silliness. "To the principals!" he grinned as he raised his beer in honest respect for his colleagues.

"To the principals!" echoed first one, then another, as each member of the group raised what was left of their beer. "To the principals!"

The early tension of the canoe trip seemed long lost in this moment of camaraderie. This was their baptism. They would do much and learn much in the days ahead. New tensions and terror would test their very fabric. But right here, right now, they were lost in a special moment.

Hopping on the old hay wagon, the Foxworthy Express, as they called it, would be one of their most treasured moments. They were now united in the sheer idiocy of being nineteen again, dripping in beer, laughing with every bump, sharing what was left of each beer with one another, and hoping the moment would last forever.

WHITE WATER, WHITE DEATH

The alcohol had transformed their wagon ride from a simple portage trip to a raucous adventure. Every bump and jostle brought a laugh or a smile. Beer splashed or was splashed on everyone. No face was clean. No body was dry. Maria in particular was thoroughly soaked after her second beer exploded in her lap. One stream of beer had shot upward toward her round chin, while the larger stream shot directly toward her chest. Her scooped-neck, light blue soccer jersey, *Madison Girls Rule,* was now slightly transparent and thoroughly soaked. Maria was perhaps the best-natured of the entire tribe, as they were now calling themselves. Having been laughed at much of her life, she was used to wearing the laugher of others, and hardly minded wearing a beer *and* a laugh with her newfound friends.

On this trip, no one was laughing at Maria. They were laughing with her as she wiped the beer from her chin and chest, then grinned and gave the now common refrain, "Yee-hah!" What she did not notice, or perhaps did not care to notice, was that her ample chest was now much more clearly pronounced. It was almost as though the beer spray had soaked her neck and right breast and had left the rest of her T-shirt dry, though dirty. Her Victoria's Secret "Sweet Nothing" bra, in fact, did almost nothing to hide what nature had given her. Even Tiffany and Ellen soon noticed the large nipple standing out beneath the beer-drenched shirt. It was a nipple erection of legendary proportions. Maria had meant to switch to her jogging bra for the first day of their adventure, but there had not even been time to shower that morning. Four A.M. had come very early, and Butch had been a taskmaster, knocking on their motel door repeatedly until everyone was on the move, out the door, and headed for the Allagash—all well before daylight.

Even amid the chaos, the beer, and the stories Jason and Butch had been sharing, it was obvious that everyone had noticed Maria's décolletage. Finally, Maria noticed it, too. She had been wondering why everyone had been looking in her direction. She wiped her face several times, thinking she still had beer foam dripping off her chin. Then she looked down.

"Oops. Wet gazoombas," she announced with an innocent grin that was remarkable for a forty-five-year-old woman in these circumstances. "Sometimes I wear my pizza there, too. Guess I'll wear my sports bra tomorrow, huh," Maria said as though she were talking about changing her earrings.

Silently, Butch, and particularly Jason, were thinking and hoping, *No! No! You look great just the way you are.*

O'Casey, too, was impressed by what he saw, but he was more impressed with her good humor, her easygoing nature, and her constant smile. "Here," O'Casey said as he took off his favorite tan Orvis fishing shirt and tossed it to Maria. "This'll help keep Jason's eyes on the road."

Everyone laughed at O'Casey's remark, everyone, that is, but Jason Foxworthy. Even though what O'Casey had said was true, Jason was pissed that O'Casey had focused the laughter at him.

"As if you weren't looking, too," Jason shot back.

Then he realized what he had said. While everyone had looked at Maria's chest, none would have wanted to admit it, particularly the other women, who were a bit embarrassed at not having said something first to call a halt to the group ogle. Jason, by being honest, was also being a jerk by getting angry at what had been a very funny moment. Somehow, his retort had fractured the joviality, the mystique, and the frat-party spirit. In the same way a fight can derail an otherwise exceptional college party, Jason's angry outburst, had, in an instant, derailed their "magical mystery tour," their brief journey back to the innocence and silliness that is often difficult for adults to find. He had transformed the atmosphere in a negative way, much as he had started the levity of the adventure with his first "Al-l-l aboard!" at the top of the dam. That was Jason—one minute the likeable class clown, the next minute the archetypal asshole.

Butch sensed the tension building between Jason and O'Casey and knew he had to intervene. He had done so in situations like this many times before, not just as a school principal, but also as a Maine Guide. Such conflicts were all too common on the fishing charters Butch guided from May through September. Sometimes, just changing the focus or the subject was enough to defuse a potentially difficult situation.

"We're just about here, ladies and germs," Butch said, hoping to inject a little humor and redirect the crew. "We've still got a long day ahead of us, so get your poopers movin'! All the gear comes off the wagon, but I want to swap out Jason's life jacket for that extra one I brought. Leave that orange joke of a jacket here with the other gear and we'll pick it up when we finish shooting the Cut."

Butch took most everything about as seriously as passing gas, which he often did without hesitation, even in mixed company. Not much bothered him, and he rarely worried about anything—which can be both a blessing and a curse for a principal. However, when it came to safety on the river, he took things *very* seriously. This was more than a second job for him. It was his calling. It was what he was meant to do. Granville Chapman belonged to another time. While he was never really much of a teacher, and some might contend not a really *great* principal, he could make parts of American history completely come to life. When he gave his lectures on Rogers Rangers during the French and Indian Wars, or the cannibalism of the Donner Party lost in a blizzard in the Sierra Nevada, students would actually sneak into his class just to listen. On occasion, Butch would find ways to bring lessons from history, particularly from the frontier, into his coaching or into his guiding trips.

As his thoughts began to refocus on unloading the gear, he reiterated, "Foxy, if you want to drown and look stupid in the process, you can bring that orange albatross of a life jacket, but I only have life jackets in my canoe for two reasons. First, it keeps me from getting a fine from the warden, who ain't here today anyway, and the second reason is to save my ass when I need it."

Jason Foxworthy hated to be called Foxy. Almost nobody would dare to, not just because he was a pretty big guy and a former football player, but because he had a very short fuse and an occasional mean streak. He'd once broken a person's nose at a frat party when the guy accidentally spilled beer on his date. Even Jason's date was horrified at the violent display. The poor guy, a geeky freshman about fifty pounds lighter than

Jason, never even saw the punch coming. It was a "rush" party, and the poor freshman knew he'd be dead meat if he blew the whistle on one of the pledge masters, especially someone with Jason Foxworthy's reputation. The incident didn't faze Jason, though. His only response when several of his frat brothers shook their heads in disapproval was to say, "What? What? That little asshole spilled beer on Margie's new sweater. I should have really kicked his ass."

Bullies like Jason had an amazingly distorted, self-centered perception of the world. He performed his job as a high school principal in much the same way he'd dealt with the freshman pledge that night. Jason never actually hit kids, but only because he'd lose his meal ticket. He found other ways to threaten and bully without breaking the law or breaking a nose while still getting that same thrill of knowing that when he walked down a hall, people moved out of his way…and that was the important thing.

"Foxy. Did you hear me?" Butch repeated again. "Leave that stupid Sears Roebuck life jacket here with the rest of the gear. If you're gonna' run the Cut with us, I want you to make it from the top to the bottom all in one piece."

Jason ignored the request and the hated nickname. He could ignore it from Butch because they were friends, sort of. *However, if that granola-head O'Casey ever calls me Foxy, I'll kick the shit out of him*, he thought to himself. *And if that faggot Angelo ever calls me anything…*, Jason pondered. Well, it was a waste of time trying to imagine Angelo having the courage to call him a name. He'd be screwed big time. Jason smiled, knowing that the Angelos of the world always got out of his way, and that's just how he liked it.

"That's it for gear, Butch," Ellen shouted as she and the rest of the crew off-loaded the last of the portaged gear.

It was amazing how much they had brought. The Chief smiled in disbelief. He had been half daydreaming and half planning the next phase of the adventure. Usually, he was the first one to lead a work party. After all, he was their Chief. *Granville* Chapman, the school principal, was not a particularly hard worker. *Butch* Chapman, the Master Maine Guide, was a workhorse and sometimes a packhorse. Right now, he was just a very happy guy, watching the rest of the tribe finish the work he would normally have been doing.

"Yeah," Maria chimed in, "everything's out of Jason's prairie schooner, but what you guys need for canoeing is back up on the hill by the dam." She and the rest of the crew had made short work of unloading the wagon, but Maria was so eager to get on with the adventure that she could have and would have unloaded the wagon by herself.

"Saddle up!" yelled Butch. It was one of his favorite commands. Every bus ride to and from every game started with those very words. Butch had often imagined himself as the lead scout in a Western movie, heading out to find a safe passage for the wagon train he was leading and protecting. That was part of what he loved about being a Maine Guide—that sense of leading a group into the wilderness, into the unknown. He never knew what was going to happen. Sometimes trips were tame. Sometimes they were more dangerous than anyone could have predicted. No one could have predicted the outcome of this trip.

As Jason ground the unwilling gears from reverse to first and the wagon lurched forward, back up the hill and toward the dam, the great Granville Chapman *history tour* began.

"Have I ever told you how the Cut got its name?" Butch asked, as though he were talking to a group of second graders. Surprisingly, these disparate adults quickly turned their heads and their full attention to him like so many eight-year-olds sitting Indian-style at story hour with their teacher. And so he was. Granville Butch Chapman had taken charge once again. The Chief was leading his tribe. A mixture of folklore and Maine history was about to be shared. As the wagon lumbered and lurched along, the tribe hung on every word.

"Aggamog Cut was really just a small stream, one-tenth the size it is now," Butch said. "In the late 1830s, Mainers got fed up with aggressive Canadian efforts to control logging in the north woods and to keep most of the profits for themselves. Besides, there had never been a clear northern border that both Mainers and Canadians could agree on. It got so bad that the disagreement became known as the Aroostook Wars. Believe it or not," Butch embellished slightly, "Winfield Scott and a small contingent of tough American troops, mostly good ol' Maine boys, were getting ready to pop those Canadians—to settle it once and for all.

"Although the Webster-Ashburton Treaty would ultimately solve the border war, the bigger issue for *us* was timber. The lakes here flowed north to the St. John River," Butch announced, pointing up the portage trail. "Unfortunately," he editorialized, "the St. John flowed northeast into Canada. Then a bunch of Maine boys did something really cool. They built a dam about fifteen miles from where we are now to raise the lake water up really high. Then they made a *cut* through the forest to connect the lake above the dam to the one below it. That's where we are now, ladies. The logs started flowing this way, right in front of us, down the river—all the way to freakin' Bangor, U.S. of A.," Butch announced with a flourish.

"Boy, were those Canadians some ol' pissed off! Just imagine plodding teams of horses and hundreds of men digging this cut, opening up the wilderness, so that Mainers could market their logs in Maine and all over the world…. What's really cool," Butch said almost reverently, "is that some of *my* family, my great-great uncle Ephraim Granville Chapman, was one a them loggers."

He smiled as his Maine accent really began to take over. "Wicked neat. Right here. Sawin' logs. Blowin' up rocks—ol' Uncle Ephraim. No shit. That's part of the reason I love this place. It feels like home."

Time seemed to stand still for the tribe as the Chief finished his tale. The details were so rich one might have thought that Butch himself had been there over a hundred and seventy years before, when it all happened. Maybe he had been. Butch truly loved the lore and legend of the woods and made it come to life. From the smell of the camp smoke to the sound of syncopated axes swinging and chopping in the deliberate way of men on a mission, the Maine woodsmen and their cause now seemed a current event. The Cut was no longer just part of a destination. It was a destiny. It was a metaphor for the new America and what it represented. Butch could work similar magic in telling about the 20th Maine Regiment and their heroic bayonet charge down Cemetery Ridge, which helped turn the Battle of Gettysburg and save the Union. But that would have to be for another time.

Jason throttled back the old John Deere just as the wagon went over a rock the size of a basketball. Ellen and O'Casey, who were sitting up front across from Butch and leaning toward him so they would catch every morsel of the tale, were all but catapulted out of the wagon. Fortunately, the wooden railing held, and Angelo's quick hands help keep them from doing a nosedive that might have ended the trip.

Jason barely noticed. He was having the time of his life. Butch could tell all the old stories he wanted. Jason was still in charge of this part of the adventure. This was the "J-Train," as Maria had dubbed it, and he was still at the helm—at least for another few minutes. Just enough time to finish his beer. Number six, he thought, but who gave a shit? It was vacation, right? If he wanted to get a buzz on, that was his business. He'd seen them all get a buzz on at one time or another. Sometimes he'd seen O'Casey have five or six double Irish whiskeys while he and Butch talked sports.

Jason was still savoring the last foamy sip of his beer when Butch's shout brought him back to reality.

"For Christ's sake, stop the tractor! Stop the fuckin' tractor!" Butch screamed. Again, everyone was jolted, but this time they were thrown forward. Unfortunately, there was no one to stop Angelo, who slammed into the front railing of the wagon. His left hand, which had stretched out so recently to cushion Ellen's fall, this time wore a rusty nail that had been protruding from the corner of the railing.

"Ahh! Ahh! Did that hurt!" yelled Angelo as the jagged sixteen-penny spike went almost completely through his palm. He grabbed his left hand and just stared as blood began to drip down his wrist.

God, that hurts! Angelo thought to himself. No wonder crucifixions were the Romans' favorite torture. Fortunately, this nail had hit the meaty flesh and missed any major blood vessels. Still, it was a very deep, painful wound, and not where you'd want to get a cut just before doing some heavy-duty white water.

Ellen and Maria hovered over him while he tried to mask the intense pain with gritted teeth and a tight-lipped smile. Their Clara Barton instincts for kindness and support were tempered by the fact that neither liked the sight of blood. However, O'Casey had swiftly opened a small first aid kit that he always kept on his belt. He had a severe allergy to bee stings and kept his EpiPen with him in the kit at all times. He and Butch were just getting ready to dress the wound when Angelo pulled his hand away.

"No, no. I'll do it!" Angelo shouted. "It's my screw-up and my blood. Thanks, guys. Just leave me alone, and I'll get it myself."

Normally, O'Casey and the Chief would have insisted. But they were both so startled by Angelo's uncharacteristically forceful reaction that they obediently handed over the bandage and Neosporin. "At least let us help tape up the bandage. That's hard to do with one hand," said Butch.

Angelo smiled at him in a remarkably responsive way for someone who had suffered a crucifixion-like wound to his palm. Had he not already braced his body with his other hand, the impact would certainly have driven the nail completely through his hand. He now seemed almost oblivious to the pain. As Butch gently wrapped the athletic tape strips around the bandage and across his palm, Angelo again smiled—mostly with his eyes—in spite of the pain. It was almost a wink, a twinkle of sorts that acknowledged both Butch's concern and the close friendship they had shared for years.

Angelo seemed more concerned about the blood than the wound. He poured most of the water from his Poland Spring bottle down his arm to wash off the copious amounts of blood that had run from his palm to past his elbow.

"I've got it," O'Casey whispered, as he used water from his own bottle and a handkerchief to help with the cleanup.

"Jesus, I'm all right! Leave me alone! I can do it myself!" Angelo snapped abruptly. He looked at the bloody handkerchief and grabbed it out of O'Casey's hand. Everyone went quiet. The river beckoned in the background with its splashing and ominous roar. The early deer flies circled overhead as the heat of the June morning grew toward noon. Everyone had been caught off guard by Angelo's uncharacteristically angry response to O'Casey's ministrations.

Even Jason was startled. He was about to shout, "You tell him, Angelo!" when Angelo himself, suddenly aware of his own behavior, found some levity in the very awkward moment.

"Didn't you guys ever see that stupid blood-borne pathogens movie? Even us ex-music teachers know better than to handle blood without gloves. For all you know, I could have freakin' cooties!"

Everyone laughed, albeit a bit nervously, both because it was funny and because they knew it had been a difficult moment for Angelo, who was about the most even-tempered person any of them had ever met. In all the years Butch had known Angelo, it was the most forceful he had ever seen his friend. That was one of the goals Butch had tried to work on with him. "If you're going to be a successful principal, sometimes you have to be more assertive. Otherwise, the kids will have you for lunch… and if they don't, your staff and parents will."

While being more aggressive would certainly have helped Angelo on many occasions as a principal, it was just not part of his style. Being nice, being kind, seemed to work most of the time. While Angelo's staff secretly wished he would be more forceful in dealing with discipline issues and recess problems, they had such great respect for his compassion and work ethic that they overlooked his other shortcomings.

When the laughter died down, someone in the group noticed the position of the tractor and the wagon where they were seated. The front wheels of the tractor were already over the edge of a small precipice. While the drop was not significant, it would have been enough to take the tractor and wagon right into the river.

"Christ almighty!" Butch shouted to Jason. "Put it in reverse…and be careful! Make sure it's reverse and not freakin' forward!"

Apparently oblivious to the near catastrophe he had almost caused, Jason dutifully put the John Deere into reverse after mis-shifting several times. The tractor and wagon bucked and lurched their way back a safe distance from the brink.

"Phew!" Ellen said. "I thought for a minute we were going swimming."

Tiffany had been silent for much of the ride, quietly thankful for having avoided her mother's party in the Hamptons. Startled back to reality, just shook her head when she realized how close they had come to a serious accident. The jagged pile of gray granite just below the rusty front wheels of the tractor was part of a steep ledge tapering sharply down to the water. Had the Chief not alerted Jason to hit the brakes, the entire trip would have been over. Their bodies would certainly have been bruised and bloodied in the fall, which could easily have been fatal for some or all of them. While most of the tribe seemed to dismiss this near-death experience as just another part of the day, Tiffany, having lived the most sheltered life of anyone in the group, seemed to fully grasp what had nearly happened. "Butch, I thought you said this trip was going to be *fun*. It looks more and more like a train wreck about to happen."

"Nah," Butch smiled as if to pooh-pooh the entire event. "The fun is just about to begin, ladies!"

He used the expression *ladies* to include everyone. Had there been six former CIA officials in the wagon, he would have used the same word. "Ladies" referred to everyone but Butch himself. That was Butch. On one hand, he was trying to be funny, and on the other, he was reminding them that they were still Girls Scouts, as far as he was concerned. That wasn't arrogance on Butch's part; it was just a fact. Most of his tribe, with the exception of O'Casey, had probably never even pooped in the woods before. But they wouldn't have a choice now. The last outhouse was on the hill by the dam and would soon become a distant memory—and a missed opportunity for the ladies, who would soon wish they had paid that fly-filled two-holer one last visit.

"Saddle up!" came the predictable command as Butch sought to motivate his fellow paddlers into action.

"Hey, Butch. So how is this thing—this Cut stuff, us doin' this river— supposed to work?" Jason sputtered, the words working their way rather laboriously from his mouth. The six beers he had consumed over the last few hours were beginning to compromise both his speech and his judgment.

"Given how hard the water's running today, I suspect we won't be doin' the river as much as the river will be doin' us. You sound a bit tongue-tied, Jason. You OK? You've been pounding the beers to you. Can you do this thing? This is a big-time freakin' team effort, you know."

"If they can do it, I can do it," Jason shot back with a nod toward O'Casey and Angelo. While he could tolerate both men and occasionally enjoyed being with them because it usually meant a good time with Butch, he would never socialize with either unless Butch were the ringleader. Butch was just plain fun to be around. They had a lot in common— sports, beer drinking, checking out good cleavage at the bars, and tales of the "good old days." However, Jason found O'Casey to be a snob—usually drinking chardonnay, Guinness, or Irish whiskey. Jason had a theory that anyone who had contempt for Budweiser or Coors beer was somehow un-American and hence an asshole. That's what he thought of O'Casey.

And Angelo ... in some ways, he liked Angelo even less. He knew Angelo was a fag. He'd heard the rumor about Angelo being chased from his last job for hitting on the board chair's kid, though Butch always swore that the kid had made it up. Butch had denied the rumors up and down, Jason felt, because he had hired Angelo and because, for some reason Jason could never figure out, Butch and Angelo were actually good friends. Still, everything pointed to Angelo's being gay. He never made comments about the girls when Jason and Butch were checking them out. And while Angelo hung out with women on occasion, Jason never believed they were dates. More like the gay hairdresser's lady friends, in his opinion. The clincher had come when he and Angelo were waiting at a bar for Butch to show up, and Angelo ordered a freakin' Dubonnet on the rocks. What a candy-ass move that was! What kind of guy does that? *A fag, that's who*, thought Jason.

Slipping back into reality, Jason looked down at the cascades of roaring white water just below him. *If freakin' Angelo and O'Casey are gonna do the Cut, I am, too—surer than shit! Yeah. Bring it on!*

"Jason! Jason!" Butch shouted. He always hated trying to bring Jason back from his daydreams and fantasies, especially after Jason had hit the beer.

"You're going with O'Casey. Angelo is riding bow for me," Butch announced as though he were reading from the lineup card that he gave to the umpires before the start of the game. He could have shouted to an anxious crowd: "And riding bow for the L.L. Bean canoe team will be Angelo Capelletti. And riding bow stroke for the Sears Roebuck aluminum canoe team will be Jason 'Foxy' Foxworthy."

Butch almost did just that, but he knew Jason was going to be pissed enough at not being in Butch's canoe. The last thing he wanted to do was anger a drunk, because that's what he knew he had right now. It was obvious to everyone but Jason.

In fact, Jason had just finished beer number six, and it was barely noon. But that was just Jason, Butch thought. He often had clients drink hard on trips. He knew that could be a bad combination—just as dangerous as drinking and driving. Still, in the woods of Maine, drinking hard was more common than not. Sometimes, his job was being one part guide, one part bartender, one part nursemaid—and sometimes, one part EMT. That was his only fear. Beer and white water were rarely a good combination. Today, with three gates now open, Black Powder Pitch would be a bear. *But it will also be fun*, Butch thought, as he readied the last of the gear and prepared for the adventure.

"Hey, Butch? How come I'm not in the bow with you?" Jason had just realized that his dream to conquer the Cut in a spray-soaked canoe with Butch was not going to happen. He had pictured that triumph many times over the last few months. Butch had told him about the Cut and about its toughest falls—Black Powder Pitch—and how great it would be to look back from below the white water and crack a beer after beating the river.

"Rock and roll, ladies," Butch hollered. He loved that expression, even if it was sexist and might tick off the entire tribe. He also did it so that he would not have to answer Jason or take ten more minutes to argue with him about riding bow for O'Casey. Sean Padraig O'Casey was a seasoned canoeist and could handle the stern almost as well as Butch. Almost. Butch had seen the deep cut in Angelo's hand and knew that under ideal circumstances it would be difficult for Angelo to pull his weight in the bow. It would be that much harder now. Butch would need every bit of his own skills to keep his canoe right side up with Angelo in the bow. He knew the same would be true for O'Casey. He shook his head. What a pair of bow stokes they'd have! Angelo could barely use one hand; Jason, who was strong as an ox, already had six beers in his tank and would want to have one in his hand while paddling through a class four rapid.

Deep in the rational part of his brain that he used more often when guiding in formal situations, Butch knew this was a mistake. But these were friends. This was not business. He didn't have to worry about having his ass sued by an uptight accountant for getting a cracked rib. These were his *best* friends. He'd promised them they'd canoe the Cut. He couldn't back out now, nor would they let him.

"Maria, are you sure that you, Ellen, and Tiffany don't want to join us? It's going to be a great time. It'll put hair on your chest," he teased. While he knew that was an obnoxious and sexist thing to say, he also knew the women would laugh and forgive him. With just a little bit of Foxworthy-type instinct, he also thought, *Ah. They love that stuff.*

Quickly, each of the women expressed their best wishes and affirmed their willingness to observe from shore. "Thanks, Butch, but after rolling my kayak this morning, I've already met my capsize quota for the trip. That's enough for today," grinned Ellen. "My hair couldn't take two dunkings in one day."

"Where's the best place to watch from?" Tiffany asked.

"About three hundred yards down from here is Black Powder Pitch. If you walk the tote road back toward where we left the gear, you'll see a big orange blaze on the left and a path down to the river. That's for people who pussy out and portage the pitch—which is probably what we should actually do today, given how hard the river is running.

"So, ladies," he said turning to his canoe mates. "Do any of you want to pussy out and portage the falls?" the Chief asked in jest. He knew what the answer would be. Even though Angelo was actually terrified of doing Black Powder Pitch, he knew he couldn't say so. Butch was so jacked about doing the Cut that Angelo just couldn't let his friend down, even if it might cost him his life. He just couldn't.

"You gals better scamper down to the overlook while we get ready to boogie," Butch said. He thought the women probably hated the word *gals* … and he was right. Butch, however, they loved; they tolerated his sexist remarks because they were harmless and were meant more to get a rise from his female counterparts than anything.

Ellen and Maria looked at each other and shook their heads in mock disgust. Tiffany really didn't care, either. She was used to hanging out with super-jocks like Butch and would hardly consider herself the *feminist* type, in spite of her self-image as a strong professional woman. She knew what Butch was doing and actually thought it was kind of funny.

As the women headed for the falls on foot, Butch prepped the team for their white-water adventure. "We'll start out on the left. Then, we'll run through a good bit of the middle of the Cut. The tough part will be going from the far left to the far right, just before the falls. We'll all need to paddle our asses off to get over to the chute without dumping."

"What's a chute?" asked Angelo.

"A chute is a rock-free funnel. It's the only safe spot to take the falls. The middle is too rocky above the falls. The left side is too dangerous and too shallow, even in this high water. Too much chance of a head injury... and you'll notice, ladies, we're fresh out of helmets," Butch grinned.

"Just listen to O'Casey and me call out the stroke. It'll either be left-left, right-right, or middle-middle if we need to go straight. No port or starboard bullshit. Foxy here could never get that straight after six beers. And Jason, for Christ's sake, if you're going to wear that orange freakin' Sears Roebuck life jacket, at least buckle it the hell up."

Not surprisingly, an already irate Jason ignored Butch. While they were good friends, Jason not only hated being called Foxy, he hated being bossed around by anyone, even Butch. As he got ready to go, he wanted to try to talk his way out of going with O'Casey and into Butch's canoe, but he knew it was pointless. He took one look back at the stern as O'Casey jumped in smoothly and pushed off.

The swift dark water pulled the bows forward and to the left, much as Butch had predicted. Each of the men took a deep breath, each thinking his own thoughts, but all felt the mystical pull of the river that had their lives and their fates in its slippery grasp.

The black swirling water was like a greedy monster sucking them in. Its many white tongues of foam licked hungrily at the bow of the first canoe. The big deep pool below the dam swirled hard to the left. Water rushed along the dark moss-lined riverbank, and the shore was littered with water-worn tree trunks that had been tossed about in the flood of the spring ice-out. Now, although the river was much lower, it was still high for June because the hydro company engineer had opened a third gate earlier in the week. The river had much more of an early-May feel. It was not a tame river today. It was not a river that novice paddlers (let alone a drunken one) had any right to be on. It would be a difficult run even for Butch and O'Casey.

"Yee-hah!" shrieked Jason as they passed through a small chute in the first big pool.

The Cut narrowed into a series of short straight runs. "Left, left!" Butch ordered as the Bean canoe shot through the first and then the second set of rips near the area where O'Casey had lost his big fish. He actually looked quickly as they shot passed the lower pool where the big brookie had thrown his fly. The green-black waters hid their secrets well. *Maybe next time*, O'Casey thought as he pulled his J stroke to stabilize the canoe, and it shot by the large boulder to his right.

"Middle now! Hard strokes!" Butch directed Angelo as the river turned to the right and forced the canoeists to follow.

"Middle, Jason! Middle, middle!" O'Casey shouted. The aluminum canoe was hardly a performance match for Butch's state-of-the-art L.L. Bean white-water special, with its high sides and Kevlar, graphite composite. The Sears special was another matter. O'Casey almost wished they had taken his Old Town cruising canoe, which he and Maria had used in the morning. Unfortunately, it was too long and heavy for the Cut. Still, it might have been better than what they were using now. Even with O'Casey's deft paddling, Foxy's old aluminum job was just plain sluggish. Then again, it was not designed for the class three, almost class four, rapids they were running at the moment.

"Middle, Jason! Middle!" O'Casey yelled in the hope that physical strength could make up for the lack of a better canoe.

Slowly, the bow came around toward the middle, but not soon enough.

Chank, clank came the scraping, metallic sound of the port bow hitting a boulder. The canoe lurched to the right and slid awkwardly into the next pool.

"Come on, Jay! Help me out here! That's it, that's it!" O'Casey shouted over the roar of the river. He knew that he couldn't push Foxworthy too much, but he needed help and wasn't getting enough. *How will we ever make the hard right across to the big chute?* O'Casey wondered as he leaned forward and almost stood, trying to get a view of the rapids below.

"Left, Angelo, left!" Butch called as the green canoe swung smartly toward the left bank and into the smooth, boulder-free foam before dropping neatly into the next pool.

Butch was surprised by the shoulder-high stack of white water that greeted them. The bow went up and then thwacked into the dark green water. The river was even faster and stronger than he'd imagined when he had reconnoitered earlier that morning. The short thick stacks kept hitting and tossing them one smack after another. *That's why they call this section The Quick,* Butch thought to himself as he absorbed one pounding and prepared for another.

The river had two sections: The Quick and The Dead. They were almost through The Quick, and doing pretty well, Butch reflected, grinning broadly. The rush of adrenaline shot up through his lower back and into the base of his brain. This was what he was meant to do. This was where he was meant to be. *Huck, honey,* he thought, *there's no place else in the world I would rather be than right here, right now.* These were the words spoken by Jim, the runaway slave, to Huck Finn as they drifted down the Mississippi on their raft. It was one of the few quotes Butch had ever remembered because it somehow sang out to him in his head and in his heart.

Angelo was hardly feeling that same feeling. If the river were not a wild and raging monster, he might think that way, but instead, he was trying to survive the moment. His hand burned deeply and wept blood, but the terror of being in shoulder-high stacks of white water made even the pain of his puncture wound shrink into the background. His terror was palpable. His mother had made him fearful of the water from his earliest days, telling him stories of children drowning in all sorts of places—pools, lakes, the ocean. She would turn over in her grave were she to see her son gripping his paddle in fear, trying desperately to follow Butch's every command.

Surprisingly, the aluminum canoe followed quickly behind the Chief's. It helped, having Butch in the lead. O'Casey didn't have to read the river as much and could concentrate on how to compensate for a slow, unproductive bow partner. It wasn't that Jason couldn't canoe or follow directions. It was that Jason was more than half in the bag. With his seventh beer almost completely gone and wedged under a tie-down strap, his reflexes were dulled even more on the river than they had been when he was driving the tractor. His strokes were clumsy and nearly ineffectual. Every stroke produced a clank against the aluminum hull. Still, the now-dented canoe followed directly behind and stayed close on the trail of the sleek green L.L. Bean special.

The lower section of The Quick gave the paddlers a short, pleasant break from the near terror of the haystacks. Smooth deep water swept along the banks and splashed the boulders along the river's edge. Butch and O'Casey scanned the river below them. Sleek water and a safe left-hand passage awaited them. Butch shot a fist up, pleased at their first big test.

Angelo glanced back quickly and caught the Chief's proud, infectious grin.

This is great! Angelo thought. "Butch, you were right. This is the best!"

"Yee-hah!" shouted Jason, responding to the triumphant gestures from the lead canoe. Almost magically, he pulled a beer from the pocket of his cargo pants. *No wonder Jason always wears those,* O'Casey thought. He couldn't believe that Jason had brought yet another beer, and was even more amazed and somewhat angry that he was trying to drain it now.

Jason even tried to toss it back to O'Casey to take a swig. "No, thanks. Save it for after the chute. We're hardly done yet," O'Casey hollered. Then, "Heads up! Heads up!"

The river had quickly turned restless again. Jason almost lost his paddle as he tried to put his near-empty beer down and return his impaired attention to the job at hand. The slow, deep water quickened as they approached The Dead section of the Cut. It was not called this because of the dead, quiet water at the end of the run, but rather because it was the area where canoeists would be found dead if they messed up on this part of the river. The calm, swirling pools they had just slid through were gone. Ahead on the left were short shallow runs and more stacks. Though smaller than those in The Quick, the stacks bounced the canoes around in a more threatening manner.

Water splashed in Angelo's face as the bow rose then dipped sharply. He was thoroughly soaked.

The stacks threw more than foam at Jason. Green water by the bucketful poured over the bow. "Yee-hah!" shouted Jason, who seemed more excited by the drama of the white water than the danger it brought. By the last stack, O'Casey could feel how sluggish the canoe had become. Two inches of water sloshing around their feet was the equivalent of a dead person lying in the bottom of the boat. Water was even worse than dead weight because it moved with the motion of the canoe, lifting the bow up as it ran to the stern and dropping the bow as the water surged forward again.

O'Casey knew they were in big trouble. While they had a small bailing bucket on board, there was no time to bail … maybe, just enough time to survive. O'Casey leaned forward and arched his back high enough to see the river's turn to the right. There ahead of them, less than a hundred yards away, was Black Powder Pitch—the most dangerous part of the Cut and the reason the section was called The Dead. Well down the bank just below the falls, he could see Maria, Tiffany, and Ellen waving with enthusiasm. O'Casey would have waved back if he were not so focused on trying to keep the canoe from rolling over.

"Get ready! Get ready! Now hard right! Hard right!" Butch shouted. The only way to clear the falls, or pitch, was to run from the far left-hand side of the river all the way across the river to the chute—the one section of the falls where a canoe could drop the five feet from the upper to the lower pool without landing on sharp rocks. The deep pool below the chute would cushion the bow in its steep descent from the upper falls. It could—and occasionally had—drowned the inept or unprepared canoeist or the unfortunate fisherman who had taken a misstep on the steep eastern bank above the falls.

Angelo responded in the bow as Butch took one power stroke after another. Cutting across the full width of the river in a scant fifty yards was almost impossible. Those who tried to cut across earlier often hit the boulders just below the surface and either capsized or were driven away from the chute and toward the steep, sharp falls to the left. While few people drowned on that side, many had suffered breaks, bruises, and severe gashes on the rocks that lurked in the water on that side.

A broken face or worse…perhaps even drowning? Angelo thought about his mother's fear of water and her terrifying tales of drowning and death. He now felt that same terror. Maybe she was right. Angelo pulled even harder with strong bow strokes, in spite of the severe pain in his palm. Blood oozed freely from his bandage, which now hung in tatters at his wrist.

"Right, Right! Go! Go!" O'Casey yelled in a panicky voice. Normally, he was calm in dangerous situations, even once when he'd had to do CPR at the beach on a teen who had gone under in strong surf. O'Casey never lost his cool, even with a crowd shouting instructions and a hysterical girlfriend screaming over his shoulder.

This was different. He could feel the canoe floundering. The water they had shipped aboard after the last rapids was literally dragging them down. "Right! Right!" he yelled again.

Butch was screaming the same commands to Angelo. Both canoes moved across the rapids in a struggle to get to the chute before hitting the falls. "Power strokes! Power strokes! Right! Right!" Butch shouted, both to encourage Angelo and to talk himself through his strategy for survival. The roar of the falls was like steady thunder now. The spray hitting the rocks created a foamy mist in the noonday sun. In less panicky times, one might have noticed the rainbows glistening in the haze.

Now! Butch thought. *Now!* He switched his power stoke to rudder mode, which started to bring the bow downstream and directly toward the chute. *Still not straight,* Butch thought as he ruddered even harder. "Left now, Angelo! Left!" he yelled, urging Angelo to help bring the bow around and directly into the chute. The timing was perfect. The canoe finished its arching swing from across the river and pointed directly downstream into the abyss. The current pulled the boat out over the chute.

For a moment, it almost seemed to hang in midair with half of the canoe literally over the falls. Then Angelo's weight and the forces of gravity dropped the bow suddenly and directly into the spray and foam five feet below. The canoe was in dive position now. Angelo instinctively dropped his paddle into the wildly swirling water on the floor of the canoe as he grabbed the gunnels. This was the most terrifying moment of his life.

Suddenly he was wrapped in a blanket of smothering whiteness. The bow shot over the falls, then dropped precipitously toward the churning water below. Angelo fought to brace his body and keep it from lurching out of the canoe. His arms crumpled under his weight and his head struck the gunnel and bounced back into a wall of water. For a moment, he was not sure whether he was dead or alive, whether he was awake or suffocating in the middle of a bad dream. He struggled to pull in a single clean breath of air. The spray and foam were choking him. He coughed desperately to expel some of the water he had inhaled. He was in full-blown panic, struggling through the most terrifying moments of his life, when he heard an oh-so-comforting and familiar yell.

"Yee-hah! Yee-hah!" came the shouts from the stern. Butch cheered in triumph as the canoe cleared the rocky edges of Black Powder Pitch. Quickly, he steered the canoe into the calm water on the far left side of the river. A small sandbar split the river in half at that point and protected them from the last of the rough water on the right-hand side just below the pitch. In all honesty, though Butch would never admit it, he was pooped. Because Angelo was a novice paddler and also had a very nasty-looking cut on his hand, the Chief had really carried Angelo through much of the last run.

As Butch caught his breath, his thoughts turned to Angelo and to his friends upstream. With the bow now pointed upstream in an eddy by the sandbar, Butch could see Angelo, still holding onto the gunnels much as he had when they'd gone over the falls. "How cool was that, Angelo?" Butch shouted over the roar of the falls above them.

"Way cool! Way cool! I thought we were goners for a minute. Boy, you are great with a paddle...."

As Butch looked up past Angelo, he could see O'Casey struggling to catch the same line across the river that had worked so well for him and Angelo. Butch watched as his protégé struggled to keep the old aluminum canoe from capsizing. It was partially full of water, thanks to Jason's earlier screw-up, and that made it almost unresponsive to O'Casey's masterful paddling skills. Even worse, Jason was in full panic mode. Even from fifty yards away, Butch could see Jason's panicky strokes, first on one side, then on the other.

At this point, O'Casey was screaming at him, trying to get Jason to power-stroke on the left side so the canoe would move across the river. Jason remembered hearing Butch yell "Left! Left!" to Angelo just before they went over the falls...or was it "Right!"? Did that mean *paddle* on the left or *go* left? In the haze of six beers, and given his disdain for O'Casey, Jason couldn't remember. He just knew that he wanted to be like Butch right now—safe and smiling in the eddy below the falls.

"For Christ's sake, paddle on the left! On the left! Left! Left!" O'Casey screamed again. He knew they were in serious trouble now. They were too close to have the entire canoe clear the huge rocks on their left side just above the falls. He couldn't bring the bow around yet because that would drive them directly into the biggest boulders and send them over the falls in the shallowest spot. *Way too much chance of a head injury, if we don't drown first*, O'Casey thought.

"Left! Left!" he screamed one last time as he tried to get most of the canoe past the great gray boulders looming like evil gargoyles guarding the falls. *Now!* thought O'Casey. *Bring the bow around now as much as you can.* "Right, Jason! Paddle on the right! Hard right paddle!"

It was no use. Jason could hear the roar of the falls just below them and feel the spray that kicked back from the breeze. Like Angelo before him, Jason simply froze. He grabbed the gunnels with both hands and prepared for the worst.

Had Jason given a few more hard strokes, most of the canoe would have cleared the boulders and the bow would have come around. As it was, O'Casey, too, braced for the impact. He was able to fend off the first boulder with his paddle, but the current was too strong and the larger boulder was just too massive to avoid.

Even the girls, who were watching a hundred yards downstream, could hear the hideous, sharp screeching sound—a fingernails-on-the-chalkboard scream—as aluminum and granite collided. Jason's old Sears Roebuck special shuddered as the force of the current took over.

Jason had been leaning forward just prior to impact as he clutched the bow in an almost standing position. The collision forced him to roll hard to the left and with him, the canoe, which capsized just as it was going over the falls. Jason bounced headfirst off the canoe as it crashed into the churning water and the boulders below. That clash with the hull probably saved his life. Had he gone face-first into the boulders, he almost certainly would have died.

For several seconds, Jason and the canoe tumbled together as he tried to hold on and also catch a breath of air. His lungs burned. He struggled in his panic to hold his breath until he could get his face above the water. The ancient life jacket, which Butch said must have come from the *Titanic*, was half off. Jason's unwillingness to wear it properly "because it would look dorky" now rendered it a useless, grotesque ornament. Its torn orange shell offered little help to Jason now—particularly since he had never secured the waist strap or chest ties. As it slipped off his chest, Jason grabbed at it frantically. Its light weight and high flotation factor caused it to disappear quickly into the rapids below him.

With his face now toward the falls, Jason could not see the large boulder just below him. The sharp thud of the impact shot excruciating pain into his shoulders and back. He couldn't hear Butch's shouts of support and assistance.

"Face downstream! Face downstream!" Butch screamed, knowing full well that there were many ways in which a river can take its toll. Jason tried to swim to the near bank well above where the girls were waiting. Had he simply looked downstream as Butch was directing, he would have seen the sandbar to his left...and with the sandbar would have come safety.

Instead, adding to his panic, the weight of his saturated Dallas Cowboys sweatshirt and heavy work boots were pulling him under. On an ideal day, Jason was not a great swimmer. Today, his feeble efforts at a freestyle stroke only tired him more. Trying to do overhand strokes in his waterlogged sweatshirt against the strongest part of the current brought him to the point of exhaustion in seconds. And the near bone-chilling water made it worse. Though it was almost mid-June, the ice had only gone out of the lake three weeks before, one of the latest ice-outs in years. Cold water and exhaustion are a lethal concoction.

Butch could see that this was a potentially deadly situation. He had seen several near-drownings as a guide and one actual drowning while fishing the Dead River many years ago. That fisherman had gone over his waders in a deep part of the river, and like Jason, was a poor swimmer.

He too had panicked. And like Jason, he did all the wrong things. He faced upstream. He tried to swim against the current. He went under within a hundred yards and disappeared in a deep eddy. His body was not found until the next day.

Butch couldn't help that drowning fisherman on the other side of the river, as he, too, was in waders. Now, however, Butch could do something. He was determined to save his friend. He knew that his best hope was to use the canoe to save Jason, since he could paddle much faster than he could swim. Jason had already drifted past the sandbar and into the rapid current.

"Let's go, Angelo!" Butch shouted, and started paddling upstream to get around the sandbar so they could then head downstream after Jason. Momentum is everything in life, and it seemed to take forever to get their canoe moving forward into the upstream current and around the sandbar. Butch had no choice but to take his eyes off Jason so that he could navigate the rapids above the sandbar and get the canoe aimed downstream again.

Just as he did so, he spotted a familiar face he'd momentarily forgotten about. Sean O'Casey had survived the falls. His high-necked L.L. Bean Class-Five life jacket had saved him. The quality jacket, all $225 worth, was designed to keep even an unconscious paddler's head out of the water. "You never know when you'll need it," he'd once remarked to a frugal friend who had laughed at his expensive taste. "What's a new head worth?" It was what his dad had said, the day O'Casey bought his first motorcycle helmet, "Never skimp on tires or brakes, or anything that might save your life." *Right again Dad*, O'Casey thought.

When their aluminum canoe went over the pitch, O'Casey ended up in the deepest and fastest part of the current. For a few seconds, he worried that he would be pulled back into the falls, into the "death roll" where the hydrodynamics of some waterfalls keep pulling the water, and occasionally its victims, around and under for minutes at a time. Sometimes, even the strongest swimmers with the best life jackets can't survive. This was not O'Casey's time to go—not yet, anyway.

He did all the right things, the way he'd been trained. He faced downstream and swam with the current. Staying alert in the cold water, he had noticed a fallen fir tree leaning out over the bank and into the river. In lower water, such trees provided perfect cover for large brookies.

Today, it provided the perfect way for O'Casey to get out of the river. He knew enough not to get caught in its upstream branches, which could be a death trap if the current were strong enough. Instead, he grabbed some of the largest branches and pulled himself around the tree and into an area close to the bank where he could stand up.

He was cold, tired, and scratched a bit from the fir branches. Otherwise, he was in remarkably good shape. As he pulled himself out of the river and onto the bank, he looked up and saw Butch. He had quickly lost track of Jason, but could tell from Butch's face and hurried efforts that a rescue attempt was under way. He caught his breath, wiped his face off with his wet sleeve, and began to work his way through the thick brush along the edge of the river, hoping to be able to help Butch save Jason.

Further downstream, the women had seen the entire drama unfold. It was almost like being at a hockey game and having seats twenty rows up from the crease as a breakaway play came heading for the goalie. First, they watched and marveled at the adroit paddling and rudder work. Butch was truly a Master Maine Guide, not just in title, but also in practice. He performed like a real warrior chief—*their* chief. Each of the women saw something exciting, almost compelling, in Butch Chapman. In that moment when his canoe had been tottering on the edge of Black Powder Pitch, Butch Chapman seemed frozen in time for all to see. He was the gladiator facing the lion. His head was clear. His heart was racing with exhilaration. He was *alive*…and from their voyeuristic perspective, each of the women could feel that adrenaline and sense that confidence that comes from knowing and doing, even in the face of imminent danger.

They had seen first Angelo, and then Jason, panic at the sight and sound of the falls. And unlike the Chief, they could see and sense the frustration of Sean O'Casey as he had tried to lead the unleadable. Now the three women were a team, trying, quite literally, to save a drowning man. They could see Jason's arm strokes getting more and more feeble. His arms were barely clearing the water. They were more hand gestures than strokes now, not the strong arm movements of an athlete swimming for shore, but rather like the pathetic wave of a dying man saying good-bye.

Although his strokes had closed the gap to shore, Jason was still at least eight to ten feet from the bank. While the current was not nearly as fast here as it was by the falls, the water was much deeper. At one point further upstream, the water was only four or five feet deep, but the current was too fast there and Jason was far too tired to stand. Now, with hypothermia setting in, his reflexes had slowed along with his will to survive.

His head went under once, then twice. He was no longer swimming. There was an imminent sense of doom about him. It was unfortunately reminiscent of the wildlife movies where the young impala, wading at the water's edge, had been singled out by a crocodile just about to grasp its prey and drag it under in a death spiral. Jason could feel the end was near. The lingering buzz from the earlier six-pack seemed to numb his fear of a fast-approaching death, as did the bone-chilling fifty-eight degree water.

Only his head was still above water. He turned downstream and saw the women. They had their backs to him and were frantically doing something else. *Why aren't they helping me?* Jason thought dully. He was too tired and too confused even to call out for help.

Barely twenty feet away, Ellen, Tiffany, and Maria gave a last heave and a tall, thin fir tree separated itself from other blowdowns. Quickly, the women turned the dead tree around, pivoting the thin end of the tree out over the river and almost within Jason's reach. His eyes were wild now. They all knew this was his only chance. Butch and Angelo were still seventy-five feet away in the canoe, and O'Casey was farther upstream, stumbling in exhaustion and trying to work his way through the brush and blowdowns toward them.

The women struggled to keep the thin tree out over the river and within reach of their drowning comrade. But each time it came close, the current would swing it downstream and away from him.

"Time it! Time it! We gotta time it!" Maria yelled as the tree swung downstream for the third time.

"Now!" Ellen yelled. "Now!"

Just as Jason drew even with the bank outcropping, the women swung their end of the dead fir tree around. The thin brown branches swung just a few inches from Jason's head. He, too, knew this was his only chance. He could barely raise his exhausted arms out of the water, but somehow managed to get first one hand and then the other onto the life-saving branches. His significant weight and the force of the current almost pulled the three women into the river. They were all flat on their stomachs now, trying to anchor the fir tree to the outcropping of ledge. They were holding onto each other and the tree at the same time.

"Hang on! Hang on, Jay!" Tiffany pleaded. "Butch is coming. Hang on!"

The women were literally at eyeball level with Jason, staring, in effect, into the eyes of a ghost. His face was more pale and gray than the sweatshirt that now covered much of his head. His eyes, in particular, signaled his desperation and despair. He tried to get a better hold on the branch, but his hands, which had been so skilled as a youth playing football and basketball, no longer responded to his commands. His left hand slipped off the branch, and for a few seconds, he held on with just his right. Then, as if in slow motion, he lost his grip or simply let go.

His eyes were the eyes of terror mixed with acceptance. He looked directly at the women and tried to say something. Then his head was gone.

"No-o-o! No! No! No!" Ellen screamed.

They quickly looked upstream and saw Butch gaining ground, but he was still at least ten critical seconds away. There was no time and no Jason.

Maria and Ellen stared in disbelief as just his arms broke the surface and flailed one last futile time, grabbing at the water and the morning air. They were looking toward the circle of water where Jason had disappeared when they heard the splash. Before they could say or do anything, Tiffany had jumped in, just as her Red Cross training had taught her: always feet first, because there's no way of knowing what's at the bottom of a head-first dive into unfamiliar water.

Tiffany did a surface dive to look for Jason, as she had been trained to do. Fortunately, this part of the river, though deep, was a slow-moving green-gray eddy. She surfaced again, grabbed a quick breath, and dove for a second time. Just as she came up again, Butch and Angelo arrived on the scene.

"Help, Butch! Hurry!" Tiffany yelled. "I've got him, but I can't get his head out. He's too heavy!"

As the stern of the canoe swung in next to Tiffany, Butch reached his arm below the waterline and grabbed a pewter gray sweatshirt. Beneath that sweatshirt was an ashen face that had been Jason's. His gray-blue pallor announced a dreadful message for his friends.

Suddenly, at the edge of the gravel bank, O'Casey emerged from the woods and waded in almost to his neck. He pulled the bow of the canoe alongside and took hold of the sweatshirt and the lifeless body and dragged it onto the shore.

Almost immediately the group began working as a veteran team trying to save Jason's life. Only O'Casey had actually saved a life before, but Tiffany had practiced CPR many times as a lifeguard on the north shore of Long Island, and Butch had actually taught CPR as part of his Master Guide's mentoring program. Tiffany counted cadence like a drill sergeant: "One, two, three, four...!"

Butch did the compressions. They were strong and sure—and done with the conviction of someone who knew he had little time to restore the breathing and circulation of a good friend. O'Casey waited his turn. *...fourteen, fifteen...* Now two full breaths; watch his chest, then wait for a fifteen count again. Even though O'Casey knew the drill, it was reassuring to have someone calling out the compression and the breathing cadence. While he knew that the newest CPR theory recommended thirty compressions before two inflations, he was more comfortable with the fifteen-to-two ratio that Tiffany was using. O'Casey knew that worked. At least it had for him years ago.

Jason's arm jerked. His head turned slightly and he gagged and spewed gray foamy water and vomit from his blue lips. His chest heaved once, twice, three times. Tiffany stopped calling cadence. Butch stopped the compressions. Everyone's eyes were on Jason's. There was movement beneath the lids, almost like REMs during a dream stage. His color began to improve. His lips quivered as the blue dissipated and life returned to his face.

Jason was alive. He had beaten the Cut...the hard way.

Aftermath

The kelly-green crushed-velvet hat refused to sink as it spun around and around in a slow dance from eddy to eddy. It worked its way through the riffles and finally lodged against the bleach-boned dry kai at the bottom of the Cut. Just above, on the last of the three sandbars, there were other hints of the "train wreck," as the tribe would call the morning's near disaster. The embarrassment of a life jacket that had failed in its only job was wrapped around a jagged granite boulder in a light rapid just above the sandbar.

It was ironic protection for a slate-gray boulder that needed little help in the rushing water, a boulder that had been blasted away from a coarse-grained granite tor that had formed the backbone of the streambed. It had been part of a large seam of rock that had been blown apart by work-hardened loggers. They had literally given life and limb to make the Cut, which eventually connected the pivotal lakes of the eastern Allagash and allowed the logs to flow southeast all the way to Bangor, Maine, rather than northeast along the St. John and into Canada. Good men had died in those efforts to save Maine logs for Maine mills and Maine-made schooners.

The boulder had come from the last major seam of solid granite, several hundred feet thick that had to be blasted away one section at a time. The area eventually became known as Black Powder Pitch because it took so much black powder to blow up those massive granite seams. The often dangerous and sometimes deadly pitch had almost taken Jason's life on this otherwise glorious June morning.

Besides the abandoned life jacket, other bits of litter announced to the keen-eyed osprey soaring overhead that intruders were in the area and that she should find her meal elsewhere along the riverbank.

The tribe had been seriously tested. They were now silently collecting both their belongings and their thoughts. The Chief knew that it was important to keep everyone busy and focused on something other than the train wreck. O'Casey was still simmering, almost seething, as he continued to retrieve debris from the morning's *fiasco*, as he thought of it. To his way of thinking, it was all Jason's fault. That stupid shithead was too drunk to have ever tried the Cut. *It's OK to have a few brewskis, even in the morning*, O'Casey reasoned, *but a six-pack before lunch is ridiculous.* All they had needed was a few more good strokes. They could have made it; two more good strokes and they would have hit the pitch straight on. They would have joined Butch and Angelo in the eddy below, proclaiming victory over the Cut in a celebration of male bonding no Super Bowl party or duck-hunting trip could ever duplicate.

Jason sat resting against the trunk of a massive white pine, one of the few first- growth pines still left at the bottom of the Cut. It has been left because it was a witch pine, its trunk fragmented and deformed 150 years ago, rendering it useless as one of the saw logs and ships' masts that had long since been harvested from the area. Its massive gnarly form and disfigured branches cast an eerie pall over the landing.

Oblivious to the tree itself, Jason leaned in complete exhaustion against the enormous pine. He still shivered constantly, even though Butch and Ellen had wrapped him in two down sleeping bags to help warm him up. He had refused to put on dry clothing, despite his friends' pleading. Instead, he sat sulking and shivering in near catatonic oblivion, ignoring everyone and everything as he reflected dully on his near-death experience.

Had he turned his head ever so slightly he would have found a sight that might have widened his eyes and stirred his very male core, even in his current state. Ellen and Maria were ministering to Tiffany. She, too, was shivering, in part because she was almost naked and being helped from her cold, wet clothing. It was nearly seventy degrees now, but it would take a while for her body to overcome the effects of the shockingly cold water. The air was alive with caddis and mayflies, and a classic June hatch of carpenter ants was also well under way, but a normally squeamish and modest Tiffany seemed totally unaware of the ants …and the eyes of her colleagues.

She was almost literally in shock—both as the result of her two-minute immersion in the fifty-eight degree water and by the immensity of what had happened. She would be called a hero, or, more correctly, a *heroine*, Ellen would add. Right now, she was just numb. Numb from the cold. Numb from the event. Had anyone ever told Tiffany, the once-spoiled blonde beauty, as she had often been described, that she would be standing half-naked on a riverbank in Maine with a carpenter ant crawling up her inner thigh and six strangers within eyeshot, she would never have believed it. None of the tribe could have imagined what had transpired, or what *would* transpire, when they had planned their jaunt into the Maine woods at the Black Rose Pub many months before.

While Jason had resisted all attempts to help him get warm, Tiffany followed every command. "Sweetie, lift your arms, I'm going to towel you off," Maria directed softly. Slowly and gently, Ellen and Maria helped undress and then redress Tiffany. She had started the morning as the cover girl of an L.L. Bean catalog. Her hair was perfect. Her Lancôme makeup was purposely just the right hue for her pink J Jill turtleneck and white mock chamois shirt from the Gap. Her Hap Hetson jeans, the turtleneck, and the shirt now lay in a filthy pile on the ground, oozing water into the moss-rich earth. Twenty-four hours earlier, Tiffany would have screamed in horror at the thought of having her favorite new "country outfit" become a muddy, sodden mess. She would have recoiled at the thought of near-strangers toweling her off, helping to unbutton her blouse, and unsnap her bra. But her fingers couldn't or wouldn't work.

Another large carpenter ant crawled slowly up the side of her calf, lingered on her quivering kneecap for a moment, and resumed its upward path, but Tiffany failed to notice its ugly black pinchers or rapidly moving feet. Her brain could barely function as she replayed the rescue tape in her head. She once again recalled the look of horror and desperation on Jason's terror-ridden face as he reached for the rescue log they were holding out. She was completely lost in the memories of that surface dive and panicky grasp for all that remained of Jason Foxworthy—the hood of his gray cotton sweatshirt. She remained oblivious to everything else, so Ellen reached gently across her still-shivering body to brush the carpenter ant away just as it approached her pubic region.

At that point, Angelo looked over and was amazed at what he saw.

What had once been an exquisitely beautiful woman by anyone's standard was now a naked and terrified girl, with wet, stringy hair and pine needles still clinging to her strong but delicate shoulders and graceful, athletic legs. To Jason, Butch, or O'Casey this might have been an erotic moment—a beautiful, fully naked woman, her body glistening in the sun. Had that been Butch standing there naked in the morning light, Angelo might have felt differently, but then again, he would have been helping Butch much the way Ellen and Maria were helping Tiffany. No, it was more like Goya's *Maja Desnuda* or another painting, which he couldn't quite recall, where the nudity of a woman had stirred him deeply in a way that was not sexual but was still profound in its impact. There was no innocence to the Maja; there was stark, naked beauty, but no innocence. On this morning, as the newfound friends worked gently and efficiently to undress and redress a near-stranger, Angelo nearly wept at the beauty, the caring, the sensitivity toward Tiffany that was almost palpable at that the moment. *Such a rare commodity in men,* Angelo thought. *Where were such men?*

As Ellen reached into Tiffany's backpack to find a dry bra and panties, her eyes met Angelo's. She looked deeply into those dark, mysterious brown eyes. Although Angelo blushed and quickly turned his eyes downward, the look Ellen had seen was not that of a leering man caught staring at a woman's nudity, it was the look of man amazed at what he was watching. Had she needed another set of hands at that moment to help, she would quickly have turned to Angelo. Ellen smiled to herself in a way that spoke of compassion and understanding rather than anger or distrust.

As the women finished dressing Tiffany, a familiar voice rang out. "Soup's on!" came a loud and friendly voice. In spite of O'Casey's anger, Butch and he had quickly gathered up almost all of the loose gear and items lost when the canoe had capsized. Fortunately, Black Powder Pitch was within a few hundred yards of the end of the Cut. It had taken little time to assemble a mini base camp, build a fire, and start one of Butch's favorite camp meals—homemade chicken soup and fire-toasted garlic bread. He had learned many, many years ago that a hunting or fishing party that is well fed and well rested is literally a group of happy campers.

That phrase was one of the Chief's frequent corny expressions, not only on the trail, but also in school. He would often start a teachers' meeting by saying, "Some of you are not happy campers. We need to find out why." Butch was not a particularly academic educator. He knew little about curriculum and cared even less. In a results-based system like he was in, Butch could have been fired many times. But his boss knew one simple thing: Granville Butch Chapman knew and understood people, whether they were teachers, parents, or students. He knew how to motivate them, encourage them, and make them laugh. He was not much of a manager. His budgets were an embarrassment. His presentations to the school committee were weak and rambling. But everyone—administrators, teachers, and parents—knew that Butch was a leader. He got things done. He knew the right thing to do at the right time.

Today was no different. "Soup's on!" Those were purposeful words. Butch knew that the warm soup would help raise the core temperatures of both Jason and Tiffany. The crispy French bread, dripping with garlic butter and featuring fire-burned corners would crunch in everyone's mouth. It would leave both a good taste and create a positive moment for everyone to rejoin the tribe, reenergize, and regain some poise after the recent debacle.

He also knew, as did O'Casey—now that he'd calmed down—that the near-death adventure of the morning was really Butch's fault. He should never have let Jason paddle the Cut after drinking a six-pack. It had been a difficult run, even for experienced paddlers like him and O'Casey. The Chief had wanted it to be the perfect moment—four rogues sitting in their canoes, cheering at the base of the pitch, having done something few people ever do: test themselves against nature and win. *That's what it's really all about*, thought Butch. In this day of text messaging and blogging, who ever takes on nature anymore? Who ever experienced what Thoreau was looking for in his trip to the Allagash 150 years ago? He and his tribe were in those same woods, looking at those same lakes, smelling those same smells. The big king pines were all but gone, but as the Chief looked over at the mammoth witch pine where Jason sat, he thought, as he often did, *Hell, Thoreau could have been right here, thinking these same thoughts and hearing these same words, "Soup's on!"*

MAKING CAMP

The soup had done what the Chief had hoped it would do. It brought the tribe back together, literally and figuratively, as they broke bread. The mood was altogether different now than it had been just two hours before. Back then, they were drinking beer and singing songs as they bounced and swayed in the "portage jalopy." One minute they were nineteen-year-old beer-splattered kids at a frat party on the Allagash. And what seemed like only moments later, they were silent and somber, paradoxically sitting by a fire on a warm day.

They sipped the hot soup and shared the crusty bread. They smiled at each other in a gentle, unobtrusive way, each seeking comfort in the food and the quiet comradeship. They had changed in a way they could not see, but each could feel. Thin white smoke curled slowly in the calm June air. Black flies began to buzz around the campers, seeking their own sustenance in a welcome ankle, ear, or neck.

Despite the flies, seven faces looked inward, looked upward, looked downward—changed faces barely hearing, seeing, or smelling the fading wood smoke. All were one...and none at the same time. For a long while, no one spoke. Each seemed lost in personal reflection. Each rewound a mental tape recording of the recent events, replaying their role in what happened and what could have happened. Nearby, a pileated woodpecker, with his red crown shining in the sun, hammered away at a rotting fir tree as he looked for lunch. Yet the campers were oblivious to the sights and sounds.

Butch knew what the silence of the tribe meant. He had a knack, honed through years of camping and guiding, for reading groups and knowing what to do when. For someone who could often be described as a showboat, Butch had another side, a highly skilled and sensitive side. He knew when to push and when to pull. He and O'Casey, though often rivals when it came to fishing, worked in silent harmony to break camp in a remarkably delicate fashion for such rough outdoor types—allowing the others to finish eating, dreaming, and healing. Once the canoes and the kayak were reloaded with gear, O'Casey tapped first one then another on the shoulder. He quietly coaxed them up from the logs where they'd finished lunch, and helped ready them for the next phase of the adventure.

It was only when the fire protested with a sharp *woooosh! sisssss! sisssss!* after several buckets of well-placed water, that the tribe began to interact again socially. They talked in low but animated voices about the great soup and crunchy bread. Ellen pulled out a large red and white kerchief and wiped some food from the corner of Tiffany's cheek. Three hours ago, such an act would have been considered intrusive and unthinkable for two relative strangers. Tiffany, the perfect Long Island debutante, had disappeared in the roiling waters below Black Powder Pitch. A new, albeit unkempt Tiffany, her hair still a damp and tangled mass, turned her face toward Ellen. She returned a beautiful, almost fragile smile and a nod that required no words to convey her thoughts and appreciation to her new friend.

Butch put Jason in the bow of his Bean canoe, not wishing to risk a conflict of any sort between O'Casey and Foxworthy. He knew Sean was still simmering in a very subtle, imperceptible way over the fiasco at the falls. Ordinarily, he was remarkably even-tempered, but Butch could tell just how much his friend despised people like Jason Foxworthy for their unprincipled, selfish attitude. O'Casey was just the opposite—too unselfish. He, like Angelo, often wore the pain of a martyr on his face. And Butch understood the source of O'Casey's pain. However, today he was in no mood to have that pain spill over and onto a pristine lake and a two-hour canoe ride that needed to be hassle-free.

Angelo took the bow in O'Casey's canoe. Sean Padraig O'Casey was the only one to hear the grunt of pain as Angelo leaned on the forward gunnel and climbed into the heavily dented aluminum canoe. As Angelo moved the piles of gear around to find a point of comfort for his small, stocky frame, O'Casey thought he noticed a redness and swelling above the bandage on his hand. O'Casey was about to speak up about it when he noticed Maria struggling to get into her canoe. So rather than push off his own canoe, he hopped out and gently helped Maria into hers. He gave the stern a firm push, jumped back into his own boat, and they were off—three canoes and a kayak working their way along the leeward shore of the lower lake.

Butch had purposely chosen the slightly longer but easier paddling route. This way they would avoid the afternoon winds, which could be significant. He just couldn't risk another capsize and possible injury, not today.

A great blue heron, flushed from his perch on the dry kai–laden south shore, looked down on the slow parade of paddlers deep in thought and working their way to a campsite they would soon call home.

Unlike their first lake paddle earlier in the morning, this one was almost conversation-free. The events at the falls were just too fresh in their minds. Each had a different mental tape to replay. Each had a different perspective. Jason's tape was the most distorted, in part because the cold water had numbed his senses. He just could not quite accept that he had almost drowned. He was mentally busy blaming O'Casey for not having gotten the stern around so they wouldn't capsize. It was typical Jason. Find blame. Avoid responsibility.

Butch, on the other hand, squarely blamed himself for underestimating the water flow and its impact on the pitch. Though he had never canoed the Cut before, he had fished it many times. He knew that three opened gates at the dam meant fast water, dangerous water. He just wanted it to be fun and memorable. That's what they had all talked about at the Black Rose when they'd planned the trip. Butch had bragged about how great the canoeing would be. He described in detail what a rush it would be to look upstream at the section of white water just conquered and know you'd "kicked ass." *It will be memorable all right*, Butch now thought, but not in the way he had wanted. *What will this do to my reputation as a guide?* he wondered. Quickly, he dismissed the thought. *We've still got the whole trip ahead of us. Let's make it fun. Let's make it great!* he decided.

As the tribe gradually approached the campground at the foot of Wilson Lake, the beauty of the spot became readily apparent. The lake was three miles long and a half-mile wide. It was in a bowl of sorts, surrounded by small hills covered in second-growth pine, fir, and spruce. As with the entire region, there was almost no evidence of human habitation. With the exception of a single hunting and fishing cabin, reserved three times a year for Power Company executives, Wilson Lake looked the same as it had two hundred years ago when the Indians speared crimson-bellied brook trout and spawning suckers in the shallow headwaters above Wilson Stream. They would smoke the splayed fish on the broad beach area that was soon to become camp for this new tribe.

The canoes slid noisily into the sand of the lakeshore beach. One by one, the group unpacked themselves amid all the gear and garb. These were not twenty-year-olds hopping quickly out of the boats and racing to stake out prime tenting spots. Rather, the forty- and almost-fifty-somethings eased slowly out and onto the beach. Still, their looks of amazement at the beauty around them could have been those of the Boy Scouts who annually made this same trek in mid-July when the water level was lower…and much safer.

Ellen sat in her kayak, a hundred yards offshore, taking mental snapshots once again as she sought to capture every nuance of color—the creamy tan beach, the long, low hillside with towering white and red pine, blue spruce, and deep-green fir. She quickly noted the solitary white paper birch at the edge of the campground and the linear contrast it provided to the array of muted greens that had filled her mental color palette. She would ask O'Casey to get this shot from a number of angles so she could paint it, or try to, during a snowy winter day when school was canceled and her painting urge came to life.

Ellen loved snow days. No school. No kids. No bells. No hassles. She smiled at just the thought of sitting by her fireplace with the snow raging outside, sipping a cup of chai tea with a dollop of Maine raw blueberry honey. She could picture the pain and pleasure of working her paints to capture the complex greens, the subtle creamy beach, and the remarkably clear, rich blue sky. She happily contemplated the idea of spending a whole day, maybe a whole weekend, just on this part of her painting. *The greens will be the hardest,* she mused, *and the sky …*

"Ellen! Ellen, get in here!" Butch hollered impatiently. When Butch was on a mission, everyone had to be on the same mission. Ellen almost rolled her kayak, *again*, as his shout brought her back to reality.

The camp was almost halfway up. She was amazed at the progress the team had made as the bow of her kayak crunched softly into the sandy shoreline. *Quenched its speed in the slushy sand,* she thought as she heard the sound and remembered the line from Browning's famous poem. Then she almost blushed. That had been the first time she'd ever heard of a Freudian interpretation of a poem. She was so naïve as a high school senior. Ellen and her girlfriends in Senior Seminar had been shocked that their teacher, Dr. Jameson—Dr. J., for short—had the courage, or nerve, perhaps, to teach Browning's poem in that way. It was all about sex, almost graphic sex. *Pushing prows,* Ellen recalled now, all hidden in similes and metaphors. At first, they thought Dr. J. was kidding. Then they saw how the pieces fit—how it all made sense. Years later, when they saw the movie *Dead Poets Society,* many of the students in Ellen's class and in other classes thought it was really a movie about Dr. J. Maybe it was…O'Casey would know. She would have to ask him.

"For God's sake, Ellen, get your butt on shore. You've been a thousand miles away for the last twenty minutes."

"Sorry, Butch." Ellen blushed at once again daydreaming and getting caught at it by Butch, who was, ironically, a daydreamer himself. The difference was that he always dreamed about fishing. Ellen dreamed about *everything.* "Butch," she continued, "sometimes, a thousand miles away is the best place to be."

"Ellen, *this* is the best place to be. Welcome to God's country," Butch proclaimed with a grin.

"Hey, Butch, we hit pay dirt! Look at all this great shit!" Jason yelled from the other end of the beach. "We hit the freakin' mother load."

"What are you talking about?" Butch asked, sprinting toward Jason.

The rest of the tribe scurried behind Butch to check out Jason's newest find. Was he ever right! Three boxes of food and a large Styrofoam cooler sat like treasure chests at the far end of the beach. Jason had, of course, opened the cooler first. It had wine, liquor, and four bottles of champagne, all swimming in a sea of melting ice, still in the plastic bags. It was amazing how just the thought of alcohol had taken a morose man still wallowing in self pity and brought him back to life.

Yum. Jason smacked his lips at the thought of the Yukon Jack drizzling slowly down his throat. "This is freakin' great!" Jason exclaimed, to no one's surprise. "Holy shit."

"That's not ours, Jason. Leave it alone!" shouted Maria. Everyone *was* surprised by the strength of her voice and the authority behind it. Maria, though a sweetheart in many ways, had successfully run a large urban middle school for a number of years, and had just jumped on another middle school student—albeit a forty-three-year-old.

"That's what's called a buzz-off box," Butch announced to the tribe.

"Say what?" said Jason.

"Most people don't fish or camp here because, as you guys learned this morning, it's tough to get here. But it's a favorite haunt for rich fishermen, corporate types, who can fly in for a day or two to fish and drink...and then fly home. Usually, Skippy or one of the other guys who run float planes will have to bring groups up in a couple of flights because they bring in so much junk—folding ovens, gas bug zappers, the works! But when the fishing gets brisk or the weather gets bad, these flying-service guys won't do a second or third run. They'll just say, 'Leave your shit for the next guy; we're outta here,' and that's just what they do. Remember last night and how hard it rained just about sundown?"

"Yeah, so?" said Jason.

"Well, it was Sunday night. The fishing trip was ending and Skippy or some other smart pilot wanted to get up and out before the storm hit. Wind shear can be amazing around these lakes. The hills funnel thunderstorms through something awful. My guess is that Skippy didn't want to come back for a second run, or couldn't. He did a grab-and-go. When he says, 'Get in the plane; we're outta here,' he means it. I've seen tents and tables and all kinds of stuff left behind and left for good. This is small potatoes."

"There's a lot of good stuff here, Butch. What if they didn't want to leave it?" Ellen asked.

"Skippy would probably just look at them and say—pardon my French—" Butch hesitated only briefly, then said, "'Long fuckin' walk back, partner. Your choice.'"

Butch grinned. He loved those bush pilots. "They don't care if the guy they're talking to is a fifth grade teacher or George Freakin' Steinbrenner. It's their plane. It's their call. And besides, most of these trips are so written off as company expenses, they could care less what they leave. It's not their stuff and it's not their money. I've found even better stuff than this in buzz-off boxes before. Let's see what else we have."

As the tribe explored through the boxes, they were amazed by what they found—more wine, bottles of both Yukon Jack and Irish whiskey, lots of bottled water, flour, apples, and potatoes. Jason had been right: lots of great shit.

Bit by bit, the camp took shape. The Chief and O'Casey were a remarkable team. They had done so much camping and fishing together that they claimed they could set up camp, have dinner, clean up, and be ready for bed in an hour. It was hard for the others to imagine either of them snoozing away at 8:00 P.M., but Butch explained that sometimes, after a ten-mile hike over steep terrain to get to a remote fishing spot, 8:00 P.M. can seem late at night.

There were four tents. The Chief had originally planned to have Angelo with him, though he didn't much care who his bunkmate was. He always fell asleep quickly, snored like a champion, and rose before anyone else. Though Butch could talk for hours, once he was ready for bed, it was lights out—literally and figuratively. As they were setting up the tents, Butch took O'Casey aside and asked if it was OK if Angelo bunked in with him instead. When O'Casey looked quizzical at the Chief's request, Butch said, "You know."

O'Casey was still puzzled.

"Look, Sean, you know that some people think...they say that Angelo—"

"Hey, Butch," O'Casey interrupted. "I don't give a crap what people say, and I don't care whether it's true or not. I'm more worried about wanting to kick Jason's ass the next time he ticks us off than I am about becoming a character in *Broke Back Mountain* for anyone here. Angelo's a great guy. He can bunk in with me any time." O'Casey smiled. "Maybe I'll get lucky, and he won't be a snorer like you."

"Thanks, Paddy," Butch said quietly with a grin.

O'Casey noted that for the second time in one day, Butch had called him Paddy. When that happened, it was like a verbal pat on the back—kind of silly, but still important stuff, even for guys who were almost fifty and dreading it.

Overall, the camp setup went well. While O'Casey and Butch dug separate latrines for the ladies and the men, everyone else gathered firewood. There was plenty to be had. Butch suggested they start with small dry kai, what people on the coast would have called driftwood. It ranged from large trees to the smallest sticks, all driven by the wind, waves, and spring ice-outs onto the shore of the lake. There was enough dry kai for fifty campfires, so they could pick and choose the best pieces. Not surprisingly, the only obstacle in the otherwise simple process of gathering firewood came, once again, courtesy of Jason Foxworthy.

"Jason, what are you doing?" yelled Ellen. He was about to swing his cruising axe into the side of a small white birch that leaned out over the edge of the beach. "Jason, there's plenty of dry kai. You don't need to kill that tree. Please, Jason!"

"It's just a freakin' tree, Ellen," Jason said with an eye roll that she would have laughed at if it weren't so juvenile. Sometimes Jason acted like one of her sixth graders. Sometimes he acted like thirteen and sometimes he acted like twenty-one. Rarely, Ellen thought, did he ever act like a high school administrator. *How the heck did he ever get the job in the first place?* Ellen wondered. It was a question that many others had asked, and one that would be asked again and again by the tribe in the days to come.

Soon the campsite began to look like the cover of an L.L. Bean catalog. In fact, most of the gear had come from Bean's. However, Ellen had bought her one-person tent at Eastern Mountain Sports, along with her backpack. That's where her brothers liked to shop, particularly for their climbing equipment. Ellen had been happy to ask her brothers for some advice, though she hadn't really needed it. She was a good researcher and could have asked Butch or O'Casey, who would have driven the three hours to shop with her any time. She was just proud to be going camping and fishing the way her brothers had done with her dad before her mother's cancer progressed to stage four.

Billy and Bruce had teased her about having to go to the bathroom in the woods ... and about the bears. "Don't be squatting over a birch when a sow bear is looking for her cubs nearby," they laughed. "You'll have a hard time running with your pants around your ankles." She knew they were kidding, or at least *hoped* they were kidding, because she was terrified of bears. Ellen wouldn't even own a teddy bear as a little girl. That was the level of her fear.

Still, it was a wonderful day when she went shopping for camping gear with her brothers. They were proud of their little sister, and she was proud, too. Even though she was forty-two, her brothers always treated her like a little kid. While that could sometimes get old, Ellen loved being their sister. For two guys who could be jerks on occasion, and not very supportive of their dad, she felt she had the two best brothers in the world. It was just a shame, she often mused, that when she was younger and wanted to go camping with them, they didn't want any part of it. Her dad would tell her, "Honey, it's just a male bonding thing. You and I will go camping sometime, just the two of us." But it never happened, and now, with her dad's poor health and drinking problem, she knew it never would.

But today she was proud to be on the trip and proud to be setting up her slate-blue "Mountain Ridge" tent with the built-in storm flap. She had rehearsed the setup many times already in her backyard, determined to be able to set the tent up by herself. She loved the feeling of independence. While she would never mind having help from Butch or O'Casey on almost anything, she wanted to show her friends that she could do some things completely on her own.

As it turned out, she had her tent up before anyone else. Ellen stepped back and smiled with pride at the sight of her handiwork. Coupled with that pride was a bit of trepidation, as she would be the only one in her tent. *I will not be afraid. I will not be afraid.* She repeated that mantra to herself again and again, hoping against hope that it would be true. Ellen had something to prove to her brothers, something to prove to her dad, and something to prove to herself. She could do it. She *would* do it! Ellen, the artist, the observer, smiled again at her handiwork.

The crackles of pine kindling igniting in the hungry flame lent a magical sound to the campground. It somehow made the experience official. Her tent was up. The fire was going. Supper would soon be on. Ellen took one mental snapshot after another. This was just what she had envisioned: the campground with the pine forest coming right down to the shoreline, sounds of firewood crackling and waves lapping at the sandy shoreline. Ellen felt complete. No wonder her brothers loved Maine. The smile on her face told the entire tribe that she was at peace, not just with *where* she was, but, more importantly, with *who* she was.

How Do You Like Them Apples?

"Cocktails! It's five o'clock somewhere!" Butch called out with his usual fanfare. He loved those pronouncements—"Breakfast!" "Soup's on!" "Supper!" That was classic Butch. He loved to showboat, but that was also why he was such a popular guide. Panache or showboating? Butch could care less. He was who he was. It was that simple, and it played well to the crowd.

Almost everyone had taken a little snooze after camp had been set up. It had been a long, physically and emotionally draining day, given the 4 A.M. wake-up, two long canoe rides, the white water fiasco, and Jason's near drowning. For most of the tribe, the shout from their chief was quite literally a wake-up call after a glorious nap.

But Butch and O'Casey had been busily working while the others slept. They had finished the latrines and fashioned a primitive toilet seat for the ladies from a large wooden box that had been part of the buzz-off trove. O'Casey had used a folding backpack saw to cut a posterior-size hole in the bottom of the box and then flipped it upside down over the latrine. He'd even created a little toilet paper holder using an empty coffee can that would keep the paper dry if it rained.

Maria, who was the first with the courage to test out the "backwoods bathroom," as she called it, came back to camp duly impressed with O'Casey's extra efforts. She had not fallen in as she had feared she might and knew she was thoroughly capable of doing. Instead, she came down the path with her usual smile, content with almost everything in life, and in particular with having been invited on such a wonderful adventure. She felt honored to be a part of the tribe. She had often been left out in life. In fact, some of her strongest and most painful memories were about being the chubby little Latina who was last to be picked for everything, even though her teachers said she was the nicest, kindest kid in the class.

Once, as a young woman, Maria had tried to take up golf. When asked by a friend, in all seriousness, what her handicap was, Maria replied with her unstoppable grin, "I am a short, fat, left-handed, Latino Catholic who is still looking for her first serious boyfriend. How's that for a handicap?" Although she'd said it with a big smile, that statement reflected more about how Maria saw herself than she actually cared to admit. Many people spend half a lifetime in therapy to articulate what Maria had shared in those few words. Such self-perceptions also became her biggest motivators. She had become a successful administrator for the simple reason that she had *earned* everything in life. Yet, she was grateful for even the smallest things—like a crudely made toilet seat and dry toilet paper.

"Ladies, you've got to try the Half-Moon Hilton!" Maria exclaimed when she returned.

Ellen and Tiffany were still groggy from their naps. The last thing either wanted to do, especially Tiffany, was sit on a box in the woods and share one of life's most private moments with the bugs and snakes. Still, Tiffany had already done several things today that she'd never thought she could or would ever do. She'd saved a life. She'd been undressed and dressed by two women she hardly knew. She'd stood dripping and naked in full view of anyone who wanted to look. She had no idea who had seen her, and after pondering it over and over during the silent canoe ride, she'd finally come to a simple conclusion: she didn't care; it didn't matter.

Tiffany surprised herself with those conclusions. She'd always been someone to whom the smallest detail usually mattered—the label on a blouse, the designer name on her handbags. She had been raised by her mother to view accessorizing as an art form. All of that seemed foreign now, and the trip was only in its first day. She wondered how she would feel at the end of the trip. She could have no idea just how much she and the others would be changed by the events still ahead of them.

"Who wants a little bubbly?" Butch, the great social communicator, asked. It was obviously a rhetorical question, as the entire crew stood in line to get their ration of California grog. "I hope you like Korbel Brut. It's nutritious, delicious, and so-o-o good for you! And believe it or not, the head vintner is actually from Coopers Mills, Maine. I met him once in the tasting room on the Russian River in California. We spent the entire time talking about the legend of Coopers Mills—Elmer Wilson and his run-down furniture barn. Gotta take you there sometime. Wicked cool. Coopah's Mills," Butch said with his best Maine accent. He laughed. "When the Korbel's runs out, I can always drop some Alka Seltzer into a glass of lake water, but it's not quite the same."

Everyone laughed at Butch, as they always did. It was one of his biggest strengths. Some might say it was his only strength, but Butch didn't care. He just loved being himself, warts and all. And he loved this—treating his friends, or his clients, to a wonderful time, doing what he liked best. Camping, fishing and hunting were more than a passion for him. They were at the core of his very being. And since he was also a very social person, the guiding part of his life was a logical extension of this passion.

The Chief and O'Casey had outdone themselves. The champagne had been a complete surprise and a gift that just added to the mystique. Both men had done enough extended camping to know it was best to have the fancy stuff on the first night, while the ice was still in the cooler. Even though they always counted on fish for some meals, they had both seen times when the dehydrated food they never thought they'd use became the final meals for the trip.

Tonight was anything but dehydrated. They started with homemade tapenade and roasted garlic on water crackers. The group was amazed to learn just how skilled both Butch and O'Casey were as camp cooks. Butch did the simple stuff, and did it well. O'Casey, on the other hand, was really a gourmet chef at heart, and found ways to make very fancy meals using a wood fire. He had put five cloves of elephant garlic into a pouch of aluminum foil. Before sealing the pouch, he poured in some extra-virgin olive oil he had packed in one of his old plastic film canisters, which he used for everything. In fact, he had perhaps ten different spices, herbs, and oils in these small canisters, which fit neatly into a small pot in his personal mess kit. He had learned that trick as a Boy Scout, almost forty years before. That simple little trick alone allowed him to turn ordinary food into a gourmet celebration.

Next, they feasted on smoked salmon with a dilled mayonnaise sauce, served on wedges of hot tortilla chips Butch had just cut from wraps and toasted until crunchy over the fire. In contrast to the gourmet fare, Butch also pulled out a bag of pickled eggs—one of his favorite camp foods. He was always incredulous when others at camp would turn down a pickled egg. That was nature's best, Butch thought. How could anyone not like a pickled egg? "Finest kind," he announced to his current group of campers.

Both O'Casey and the Chief loved to have contrasting foods on their trips. Sometimes, they'd start with thirty-dollar-an-ounce caviar and follow it with hot dogs and beans. That dietary discord really connected them. They were both smartasses at heart, though radically different men. Butch lived in the here and now. He rarely read unless it was a historical biography or his favorite hunting and fishing magazines, which he devoured from cover to cover. O'Casey was his fishing "partner," a term they had used for years until it developed a sexual connotation. In fact, after Butch once introduced O'Casey as his partner to some friends he hadn't seen in years, he was asked later on by one of them how long he and O'Casey had been lovers. Butch had turned scarlet and spent the remainder of the evening trying to explain what he meant and what his true gender preference was. He often wondered whether his friends believed him, but he never used the term again to describe his friend O'Casey.

Sean Patrick O'Casey could not have cared less. Though he was very much an extrovert like the Chief, he was far more cerebral. He loved music, particularly blues and classical, and, of course, he also loved Irish music of all kinds. The most difficult music for him to listen to was opera. His wife, Catherine, had been a well-respected opera diva, and although he loved to hear her perform, no matter how many times he listened to opera, it was the woman and not the music that sang to him. When his wife died, O'Casey just couldn't listen to it anymore. She *was* opera to him. Her death made the melancholy of most opera all the more painful to hear.

"So who wants to try one of my famous pickled eggs?" Butch prodded. He enjoyed cajoling the squeamish into making a culinary leap into the unknown.

"I'll try a bite or two," said Tiffany shyly and to everyone's surprise.

That broke the ice. Almost as quickly, the eggs disappeared much the way the roasted garlic, tapenade, and smoked salmon had.

For the main course, O'Casey had dusted off his best culinary talents. While Butch grilled sirloin tips that O'Casey had marinated in his favorite teriyaki sauce, O'Casey worked on his pièce de résistance— fresh Atlantic scallops *Diablo* with a cream sauce of butter, sherry, Triple Sec, and chipotle pepper. O'Casey had the meal down to a science, even plating it with some fresh parsley sprinkled around the light orange-pink cream sauce. Who else would think to plate such elegant-looking food on paper plates?

Everyone was nonplussed by the extravagant meal and by Butch and O'Casey, who could certainly take this show on the road, according to the highly satisfied customers on the shores of Wilson Lake.

The entire setting could not have been more perfect. The bugs, which were often brutal in mid-June, were very cooperative and almost nonexistent. The afternoon wind was just a light breeze keeping the campsite cool and bug-free. As the sun began to set and the last morsels of dinner were being consumed, the champagne began to make its cerebral impact known. What was fun became funny. What was funny became hilarious. Just after the last of the eggs was finished and everyone acknowledged their culinary value, Butch grinned and said with great pride, "They also have great medicinal value. They make you fart."

Normally, this would have been considered a crude remark, even for Butch. Now, however, with the tribe well into the third bottle of champagne, anything was fair game. Butch had timed the remark to coincide with Ellen's finishing the last of the eggs, and his timing was perfect. It made the situation all the more hilarious. As if on cue, Maria let out a barely audible *pfft*. With that, the house came down. Even Angelo, the quietest member of the tribe, laughed loudly. Maria, forever the good sport, was used to wearing people's humor. This time, however, she knew the laughter was from love and just the circumstances of the moment. Then Angelo too, let out a blast even louder than Maria's. Tribe members had been sitting on a bench that Butch had fashioned out of flat rocks and a log he had trimmed with his cruiser axe. With Angelo's blast, they all fell off—first one, then another, holding their stomachs in laughter.

For the next hour, the hilarity continued, and the champagne flowed until the last drop was gone. Whether it was the eggs, post-hypnotic suggestion, or, most likely, very good and highly adequate quantities of champagne, they all suffered the same indiscretion—all but Tiffany.

She had suffered enough indignity for the day, so her friends graciously picked up the slack. Tears of laughter flowed.

Even Jason had been reintegrated into the social setting. He contributed his share to the body orchestra and had graciously been laughed at, and he had not flinched. But, then again, Jason had a varsity letter in being crude. While this was sociologically foreign territory for the women and for Angelo, Jason was cognitively and socially at home now. O'Casey was rarely crude around women, though he could swear like a trooper when he was really angry. Tonight, he was anything *but* angry. He was as happy and at peace as he could remember being in a long time. The pain of the accident seemed a distant memory now, though it was a pain that rarely went away.

The sun was now squatting almost precariously on the horizon. The deep red was remarkably easy to look at and not painful to the eye. Slowly, magically, the western sky worked its way through a range of crimson, then to peach, and finally to a pale, very thin pink that got lost in the gradually darkening night sky. As the air began to cool and O'Casey got ready to build the "night fire," Butch hovered for a minute by the far edge of the fireplace.

"Voilà!" he proclaimed. Slowly, and with painstaking care, he unwrapped and served piping hot baked apples. He had cored some of the apples from one of the buzz-off boxes, added maple syrup and rolled oats he'd be using for future breakfasts, sprinkled on some cinnamon, placed a few dabs of butter, and baked them in an aluminum foil oven he'd crafted. The tribe laughed and ate, laughed and farted, laughed…and laughed and laughed.

O'Casey quickly took the small, efficient cooking fire and turned it into a wonderful, well-controlled bonfire. The light and heat added to the beauty of the evening. Golden sparks flew into a glorious night sky that had quickly transitioned from a postcard sunset to the blackest of moonless canopies. A brilliant Jupiter and a faint and ruddy Mars announced their presence to a grateful audience. O'Casey pointed out first the two planets, then Sirius, the Dog Star, which often looks like a sparkly Venus. Later, a spectacular Big Dipper poured its contents into the deep and mysterious western sky.

O'Casey's uncle, a self-taught astronomer, had made his own telescope by hand, grinding his own optics with a pumice rub, and had taught his nephew most of the major constellations. O'Casey, in turn, had started teaching his young son, Matthew, the very same lessons. He would carefully climb up onto a flat-roofed addition to his farmhouse with his son working the steps of the ladder just ahead of him. O'Casey would then spread out a sleeping bag and the two would, as he explained it to little Matthew, read the night sky together.

After the accident, it was sometimes very painful and at other times healing for O'Casey to read the sky by himself. He wondered and sometimes prayed that Matthew could hear him say, "Hey, Buddy, how do you like Orion tonight?" And on this night, as he pointed out Orion to the tribe, Sean Padraig O'Casey said a silent hello to his little guy, Matthew. He was glad that he was sitting at the outer edge of the fire's light. He had purposely let it die down so that he could point out the stars. No one noticed in the growing darkness of the Maine woods the tears that welled up in his eyes. However, as Ellen stood up to stretch, she turned toward him and saw a single large tear run down the side of his cheek. He unconsciously wiped it away just as Butch threw some more wood on the fire.

The comedy club atmosphere died down slowly as each member of the tribe savored the last bites of their baked apples and a small box of truffles Butch had kept hidden in the cooler just for tonight.

Maria sat next to her new friends with a smile as broad as any she had ever felt. "I hope and pray that heaven is even half this good."

"Amen, sister," Tiffany said in a quiet, almost inaudible voice.

Maria heard her and was startled by the comment. She and Tiffany were about as different as any two women could possibly be. Tall and gracefully thin, Tiffany Goodrich had been born into a quintessentially upper-crust Long Island home. As the only child of a successful plastic surgeon and a mother with a Harvard law degree, she'd been given everything she ever wanted. Tennis, swimming, and ballet lessons, the best private schools, ski trips to Vail, Innsbruck, and British Columbia. Her education at Connecticut College—her mother's alma mater, of course—had been fully paid for, too. But after visiting friends at Bates and Bowdoin, Tiffany wished she could have gone to school in Maine. She loved the freshness, simplicity, and genuine energy she felt in Maine. Just like her friends there--real and honest. Her mother would have none of it. As always, Mimi Goodrich got her way.

At times, Tiffany wanted to scream, and she often felt empty and alone. She hated the fact that people saw her as a clone of her prejudiced and opinionated mother. She hated the fact that she'd been brought up to judge people by the labels on their jackets and the color of their skin. As an adult, she was determined to become her own woman and bury those attitudes with her mother's generation.

Sitting next to Maria at that moment by the campfire, Tiffany felt wonderful. She loved Maria's spontaneity and smile. She loved the fact that Maria could cheerfully encourage her to use the Half-Moon Hilton and was not embarrassed at passing gas after eating pickled eggs. Her mother's skin would crawl at the thought of Tiffany in dirty clothes that didn't match, her hair half brushed and matted, sitting next to a short, chunky Latina who looked more like the family's help in the Hamptons rather than a newfound friend. Tiffany smiled contentedly to herself and was truly glad that she was here with the tribe and not at the Hamptons.

Ironically, Maria had just been thinking similar but polar opposite thoughts. Here she was, sitting with a great group of friends who weren't judging her by her looks, her poor upbringing, or her heritage. They were fun, fine people enjoying a magical experience together. She had been taken aback by Tiffany's "Amen, sister" comment and the sincere warmth that came with it. And just as spontaneously, Maria sang out, "A-a-a-men. A-a-amen. A-a-men. A-men. A-men."

From across the fire came a delicate, almost ethereal tenor reply: "Halleluiah now! A-a-men. A-men. A-men."

And thus began a poetic, lyrical dance of voices, one to the other— kind heart to kind heart. Two adults, Maria and Angelo, though different in so many ways, had risen above loneliness and ridicule in their similar childhoods to find goodness in others and share their inner beauty in the music they felt in their souls. Now they were trading spirituals in light and lovely a cappella style.

The tribe sat mesmerized as the music flowed like a quiet brook, sometimes bubbly, at other points soft and silky. Angelo, like Maria, had been moved by the friendship and beauty of the moment. He marveled at where he was and who he was with. And he too was struck by the acceptance of the tribe. He respected and admired that quality of acceptance, in particular, about Butch. He loved Butch in a way that he could barely describe. The fact that Butch did not love him back in that same way was unimportant.

Butch had supported Angelo at every turn. As he told his superintendent once when pressed to fire his friend, "This is all bullshit. Angelo is a great teacher. The kids love him. The parents love him. I don't know about his sexuality, and I don't care. He would never touch a student here and never has. I would trust him with my life. If you want to fire him, you'll have to fire me. If you go to court on this, I will be your worst enemy and most hostile witness. If he goes, I go, and I will tell the entire world and the court that this is pure prejudice and nothing more. And if he doesn't sue your ass for wrongful dismissal, I will. You asked me how I feel. There it is. Fire me now or leave us both alone."

Butch was right. It was pure politics. Fortunately, in this political game, Butch was holding a full house. The superintendent folded his hand. Angelo stayed and smiled at the man who stayed by him when others turned away.

And now as Angelo's voice soared with the Maria's into the night air, thoughts of backroom politics and school committee hearings were the furthest thing from anyone's mind. They were no longer principals dealing with budgets, buses, and buttheads. They had been transformed in place and time. Perfect pitch and perfect harmony mingled with campfire smoke and the crackle of a pine fire.

Ellen, in particular, was struck by the purity and elegance of the moment. *How could I ever paint this?* she mused. It was such a multisensory moment. Maria had a remarkably deep, resonant, and occasionally sisters-of-soul voice. She could even do a reasonably good Aretha Franklin when she and everyone else had had enough to drink.

By contrast, Angelo was a gifted, classically trained tenor. His mother, a first generation Italian, had made him listen to old Enrico Caruso recordings for hours at a time. She had worked two and sometimes three jobs to provide for her sons. Her husband had left her when the boys were young, and he'd had little positive influence on their lives, Angelo's in particular. Some children realize early where they fall in the order of parental acceptance, and Angelo could see that every time he played catch with his father and older brother, Marco. Angelo wanted to catch every throw and earned more than one black eye and fat lip trying. Later, he remembered reading James Joyce's *A Portrait of the Artist as a Young Man* and shivering at the parallel he saw and felt. In one sequence, young

Stephen Daedalus was playing, or trying to play, schoolboy rugby. He had kicked at the ball and missed, and the play continued down the field. Suddenly, Daedalus saw the futility of it all—that he would never be one of the guys; he would never be a man's man. *What's the use*, he thought, and stopped running.

Upon reading those words, Angelo had said to himself, *That's me. I am Dedalus*. So, like young Dedalus, Angelo stopped running. He stopped trying to be his brother Marco. He knew he disappointed his father every time he tried to field a grounder or to hit the ball. This was painfully confirmed when his father once remarked after Angelo muffed a slow grounder, "You're not your father's son." The words were as much metaphorical as real. Angelo would rather have taken his father's fastball in the face and broken his nose. A few weeks later, most of the pain and the bruises would be gone, but the pain of those words *never* went away. His father did, however: Guido Capelletti left home that winter and never came back.

So, at seven years of age, Angelo turned to music and relied on his mother for support and recognition...and for the one skill that he did have—perfect pitch. How ironic, Angelo thought many years later. His *pitch* was perfect. He could *hit* every note on the scale flawlessly. Yet he couldn't throw a ball straight or hit his father's slowest pitch with a Whiffle-ball bat. Life was strange.

On this night, by the light of a campfire, there was not a single note that Angelo missed. The first act of the impromptu concert was nothing short of stellar. Distant Sirius twinkled in approval. The fireside crowd marveled at the hidden talents these two shy members of the tribe shared. They slipped gracefully from song to song and genre to genre, exchanging melodies and harmonies. One led and the other followed... like the distant flashes of lightning and low responding thunder miles away in the night sky. They sang show tunes and classics, then Simon and Garfunkel, James Taylor, and other tight a cappella harmonies.

Jason, who was not much for anything intellectual, including music, created a typical Foxworthy moment when he asked, "Can you sing 'Stairway to Heaven'?" Even in the semidarkness, he could see and almost feel the eye rolls of disdain, especially from O'Casey.

"What? What?" he protested, as though it was a routine inquiry that anyone would have asked. "How about some country music?"

Just about the time O'Casey was ready to throttle Jason, Maria started singing Kenny Rogers' "The Gambler." Surprisingly, first Angelo came in with back-door tenor harmony, then everyone chimed in, filling the night air on the eastern end of Wilson Lake with what Angelo would later describe as "almost music." The final notes of the chorus came not from Angelo or even Maria. Just as the two were about to add the very last notes, from the lake edge not a hundred yards away came a melancholic, almost mournful reply to their chorus. Two loons sang their own ancient vibrato like an offering, one to the other, a lonely, romantic harmony perhaps a million years in the making. It was the perfect wilderness harmony—nature's curtain call. The loons' tremolo melted joyfully into the darkness of the Maine sky.

"And on *that* note," Butch grinned, "it's time for beddy-bye."

Reluctantly, the tribe dispersed. The ladies took a flashlight and took turns standing guard below the Half-Moon Hilton as first one and then the other completed their nighttime *toilettes*. Tiffany and Maria were first into their tent. They squirmed and twisted in the confines of the small tent to get their sleeping bags and air mattresses in sync amid the backpacks and other sundries they had brought. And although they were both neophyte campers with deep-seated fears of the wilderness, they were soon fast asleep.

For Ellen, however, it was a different matter altogether, though she had put on a brave face. Although she was one of the first invited on the trip, she had been the last to confirm she'd be going.

Her dad had been ill and hospitalized for a variety of ailments that were all complications of his heavy drinking. He had been a wonderful father, and truly loved his "little princess," as he still called Ellen on occasion. However, even her continual pleading had not convinced him to stop drinking.

He had never had a drinking problem until the final stages of her mother's illness and then her death. From that point on, the alcohol seemed to be his only source of comfort. In fact, those were exactly her father's words at one point. "Please, Ellen, just leave it alone. That's how I get through the day. I miss her more than you can ever know!" They had been childhood sweethearts, and although there were times when their marriage got rocky and the fights were pretty significant, they were, as Ellen noted once, almost like the alpha and omega symbols that decorated the altar at Saint Bart's Catholic Church—so very different and yet united, connected even in death.

Listening to the renewed wail of the loons, Ellen, alone in her little tent, could almost hear her father calling out to her mother, "I miss you." And from the farthest end of the lake, in a thin tremolo, came the mate's reply, "I miss you, too." As wonderful as the evening had been, she could not get past the feeling of loneliness and melancholy. Loons do that to some people, while for others their music is an elixir that sings to their heart and soul.

In the men's tents, it was another story. Although Butch and Jason could talk for hours if anyone were willing to listen, both were asleep in five minutes. Butch had two speeds—fast and off. He hit the off switch two minutes into the rack. In five he was snoring contentedly. Jason, too, was asleep almost immediately. As usual, he had had *his* share of alcohol and some of everyone else's besides. This was standard operating procedure for Jason. It was one reason why his mouth got him into so much trouble, but that was how he was raised. His parents were essentially alcoholics who fought and argued constantly. Like Jason, they were very hospitable and could be very, very funny and fun people to be around, but they could also be crude and mean-spirited. So, for better or for worse, that was who Jason had become.

Some people tend to resemble one parent or the other. While some embrace that parental resemblance, others try to run from the parent they have become. Maria, for example, was much like her mother—solid, not only in appearance, but in character, work ethic, and integrity. To be called her mother's daughter would be a compliment of the highest order. Though Maria could be very tough when she had to be, which was fairly often as a middle school principal, she could also be the most kind and tender of souls. She loved even her toughest students; in fact, that was her specialty—loving the kids everyone gave up on in school. Maria not only kept in touch with students she had expelled, she often then fought to get them back into school. Over her career, she had helped a handful, not only to graduate from high school, but a few to graduate from college. She would never quit on kids, even when they had quit on themselves.

Once, when O'Casey and Butch were talking about Maria's determination and work ethic, Sean turned to Butch and said, "She is just like the mules in Faulkner's novels." Butch looked at O'Casey with such a blank stare that Sean realized he'd made an analogy that would take an hour to explain. In fact, O'Casey knew that it would take fully ten minutes for Butch to fully understand what an analogy was, let alone what it meant. Since O'Casey routinely looked at life in metaphors and analogies, such insights were routine, though perhaps sheer confusion for his best friend.

What O'Casey wanted to share with Butch had to do with William Faulkner's Pulitzer Prize acceptance speech. Faulkner distilled the heart of his writing and life's philosophy into a simple metaphor of his own—that the characters in his novels that he admired most were his mules and the black grandmothers, because of their silent and noble toil. "They would," as Faulkner contended, "not only endure, but prevail." That was how O'Casey viewed Maria. She was for him the most noble of creatures, one who did all the work, was given little credit, and without whom, the world would never get any better. "One day," O'Casey thought to himself, "I'll have to tell her that." Little did O'Casey know how soon his own life would hinge on the ability of Maria and the other women, not only to endure, but to prevail.

In the fourth tent, O'Casey was wide awake and concerned about Angelo, who was struggling to put a clean Band-Aid on his wounded hand.

"Let me see that," O'Casey ordered.

Given the no-nonsense directive, Angelo complied at once.

O'Casey, who was comfortable with almost any first aid situation, cringed at what he saw. The initial cut and puncture wound had been deep, jagged, and about two inches long. The rusty nail had slid along his thumb and buried itself almost completely, and the wound was now red and swollen. Whether it was because of the initial cut, the result of having been in the river water, or due to the dirt-laden activities of the day, the bottom line was simple: the cut was already badly infected.

"We've got to clean this up," O'Casey said with the certitude of an emergency room doctor. In fact, that was a life goal that O'Casey knew he would never achieve. He had always wanted to go to medical school but never received the support or encouragement to pursue that dream. Still, in moments like this, O'Casey could work with the skill and demeanor of a career physician.

Angelo had immediately insisted that O'Casey use the latex gloves that dangled from his fanny pack, and as he worked to cleanse and dress the wound with his well-stocked first aid kit, he was struck by just how infected Angelo's hand had become. Half in jest as he delicately worked to finish wrapping the wound, O'Casey asked, "Do you always get infections this easily?"

Angelo looked down silently and O'Casey realized he had hit a nerve far deeper than any in Angelo's hand. For what seemed like an hour, but was perhaps just a few minutes, Angelo stared in silence at his newly wrapped hand. O'Casey finished putting his first aid kit away and was just straightening out his sleeping gear when Angelo responded in a slow and clearly painful admission.

"I have a compromised immune system. Yes, I do get infections easily. I just never thought I'd get hurt on this trip. It sounded like so much fun, I just couldn't say no."

"Well, you need some sleep. Doctor's orders!" O'Casey said lightly. "I'm just going to hit the head and then sit by the fire for a bit. Don't wait up for me and don't keep the lights on," he joked as he exited the tent. *Compromised immune system?* he repeated to himself. Pieces of the puzzle were starting to fit. However, Sean Padraig O'Casey was reluctant to make that leap quite yet. It would not be fair to his friend Angelo.

Unlike almost everyone else in camp, O'Casey was not a good sleeper. He always had way too much on his mind. Even though it had been almost five years, the accident was never far below his conscious level. His limp was all but gone, as was the pain in his back that had been almost crippling for the first few years. At one point, he'd been so distraught over the loss of his beloved wife and son that he had thought he might go mad, or, better yet, end it all. Butch and the fishing trips had been a great help. More than anything, he had needed time to work through his anguish, and casting for trout proved far more helpful than the therapists he had tried several times. O'Casey almost laughed to himself at the thought of his last therapist's questions.

"You seem like a very angry man, Mr. O'Casey. Why do you think that is?"

"You have my history, Bozo. Why the fuck do you think I'm angry? My wife and son are dead! I did it. I was the driver. My wife and son trusted me to get them home and I let them down. If I'd seen that asshole coming, they'd still be here. Matthew would be in fourth grade. Fourth freakin' grade."

"You're being way too hard on yourself," the therapist responded in a voice so insipid and rehearsed that O'Casey stood straight up.

"I'm out of here! Go play psychobabble with someone else," O'Casey shouted angrily.

"But we're not done yet. We just got started. Where do you think you're going?" the therapist asked in such a rhetorical, nonauthoritative way that it barely called for a response.

O'Casey turned around with a slight grin and said, "Fishing. I'm going fishing." And that's just what he did. He fished all through that day and late into the night. At one point, he looked at the end of his fly line and realized that he didn't even have a fly on it anymore. He didn't care. It was what he needed, a fly rod in his hand and water bubbling past—that, and a little sip of Irish whiskey, a wee drop of the *creathur.*

Wilson Lake and this trip were the best therapy of all for O'Casey. He knew that it wasn't good to be alone so much, even when he was fishing. Being part of this group of principals was, in many ways, better than he thought it would be. In fact, it was great, with the exception of Jason Foxworthy.

The loons were singing again, now offering their famous "laugh" rather than their soulful wail. *It's amazing,* O'Casey thought, *just how different those two loon songs are, and how many emotions they can evoke.* Then he thought of the juxtaposition of feelings he often had, of being happy and carefree one minute and lonesome and aloof the next. The loons knew. They knew what life was all about.

As he sat by the fire smiling at the wisdom of two birds who had mated for life and sang sad, sweet songs to each other in the darkness, he heard another sound, even more penetrating and evocative. First one, then two, then a pack of coyotes began to howl in another ancient song of the woods. O'Casey was glad the ladies were all asleep. Even hardened campers like himself and Butch would bolt upright when the coyote howls were close to camp.

Although there was apparently no recorded case of an adult ever being attacked by a healthy coyote in the woods of Maine, it was hard to believe that to be true when several were howling within a rock's throw of camp at two in the morning. While Butch had joked that the pistol he always brought on camping trips was to scare off a hungry bear looking for a cooler full of trout, O'Casey had noticed times when Butch moved a bit closer to his holster on nights when the coyotes were howling.

As O'Casey got up from his seat by the fire to head off to bed, in the one-person tent fifteen feet away, Ellen shivered, not in the cold, but in near terror. *I can do this. I can do this*, she sobbed quietly to herself, as the crackle of the fire died down with the nighttime harmonies—first of the loons and then of the coyotes.

Fortunately, she could not hear the deep grunts of Brute, the huge black bear searching for food several miles away, or the sow and her cub even closer and in equally desperate need of a meal.

First Fish

"Breakfast! Breakfast!" came the newest of the Chief's now famous shouts. For some, the sound of this classic pronouncement came as a wonderful and energizing call to action. For others, it had all the poetry of a drill sergeant punctuating the shock of the reveille bugle with orders to get up and get up *now*!

As always, Butch had been up at first light. Camp was spotless. Anything that had been left out or strewn about was now organized by tent and by owner. Though he was rarely this meticulous as a principal, camping and fishing in the wilderness were another entity, altogether. They were his first love, his true calling. In another life, he might have been the lead scout working with Sacagawea on the Lewis and Clark Expedition. It didn't matter that this was just a group of friends rather than a high-paying trip with executives from Intel. He took his role as Master Maine Guide very seriously, whether he was getting a hundred-dollar tip for netting a trophy trout or taking a group of friends fishing. He had screwed up once on this trip, though, by running the Cut with a drunk in the crew. He did not plan to screw up again.

Slowly, the campers emerged from their tents and moved like honey in January, grumbling as they approached the campfire.

"Oh, man," groused Tiffany, looking at her watch and sounding more like one of her sixth graders than an elementary principal. "My God, Butch. It's only six o'clock in the morning!"

"Hey, Tiffie. The fish don't wait. They like to eat early and often. By ten A.M. *they're* not very hungry. But if we don't catch some fish on this trip, at some point we're *all* going to be hungry. Besides, it's a beautiful morning. Look who's already up and having breakfast."

Tiffany blinked, rubbed her eyes, and then blinked again. She was almost not sure what she was seeing. Just as her brain and her eyes were getting synchronized, Jason all but shouted, "Look at the freakin' moose! Where's your gun, Butch?"

At that, everyone who was not yet out of their tent scrambled to Jason's side. Less than a hundred yards away stood a bull and a cow moose, knee deep in a bog on the far side of Wilson Stream. They were calmly browsing on their favorite forage, new catkins and young water lilies along the sphagnum bogs that bordered much of Wilson Lake. O'Casey, who had been up shortly after Butch, was surprisingly absent as the others marveled at the size and paradoxical homely beauty of the two moose. Ellen, who'd gone back and put her contacts in so she could see the morning visitors, was the first to notice something she was more anxious to see than the moose.

"There's O'Casey!" Ellen whispered, pointing him out to the group.

Just where the woods met the headwaters of Wilson Stream and less than a hundred feet from where the moose were browsing, O'Casey squatted in a near- motionless position, almost hidden in the alder thicket along the riverbank. He had actually been the first to notice the moose that spectacular morning. Given the fiasco with Jason and the twin fawns the day before, he had purposely not awakened the tribe. He had long since taken his camera equipment and stealthily moved as close as he could possibly get to the coveted prize. The tribe could not see the sweat on his face, nor could they see the slight tremor that caused his usually steady hands to shake. This was the dream of a lifetime. The low side-lighting of the sun, which had just come up, was perfect. It gave his shots great contrast and depth, particularly for the bull moose.

O'Casey had many good shots of moose he'd taken on the Airline, east of Bangor, and on the Golden Road, north of Greenville. These, however, would be *great* shots. The midmorning breeze had yet to come up. The soft blue mirror barely rippled with the duplicate image of the towering bull. His occasional movements rolled the reflecting image across the water and added even more dimensionality to the digital images O'Casey snapped almost continuously. The cow moose browsed nervously on the lily shoots, picking her head up frequently and sniffing the air. The bull seemed unfazed and either unaware or unconcerned by having campers watch his morning routine.

While the bull was not huge by Maine standards, maybe 800 pounds, it was impressive, even for O'Casey. Its rack was still in the early growth stage, and the velvet would not come off until the fall during the rut, when he would announce to every cow within bellowing range that he was anxious and available. By then, the bull would have cleaned every bit of velvet from his intimidating chestnut-colored three-foot rack. During the rut, the bull's grunts, bellows, and pervasive urine scent would challenge other bulls for the right to leave his genetic marker for generations to come in the Wilson River Valley.

O'Casey's cherished moment suddenly got even better. From the edge of the mouse-eared alders just across the stream, a wobbly-legged spring calf perhaps no more than six weeks old emerged into the sunlight. That explained the cow's nervous behavior. She made a low snorting sound and the calf walked awkwardly toward her flank to nurse. Although O'Casey had seen calves before, he had never seen one nursing. He also did not have a single picture of a bull, a cow, and a calf together. *This is priceless*, he thought as he silently snapped shot after shot with his Nikon and favorite telephoto lens. His new 8-gig card could hold 2,000 shots, so he was not frugal about how many he took. He might never get this chance again. How many photographers would? He snapped and smiled, smiled and snapped.

Back in camp, Jason mused with the tribe about how he could probably hit the bull moose with a well-placed rock. Without his usual affable grin, Butch whispered back that he would more likely shoot Jason than he would shoot the charging bull or cow angered by that rock.

"Believe me," Butch whispered, "you wouldn't want to piss off the cow *or* the bull, and I suspect that O'Casey would be charging at you faster than either of them—and that's before the ladies got a hold of you." Almost in unison, the women nodded in agreement, and Jason fell silent.

Finally, the three moose had eaten their fill and turned away from the bog and headed back into the forest. When O'Casey returned, he shared digital glimpses of the moose in various positions and close-ups. Several were truly of prize-winning quality. Even Butch, who rarely complimented his friend, grinned and announced, "We have our own Ansel Adams here."

"Thanks, Chief," O'Casey smiled. He chose not to explain that Ansel

Adams was not a wildlife photographer, though he had undoubtedly seen many moose on the Snake River tributaries. But it was unlikely that a moose or a deer would have held still for a photographer hauling a forty-pound 8 x 10 camera and tripod. Glaciers, on the other hand, didn't much care what anyone carried or shot. Their movement was far more predictable and less temperamental than a charging bull moose.

As thoughts moved from moose to more mundane matters, the smell of freshly brewed coffee invigorated the campers. Though Butch was often one to prepare elaborate, almost elegant breakfasts, he rarely did so on the first morning of camp. Everyone had a choice of hot or cold cereal, oranges, and coffee. The piping-hot coffee was refreshing in its warmth, since the valley had not yet heated up with the early summer sun. The robust Arabica beans sent a magnificent aroma into the still morning air. However, the coffee tasted a bit strange to all but O'Casey, who was a veteran of the Chief's camp coffee.

Maria spoke up first. "Hey, Butch, there are lots of grounds in my coffee and I thought I found a little piece of shell in my last sip."

"You did," grinned Butch. "That's camp coffee. I don't use a basket. That's the real way to make coffee at camp. I just toss four *big* handfuls of coffee into 'Ol' Blue,'" the Chief said, gesturing to the big chipped porcelain coffeepot he'd had for years. "I keep her just under a boil for about ten minutes and let her cool just a bit. Then I toss in a handful of eggshells and *presto magico*: the eggshells grab most of the coffee grounds when the coffee is done. Besides, it adds a bit of flavor and protein. You've just had Ol' Blue camp coffee," Butch concluded as he tapped the treasured coffeepot. "Now, who wants more to heat their cup?" he asked, anxious to see who had the strongest stomach.

Ellen was about to ask, "Is that safe?" but she figured, after all, Butch was the Chief. He knew best. So instead, she smiled and said, "Fill me up, Buttercup."

Everyone followed. They were all learning to trust Butch and, to a similar degree, O'Casey. No one trusted Jason, who could not have cared less anyway. He actually liked to be the bad boy. He loved to see himself as James Dean, the ruggedly handsome rebel in the white T-shirt. Of course, that was his perception…the one he'd share with any woman who would listen.

Breakfast was hardly over when Butch started cracking the whip again. In just a few minutes, he and O'Casey had backpacks and fishing gear ready for what seemed more like a forced march than a day of fishing. "We're off for the day and won't be back until late." Butch told the tribe. "Take what you need. I've got lunch, toilet paper, and fishing equipment. Bring your own water bottles from the cooler and whatever else you want. It will be a long day. Bring a book if you like." He didn't bother to tell them that they'd be walking for a half hour before even seeing much of the river.

Only Jason grumbled about why they couldn't just fish from camp at the head of the stream. "You can if you want to catch chubs and suckers," Butch said with his usual grin. "The headwaters get pounded pretty hard, especially by the rich boys who get flown in to this camp. They're too lazy to go where the real fish are, but we don't mind, do we gang?"

The question was meant to be rhetorical, but the women laughed and said how much they wanted to hike and see the wilderness. Maria's quick-witted response was the best, however. "Nope, Butch. I don't mind at all. If we keep exercising at this pace, in another two weeks I'll be a size four. Of course, I'd also have to grow about six more inches as well."

Periodically, when the path led them right to the water's edge, someone would ask, "Are we there yet?" and Butch would just say, "Not yet," and keep moving. Though it was technically called Wilson Stream, it was in many ways a river, and as they would soon discover, it behaved in a way that few streams ever did.

After what seemed like a very circuitous route, the path, as if by magic, brought them back to the river's edge right at the point when everyone needed a serious break. "Here we are," Butch announced in triumph.

He had good reason to feel triumphant. The scene before them was breathtaking. For some, it was as if they were eight-year-olds sitting above the dugout in the first base box seats at Fenway Park as the Sox took the field for game one of the playoffs with the Yankees. For others, it had the impact of being in the front row at the Met as the curtain opened and the Bolshoi Ballet began dancing *The Nutcracker*.

Before them lay what appeared to be a bottomless pool of emerald-green water framed by a garnet-laden beach of sand and small granite boulders, worn by thousands of spring floods and summer rains. Above them for at least a hundred yards ran a series of shallow, waist-deep rapids sparkling like Waterford crystal in the June morning sunshine. The area directly below them was a series of cascading pools of various widths and depths. A master fly fisherman might feel greedy in describing this ideal mix of water—fast and slow, shallow and deep, transparent and mysterious. There was more than enough room for the entire tribe to spread out and fish the length of the magic before them…and so they did.

Butch and O'Casey quickly assembled all the gear as though they'd rehearsed the dance of lines and bobbers, hooks and worms, just for this very moment. Butch explained both the process and the etiquette of bait fishing for brook trout. *Who knew*, the women thought to themselves, *that there could be so much to drowning a worm.*

"What we keep, we eat," Butch said. "The stream has an abundance of fairly small fish. We're probably not going to get many trophy fish here. But once we have about a dozen or so keepers, we'll release as many more as we can catch."

Generally, Butch didn't "kill" many fish, as he and O'Casey would describe it. Mountain brook trout were delicious, but if they were not thinned out by fishermen, they would compete to an unhealthy level for food. This was especially true in August when warm water temperatures would force them to congregate in the diminishing areas of cold water and high oxygen levels. Such conditions were hardly a problem in June, as the spring runoff and brisk water temperatures were ideal for the trout and for the tribe.

Had it just been the four men, Butch would not have set up the bobber rigs he and O'Casey were so busy tying. He would have taught Angelo and Jason how to drift-fish "garden hackle," the name most fly fishermen used for worms or night crawlers. However, drifting a worm and a split shot took both time and patience, and Butch wanted to ensure that the women, in particular, really got into the fish. "You just toss the bobber up into the current and let it drift," he told them. "The key is in knowing when to set the hook. When a fish is nibbling the worm, the bobber will bounce, but you've got to wait until it goes under the water for a two count. Not one, not three, but a two count."

"You're kidding, Butch. I know you are," said Maria. "What does a two count have to do with catching trout?"

"I'm dead serious," he replied "On a one count, the fish just starts to run with the worm but may not have put it in his mouth. Set the hook and you'll wear the bobber and not the fish. Set the hook on three, and the fish will have swallowed the hook. You'll have to kill the fish because the hook will be in its stomach. Once we've caught lunch, we won't want to kill any more fish. At least that's how I look at it, and hopefully you'll agree once you've caught enough.

"Here are the other rules of the day," Butch went on. "The *first* fish caught means no dishes for that person for the entire trip. The *most* fish means you get to wash the dishes tonight because you had the most fun today, and the *biggest* fish means you get to fill the latrines when we break camp. That helps to keep everyone humble."

Although he knew that Jason would be eager to catch the first fish, both for bragging rights and because he hated to wash dishes, Butch had other ideas. He and O'Casey had purposely rigged up only three rods to start and fumbled as they rigged up the next two. Long after each of the women had landed their first fish, Jason was still whining like a schoolboy, pestering Butch to hurry up with his rod before all the fish were caught.

Butch and O'Casey were both aware of the trauma that Tiffany had experienced after saving Jason at the falls. While neither had actually seen Tiffany naked, they had seen her being dressed by Ellen and Maria and knew that allowing such an intimate act reflected a woman who was in an emotionally fragile state. They knew she needed to be reenergized, and few experiences were more transformative than catching one's first fish. Butch gently eased in next to Tiffany to help cast her Shimano ultralight spinning rig into the current just at the head of the "big eddy," as he called the pool nearest where she was standing. While both Butch and O'Casey knew the real Big Eddy was a legendary fishing hole on the Penobscot River many miles to the southwest, the name somehow seemed to fit this smaller pool, too.

"One thousand one. One thousand two. Oh shit! Oh shit! What am I supposed to do, Butch? I forgot. I've got a fish! I've got a fish!" Tiffany squealed.

Before Butch could remind her to reel the fish in, Tiffany had instinctively backed up. Within seconds, a crimson-bellied brook trout bounced its way along the shallows at her feet. O'Casey waded into the riffle and scooped up the fish, using his thumb and forefinger to grab the fat eight-inch brookie by the lip.

"Nice fish, Tiff!" he shouted with pride. In less than a second he had unhooked the wriggling brookie and brought it right up to Tiffany's face. "You've got to give it a kiss. It's your first trout, right?"

"Yuck! I don't want to kiss a fish!" she protested, though she knew she had no choice. "Well, OK," she laughed and quickly kissed the squirming brookie, his golden spots and orange-and-crimson fins twitching wildly in the morning sun.

Tiffany had instinctively yanked on the rod on *one thousand two*, and the brookie had been hooked neatly on the outer lip. After the official smooch, O'Casey gently brought the brookie into the shallows and released it as though letting a butterfly drift back into the warm moist air of the rainforest. For O'Casey, there was something almost sacred about releasing fish. Though he had kept and eaten perhaps hundreds of fish, both he and Butch did so with the same reverence for the fish that the Native Americans had had for the buffalo. It was at once a source of food and a spiritual source of renewal and sacred majesty that could not be captured in words or on film.

"I've got one!" Maria shouted.

"Me, too!" squealed Ellen in an almost childish voice. She had dreamed of this moment for years and years. She had begged her father and brothers so many times she couldn't count them all. Although the squirming brookie was only ten inches long and was on the line for just thirty seconds before Butch had brought it up for the ritual kiss, Ellen would remember the moment forever. It was not a disappointment. She could see why her brothers and father loved the experience. It *was* magical. The many shopping trips her mother had taken her on had no such magic in spite of her mom's best efforts to the contrary. It was not the fish. It was the experience. It was the thrill of the doing and the being. It was the rules and the rituals…and it was just great. Ellen beamed as she watched Butch release her fish in the same delicate fashion O'Casey had used with Tiffany's.

No one was surprised when Jason became the first of the tribe whose fish had swallowed the hook and needed to be killed. He had purposely counted to five to ensure that it would be the first keeper, regardless of its size. He wanted none of that catch-and-release crap.

Butch and O'Casey had planned to have fish for lunch and knew from experience that many of the fish on this first day would be badly hooked. That was also one reason why both veteran fishermen almost never used worms. Perhaps forty percent of the fish caught that way were hooked too deeply to be released and would die shortly afterward.

Instead, they often used #14 or even #18 flies that were so small they rarely resulted in the death of a fish. Often, the two fishermen released forty or fifty fish before having to keep and kill one. For both, there was a sense of loss and almost failure when a fish, particularly a large one, was *creeled,* a term that came from the days when fishermen carried wicker creels and routinely filled them to the brim with deep-bellied fish. It had taken several generations of fishermen like Butch and O'Casey to alter that ethic, and both men had lobbied on behalf of catch-and-release legislation they had helped to craft. This new ethic now permeated their personal philosophy. At meetings where they encouraged such ethics, they were occasionally harassed by NRA-types who laughed at their *pussy behavior.* Didn't they know that real men killed fish, and deer, and bear? Once at a legislative hearing on Maine's "catch and release" policies, O'Casey and the Chief were harassed by an NRA lobbyist. His condescending words and behavior toward them suggested the snide attitude of, "Why don't you limpwristed Massholes go home where you belong?"

Butch smiled at the lobbyist as he detected a slight Virginia or Carolina accent. "My great, great grandfather fought with the 20th Maine," Butch grinned ..."and he probably kicked your rebel great grandfather's ass in the process. My guess is that gives me a lot more right to be in this hearing than some right-wing cracker with a bible college education. That just proves that you can't send a Bob Jones University boy on a man's errand." Butch knew that those were fighting words. When the lobbyist stood up, so did his friend O'Casey, who had never been afraid of a fight. The lobbyist could see a fire in O'Casey's eyes as well that told him he had grossly underestimated the conviction and heart behind the two Maine boys. Some of the Maine legislators heard the exchange and smiled.

"Good to know the 20th Maine was still alive and well in a few good men," thought the presiding senator nearest to the exchange. Although he had been somewhat ambivalent on the catch and release legislation, and some of his own constituents might oppose it, the senator soon spoke on behalf of the legislation, moved in part by The Chief's strong exchange with the lobbyist and a deep-seated distrust the senator had for high paid *suits* trying to buy votes in his beloved Maine. The legislation passed, as did an extensive awareness campaign to encourage a catch and release ethic, which was central to the fishing experience for the two good friends.

While Butch and O'Casey practiced it on most of their fishing trips, the also knew that on *some* rivers and on *some* trips, "culling" fish was akin to thinning crops in a garden. It was a necessary evil that, as a fringe benefit, provided a nutritious meal for the fisherman. On this day, a number of fish needed to be killed to provide their planned lunch of pan-fried trout, but somehow the "two count" seemed to work like magic. Fish caught on the two count were almost always released safely.

Everyone caught and released a number of fish, including Butch and O'Casey, although they were the last to gear up and gave themselves the poorest quality water. Angelo, who would have been content just to watch from the sidelines, originally seemed to be the least enthusiastic fisherman. He was such an unselfish person that he only threw his line out after the women had caught and released a half dozen fish apiece at the head of the big eddy. Finally, Butch insisted and all but dragged Angelo to a premier spot where he knew Angelo might take a nice fish.

After several failed casts that barely put his bobber into the current, Angelo gave his rod a mighty heave. The light tackle shot completely across the stream in a sweeping arc to the far end of the pool. Since there were ample fish within fifteen feet of shore, no one had even made an effort to get their worm that far out. Seconds later, the bobber disappeared, and Angelo, who had almost never fished before, wasn't even looking. It wasn't until his rod dipped once and then more forcefully a second time, that he noticed that his bobber had disappeared.

"Butch," he called out, "I think I'm caught on a rock or something. My bobber's gone."

Just then, a beautiful sixteen-inch brook trout shot out of the eddy directly below where the bobber should have been. "Wow! Did you see that, Butch? Did you see that?" Angelo shouted excitedly. And that was precisely the enthusiasm he displayed throughout the battle. For someone who was so often reserved, he showed the giddiness of an eight-year-old. Even Jason cheered as Angelo followed Butch's instructions for landing the fish.

"Don't horse him! Don't horse him. Let him run! Now reel. *Reel!*" Butch ordered. "Keep your rod tip up!"

Butch shouted first one directive and then another. Angelo had no idea what most of them even meant, but somehow he managed to swing the feisty brookie into the shallows, where O'Casey grabbed the leader and slid his hand down to the hooked jaw of the big male trout. Though it was small in comparison to the trophy fish O'Casey had lost the day before, it was still a magnificent fish for a stream or river of this size. It shook back and forth with such strength that even in O'Casey's skilled hands, the fish almost leaped to safety on several occasions. Angelo knew the routine now and needed no prodding. He splashed his way to O'Casey's side, almost falling in several times as he struggled to give his fish a kiss before it was released.

"Smile!" Ellen hollered as she snapped a picture of Angelo smooching the fish. "One more! One more!" she shouted, struggling with the thumb-wheel to advance the film to the next shot.

Just as Angelo turned for a second kiss, the still vigorous brookie thrashed one last time, and O'Casey, sensing its panic, simply loosened his grip. The slippery fish went airborne and quickly splashed its way to freedom. It wriggled, splashed, and leaped like a salmon at low water seeking a spawning ground. It rolled once in a pool barely three inches deep. The crimson flank and bright yellow spots exploded with color in the morning light. Bursting with a newfound energy, the trout made two strong sweeps with it tail and disappeared into the depths of the big eddy below. A brief swirl of dark water and thin white froth painted the solitary trace of a fish that had given its captor the thrill of a lifetime.

Angelo was overjoyed both by the battle and by the final outcome. He had kissed but not killed his first fish ever…and what a fish! Now he knew why Butch and O'Casey were such devotees. Angelo felt an exhilaration that, as a rule, only great musical moments could produce. He smiled broadly in a way he rarely did in public. It was not that he wasn't a happy person, but his happiness was often internal. He had been criticized so often by his father for his failures in sports and by his mother for his failure to be perfect in piano practices, that even when he was successful, he often second-guessed even his best efforts. Now, however, everyone had seen the fish. He had done it! There would even be a picture. *How cool*, he thought. *What a day!*

Although the successes of the others were less momentous, each member of the tribe caught their fill of trout that morning. Butch had known that, given the time of year and the water conditions, they would take fish. At least he had hoped so. Occasionally, he was wrong, as are all guides at times. Sometimes, the fish "just don't show," as he would explain it to clients. More often than not, however, Butch was right, and today was no exception.

THE PARTRIDGE AND A BEAR TREE

Butch had toyed with the idea of having lunch on the big eddy, but he realized that after lunch everyone would be ready for an afternoon snooze. It would be far more comfortable for that to happen at camp, especially after getting couch potatoes to rise so early. So, despite some grumblings of protest, Butch led a "forced march" of the tribe back to camp.

The lingering excitement of the morning's events made the trip more palatable than they had envisioned. Everyone bubbled with talk of his or her own fish. They were all amazed at how much fun the fishing had been. Even Angelo, who was rarely gregarious, chattered away like a schoolboy after a birthday party, and he and Maria often roared with laughter as they shared their angling experiences.

For Angelo and Maria, being part of the crowd, or this case, part of the *tribe*, was a rare and valued experience. Just showing up at Butch's house with a car full of camping gear to meet a whole new group of friends had been a personal victory for each of them. And when one has friends, when one feels truly wanted and needed, the air somehow seems fresh and pure, the skies a deeper blue. In spite of the painful throbbing in his injured hand, Angelo felt totally alive and totally at peace.

The others, too, personalized the morning's experiences, talking simultaneously to the person in front and the person behind as they walked the narrow *freeze-out* road they followed back to camp. The road, though longer than their earlier path along the river, was an easier walk. As a veteran guide who thought out even the smallest of details, Butch knew that tired legs and narrow paths could mean trips and stumbles.

Trips and stumbles created sprained ankles and twisted knees, and one serious injury could ruin an entire trip.

On walks like this, either Butch or O'Casey would take the point and the other would follow at the end as the sweeper. It was not at all uncommon in such treks for a person to fall behind to tie a shoe, take a drink, or, more frequently, stop to take a quick pee. While the freeze-out road was generally easy to follow, it had its forks. One wrong turn and a lollygagging hiker could get separated from the group. A second wrong turn could prove fatal. Given that the nearest paved road was twenty-five miles away and the closest town was forty miles away, there was little margin for error. People who got lost in Maine's "big woods" could be lost forever.

And besides, there were bears—big black bears. One time when O'Casey was visiting a friend at Grand Lake Stream, near Calais, Maine, they had driven his old Honda Civic to the local dump at night to watch the bears feeding on the garbage. He had seen a large male bruin that seemed to be as big as his Civic. He never forgot its size. O'Casey knew that while bear encounters were infrequent, the tribe was right in the middle of bear country now. He also knew the two most common reasons for black bear attacks: something or someone threatening a sow bear's cub, and an injured bear looking for large, easy-to-catch prey such as a wounded animal…and rarely, a careless camper.

As O'Casey was reflecting on his bear encounter at the dump, from his sweeper spot on the trail Butch shouted out, "Hey, guys, check these rake marks!"

"What the hell are rake marks?" Jason asked, as he looked at the broad white stripes that started almost eight feet up in a fir tree and ran halfway down the trunk.

"That's just a big ol' black male bear—a boar—trying to say hi to the ladies. That semi-disgusting smell is his other calling card. He's saying to the ladies, 'Bubba is back,' and he's saying to the other male bears, 'Get your ass outta town.'"

Ellen felt the hair on the back of her neck stand straight up. Just before confirming with Butch that she wanted to go, she'd asked him about bears. He'd told her that they'd probably never even see one. "Butch, I thought you said we wouldn't see a bear on this trip," she said with the same trepidation most of the tribe was now feeling.

"Haven't seen one yet, have we?" Butch said.. "Doubt we will. They are primarily nocturnal feeders. As long as we're smart in dealing with our food and garbage, and none of you ladies are having your period, we're safe." He knew that last statement would probably terrify the women, who were no doubt suddenly trying to figure out where they were in their menstrual cycles.

"Look, guys," he continued, "in all my years in the woods, I've only seen four, and I've only been chased once. Me and O'Casey. We ran like hell. But either he wasn't hungry or he didn't like the smell of my Irish friend." He grinned at O'Casey. "That's why I bring my friends Mr. Smith and Mr. Wesson."

From deep in his fanny pack he produced a .38 caliber Smith & Wesson revolver. "It's mostly just for the noise. I also use it when I can't get campers up in the morning. It's amazing how effective several gunshots are at six A.M. right outside your tent—especially when I'm shouting, 'Bear in camp!'"

This was the Chief in rare form. With the exception of O'Casey, who had heard all this before, the entire group was spellbound and scared at the thought of a bear that could reach up almost eight feet to make the claw marks on the tree before them.

"Relax, ladies," Butch said, directing the remark as much to Jason and Angelo as to the women. In a metaphorical way, "ladies" was Butch's way of making his own claw marks on the tree. He was the Chief. He had the knowledge, the confidence, and, of course, the gun. "You don't have to worry. And besides, that's why I always bring the pickled eggs. The farts keep the bears away."

"Really, Butch?" Jason asked as if on cue. He was not trying to play the straight man. He had just been suckered in by one of the Chief's favorite lines.

"No, I'm just kidding. Bears smell so bad themselves that a fart would seem like Chanel Number Five to them."

Everyone roared, including Jason. Butch was glad that he'd been able to add a bit of levity. He had purposely drawn the group's attention to the rake marks on the tree. It was important for everyone to have good "bear sense." This was, after all, bear country, and the humans, and not the bears, were the tourists.

Bears were hardly the only worry in the Maine woods. Even on easy hikes like this one, it was imperative for a good guide to be watchful, to point out slippery rocks and broken branches at eye level. As the point person in the trip back to camp, it was O'Casey's job to follow the correct trail, and it was almost as important to watch for trailside problems that could lead to injuries.

O'Casey had nearly lost an eye once while returning to the car after fishing a bit too late at a favorite pool. As he hurried along a path he knew as well as his name, his thoughts had turned to the wonderful evening of cream-colored caddis flies and the many fat brook trout he had fooled. Suddenly, he felt a severe pain in his eye and knew at once that a branch had scraped his cornea. He didn't realize just how severe the laceration was until he got back to the car and looked in the mirror. His left eye, his really good eye, was already filling with blood.

O'Casey, who had broken, sprained, or dislocated almost every part of his body playing rugby in college, had a high pain threshold, but the pain in his eye was excruciating. He recalled with an almost comic sense that when he arrived at the emergency room, the nurse had shouted out, "We need a doctor, STAT!" O'Casey had wondered who they were talking about until he realized it was *him*. It was his eye, now totally full of blood, that had shaken the usually unshakable emergency room nurse. Almost miraculously, O'Casey thought, the eye had suffered no long-term damage. He looked like hell for weeks, but he was fine.

Unfortunately, the bloody eye became a terrorizing factor back at school. No one wanted to get sent to see Dr. O'Casey, or Dr. O, as the students called him. His reputation for giving kids the "evil eye" had been magnified five-fold. For several weeks after the bloody eye incident, student behavior had been near perfect. While O'Casey quickly forgot about his blood-filled eye after the pain went away, his students lived in fear of having to visit Dr. O and see a bloody eye staring back at them. While most of the kids liked Dr. O, his near-tragic eye injury had created a new sense of respect that he found more humorous than his kids did.

Still, the incident had created a lasting impression on O'Casey, which he mulled over as he walked point back to camp. He had always had a strong "boy scout" or "principal" gene, as those who knew him described it. He could see a problem or danger half a mile away—a broken bottle or a child about to walk into traffic. He would occasionally stand by a spill in a grocery store or restaurant until an employee noticed and dealt with the problem. It wasn't that he was a do-gooder. He just hated the thought that someone might get hurt on his watch. He was that way as a boy and as a Boy Scout. He was that way in the Marines—it had made him a good sergeant and had helped him to bring home soldiers who would otherwise have died from a lethal dose of stupidity. And he was that way as a school principal. Now, as he walked along, leading the tribe back to camp, he kept that same watchful eye out. Somehow, O'Casey could carry on a conversation while walking the trail and still point out a dangerous rock, notice a pileated woodpecker high up in a tree, or hear a saw-whet owl in the distance.

Ellen, who had deliberately fallen into line behind O'Casey, enjoyed walking behind him. In fact, she now considered him a *hunk*. A lot of women did, in spite of the large scar that was a permanent reminder of his accident. When O'Casey had been fishing at the base of the dam, Ellen and Maria had felt like schoolgirls, first talking about him as though they were watching from the stands at a basketball game. Later, they'd had a similar conversation about Butch. Even though Jason was easily the best-looking man on the trip, they were turned off by his narcissistic opinion of himself. He was a pretty boy who had always been able to get the girl, and it was obvious that he had already been trying to work his magic on Tiffany. Even now, as they walked back to camp, Ellen could hear Jason's loud boastful voice, talking about himself almost in the third person.

He was like Jimmy in the *Seinfeld* episode...or George W. Bush talking about himself in the third person as "the President." Ellen was amazed that any woman could find such conceited men attractive. She wished that Jason Foxworthy would fall on his face on a muddy section of the trail. That would serve him right. Maybe then, Tiffany would see what a loser he really was.

Ellen was actually surprised at how much she liked Tiffany. Until Tiffany's rescue of Jason, Ellen had thought of her in somewhat the same way she viewed Jason—a shallow "pretty girl," the rich spoiled blonde daughter of a rich spoiled blonde. *Rich bitch* came to mind, but Ellen got mad at herself for even thinking of a put-down term like that.

First impressions can certainly be wrong. She now thought of Tiffany in an entirely different light. After the rescue, she and Maria had seen a marvelous dichotomy—a powerful, confident woman capable of rescuing a drowning man and a frail little girl who had been shaken to the core by a near-death experience. Tiffany was now a sister of sorts, a person Ellen hoped would be a long-term friend. As she listened to Jason cluttering the trail with his noise, Ellen also hoped that Tiffany would see Jason for who he was—shallow, obnoxious, and pathetically self-centered. He was after only one thing: sex—of the most carnal and selfish variety. While sex was something Ellen could really use right now, because it had been a long time since she'd had a sexual partner and a *very* long time since she'd had anyone she really loved, the thought of sex with Jason Foxworthy was nothing short of repulsive ….

Suddenly, the world seemed to explode! Dirt flew in Ellen's face and behind it came a loud whirring, thumping sound and tan wings that terrified her as the bird flew right at her. *"Ahhh!"* she screamed as she instinctively covered her face with her arms. Just as suddenly, Angelo fell forward, landing on top of her as one domino might land on another. *What the hell happened?* Ellen thought as she untangled herself from a very embarrassed Angelo. Slowly, she got to her feet, mentally checking her vitals to make sure she was uninjured.

"Partridge," O'Casey laughed as he dug himself out of the bushes. The bird had been scared from its trailside nest quite literally into Ellen's face.

"O'Casey, why the hell did you jump into the bushes? I wouldn't think an old hunter like you would be afraid of a little partridge," the Chief joked from the back of the line.

"Christ, it's my old Marine jungle training. It never leaves you. Walking point on a trail in Cambodia near the end of the war, if I didn't learn to dive for cover when the bushes rustled like that, I would have been dead at least ten times, and you guys would have been coming back in black plastic body bags."

The Chief was caught off guard by O'Casey's remarks. Even though he had known for a long time that O'Casey had been a recon Marine as an eighteen year old kid, he had almost never, ever talked about it. On one or two occasions when Butch had pushed O'Casey for details about the war, O'Casey had pushed back. "If I ever feel like talking about it, you'll be the first to know," he would say.

It was the same thing with the accident. Butch had not known O'Casey well when his wife and child were killed, but he had heard the stories. O'Casey's wife had apparently been a beautiful and wonderful woman and a magnificent opera diva. They were driving home from her concert at Carnegie Hall—Carnegie freakin' hall, Butch had noted to himself—when it happened. Apparently, at the last minute, their son had begged them to let him come. "Please, Daddy, I want to hear Mommy sing. Please?" he'd implored.

O'Casey, who was a notorious softy, had given in. He had wanted to stay in New York with Catherine and make it a special event. The baby sitter, who loved little Matthew, had even planned to stay for the weekend. But four-year-olds can be very persuasive. "It's OK," Catherine had insisted. "I may never get to sing at Carnegie again. I don't know how I managed this. You and Matthew may be the only people in the audience, but no matter how many people are there, you'll be the most important."

Butch didn't know much about the accident itself. On rare occasions when O'Casey would get into the Jameson's whiskey too much, he would share bits and pieces about Catherine, but almost never about the accident. What Butch knew, he had learned from others. Apparently, Catherine had been brilliant. She had received three curtain calls and a five-minute standing ovation. The mayor of New York and loads of other celebrities waited backstage for a congratulatory hug or photo op with her. It had been the perfect night. Sean had suggested that they spend the night in the city, but Catherine wanted to tuck Matthew into his own bed. Sean had driven the hour-long route from Manhattan to Westport many times, even at five in the morning. He felt sure he could do it. That was the last thing he remembered.

He had confided to Butch that amnesia was the only blessing of the night. He had no recollection of the accident. He never remembered seeing the drunk who was driving in the wrong lane. He never remembered seeing his dead wife or dying son. His own coma lasted more than three weeks, long after his wife and son had been buried. He never had a chance to say good-bye to the people he loved most in life. But he understood why his parents and Catherine's parents had made the decision to go ahead with the funerals. Everyone, including the doctors, were surprised that Sean had survived. His injuries had been potentially life threatening—a fractured skull, a broken hip and femur, and a lacerated spleen that was eventually removed. Only his strong constitution and will to live had apparently saved him. Many times, Sean had said to himself, and on rare occasions, to others, that he wished he had died with his family.

Still, O'Casey had found great solace in his job...and in his fishing. He loved his students at school and he actually loved his teachers as well, which was pretty unusual for most of the principals O'Casey knew. He stayed busy with his work as a way to keep his mind off the otherwise constant pain, not so much from his injuries, which continued to give him physical pain, but rather from the numbing loss of the two people he treasured and worshipped. For a while, he had to put their pictures away. On too many nights he found himself holding a favorite picture of the three of them in one hand and an Irish whiskey in the other and drinking himself to sleep. When he found it affecting his ability to get out of bed and get to work, he put the picture and the whiskey away. While on occasion both would reappear, O'Casey had found ways to control his grief and to live a life "mixed with blessing and sadness" as he would occasionally say to his closest friends. The blessings were his job, his good friends, and his fishing. The sadness was self-explanatory and ever-present.

Often, Butch could tell that his friend had the accident on his mind and would just kidnap him for a day or even a weekend of fishing. Though they were different in a number of ways, Butch and O'Casey were still fast friends. Butch admired him for many of the things he was not—bright, modest, musical, mellow. Once, when a mutual friend described O'Casey as a true "Renaissance man," the Chief was afraid to ask what that meant. Though he could never express it formally—he was not the hugging type, nor were most Maine men—Butch loved and admired his friend. He always felt good at helping O'Casey to get over his down periods. That was his way of being the Chief with O'Casey. Though Butch knew he was no Sean Padraig O'Casey, he was still very comfortable in his own skin. Granville Butch Chapman liked the person he was. He liked being a principal, a coach, and most of all, a Master Maine Guide. And he loved being called *their Chief.*

Now on the trail with the tribe somewhat in disarray, it was time for him to be the Chief again. The incident with the partridge had disrupted the march. Butch knew they needed a break, but a muddy thicket with buzzing black flies was not the place. So he pushed his grumbling group on for ten more minutes. Fortunately, they were almost to Indian Springs, a term Butch and O'Casey used to describe a small but very active spring that bubbled up from a granite outcropping on the side of the trail.

"This is a great place to fill our water bottles, guys," said Butch. "Just make sure you don't fill up in the pool area below. Get your canteen right up against the rock where the water bubbles out. That way it's good, fresh, and most importantly, safe to drink."

As the thirsty campers filled their water bottles and canteens one at a time, Angelo bent down and thrust his hands into the cool water in the rocky pool below the spring. Butch was the first to notice how carefully Angelo tried to wash the black bog mud from his wrist just above his frayed bandage.

"Let me see that," Butch ordered.

"It's fine, really," Angelo responded.

"Give it here! That's an order," Butch laughed, only half in jest. In a flash, Butch had his knife out and cut away what remained of the blood-stained and mud-soaked bandage.

Angelo pulled his hand back as Butch tried to cleanse the wound. "Universal precautions! You taught us that at staff meetings," Angelo responded defensively.

"I won't get your cooties," grinned Butch, trying to lighten the moment. "Look, I'll pour the water. You just wash it off with this gauze." It was clear that Angelo was reluctant to have Butch look as his injured hand, and even more reluctant to have Butch touch the wound.

As a guide, Butch was always prepared, and he had a small green fanny-pack first aid kit with him at all times, even fishing. "I never know when I'm going to get a bloody nose...or my period," he joked as he pulled out a thick gauze pad.

Butch was startled by the angry-looking wound that was starting to ooze a light yellow fluid. *Not good*, Butch thought immediately. It was significantly worse than when O'Casey had dressed it the night before. The surprise and concern reflected in his hoarse whisper was more than Butch had wished to betray. "Christ, Angelo, that's really infected! Didn't you notice?"

"Yeah, Butch," Angelo said timidly. "I figured it was, but I didn't want to bother you, and I thought it would just get better with time."

"OK. Let's get it cleaned up." Given Angelo's *universal precautions* reprimand, Butch put on his latex gloves. This obviously pleased Angelo, who then seemed more comfortable with the skilled care Butch showed in working on the wound. First, he thoroughly cleaned the wound with hydrogen peroxide, which he always carried for such purposes. Next, he applied a liberal amount of Bacitracin. Finally, he dressed the wound with the skill of an ER physician and the kindness of Mother Theresa.

While the others were slightly aware of the first aid treatment taking place, only O'Casey had noticed the concern in the Chief's face. *It must be getting worse*, O'Casey thought to himself.

He and Butch had worked in tandem several times when fishing buddies had gotten injured. Both were comfortable providing first aid and both had significant training as well. While O'Casey had not glimpsed the wound itself, he could see from the look on Butch's face that it had, in fact, gotten significantly worse. He could also tell from the Chief's thoroughness in dealing with it that it was a growing and serious problem that might have consequences for the entire group, consequences none of them could have anticipated.

The tribe finished the journey back to camp with lots of laughter and a good-hearted spirit. Ellen was well covered in mud (and a few feathers) from her run-in with the partridge. Inwardly, she laughed at her wish earlier in the day about having Jason be the one to fall in the mud. *God must have a good sense of humor*, she thought. *That's what I get for wishing ill on someone else.* She had a remarkable self-deprecating perspective. She could laugh at herself and didn't mind being laughed at, on occasion. It was one reason why she loved Maria, who seemed to have a varsity letter in self-deprecating humor. As Maria often said of herself, "I was teased so often that I learned to laugh *with* people; otherwise, I would just feel laughed *at*. Because people liked my laugh, they somehow seemed to tease me less. It was a survival mechanism, but it worked."

Ellen was laughing to herself as she headed off to her tent to get out of her muddy clothes. *So much for wishing ill on someone else. Next time, I guess I'll wish Jason hits the lottery. Maybe then* that *will happen to me instead.*

REFLECTIONS

Afternoon at camp, like the lake itself, was a near motionless calm. Campers self-selected their own level of comfort, choosing to play, relax, read, or sleep. As always on Wilson Lake, fishing dropped off almost completely in the afternoon sun. The bugs were surprisingly in short supply, as was the usual prevailing summer wind that tended to pick up throughout most June afternoons. The sky was a deep, mysterious blue. Occasional billowing cumulus clouds slid by along the northern rim of the bowl created by Wilson Lake and the hills on the north shore.

O'Casey was giving a mini-seminar of sorts to Maria and Ellen, who were fascinated by his Nikon D70 and the pictures he had captured. He had attached a polarizing filter, once a few puffy clouds had arrived, and showed the two women how to accentuate the blues in the sky and the clouds by choosing the angle at which to shoot and the intensity of the filter being dialed in with the adjustment ring. Maria, in particular, seemed fascinated by the physics behind the process. She had taken a science minor in college. Her love for science, however, came with a very unceremonious and auspicious start.

She would never forget the remarks from her first science teacher there, Melvin Lee Barney, who had immediately shown contempt for her transfer from a barrio school to the one most of the white kids attended. "You don't belong here!" he had told Maria. "You don't belong in this class. You don't belong in this school," he had said after class on the first day of school. "In all honesty, you and your kind don't even belong in this country," Mr. Barney stated flatly. It was that simple, as he viewed it. They didn't belong. She didn't belong. This was America. It wasn't

Mexico. Swim the freakin' river. Get the hell out. I'm not a racist. I'm an American."

Maria's mother had insisted that her daughter attend Rio Seco Middle/ High School. They certainly lived close enough for her to attend. Even though Maria was told by some of her peers at school that she should go back with "her own kind," Maria knew that it was the right school for her. Less than ten percent of the students in what was essentially the barrio high school on the other side of town went to college. That was Maria's dream—to attend college—mostly because it was her mother's dream. In spite of the insults she received about her ethnic background, her religion, her weight, her appearance, and her gender, Maria never lost focus. She never lost her sense of humor. Most importantly, she never lost the dream she and her mother shared. Maria loved the whole notion of the "American dream," even if Mr. Barney and many classmates felt it was a dream reserved for white Texans.

Maria was incredibly determined, particularly in Mr. Barney's class, where she had to work twice as hard to get the same grade as other good students in the class. But she never got less than an A-minus in science, despite Mr. Barney's best efforts to the contrary. Maria liked science in part because the answers were either right or wrong. If she knew that the symbol for lead was Pb, her teacher couldn't mark it wrong, even when he wanted to do so. Once, she got a C on a twenty-page paper she had written on the fragility of the desert ecosystem. She loved the topic, wrote three times as much as any of her classmates, and knew the paper deserved a better grade.

Without ever letting on her reason, she gave a copy of her paper to the high school science department chair, Dr. Patricia Simpson, who had learned a thing or two about the difficulty of being a woman in the field of science. "I'd be glad to read it, dear," Dr. Simpson had said with a smile Maria could still remember. In fact, it was that smile, Maria later realized, that had changed her life forever. A week later, when she met with Dr. Simpson, she was told, "That would get an A in my Senior Seminar. What did you get, dear?"

In fact, Dr. Simpson already knew. She knew Melvin Lee Barney better than Maria did. Dr. Simpson had, ironically, been taught by "Big Butt Barney," as the kids had called him for years. Now she was Melvin Barney's boss. She had tried unsuccessfully to have him fired, but the old boys club on the board had just been too strong. Dr. Simpson had gone into Barney's class to do an observation and had found him clipping his toenails—during class. The kids were all talking or reading the sports page about the big football victory on Saturday night. Barney hadn't even flinched when Dr. Simpson had come in. He had actually planned the move as a way to show Pat Simpson what he thought of her as his boss. Who the hell did she think she was? Miss Ph.D. She couldn't get a guy, so she got a doctorate as a consolation prize—that's how Barney figured it. What did that have to do with teaching, anyway?

Dr. Simpson had shown up for the disciplinary meeting with Barney and the superintendent only to see Barney leaving the office five minutes before the meeting was supposed to have started. "Melvin Lee, you tell your daughter Tammy she's one hell of a cute cheerleader! See you on the nineteenth hole," Superintendent Jimmy Johnson said with a snicker, knowing that Melvin Lee Barney could always be found at the Arroyo Seco Golf Course bar, where Johnson was also a frequent visitor.

After Barney left the central office building, Johnson, who had been Dr. Simpson's former principal, said, "Now, Patty, don't get your sweet ass in an uproar over a few toenail clippings. Melvin Lee Barney has been in this district for thirty-four years. He's going to stay until he wants to leave. He's no Patty Simpson. I know he can't spell Celsius, let alone calculate it from Fahrenheit. That's why I hired you. But don't ever tell me any more bullshit about Melvin Lee unless he kills Pastor Bacon's hound dog, in which case I'll buy him a drink."

While Dr. Simpson learned that she couldn't win the war and get Barney fired, she knew she could certainly win a lot of battles along the way. She controlled the schedules, and she controlled student placements. Melvin Barney would learn the hard way who the real boss was as he received one miserable schedule and class load after another—kids with piss-poor attitudes—just like his own.

Thanks to Patty Simpson's intervention, Maria's grade was changed from a C to an A. Although Mr. Barney rarely even looked in Maria's direction again for the rest of the year, she got the grades that she earned, an A every quarter. She also got a personal mentor, coach, and role model in Dr. Simpson. Although she did not become a physics professor as Pat Simpson had hoped, Maria became something even better—a middle school science teacher, just like her hero, Dr. Simpson. Eventually, Maria became a principal so she could have even more of an impact on kids and on the hiring and firing of teachers. There would never be a Melvin Lee Barney in her schools. "Not on my watch," she had promised herself.

Today, as she played with the polarizing filter, looked at the clouds, and listened as O'Casey talked about hatches of cadis, damsel, and mayflies, thoughts of Dr. Simpson and science classes past filled Maria's mind. As she dialed the polarizing filter to maximum and then saw its impact on a shot she had just taken, she smiled with a contentment and pleasure that was almost indescribable. A fat little girl from the barrios of West Texas was now standing on the banks of a beautiful lake in Maine on a June day, hanging out with friends who liked her for who she was. She had a job she loved and was doing something she could only have dreamed about. *Lord, I am thankful,* she said to herself, repeating the simple prayer her family always recited while still holding hands after grace.

"Amen, sister!" replied Ellen.

"What?" All of a sudden, Maria realized she had said her "silent prayer" out loud.

"We used to say the same thing at my house after grace," Ellen shared with a smile.

"And mine, too," said O'Casey.

When the girls looked incredulous, O'Casey insisted, "Really! Honest! We had lots of pagan rituals, but that wasn't one of them." He grinned.

The "three amigos," as Maria would later refer to the group, spent much of the afternoon taking pictures, talking, and just having fun. Ellen, in particular, was really having fun. She was enjoying being close—very close—to Sean Padraig O'Casey without his even knowing just how *much* she was enjoying the day and the face she was rapidly growing to like. O'Casey was usually oblivious to the advances of women, who found him handsome in spite of the jagged scars on the left side of his face where the door of his car had collapsed with the impact of a pickup truck going eighty miles an hour in the wrong lane of the Connecticut Turnpike. He would never know just how hard he had tried to veer out of the path of a driver who had been determined to take his own life that night, even if it also meant taking the lives of innocent people. Ellen looked beyond the scars to the kind man who found this day on a lake in Maine a wonderful narcotic to dull his daily pain.

Angelo was reading a biography of Tchaikovsky. Although opera was his favorite music, he loved all the great composers. He had studied the lives of Beethoven and Mozart, and found it fascinating how their lives shaped their music and how their music shaped their lives. That's how he felt. Music was his life. It was the only thing he was ever good at and the only thing he had ever wanted to do. Even as he read on this summer afternoon, he pictured a real-life Swan Lake with dancers floating across the water in a magical ballet. He closed his eyes to imagine it further, but the pain of a throbbing hand brought him back to a reality he could never quite escape. Still, it was a lovely day.

At the campfire area, Butch was working diligently to fashion a McIver-like invention. The hot bread from last night's dinner had been so successful that he was trying to make a reflector oven from scrap metal he had found near the campsite. Butch loved a challenge. He was really a throwback to another era. In another life, he would have been a Jeremiah Johnson–style reclusive trapper and hunter in the days just following the Lewis and Clark Expedition when a muzzle loader, a long knife, and the patience of Job could allow a man to see vistas few white men had ever seen. Butch was that kind of man. Often, in the Maine wilderness, particularly at night, when the coyotes, the loons, and the screech owls sang their eerie songs, Butch could imagine himself two hundred years back in time and feel very much at home.

Farther up the beach, Butch could hear the rhythmic, ever-so-slight splash of a serious swimmer. Tiffany was not just a good swimmer. It was no accident that she had rescued Jason. In high school, she had been the captain of both the swim and tennis teams. Actually, she'd been a nationally ranked swimmer in high school—eighth in the country in the 200-yard freestyle. She was also superb in the butterfly. However, her mother had convinced her to stick to just one sport, tennis. "Now, honey. As good as you are in swimming, you don't want to get too dyke-y looking. That's what happens to girls who swim too much, especially events like the butterfly. First, you get very big shoulders. The next thing you know, the boys stop calling, and *other types* of girls are starting to hang around the locker room. Now I know you don't want that, do you, honey?"

Mimi Goodrich had said all this with the same plastic smile and plastic voice that Tiffany had grown to dread. If only she could stand up to her mother, but she never could. She just couldn't. Her father couldn't. Few people could, and when they did, they paid dearly. It was a victory just to be hiding out in Maine now, far from her mother's legendary opening-the-Hampton-house party. As she drifted into the rhythm of her freestyle strokes, Tiffany remembered the first time she'd read Niccolo Machiavelli's *The Prince*. *That's my mom*, Tiffany thought.

At that, she changed her stroke from the rhythmic cadence of the freestyle to the powerful and taxing dolphin-like moves that make the butterfly such a grueling and remarkable event. Amid the power and the pain of her burst of energy, Tiffany smiled just a bit to herself at her mother's aversion to the butterfly and her own victory at being in Maine. She was tempted to tear off her bathing suit and rub mud in her hair. *What do you think of that, Mommy Dearest?*

Just as everyone turned to watch Tiffany's burst of power and talent, she switched to the sidestroke, a graceful old stroke that few people did anymore. Tiffany liked it because it allowed her to drift off into happy thoughts, thoughts of her morning with her new friends, and thoughts of a new freedom she was discovering here in Maine. The cool clear water washed over her body, her face, and down her legs. It felt good, simple, and clean.

Someone else was enjoying Tiffany's swim. Jason Foxworthy studied every bit of Tiffany as she swam. He imagined her nude and himself swimming below her, watching but not yet touching. The watching was almost the best part for Jason. Everywhere Tiffany had gone during these past two days, Jason had watched. He had seen her go into her tent a little while ago, but had no idea she was getting into her bathing suit. Just maybe, he thought, the light would silhouette her gorgeous body when she went back into her tent in a few minutes. He'd be watching for sure.

And so it went for the afternoon—each person doing something they enjoyed. The activities reflected something about each of them. Maria, the student, the scientist, the friend and listener soaked up the camaraderie of her newfound friends. O'Casey, the storyteller, teacher, photographer, and naturalist thoroughly enjoyed his afternoon. If he were only teaching the women how to cast for rising trout, he would truly be at peace.

Ellen was enthralled by the afternoon activities and also with O'Casey.

She had always dreamed of being on a wilderness lake in Maine, camping and fishing the way her brothers and father had done for years. Now she was doing it with new friends—great friends—and was standing next to a handsome man who was oblivious to her longing glances and admiring smiles. She could smell O'Casey's strong, sensual male odor. While she had never given any credence to the notion of pheromone attractions before, she did now. She was *almost* in heaven.

Butch *was* in heaven. He had succeeded in making a reflector oven out of junk he found in a logging camp dump near the end of the beach. *This will do for sure!* he thought. He had almost expected to find a buzz-off box at this particular site. He usually did in late May and early June, when the bush pilots were at their busiest running corporate types in for a weekend of fishing and drinking. While the champagne and the rest of the liquor had been a pleasant surprise, Butch routinely found things like flour, apples, bread, and beans—that is, if the bears hadn't gotten the stuff first…and needless to say, he didn't share that thought with the rest of the tribe. This campsite was often "bear central" due to all the food that got left here. Butch whistled as he mixed his homemade bread recipe, using the flour from the buzz-off box with the small bag of sourdough starter that he always brought with him, as well as some oil, an egg, canned milk, and a hint of Maine maple syrup, one of his favorite, subtle ingredients. *Time, that's all it needs*, Butch thought. *Plenty of time to rise.* There was still much of the afternoon and early evening left—plenty of time for great sourdough bread.

Angelo, too, was thinking about time. That was all he needed for his hand to heal, for the throbbing to stop. Time. Butch and O'Casey knew what they were doing. It would get better soon. Angelo knew it would. He had faith in his friends and faith in God. Time.

That's all it is. Just a matter of time, Jason said to himself, *before that babe will be jumping into my pants or I'll be jumping into hers.* He ogled Tiffany one last time before she closed the tent flap to change. Jason had thought about sneaking up to her tent and finding a lame excuse to open the flap and enjoy all of Tiffany for the first time, but he knew Butch would probably see him first and would certainly hear any ruckus that might ensue.

Jason returned to his fishing. He was drowning worms, using a bobber rig to catch chubs and suckers near shore. He'd then thrown them up on shore and watched them flop around until the sun dried them out and they suffocated from lack of oxygen. Jason thought it was funny to see them struggle for breath. *How weird,* he thought. *Breathe, you suckers. The more you struggle to breathe, the less air you get. Pretty funny.*

When Butch finished making the bread and went down to the shore to wash his hands off, he saw what Jason was doing. "Why are you just killing those fish? What are you going to do with them? We can't eat 'em. The chubs taste like shit and the suckers are too wormy this time of year, though a month ago they would have been good."

"I just thought I'd leave 'em for the seagulls," Jason shrugged.

Butch could barely believe his ears.

"We're a hundred and twenty miles from the ocean! Not many seagulls here, Foxy. But it sure would attract the bears, so unless you want to be a bear's breakfast, I suggest you take those dead freakin' fish just as far up the beach as you can and then throw them as far into the woods as you can. The last thing I want to do tonight is dance with a hungry black bear. OK?"

Butch gave Jason a sarcastic look that only he could get away with. Jason and Butch were both former football players, so Jason knew all about alpha males. He was one himself, but he knew who the king of this hill was. So he started to pick up the fish one at a time, sliding a stick through their gills so he could carry them all at once.

Suddenly, he had an idea that made him smile with the glee of the high school bully giving a little seventh grader a swirlie—putting his head in the toilet and flushing it while the kid screamed. Making sure that no one was watching, Jason lugged the stick full of still-wriggling suckers and chubs toward the women's Half Moon Hilton. *This could be fun,* he thought with a smirk. *This could work.* If it did, it would be great. "Time—just a matter of time," he muttered, giving the fish a heave in the direction of the latrine.

Meanwhile, Angelo read in the warm afternoon sun. Tiffany took a little nap. Butch continued to have great fun making camp "just right" for everyone. This included occasionally punching down the dough and giving it the attention and kneading necessary for a masterpiece. The three amigos talked and laughed, sharing stories of school, of childhood, of dreams, and of times past. The full-bodied cumulus clouds darkened as moisture started to fill them to a point of intimidating gray-black saturation. There would be thunderstorms somewhere today. Jason returned to the shore where he'd caught all the fish and skimmed thin shale quarters and half dollars across the darkening water. He counted the skips and also counted the time, just waiting for dark...and hoping... just hoping.

RIGOLETTO AND RIGATONI

The flies near the Half-Moon Hilton had found another area of congregation less than twenty feet away. They swarmed around the long alder branch Jason had half-dragged, half-thrown into the woods. This was not an unconscious act of laziness on Jason's part, though his directive from Butch would have meant a much longer walk to get the dead and dying fish well away from camp. Jason was certainly capable of the laziest of actions, routinely throwing an empty beer can from his moving car or discarding fast-food refuse right where he'd finished eating. True, he had a varsity letter in slovenly behavior, but this act, like many in his life, was designed for a selfish outcome that only Jason would want...and so, in his typical style, would be done at the expense of others.

The chubs on the stick died almost immediately. The thick alder branch jammed through their gills and out their mouths destroyed their last chance to take in oxygen, even had one of the women noticed and thrown them back into the water. The impressive, five-year-old sucker, perhaps twenty inches in length, had struggled much longer, trying its best to flop its way back to the water. But with ten other fish on the stick, and the water almost a hundred yards away, the sucker was quickly exhausted. Its flopping and squirming were pointless. After several last gasps, it died an unpleasant death on the hot, humid forest floor. The heat quickly began to putrefy and decompose the fish. The flies were the first to notice.

A half mile to the south, another creature would eventually notice the smell of fish that was not too decayed to become a late-evening meal. The seven-year-old black bear and her spring cub were foraging along a former clear-cut, nibbling the shoots of small maple and beech trees struggling to compete for space, growth, and survival with the more rapidly growing gray birch, fir, pine, and alder on the lower ridge. The sow was very hungry this time of year. The wild blueberries and strawberries, when she could find them, were still weeks away. The beechnuts and acorns of last fall had long since been eaten by the deer, red squirrels, and chipmunks in their efforts to survive the brutal Maine winter and wet, unfriendly spring. The sow sniffed the late-afternoon air and smelled something intriguing.

To better educate her highly skilled, thick black nostrils, she stretched her lean, muscular frame up onto her hind legs to get a better sense of these new smells. Though not massive by any means, and still thin from lack of adequate food and a cub always anxious to nurse, the bear reached close to six feet into the air. The large, shaggy black boar that had fathered the sow's cub last fall and had made the rake marks seen earlier in the day by the tribe, stood well over six feet tall and could easily rake branches eight feet high. This sow was not nearly so massive. However, her intimidating shape, large teeth, and claws sharp enough to open a tin can with a single swipe, were certainly sufficient to terrorize a camp or even kill if that were necessary.

She stretched and stiffed again. Wood smoke for sure. Strange food smells near the fire, people—lots of people—and fish, decomposing fish. She had found supper. There was no hurry. Perhaps a light nap with her cub first, and the decomposing fish would still be there. They never moved. There was no hurry. Late-night meals were the best…and the easiest to get. Time, not yet time.

The late afternoon had quickly melted into early evening.

"Supper!" Butch shouted. He loved to do that, to rally the tribe to the fire. Given the incredible feast from the night before, everyone came running, anxious to see what miracle Butch and O'Casey had worked up. When they were all assembled and drooling with anticipation, Butch announced the cruel hoax. "Actually, supper's not quite ready yet. But I do need *lots* of firewood, and I figure that a little work before supper will be perfect for your appetites."

"Oh, Butch. You meanie!" Ellen complained.

"Meanie? How old are you?" Jason chimed in. "I was thinking more like 'freakin' asshole.' Butch, I was sleeping and having a *great dream*. Tell you about it later. You'd like it...or maybe you wouldn't..."

"Go dream about the wood you're going to get for me right now. I can't finish cooking if I can't feed the fire, right?"

While the tribe wandered off with varying degrees of enthusiasm and complaint, Butch continued with the cooking. Actually, his bread was not quite done. While he did need the wood, he could also see a bit of boredom setting in, and boredom, Butch had found, often led to conflict, whether it was in school with kids, or in camp with adults.

Camp cooking is a difficult and delicate process. Success is not just a question of the cook's skills, but also what the cook has for provisions. Both Butch and O'Casey knew this would be their last night at this campsite. In the morning, they would begin a two-day canoe ride down the river and be at the landing at the south end of Granite Lake on the third day. Tonight, like last night, would be a special meal. The plan was always to have the heavy food, AKA the "good stuff," on the first few nights and to save the fish, when they were lucky—and they were almost always lucky—for the last few days. Even if they weren't lucky, they had enough dehydrated beans, rice, and soups to keep them all fed as long as things went well—and things almost always went well.

"I'll let the wine breathe for a few more minutes," O'Casey said to Butch in an affected British accent, as though he were the butler at an eighteenth-century estate preparing dinner for evening guests. "The caviar, mushrooms, and sardines are all ready as well."

"Sardines?" Ellen chimed in with mock incredulity. "Caviar and sardines? You're kidding, of course"

Again in his not-very-good British accent, O'Casey responded, "Sir Butch...er, Sir *Granville* and I never kid about the gastronomic wonders we serve our guests here at Lakeview Castle, madam."

The rest of the tribe had dropped off the last of their firewood and were now listening to Sir Butch and his humble manservant O'Casey hold court. They had these events down to a science, having done this so many times with friends and, on occasion, with Butch's customers. Usually, O'Casey did not join Butch for his guide trips. However, if Butch noticed that O'Casey really needed some fishing to maintain his sanity when the pain of the accident went from subtle to alarming, he would ask him to come along. As O'Casey's best friend, Butch would make up an excuse, saying that the customers really needed one-on-one coaching and that O'Casey was as good a casting coach as Butch was himself. While O'Casey could usually see through this, he always appreciated the invites and refused to take any of the tips he was offered.

"Our sommelier will be starting you out with a lovely '89 Baron de Rothschild Bordeaux—a nosy little wine with a deep plum and cherry start and a full-bodied, slightly apricot finish. A little bit fruity and mysterious, but wonderful with the caviar and even better with the sardines." Butch tried very hard to affect the same British accent but came across more like a clamdigger having lunch at Moody's Diner. That made the exchange all the more wonderful. Actually, the wine that had been left in the buzz-off box was really quite a lovely St. Michelle merlot and nothing to sneeze at.

"The caviar, of course," Butch went on, "is authenticated Beluga first-run, black Russian caviar. A bit too salty for my taste, but the Amish Farms organic chèvre cheese will offset that quite nicely. They, like the delicate snack to follow, will be served on our finest Imperial Water Biscuits—light and lovely as always. The sardines, naturally, are a palate cleanser for the fresh shiitake mushroom pâté to finish the appetizer portion of our meal."

Although the caviar was hardly high-quality Beluga, it was still caviar. Serving both caviar and sardines on the same night was typical Butch and O'Casey, occasionally referred to as Butch and Sundance, though neither used or particularly liked the analogy. However, by now, Ellen had seen a Robert Redford resemblance in Sean Padraig O'Casey, fed more by the wine and a growing interest in O'Casey than anything based in fact. O'Casey would have cringed at the comparison, having long since convinced himself that he was a scarred and fairly unattractive man who would probably remain single—and unfortunately celibate—for the rest of his life.

The tribe devoured the hors'doeuvres so quickly that Butch and O'Casey barely got any before Maria had to speak up. "Come on, guys. Let's leave a few for the chefs. We can't afford to have them fall over from starvation. Where would we get our next meal?"

"And now," Butch announced, "the pièce de résistance! Rigatoni al O'Casey-o!" He grinned as he tried to mix metaphors and switch from a British accent to an Italian one. His ineptitude at this added to the comic relief and the fun of the moment.

The rigatoni was actually spaghetti with homemade meatballs and marinara sauce that O'Casey loved to make. His mother had taught him how to make it many years ago. Although his mother was first generation Irish, the recipe was authentic Italian. Giuseppe and Maria Luppino had lived in the apartment above O'Casey's family when they lived in a poor section of the North End. O'Casey loved the fact that an Irish kid was such a good cook of Italian food. Even his Italian friends were impressed. "Mama," they'd say, "the Irish boy can cook good like you." O'Casey always knew this would be followed by a squeeze of his skinny cheeks. "You a nice-a boy. Too skinny, but-a nice. Why you nice-a mama no put some weight on-a you?" O'Casey relished those memories of the Italian neighborhood, and although he treasured his Irish heritage and his Boston upbringing, his formative days as the skinny Irish boy in a North End Italian neighborhood were special to him.

"Why you no take-a more sauce? And no more rigatoni? You get-a too skinny!" O'Casey sputtered as his boyhood memories spilled into his effort to cajole Tiffany into having more for dinner. The others had hardly been shy in their portions, but Tiffany's small portion brought out O'Casey's poor Italian accent and sincere desire for her to eat more. "You're going to be getting one heck of a workout once we head downstream, so *mange* girl, *mange*."

Angelo, too, though his body shape would have indicated otherwise, had taken a fairly small portion and had eaten only half. While the food was delicious, Angelo was just not feeling "tip top," as he would have described it. His hand was feeling quite warm now, almost hot. And while there did not seem to be any more pus leaking from the wound, Angelo knew he was in trouble. His cut was very infected and his hand throbbed constantly.

His mind wandered, and he got lost in boyhood thoughts of his own Italian heritage and the rare Sunday dinners with his father's family, which he had so longed for as a boy. They were rarely invited to the in-laws', though occasionally, his father would take Marco after a Little League game, if Marco had pitched, but he almost never took Angelo. Still, Angelo loved his Italian heritage, and particularly the opera. His opera. It had spoken to him from his earliest days, the music filling his head and his heart. Often, when he couldn't sleep, especially after the screaming between his father and mother, Angelo would imagine himself singing, not in a large opera house in Florence or New York, but in a little Venetian café entertaining elderly couples having dinner.

He began humming a favorite aria, oblivious to his surroundings. The humming grew louder as Angelo drifted more and more into his fantasy.

"Hey, Angelo! How about some *Rigoletto* with our rigatoni?"

Angelo blushed as Butch's request brought him back to reality.

"I'm sorry. I didn't realize that I was singing. I'll stop. Sorry about that."

"Are you kidding? That sounded wonderful! Seriously, if you don't mind, we'd love to hear you sing. "*Rigoletto, Carmen, The Barber of Brazil,* anything," Butch suggested with a straight face.

While *The Barber of Brazil* went completely over Jason Foxworthy's head, the others tried not to laugh. They knew Butch was sincere in his request and they didn't want be seen as laughing at his lack of sophistication.

"Well...I don't know," Angel said. "I'm not exactly on top of my game tonight."

"Please? Pretty please?" first Ellen and then Maria begged.

Angelo smiled modestly. Then in a soft, almost boyish voice he began to fill the camp with "La Donna é Mobile" and other lovely pieces from Verdi and Puccini. His pure voice lacked only in volume. His shy, tentative nature gradually disappeared into the night air. Rich and robust notes, confident notes, perfect pitch—all swirled around the glow of the campfire and the faces mesmerized by a talent too often hidden in a timid, kind man.

And in spite of his serious illness and spreading infection, Angelo felt a confidence that seemed to stir his soul and transport him in an almost palpable way to another place and time. He was in Venice. He was dreaming as he sang. Elderly Venetians were hanging on each syllable. He wasn't just hitting notes; he was *insinuating* them—sliding into and out of notes in perfect pitch, much as a great violinist slides into rather than simply hits the perfect note.

Because Maria had spoken to Angelo about her wish one day to see *Phantom of the Opera* on Broadway, Angelo began the tenor portion of the famous duet, "The Music of the Night": *Slowly, gently, night unfurls its splendor... turn your face away from the garish light of day...*

To everyone's amazement, Maria began to weave in like a thin, silvery thread: *Here in this room, he calls so softly...*

Her voice, though not flawless like Angelo's, was still nothing short of exquisite. The rest of the tribe was frozen in the delicacy of the moment. The unrehearsed harmonies were a pure, miraculous celebration. Here in a simple campsite in Maine, two adults who were almost strangers to each other, vocally made love to the music and to each other, transforming the night.

The last notes echoed through the valley. Everyone was so transfixed by the singers, they had scarcely noticed that O'Casey had turned away from the fire. He sat silent and alone with his Irish whiskey. He was almost hidden on the edge of camp, sitting on a log in an unplanned retreat, sipping through his thoughts and pain. O'Casey knew it would be a long and lonely night. While Maria was hardly a match for his beloved Catherine, she and Angelo had both sung with a wonderful passion that transcended their varying degrees of talent. Angelo, with more training and support growing up, could have been a masterful tenor. As it was, his delivery of certain notes, his execution, and particularly his pitch were sheer luscious perfection.

It brought back loving memories of Catherine—the beauty of her voice, her hair, her soft green eyes, and a gentle touch O'Casey was almost embarrassed to admit he loved the most. They would sit by the fire and hold hands for hours, scarcely talking, yet communicating a rare love as subtle and delicate as the distant glow of a firefly in the meadow. First it was there, soft, beautiful, mysterious...and then it was gone. Was it there? Had it been there? Catherine, like the light in the meadow, had filled O'Casey's heart with a childlike sense of wonder and joy.

Where is she now? he thought. She was gone. The light was gone. The joy was gone. The music was gone. Tears rolled down his rough, scarred cheeks. Only Butch and Ellen had noticed O'Casey's departure from the firelight. Butch knew that he'd made a mistake ten seconds after he had asked Angelo to sing. While it would bring joy to the rest of the tribe, it would bring a deep sadness to O'Casey that Butch could not understand. But he knew his friend. He knew what the head down and back turned meant. He had seen O'Casey get up and go to the tent and knew the Jameson's would soon be sipped deep into the darkness.

Ellen only knew tiny bits and pieces about his past and only rumors about the accident. Few knew the details, which was how O'Casey wanted it. Now this strong, aloof, attractive man had caught her eye and was also catching her heart. Quietly, almost awkwardly, she got up from her place by the fire. She went and stood next to O'Casey for what seemed like minutes. Gingerly, tentatively, she put her hand on his shoulder—first on the outer edge of his clavicle, and then just on the inner edge of his neck. She needed to touch his skin, to feel the warmth of his body, to let him know in some small way that she cared for him and wanted to ease his pain.

No one moved. The fire crackled. Sparks snapped from the small pine branches Jason had thrown on top of the dry kai that formed the bulk of their night fire. Angelo breathed deeply and slowly. It was not Venice, not Florence. They were not elderly couples alternating sips of espresso and Sambuca. But it was his dream of sorts. He had filled the air with magic, a magic and beauty of his own creation, and shared with an audience he had grown to love. He looked across the fire to see a man who meant more to him than any on the planet—a man he loved more deeply than he could or would ever show. It was unimportant that Butch did not really know or understand opera—or that he did not know or understand Angelo's love for him. Angelo could see that he had moved Butch in a deep and profound way. A rarity, Butch was actually speechless, as were the women. They were all caught up in a moment of sheer poetry and perfection.

On the horizon, first heat lightning and then deep searing flashes—jagged bolts and booming thunder—filled the very edge of the landscape, miles away. Then a voice, less loud, began another nighttime harmony like two lovers talking alone—one almost whispering to the other. A thin, mysterious tremolo from one dark form echoed across the lake, followed soon by the soft, sad, delicate reply of its mate. Back and forth they danced their songs from one canyon wall to the other. When the pain of the loons' song was almost too great for him to bear, O'Casey reached back and touched two fingers to Ellen's extended hand. Her heart stirred at the touch. She moved closer and felt O'Casey lean back and shift some of his weight against her. The loons sang again and again as the storm slid slowly by them to the north.

With the crackling of the fire, the rumble of the thunder, and the deep, almost heavy breathing of the tribal family lost in their own thoughts and images, none could hear first the grunt and the almost imperceptible growl of a hungry bear moving quietly toward camp.

"Bear in Camp! Bear in Camp!"

B eddy-bye time, ladies!" Butch proclaimed. The Chief was not shy about taking charge, and everyone began to respond...almost everyone, that is.

Neither Ellen nor O'Casey moved a bit. Ellen's heart was pounding at his response. It was more than she could ever have hoped for. Although she had known O'Casey for several years through conferences like the one when the trip was planned, she'd never thought of him in a romantic way. It wasn't that she didn't find him attractive. She just knew that he was "out of bounds" and unavailable, much like the husbands of her good friends, or several handsome but gay teachers in her school. She was a realist about whom she could seek out and who might seek her out. Standing with her back to the fire and Sean's hand on top of hers was a moment she would always remember. She didn't want to move a muscle for fear that she would reawaken O'Casey's defensive self, and the moment—like an exquisite reflection on the lake's surface—would be there for a second and then gone forever.

The sow bear was getting cautious now. It could smell the fish, the fire, and the human odors that were often present at this particular campsite, one of her favorite haunts. The hairs on her back were starting to stand up as adrenaline began to surge through her veins. Her own hunger pangs and those of her nervous cub were an undeniable driving force now. Yet the sow's hunger was being tempered by caution and by a distant, horrible memory. It was of another cub that had been caught briefly, teased, and then killed by a human who'd been bitten by the terrified little bear. But now, the decaying fish were a stronger motivator.

The sow circled behind the camp; she growled quietly to her cub, keeping her close but at a safe distance behind her.

Angelo headed for the tent he shared with O'Casey. He was anxious to get back to his bunk. He had taken two aspirin earlier in the day, which had helped with the throbbing pain in his hand. Butch, too, wanted to head off to bed. Everyone tended to forget that it was always the Chief who was first up in the morning to get the fire going, to start the coffee, and to organize breakfast and the day ahead. In order to break camp in the morning by eight at the latest, Butch knew that he'd need to be up by five. It was already almost 10:00 P.M.—way past his bedtime, especially when he was camping.

"Hey, Tiff, I'll warm up the seat for you…and chase away the bears," Maria shouted with typical good humor. Actually, she had not thought much about bears until she saw the rake marks and learned that bears were nocturnal feeders. *I'm not worried* she thought. *What are the chances that a short, fat, homely Mexican American is going to be supper for a Maine black bear tonight?* She was far more concerned about the distant thunder that she heard. From the time she was a little girl, one of her greatest fears had been of being hit by lightning or sucked up by a tornado. The violent weather that hit West Texas from time to time would do that to a little girl and impact her memories for years to come.

Even as she heard crackles of thunder in the background, Maria walked with an unhesitating gait up the now well-worn path to the Half-Moon Hilton. She was glad, however, that she only had to pee. Being a heavy woman sitting astride a wobbly box that was masquerading as a toilet seat was unsettling enough. Having to put her flashlight down in order to help in that balancing process and allow her to do what she needed to do became a test of her courage. She quickly pulled up her pants and scurried down the path toward the flickering light of the campfire.

"The seat is nice and warm…and the coast is clear," she called out to an anxious Tiffany, who was waiting by the fire. Tiffany was hardly excited about using the Half-Moon Hilton even in broad daylight. Until the trip, she had never peed in the woods, even once—and poop? Well, that was unthinkable. As a child on a sleepover, she would often wait most of the weekend before doing more than pee at a friend's house. Tiffany knew she had lived a sheltered and privileged life. However, the trip, while originally terrifying in its lack of bathroom amenities, had become a magnificent and energizing experience. She had already learned more about herself, her capabilities, and the kind of friends she would now want than she could ever have imagined. In college, or especially in high school, the thought of befriending a short, chubby Latino girl with kinky hair would have been social suicide. She could just imagine Maria walking through the door of her East Hampton home and hearing her mother say, "Señorita, cleaning day is tomorrow, not today."

Her mother would be incapable of understanding Tiffany's profound admiration for her new friend. Here she was, bounding out of the woods, alone and unafraid, just having warmed up the toilet seat for her! Tiffany was tempted to ask Maria to be her escort to the Hilton, the way girlfriends out on a double date head off to the bathroom together. But this was not the kind of trip those girlfriends would go on. Straddling a wooden box over a hole dug in the dirt was hardly a moment to be shared with a friend. Still, Tiffany knew that her bladder could never make it until morning. The two shots of Yukon Jack that Jason had all but insisted she drink gave her just the extra courage she needed. She was now glad that she had purchased L.L. Bean's best camp flashlight.

Squaring her shoulders, she reluctantly began her walk into the foreboding woods. When Butch first built the Half-Moon Hilton, she had wondered why it was only a hundred yards from camp. It seemed so close. During the daytime, from just the right angle while sitting on the throne, she had been able to see part of the beach. That meant that, at just the right angle, someone could see her. Now, as she walked up the hill and along the winding path, she wished the Hilton were only ten feet from camp. In fact, now she wished that she had just hidden behind some bushes ten feet from camp and peed away.

Tiffany was amazed at how much her modesty threshold had changed in just a couple of days. Right now, she would almost rather pee in the middle of camp than continue any farther. The alders overhung the trail like the arms of monsters in a haunted forest. She thought of Maurice Sendak's children's book, *Where the Wild Things Are*. Well, the wild things were here right now. This trail and these woods were wild, and unlike the boy in the story who embraced the wild things, Tiffany could feel a sense of terror and dread building within her.

Suddenly, she heard the sharp snap of a twig. She froze. She waited for another sound to help her identify the direction. She strained to hear. But other than the pounding of her own heart, all she could hear was the distant thunder, the occasional crackle from the campfire, and the wind, which was now blowing up the hill and rustling the leaves in an ominous fashion. *I can't do this*, she almost said aloud. As she started to turn around to head back down the trail, the beam of her flashlight landed squarely on the Hilton seat, a tired wooden box with a crude hole cut out to make the primitive toilet. But it had become a welcome sight for the women, who would not have to take off their pants and squat like dogs to go to the bathroom. It lent a bizarre sort of dignity to a natural process that, in the woods, can be anything but dignified. There were even two magazines in a plastic bag that Butch had found by the buzz-off box. *That Butch!* Tiffany thought. The familiar sight had given her a sense of comfort that allowed her to focus on the task at hand. She undid her pants and sat down. The tension that filled her body tightened her pelvic muscles just enough to keep her from emptying her bladder quickly. *Oh, hurry up*, she thought. *What a time to have to wait.*

Others were not waiting. Hunger had finally overtaken caution.

With the distant lingering memory of her previous cub's death at this campsite, the sow had been reluctant to return. But hunger was too dominant a force for her to ignore. Newly killed fish, not yet rotten, would make a good meal for her and her cub. She was very close, almost there. The wind, which had been blowing down the hill, shifted suddenly. The thunderstorm in the distance began to swirl and drive the wind down the lake, over the beach, and up the hill.

The Amarige perfume Tiffany wore caught the sow's attention first. Even the cub noticed, stood on its short hind legs, and sniffed the air. It let out a muffled grunt much like the bleat of a young goat, only deeper. The sow, comfortable that the cub was well behind her, grunted her acknowledgment of the scent. Then another smell filled the air and sent terror into the heart of the anxious sow. It was an ominous smell—sweaty, masculine, and sinister. When her cub had been killed, she had been forced to retreat into the woods. She had come back hours later when the hunters had left the area. Her cub was not only dead, but it had also been skinned. All that remained was a small, savaged carcass. She had sniffed and pawed at the carcass, but it didn't move. All she could smell was that same sweaty, masculine, sinister smell that filled the air now. The hairs on the back of her neck stood straight up. Her jaws opened and her sharp yellow fangs were at the ready.

Part of Jason's plan had already worked. Tiffany was almost half in the bag, and, if he was lucky, half naked and sitting with her legs spread wide apart over a wooden box waiting for nature to take over. His heart beat with anticipation. He continued to tiptoe up the trail, careful not to break another twig as he had done only moments ago. He had actually hoped that a bear or coyote would find the fish about the same time one of the women was seated on the toilet and she—whoever it might turn out to be—would come running down the trail, naked from the waist down, dragging her pants behind her. *How funny would that be...and how hot!* Jason thought.

He couldn't get too close to the Hilton because he wanted to see and not be seen. Having been a hunter for years, he had very good night vision. It was all a matter of training and motivation, he thought. He had done a considerable amount of stand hunting for bears. However, that was not how he'd gotten the trophy bear gracing his game room floor. He had killed that bear at the town dump in Grand Lake Stream. Unbeknownst to Butch and O'Casey, who had never been to Jason's house, he had shot the bear illegally at point-blank range from his pickup truck window while it foraged for garbage at the dump. It was the same massive bear O'Casey had seen several years before at the same dump site. Of course, Jason's story of how he had killed the bear was significantly different from the repulsive method he had actually used. His account all but involved hand-to-hand combat with the giant bear. By contrast, Jason rarely talked about the small bearskin that he had on the bathroom wall. "That's another story," he would tell his friends, but he never told about the wailing cub he had dragged down from the tree and shot when it had bitten him in self-defense.

There she was. Jason could see Tiffany's profile through the trees. She had to put the flashlight down to wipe herself. The light aiming out into the woods created a distorted but erotic silhouette, to Jason's way of thinking. He crept closer so that he could see the good stuff, what he had hoped his plan would provide.

Just as Tiffany picked up the flashlight and moved to stand and pull up her pants, the wind shifted slightly. A strong breeze blew in from the lake, picking up Jason Foxworthy's scent as it came up the hill and toward the bear's dilating nostrils. The sow, in near panic, stood on her hind legs and sniffed the air frantically. All her senses were on highest alert. Deep in the recesses of her instinct-driven brain, the sow recalled that smell. It was the same loathsome stench that had permeated the carcass that had once been her cub. It was the same hunter. He was here!

Every fiber in the bear's body reacted. Standing on her hind legs, she roared in anger, then roared again in fear for her cub. She turned her head to locate the small bear. As she did so, a blinding light flashed into her eyes. Tiffany had, of course, heard the bear and instinctively turned her hand and body toward the sound. As the light caught the full image of the enraged bear standing only twenty feet away, Tiffany screamed in terror. She screamed again and again. Although her pants had come up and were just buttoned as she turned toward the bear, she seemed frozen with fear.

"Run, Tiff, run!" Jason yelled from farther down the path. "Run!"

Jason's shouts broke through the barrier of terror and in a flash, Tiffany ran past Jason and toward the beach, screaming for Butch.

"Bear in camp! Butch! Bear in camp!"

The bear turned again to be certain that her cub was safely behind her. She stood on her hind legs again, bared her vicious teeth at Jason, and thundered down the trail directly toward him. Jason ran in a panic and terror that eclipsed Tiffany's. Almost instantly he had recognized the yellow-brown streak that ran along the bear's flank. It was Yellow Patch, the big sow that he had seen in the field glasses on the south ridge a couple of years before, feeding on beechnuts with her cub late that fall. It had probably been her cub that he had eventually killed. Somehow now, Jason knew that she was after him…and she was.

His heart seemed to be leaping right out of his chest as a massive adrenaline surge took over. Fighting was not an option, not without his hunting rifle and two hundred yards of safe distance to fire. Now the bear was just ten feet away and would easily have overtaken him if it had not also been concerned about its cub's safety. It would not lose another cub. It would *not*. Jason dashed headlong into a tree, knocking the flashlight from his hand. The collision gashed his forearm, bent his wrist back, and lacerated his forehead in several places. Stunned for a moment, he crawled on his knees, grabbing for his flashlight. Dirt flew into his face, his mouth, his eyes. He could smell the bear now, almost on top of him.

As he rolled his hips on the ground and turned the long metal flashlight upward, he looked into the face of rage.

The bear towered directly over Jason Foxworthy. Her thick nostrils sucked in the stench of the figure below her. She roared again in anger. Her teeth dripped with yellow foam. Her adrenal glands helped her attack instincts prepare for one vicious bite to Jason's neck and the meal that would soon follow.

Jason struggled to get to his feet, pushing himself away from the sow in a backward crawl, bouncing off a small alder stump and upward, away from the bear. Then, for a brief moment, they were face to face. Jason, in utter terror, screamed out a high-pitched shriek. He could see and feel the rage in the bear's black bulging eyes. The powerful beam of the flashlight rose reflexively into those terrible eyes. Momentarily, it seemed to paralyze the bear, whose otherwise great night vision was almost incapable of dealing with such a powerful light from only a few feet away.

Jason threw the flashlight at the bruin, hitting it squarely on the nose. The shock of being hit startled and enraged the bear even more. It lunged for Jason, who dashed the last few yards to the clearing by the camp. The sow was at Jason's feet now as he kicked away one savage blow from a massive paw and then another. The bear contracted all her muscles and readied herself to lunge for Jason's throat.

An enormous explosion rocked the air. Then another and another. The bear stood up on her hind legs and roared at the flashes in the night sky. She roared again at Jason and showed her fangs in a terrifying gesture of dominance. Another shot rang out along with a blinding flash…and just as quickly, the bear was gone.

Jason lay on the ground trembling and shivering with fear and shock. His heart pounded. He felt as though it might explode through his shirt. As he slowly came to his senses, he could feel blood running down his sleeve and down his forehead into his eye. "You all right, Bucko?" Butch asked as he threw two more shells into the empty .38 and readied a third to load.

"Why didn't you shoot the fucker? She was trying to kill me!" Jason yelled up at Butch as he lay on his back still trying to recover from the attack. His head wound was now bleeding freely down his face and nose.

"This ol' .38 probably wouldn't kill it. I'd need eight or ten shots before it'd be dead, and by then…you would have been breakfast. The bear's gone. This thing isn't very powerful but it makes as much noise as a cannon. That's why I bring her along. I'd use it for crowd control at lunchroom duty if I could get away with it," Butch said with a grin as he tried to lessen the terror at camp. "Boy, that bear was some ol' pissed at you. What did you do to piss her off? I've never seen anything like that. Bear attacks are pretty rare, even up here."

Lying on the ground, thinking back on his incident with Yellow Flank, Jason thought he knew why he had been attacked, but he never told anyone, not that night and not ever.

As O'Casey silently, almost reluctantly, began to clean Jason's head wound and stop the bleeding on his forearm, Tiffany knelt down beside him. "He saved my life. Jason saved my life!" Tiffany said with the conviction of someone who had been rescued from the jaws of death—quite literally.

Jason, always one to sense opportunity, even flat on his back, smiled at Tiffany, squeezed her hand, and, through a wince of mock pain, rewrote history. "Just as I was about to throw a log on the fire, I heard Tiffany screaming bloody murder. With the log still in my hand, I ran up the trail toward the screams. This huge bear was towering over her, pawing the air above her head. Just as he was about to eat her, I took the log and smashed it over the bear's head over and over again. That's why he was so angry and wanted to kill me. The log finally shattered and I couldn't find another. He was really pissed at that point, so I took off to get Butch and his gun."

"She" O'Casey said quietly. "It was a *she* bear, a *sow*. She must have had a cub nearby because when she stood up you could tell that her teats were full of milk. That's probably why she was angry and attacked. Sows are very protective of their cubs."

"Whatever," Jason shot back with a look of contempt at O'Casey for ruining his tale. "All I know is that it was a big fuckin' bear and it would have eaten Tiffany for breakfast if I hadn't been there."

Jason was thrilled with his story. His plan, which had gone completely wrong, had turned out even better than he could have imagined. Although he had not gotten to see Tiffany's good stuff as he had hoped, ~re would be plenty of time for that now. He smiled in contentment as ' stroked his hair.

ich! Go easy, will ya!" Jason complained.

O'Casey continued to dress the wounds, and by this time wished that he had straight iodine to pour right into the deepest cuts to make Jason cry with pain. While O'Casey *literally* hated to hurt spiders, he sensed a spider that he would like to hurt right now. It bothered him to see Tiffany, who had proved to be a wonderful woman in spite of his earlier misgivings, suckered in by Jason. *So how could Jason have scripted this? Where did he rent that bear?* O'Casey mused to himself. Somehow, all the pieces didn't fit, but he was way too tired to play detective now.

"I hate to break up the party, ladies and germs, but the bear's gone and *he*, or rather *she*, won't be back. I plan to stay up all night standing guard with Mr. Smith and Mr. Wesson here," Butch said, holding up his prize pistol to demonstrate, particularly to the women, that the Chief was in charge once again. He turned to finish reloading the revolver, which now had five shots in the cylinder, but was interrupted by Ellen, voicing her concerns about being alone in her tent.

Butch would forget to add that last bullet to the six-shot cylinder. This quick mental lapse would become just another very costly error for an otherwise conscientious guide.

"Ladies, I suspect you wouldn't mind partnering up, just for tonight, with the men. I know they'll all be good doobies and behave themselves. I know you'll want to get at least a little sleep, and now that you have your hero, Daniel Boone here, and his buddies to keep you safe and warm you may sleep a bit better."

Jason loved the new moniker "Daniel Boone." He would use this story forever. *What a great chick line—not that I ever need one,* Jason thought. "Let's get some shut-eye, Tiffie," Jason suggested with a cockiness that made everyone but Tiffany want to vomit.

As Jason grabbed Tiffany's elbow and began to saunter off toward her tent, Butch frowned. "Hey, Jason. You behave yourself," he admonished.

"What? What?" Jason replied, as though he were an eighth grader who had just been caught grabbing a girl's ass in the lunch line.

THE CALM BEFORE...

As so often happens after a severe thunderstorm at night in the Maine woods, the next morning, the air was remarkably clear and invigorating. Much like a tropical rainforest, the woodlands steamed from the moisture of the night before; hatches of insects were in abundance both in the woods and on the water.

Butch was, as usual, the first to wake up. He was wet and, not surprisingly, uncomfortable from sleeping outside against a log in the driving rain. His bottom was almost paralyzed from sitting all night in that same position. Yet somehow, he felt invigorated. This is what he lived for—night watch, pistol in hand, protecting the tribe from a possible marauding bear.

He found a special magic in being the first one awake. He loved this time of day. The sun had not yet risen. The loons who had sung their songs of sadness and romance the night before now fished together just offshore. *If O'Casey were awake now*, Butch thought, *he could be getting some great shots.* Then he smiled. No, O'Casey was right where he needed to be—warm, dry, and happy—in Ellen's tent.

Butch disrobed and changed into dry clothes right by the fire, knowing that the other campers would probably still be asleep. If they weren't, they could just deal with what they saw. The Chief was very matter-of-fact about his own modesty and that of others. Nakedness for him was part of the wilderness; no big deal.

After running through his usual routine of getting the fire going again, planning breakfast, and picking up the various and sundry gear that the tribe always left where they dropped it, Butch headed for his morning ritual on the toilet. As he bounded up the hill toward the Half-Moon Hilton, he replayed the previous night's timeline in his mind, between what Jason had shared versus the events as he remembered them. It had seemed only a few seconds from the time Tiffany first screamed and the time she ran headlong into the camp clearing—certainly not enough time for Daniel Boone to grab a log, run up the hill, and fend off the bear while she ran back to camp. *Interesting…*, Butch mused. Then he saw something more revealing. Several turkey vultures circled overhead, just above the treetops. *That's odd*, he thought—until he looked ahead in that direction.

"That stupid son of a bitch!" Butch said out loud. "That explains everything; well, almost everything."

Directly below where the vultures were hovering lay the long alder branch with the decaying fish still attached. Butch decided to forgo his trip to the Hilton long enough to drag the repulsive, now maggot-ridden fish down to the end of the beach and well into the woods, way away from camp, where they belonged in the first place.

When he got back to camp, the first of the tribe began to roll out. Angelo moved slowly toward the warmth of the campfire, squeezing his throbbing fist as he walked. His hand, which had continued to get worse throughout the night, needed immediate attention. The Chief quickly read the situation and was seriously concerned. He had actually considered spending one more day at the campsite. It was such a beautiful spot, and the tribe seemed to be having such fun, in spite of the bear. He was also no longer concerned about the sow's coming back to camp. Now he knew why she had startled or been startled by Tiffany. His bigger concern at the moment was Angelo. Should they head back up the way they had come? It was the shorter route, but not much fun. He had hoped to take everyone down Wilson Stream and exit at the far end of Granite Lake, where their other cars were parked. It would take about a day and a half if they pushed forward, versus a long, very boring day if they went back the other way.

He posed the question to Angelo, which he should not have done.

"Butch, I'm fine. Really. My hand looks worse than it feels. It's not as sore as it was yesterday. I'll be fine. I'll let you know if I think it's getting worse." Of course, none of this was true. His hand hurt like hell, but he figured that adding only half a day to the trip would not make much difference in the healing process. "Besides," he argued, "the Granite Lake landing is only an hour from Bangor General Hospital, a much better hospital than the little community hospital in Greenville."

That was true, and it was enough to convince Butch to move on with his plans.

O'Casey and Ellen rolled out of bed soon afterward. They stood together just barely leaning on each other. Her brown curly hair was matted from the night's slumber, and seemed to stick almost straight up. Sean noticed and pulled his treasured Red Sox hat off and adjusted it to cover Ellen's disheveled tresses. They were both oblivious to the fact that Ellen had forgotten to put her bra back on. She was so smitten with standing next to O'Casey, leaning on his shoulder, and sipping hot coffee that nothing else mattered. The loons made a guest appearance right in front of the tribe, swimming slowly and unafraid. O'Casey, content with his current status, made no attempt to dash for his camera as he otherwise might have done.

The peace and quiet of the morning ended abruptly as Daniel Boone followed Tiffany from the tent. Just as she was exiting the outer flap, Jason put his hand on her backside like an Italian sailor might do to an unsuspecting woman waiting at the bus stop. Even Tiffany was taken by surprise. "Jason!" she whispered. Jason, who knew few social boundaries, had assumed that a night in the tent with Tiffany after "rescuing" her from a savage beast somehow entitled him to whatever physical contact he wanted.

The rest of the tribe was appalled, and sought diversions from Jason's actions, lest Tiffany be further embarrassed.

Butch took immediate control of the situation. He did not want to make anyone anxious, least of all Angelo, but he wanted to get moving and stay on his adjusted timetable—a day and a half to the far end of Granite Lake, where his Jeep Cherokee and Jason's old hunting truck were parked. They had left O'Casey's Wrangler and Angelo's new Jeep Laredo at Teapot Landing where the trip had started.

Butch divided the workload quickly, and to everyone's amazement, they were in the canoes and ready to roll in less than two hours. Gone was the fancy breakfast and culinary aplomb of the day before. "We have oatmeal, and we have oatmeal," Butch announced.

Jason sneered and groused, "I don't eat oatmeal."

Butch, given his lack of sleep and his discovery of the fish that morning, was in no mood to take any bullshit from Jason Foxworthy. "Well there, Mr. Boone. You can eat whatever the freak you want, but A, you can cook it yourself, and B, you can do it after all your work is done breaking camp."

Ouch, thought Maria. *Not a day to short sheet the Chief.*

Butch loaded each canoe personally. Even O'Casey, a veteran camper himself, deferred to Butch. He could see that the Chief was a man on a mission. O'Casey had enough respect for his friend to simply hand him gear as Butch adjusted and readjusted every item.

"Here's the deal, guys. We're going to do over half the river today. I know it's called Wilson Stream, but it's really a river. It's usually pretty lazy by mid-June, but it rained hard last night. It also appears that it must have rained even harder in the upper valley. They probably had to open another gate to keep the water behind the dam from getting too high. That means we've got to be smart. I don't want to dump any canoes or lose any gear. Let's stay close and follow my lead through each rapid, even though they won't be nearly as bad as the Cut. There are several pretty good falls, but we'll portage them if we need to, and we may not get to them until tomorrow. Today is the easier part, but it will give everyone a chance to get used to the river and to how each of you paddles. Everyone grab your paddle now and touch them to mine."

"What?" Jason said.

"Just do it," Butch directed, clearly tiring of Jason now.

Seven paddles touched at the tips. "*A wah nee hota. Ne we chata!*" the Chief said quietly. "That was a Lakota Sioux invocation to the Great Spirit for their equivalent of teamwork. That's what we need. 'Mario Lanza' here needs to have his hand looked at," smirked Butch with a nod toward Angelo. "And 'Daniel Boone' here needs to have his head examined."

As Butch turned toward Jason, it was clear to the others that something had been lost in the translation. Clearly, Butch was mad at Jason once again, but Butch did not push it further. But the mere fact that Jason did not do his usual "What? What?" made it obvious that he knew Butch had something on him, but the tribe would never learn what that something was.

The morning was peaceful and warm as they pushed off. No one, with the possible exception of Angelo, wanted to leave their beloved camp. It had been perfect. Great food. Great fellowship. Great music. But even Angelo, despite the intense pain in his hand and arm, hated to turn away from the beach and head downriver. As the last vestiges of the camp disappeared, he leaned back in his canoe trying to grab one last memory of the stage on which he had performed *Phantom*. It had been, for him, a dream come true.

The river—a stream in name only—had risen several feet in less than twelve hours. The tribe made great progress down the first few miles where it was wide and had few rapids. As with many big streams and river valleys, as the terrain dropped toward sea level and the banks got steeper, the river became less forgiving.

Butch had insisted that Angelo be in the bow of his canoe once again. Butch was the only member of the tribe who could handle a loaded canoe single-handed. He was a master canoeist and had actually won a number of canoe races on the Kennebago, the Rapid, and the Dead Rivers. He would need those skills today, as Angelo could barely hold his paddle in spite of his best efforts.

The Chief had O'Casey in the last canoe with Maria. Butch would be running point, surveying the rapids; Sean would be the sweep. If anyone dumped, O'Casey could be counted on to help with the rescue. Butch knew that he couldn't leave Angelo, so his challenge was the second canoe. Naturally, "Daniel Boone" was thrilled that he could be with Tiffany again. He'd show her a thing or two about canoeing. However, when Butch assigned him to the *bow* position, Jason was incensed. "I can handle the stern. I've done that a hundred times!" Jason bragged in protest.

The Chief, forever the strategist, whether it was with noncompliant students or arrogant executives on a fishing trip, handled Jason with ease. "I know you'd be great in the stern, but if Angelo drops his paddle or falls out, I'm *really* going to need your help. You're strong enough to grab him and hold on until we get to shore. Who else could do that?"

The ploy catered to Jason's sense of self-importance and masculine pride. He smiled at Tiffany, glad that she had heard Butch speak of his strength and skills.

The Chief knew that Jason Foxworthy was the antithesis of Daniel Boone. He was a self-indulgent, lazy, self-centered son of a bitch who would never be invited on another trip—not even to a shopping mall.

The last thing he would want to do was put Jason in the stern of the canoe, which had most of the important supplies. Tiffany was the key person he was counting on for help. She was obviously in top physical condition, and even though she had little prior paddling experience, she was a quick study. Besides, if she could rescue a drowning Jason Foxworthy, Butch felt, she could do anything in life.

Soon, the big hole where they had caught all their fish the day before was just around the bend. Butch knew that this would be a critical first test, so he had them pull into the slow water just above where they had fished.

He called out, "Watch my lead, Jason! Good hard bow strokes. You're leading number two." While none of that was exactly true, it was the Chief's way of saying, "Pay attention!" But he knew that Jason was such a baby, he'd react negatively to anything but a compliment. And it worked.

Butch surveyed the short set of rips and saw a sluice, a safe narrow passage, they would have to hit right on. While the sluice was only slightly left of center, there was a lot of water to cover before the bows could get squarely headed downstream into it.

Butch shoved off and headed for the line he'd need to get everyone through the sluice. Normally, he would have been yelling to Angelo, "Drive! Drive!" However, he knew that's just what Angelo would try to do. He could hear, see, and feel Angelo wince with pain at every stroke. Angelo was trying not to cry out as the paddle forced his cut wide open. At one point, Butch could even see pus and blood running down his forearm, but he never complained. When it was obvious that they were going to hit the sluice perfectly, Angelo even turned and smiled, as if to say, "We made it, Butch!"

Tiffany was everything Butch had hoped she would be and then some. She was remarkably strong and coordinated. She studied his every move and noted when to rudder and when to stroke. As one point, she over-ruddered and the canoe started to drive sideways, but she quickly self-corrected. To Jason's credit, he made some strong bow strokes, and with Tiffany's adroit rudder skills, the number two canoe also hit the sluice perfectly.

Although the plan had been for Ellen to go last, since she had the least gear and was pretty good with a kayak, O'Casey insisted that she go ahead of them through the sluice. A large boulder protected the head of the sluice. In low water, it was a great place to fish, O'Casey recalled, but it was a dangerous place now. If a paddler were to undershoot the sluice and hit the edge of the boulder, he, or she in this case, could get hung up sideways. For a canoe, that meant a dump. For a kayak, it could mean a roll-under, possibly pinning the kayaker in a death grip against the boulder.

The strength of the current brought Ellen downstream much faster than she had anticipated. She thought she had time to get in a couple more strokes downstream, but instead of digging deep into the water with a power stroke as she'd intended, the stroke bounced off a rock, upsetting her balance and almost dumping her in the water on the upstream side.

O'Casey knew she was in trouble in a minute. He was now glad that he had backwatered so much before hitting that portion of the run. Ellen's kayak was now in a sideways fetch, hung up with the large boulder amidships. She tried to push off, but with hundreds of foot-pounds of water pushing equally on her bow and stern, she was stuck.

O'Casey screamed, "Don't move! Don't do anything!" Then, "Maria, we're going to aim right for her! Power stroke! Power stroke!"

Maria drove the paddle in again and again. Though she had little upper body strength, she had tremendous determination, and her strong bow effort was perfect.

"Sean, we're going to hit her! We're going to hit her!" Maria yelled frantically, as the bow aimed right for Ellen's kayak.

Even Ellen, who had great faith in O'Casey, was afraid his canoe was going to cut her kayak in half and crush her against the rock. She was already loosening her spray skirt in preparation to bail out.

"Now left! Go to the left! Left!" O'Casey yelled, and Maria was able to drive three hard strokes in on the right side, forcing the canoe to the left.

Along with O'Casey's hard ruddering, it made just the difference. While it first appeared that their bow would actually hit the kayak at a right angle, instead, it hit with a glancing blow near the bow, which was just what O'Casey wanted. He hoped and trusted that Ellen's kayak could handle the impact, but he was counting on the collision for help. The impact drove the stern of the canoe toward the stern of the kayak. For a second, the two were side by side and parallel with the rock, and O'Casey grabbed Ellen's stern line, which had been trailing in the water, and wrapped a turn around his wrist. He held on as his canoe shot by.

Although it almost pulled his arm off and the rope cut deeply into his hand, the move worked. The weight and momentum of O'Casey's canoe pulled Ellen's stern off the rock and aimed her bow downstream again, right toward the sluice. The kayak shot forward and almost ended up in O'Casey's lap. For just a moment, it looked as if both would go over. Maria kept using driving strokes to help keep the canoe stable and moving forward. First the canoe and then, almost simultaneously, the kayak shot through the sluice. In a moment, they were all through and all safe.

"Holy shit!" Maria shrieked. "We did it! We did it!"

"Yee-hah!" shouted O'Casey enthusiastically, raising his paddle over his head.

"Yee-hah!" Ellen cheered as she winked over at O'Casey, who had immediately looked in her direction. Their eyes met briefly and shared more information than anyone else needed to know.

The tribe pulled off into a slow, shallow eddy to catch their breath and collect their senses.

"That was our first big test," Butch announced. "Great job, everyone. O'Casey, I thought you were going to cut Ellen's kayak in half. I figured she must have been snoring awfully hard last night for you to be that mad! Good rescue move."

"That was mostly good bow stroke, Maria. Great job, Superwoman!"

Maria's smile could not have been broader. Though it was difficult to tell from her dark and suntanned skin, she appeared to be blushing and actually put her head down. For a moment, Sean almost thought he had said something wrong. Then he realized that along with the smile were some tears of joy.

Maria could not have imagined a better compliment than being called Superwoman. She could not have been happier or more proud. Even though she knew that O'Casey was being gracious, she also knew that she had played an important role in Ellen's rescue. She could feel the canoe responding to her strokes. It was a type of "women's liberation" she had never encountered or expected, but it felt...magnificent.

"I *think* we've only got one more set of challenging rapids before we get to our campsite," Butch told the group.

Only Jason picked up on the *I think* portion of the statement. The rest of the tribe had such supreme confidence in the Chief that his uncertainty was almost irrelevant. He could get them through anything. He was *the* Chief. He was *their* Chief.

"What do you mean, you *think*?" Daniel Boone asked in a way that seemed to challenge the Chief's authority. The others noticed the tone and waited for The Chief's reply.

"It's simple," Butch said. "I've never canoed the entire river, though I've fished most of it. I know the river very well just down to where we'll camp, about four miles below where we are. I have a map of the river that O'Casey and I will study tonight at camp. We'll be fine with that part, I'm sure. But when the water rises, everything changes. The river is probably up several feet right now from where it would have been before the thunderstorms of last night. I have no doubt that they probably opened at least one more gate at the dam. They can do that automatically now; that's why there was no one at the dam the other day.

"When the water gets too high on the lake side of the dam, it sends the information to Bangor Hydro. They open the gates if they want to, releasing millions of gallons of water—coming right toward us. That's just what's happening. Fortunately, the river can handle that right now, but even small drops in elevation can change significantly with more water. That sluice you ran just a minute ago would have been a few bare rocks and a set of riffles, not rapids, two days ago. Jason, I *think* we may only have one more set of big rapids before we get to our next campsite. I *think*, but I'm not sure. Please let me know if *you* 'think' differently, now that you're freakin' Daniel Boone."

Even O'Casey, who detested Jason Foxworthy, almost winced at the sarcastic tone in the Chief's voice. *I wonder what Jason did to put a hair across the Chief's ass like that?* he thought. He knew Butch better than almost anyone, and it was rare that Butch got that way. He never had with O'Casey. While Butch was not always the most complimentary person, particularly with men, he was also rarely sarcastic—that is, unless someone really pissed him off. Clearly, Jason must have done something to tick him off, especially given that Butch had called him "freakin' Daniel Boone." *I wonder*, thought O'Casey. *I wonder...*

"Hey, Butch, I was just curious, that's all," Jason responded in a deferential voice. "I'm not questioning your judgment. You just seem to *know* everything about this area. I was surprised. I assumed you had done this river many times."

"Well, I haven't, OK?" the Chief shot back. His patience was short because he'd had so little sleep. He was also very worried about Angelo, who could barely hold his paddle. If Butch could have had his way, and if they could have pulled it off, he would have medevac'd Angelo to Bangor General. If it were later in the week, Butch would have stayed at camp. He had actually considered that. If he'd thought Skippy or one of the other bush pilots was flying in the area, he would have tried signaling them to get them to land. As a rule, most of their activity would be at the end of the week. However, with the high water likely to drive the fish down for the next few days, the likelihood of a fly-by was small.

As Butch cooled down and reflected on his options for Angelo, the rest of the tribe started to fidget. Even though it was only midmorning, the temperature had risen to almost eighty. The cool water was already looking like an invitation to swim. However, Butch knew that he had crossed the line in his frustration with Jason, and they all needed to forget that and keep moving. "Come on, guys. Let hit the last set of rapids. Then we'll set up camp and catch some fish."

"Let's do it!" shouted Maria, now that she felt like she could contribute to the cause. *Superwoman*, she thought to herself. *Cool freakin' beans!*

As is typical for many rivers and streams, the middle of Wilson Stream was somewhat slow and meandering. However, the prior night's rain combined with a release of dam water that was more significant than Butch had expected, gave the river the feel of a class two rapid. There were fewer slow spots and eddies and far more fast runs. However, it was still the best part of the river for the tribe to hone their canoeing and kayaking skills. Ellen got a much better sense of what she could and could not do with her kayak. She learned quickly that when she had to traverse from one side of the river to the other, she had to paddle very hard at the beginning to offset the downward force of the current at the midstream point. She also learned that by rotating her hips to the upstream side, she could dig into the current and force the bow across the stream. Much like a skier digging the inside edge of the downhill ski into the slope, Ellen learned that this ever-so-slight leaning move would help her slip across even a strong middle current.

Tiffany was proving to be nothing short of amazing. Butch had always enjoyed coaching more than teaching. He knew that practice was the key to honing any skill, whether it was a wrist-deflection pass in hockey or a shoulder brush on the gate of a slalom run. He also knew that Tiffany would need a lot of practice before she hit the last big rapids of the morning. So rather than take the shortest and easiest line downstream, he pretended that the safest route was almost always to go from one side of the river to the other. Ordinarily he would not do this, nor did he need to. However, he could see the water continuing to rise, and the current continuing to build in strength. He knew that everyone would soon need to bring his or her A-game, but since Tiffany had never really canoed before, she would need to rehearse every stroke now.

She proved to be the quickest study Butch had ever seen. She watched his every stroke and literally counted where and when he did power strokes versus J strokes and on which side. She studied his ruddering techniques. She noticed that Butch would even do a double pull or push stroke if he needed more force than just ruddering to get the bow across or downstream. Wherever Butch went, Tiffany went. Whatever Butch did, Tiffany did. Butch was taken aback by her upper body strength. Her years of conditioning, particularly for swimming, had given her remarkable strength and stamina. To his great satisfaction, Butch realized that his decision to put Tiffany in the stern of canoe number two was the best decision he could have made.

What could have been a long and difficult morning soon became a fun and exciting time. Butch was surprised, however, that they were hitting more sluices now, areas of tight, funneled water every time the river straightened. These were really haystacks now—sluice openings with two- and sometimes three-foot walls of water on either side. He never would have thought that the tribe could be capable of handling such water with full canoes, but somehow, they did.

Though Angelo could barely hold a paddle, he struggled to contribute. By contrast, though Jason had neither the heart nor the head to be a good paddler, he had the strength. Tiffany more than made up for Daniel Boone's inadequacy. The third canoe was fine. Maria was so excited about being dubbed "Superwoman" that she began to believe it. No longer the tentative butterball, she now saw herself as having an important role. She could feel her paddle digging in deeper as she followed O'Casey's every directive. Given his masterful rescue of Ellen, Maria felt that if he told her to jump ship, she would. Her skills soared, along with her self-confidence.

And Ellen was becoming a pro with the kayak. She leaned into the current enough to help the track and glide. She learned when to power stroke and when to rudder, all this intuitively, since there was no one to direct her strokes or help her with her skills. She, too, felt an important part of the tribe. She also felt invigorated and alive. After breezing through a set of haystacks three feet high, she gave out her own "Yee-hah!" and pumped her clenched fist in the air.

Back and forth they went. With spray in their faces and wind in their hair, the women became indistinguishable from the men. At one point the Chief turned back and realized that if he fell overboard, the tribe could and would make it. Like every great coach, he could smile just a bit knowing that his team, his tribe, was now as prepared as he could make them. For a moment, on a slow traverse across the river, he looked up. Tiffany was no longer on his heels watching his decision-making. She was calling out strokes to Daniel Boone. "Hard left! More left. Now power right. Power! Power!" Tiffany was able to get away with more ordering of Jason than anyone ever had or ever would. He was so excited about and so determined to have sex with Tiffany that he didn't want to jeopardize anything.

Jason drifted back into his thoughts of last night. His hand had been in Tiffany's pants for just a brief second—just long enough for him to feel the shaved area of her bikini line. He didn't go further because he was afraid that if she woke up, she might freak out and scream for Butch or, worse yet, his nemesis, O'Casey. Then he and O'Casey, or maybe even Butch, would do battle for sure. Jason imagined tonight with Tiffany. He would again remind her of his great rescue. He was Daniel Boone now. She was the white woman he had rescued from the Indians. She'd be safe with him. *Ya, right!* Daniel Boone was smiling...almost drooling.

"I said *left*, for Christ's sake! Left, Jason! Left!" Tiffany, too, had let her guard down because they were in such an easy section of water. There was a boulder that they needed to go around. It was only about the size of a freakin' bathtub. Surely, Jason had to see it. Bang! *Scrrr...raaaape!* The canoe hit the boulder almost head-on. Had there been any degree of current, Tiffany would have been thrown right out of the canoe and into the river. They actually hit with such force that it pushed the front of the bow in almost two inches and opened up a small seam in the top weld. Water began squirting into the bow area forward of Jason's feet.

"Come on, Jason! We were doing so well!" Tiffany hollered in frustration as the canoe slipped off the rock and headed safely downstream again. She was glad that Butch wasn't looking, and she wasn't sure if anyone else had seen their screw-up. By this time, everyone seemed to have this section of the river well in hand. Each of the teams was actually picking their own line for navigating the rapids. Tiffany took a deep breath to control her anger and frustration. She really wanted to like Jason. He was *very* good-looking, though he now had a beer belly and was obviously out of shape. Still, he was very funny and a jock like she was. Although her mother would cringe at the thought of bringing home such an obviously blue-collar guy, Jason had potential. *That's what he has*, she noted to herself. She had already learned on this trip not to judge a book by its cover. Maria was now one of her best friends, she mused, but never would have been before this trip.

As she looked again at Jason—the handsome, overgrown teenager in the bow -smiling and trying hard to make amends, she acknowledged that they had much in common. She really did want to like him. After all, he had saved her life. Well...when she'd awakened in the morning she wasn't totally sure about that. The cloudiness of the wine and Yukon Jack made it all seem a blur. She remembered the terror of seeing the bear. That memory was way too vivid and would be with her forever— the huge black body, and giant fang-like teeth; it was something out of a horror film, she recalled with a shudder.

It just seemed that Jason had arrived almost instantaneously. That was strange. And because she ran past him, she hadn't seen him hit the bear, though it was very obvious that the bear was mad at him. That *must* have happened because the bear was wild at Jason and went after him and not her in camp. *Thank God*, she thought. *Thank God Jason was there.* He could be an asshole, but maybe he was right. He had saved her life. She needed to lighten up. "My bad, Jason. I should have seen that rock. Sorry, *Daniel Boone!*"

Jason beamed with pride. Finally, Tiffany had seen the light. Jason grinned from ear to ear. Tiffany could scarcely have understood the meaning behind the smile that came back toward her.

"Pull over! Pull over!" Butch yelled.

As the canoeists paddled over toward a right-hand eddy, they could feel the current suddenly strengthen. Ellen, who'd been having fun practicing her hip leans, was not paying attention. "Pull over! Pull over!" Butch screamed at her again and again. He was already out of his beached canoe and running for the bottom of the eddy. Ellen had gone by the canoes before she realized what was happening. She was heading for a high, funnel-like chute and a huge waterfall—almost twice the height of Black Powder Pitch—just fifty feet in front of her.

O'Casey was right behind Butch, who used his paddle to help grab the floating bow line of Ellen's kayak just as it was about to shoot past and into the final set of rapids above the falls. Her bow swung around completely, forcing the kayak into an upstream position. Butch was, pound for pound, the strongest person O'Casey knew. He could bench press almost 300 pounds. More impressive for his students, he could lie on the floor, reach his arms as far from his body as he could, and then do pushups. Not the strongest kid in the school, not once, not ever, could duplicate that feat...and yet Butch was about to be pulled over the falls with Ellen, perhaps to their death.

Just as the Chief could sense his feet slipping out from under him, he felt a set of hands pulling him back toward shore. O'Casey had his arms around the Chief's waist and was driving his legs hard into the rocks below him. Tiffany then grabbed onto O'Casey and gave him additional stability and strength. They all pulled together, bracing their legs against the raging current that sought to pull Ellen and perhaps the entire group over the falls. Ellen frantically drove her right paddle in and then her left with strong, powerful strokes. Her positive inertia with the kayak proved just enough for the human chain to get more leg drive.

And suddenly, there she was. Ellen and the kayak together, dragged up onto the last sandbar. As with the bear incident and Jason's rescue on day one, everyone took a minute just to recover. Adrenaline does funny things to the body. While it gives a person great short-term strength, it also eventually produces that classic weak-in-the-knees feeling and a sense that one might pass out. Each member of the tribe reflected on what had almost happened. In another second, Ellen would have been in a closed chute, an area she could not have escaped from or bailed out of safely. Past the brief chute was a straight drop-off of at least ten feet, maybe fifteen. Without a helmet, and maybe even with one, Ellen and, quite probably, Butch, would likely have died.

"Holy fuckin' shit!" Ellen exclaimed.

At that, everyone howled with laughter. Whether it was the adrenaline release, the near-death experience, or the fact that Ellen had sworn and in a way she never had in her entire lifetime, everyone just lost it—pee-in-your-pants lost it. Sometimes, laughter can be rooted in a great line, great timing, or a very funny incident. This laughter was just the spontaneous, uproarious howling of a family, a tribe, who were now one and had bonded in that second...forever.

It's Official

A portage, even one of fifty feet, is never a fun process, but it certainly beat the alternative. Going over the falls was simply not an option. The falls were on the edge of a small granite bluff with just enough of a trail on the side so that the tribe could portage the gear without a significant delay. The short switchbacks on the trail did not present a problem for carrying the gear, but they were really too short and steep to be able to bring the canoes around. That meant that the group had to hand-line the canoes down the face of the short cliff to the eddy below.

It seemed strange to see the empty canoes being lowered down the face of the cliff. All Ellen could imagine was *herself* in that headlong position, aiming down the falls and into the rapids and the rocks below. *I would have been dead meat*, she thought. As her kayak was then lowered down the face of the rock, it bounced slightly several times at the bottom of the ledge, and she could almost feel her body bounce with it. She tried to imagine her broken bones and shattered face being swept around in the wild foaming current at the base of the falls...and the red froth and foam that would be her signature of a life lost. The thought sent shivers down her spine.

Just as quickly, it was replaced by an overwhelming sense of gratitude that washed the negativity away. "Hey, Butch," Ellen whispered, "thanks for the rescue. That would not have been fun going over the cliff. I owe you one!"

"Ellen, it all works out over the length of the friendship. Maybe you'll do the same for me one day," Butch responded with his usual broad grin and enthusiastic voice. Little did he know how true those words might be.

Because it was already exceedingly warm, Butch was anxious to get to the next campsite. Although he knew this part of the river in general, he had been surprised at how quickly the falls had come up. It had caught him off guard. While he knew it was there, the speed of the current had carried them to the falls much more quickly than he had expected. He also noted that the river level was much, much higher than he'd anticipated. The dam must have opened another gate.

Butch could not have known that the thunderstorm the night before had created significant stream flooding in the valleys above the dam. Bangor Hydro was now running "spring condition" dam levels, with all but one gate now wide open.

"Saddle up," Butch ordered as he loaded the last of the gear back into the canoes. He was a bit less concerned about load placement this time. He knew the section below the falls quite well and was also less concerned about his now seasoned crew. The run from the falls to the giant sandbar that would become their campsite took less than an hour to complete, and the trip was almost idyllic. On several occasions, Butch and O'Casey noticed big brookies rising to slurp down emerging mayflies. Both knew that this was not the time to fish. However, it was hard to move past rising fish and deep pools that could hold four- and five-pound trout.

They rounded a big sweeping bend and right before them lay another magical spot—a smooth oval sand bar tucked into a dark, mysterious forest of tall white pine, smatterings of blue spruce, and stubby red cedar. The land surrounding the river was much higher here, and more foreboding than their prior campground. The ridges of the small valley were pink-and-gray speckled granite with mica flecks occasionally catching the sparkle of the sun. The location almost seemed more in keeping with a western settling, perhaps a bit from an Ansel Adams Salmon River photograph. The heat, too, was not typical of a Maine day. It was not yet noon and the temperature was approaching ninety degrees, a rarity in an area that could fall into the high thirties on an early June night with a full moon. The life vests that Butch had insisted they continue to wear until they reached the sandbar had rendered all of them soaked with sweat. Quickly, vests and long-sleeved shirts came off, as did the zippered bottoms of the cargo pants most were wearing.

Butch and O'Casey led the camp setup process on the highest point of the sandbar, about eighty feet from the water's edge. Interestingly, everyone seemed to want to continue the coed sleeping arrangements. Although it meant that the Chief would again be alone at night, he didn't give it a second thought.

While Angelo would have loved to share a tent with Butch, he knew that could become awkward for a variety of reasons. Besides, he just couldn't tell Maria that he wanted to change roommates.

More importantly, it would be almost impossible to share limited tent space with a man he was deeply in love with. He was not even sure if Butch knew he was gay, a fact he had never shared with anyone outside of a very limited group of similar friends who lived many miles from his school. It had been his burden throughout life to hide that most important part of who he was. It was as if he were trying to hide his love for music. He was a gay man who loved music. He could share one part of his self and soul, but not the other. Even these, his newfound friends on the trip, did not know, or so he assumed. Angelo felt certain that the Chief did not know how much he loved him. Being in a tent with Butch and not being able to profess his love would have been more than Angelo could now stand. So he would be the Phantom of the Opera one more night. He didn't mind. Maria was great.

While the guys were setting up camp, the ladies made the sandwiches. Butch didn't care if that appeared sexist. It was work that needed to be done. He did breakfast and dinner. They could do the lunch, Butch reasoned. Political correctness was not a part of his thinking. He had put Tiffany in the stern of the number two canoe, not as a feminist gesture, but because she was the best "man" for the job. If she were less capable than Daniel Boone, she would have been in the bow. Fortunately, his instincts had been correct and Tiffany had done a kick-ass job. The real Daniel Boone would have been lucky to have had such a sidekick. Tiffany was tops.

Butch was so pleased with their day's progress down river that he decided to finish the last small piece and then the lake trip for the morning. Given the afternoon heat, the Chief figured a short afternoon hike and some big-pool fishing might be an ideal last bit of fun. Angelo announced privately to Butch that he did not really feel up to joining them. It was obvious, as Butch had suspected. Angelo's hand was fully involved and compromised. Upon closer inspection, it appeared that the infection was starting to travel. That was the Chief's greatest fear. Although he did not see a line up Angelo's arm yet, he could see some swelling and feel significant warmth above the wrist and well into the forearm.

Butch knew that it was too long a trip to make it to the end of Granite Lake today. Besides, he thought, it would be better to let the rising water begin to subside, which he hoped would happen later by morning. The one good thing about dam-induced rises in the water was that they could go down as quickly as they went up. Often, the dams were opened in the morning after a big rain and then closed down in the afternoon. It would be just a matter of hours, the Chief reasoned, before the high water would drop. Since the most challenging part of the trip was still ahead, Butch decided that waiting until morning would be the best course of action. Still, he was very concerned about Angelo's infection.

"I'm going to leave the largest water bottle with you, Angelo. Stay well hydrated. I know another spring about half a mile below us, and we're going to fill up all of the water bottles there. Stay out of the hot sun, too. We'll only be gone an hour or two. If you really need me, fire my pistol three times. I think we'll be able to hear it. Otherwise, just yell 'SUPPER!' as loud as you can, and Jason will be here in ten minutes," the Chief said with a reassuring grin. He didn't want to overdramatize the situation, knowing that Angelo hated to have any attention called to him and was truly a team player.

"Are you sure you don't mind? I'd just like to relax and read. This autobiography of Tchaikovsky is terrific."

"I want it just as soon as you're done," Butch said.

Angelo returned the Chief's smile, fully aware that while Butch actually did like historical biographies, composers weren't a likely choice for him—unless the composer also happened to be a Civil War general or a Spartan warrior.

Off they went—like six little kids with the oldest at the front of the line and the rest playing follow the leader. Butch didn't even give them his usual briefing about where they were going, what they'd be doing, and when they'd be back. They had food, water, and their leader—and a few fishing rods thrown in just for good measure. That's all they needed to know and all they cared about. The adventure would continue. Butch also knew they needed just a little stress free time, given what they had already been through and knew, too, that Angelo needed some alone time to sleep and to heal.

Each was thrilled with his or her own experiences on the trip. Maria was now *Superwoman* and Jason was *Daniel Boone*. One deserved the title. One didn't. In Jason's case, he didn't care. He'd use it anyway. *And besides*, he thought, *I got the girl.* Tiffany had saved Jason and had then *been* saved, or so she thought, by him.

O'Casey and Ellen were, when they could, walking side by side and briefly touching hands when the opportunity allowed, though it was almost always initiated by Ellen. O'Casey was much like an eleven-year-old boy, on the one hand excited about the prospect of a girlfriend and at the same time terrified by it. He continually pondered a dilemma he could not resolve. He knew he would never get over Catherine's death. No one could replace her. Not even Ellen. Yet he was so lonely. Drinking Jameson whiskey late into the night was certainly not the answer. He knew that. Fishing certainly helped, but right now as he walked down the trail with Ellen either by his side or walking just ahead of him, Sean Padraig O'Casey actually felt happy for the first time he could remember since the day he awoke from his coma. His shy smile was firmly in place.

The Chief was always happy when he was in the lead. His tribe, walking Indian file behind him, gave him a sense of purpose that filled his heart with joy. While he enjoyed being a school leader, being a guide or being the Chief was an even more rewarding experience. It spoke to his heart and to his first love—the wilderness. He was taking them to the biggest pool on the river, the last really slow spot before the final five miles. While he'd never been below this big pool, he could tell from the topographical map and the discussions he'd had with other guides that the stream quickly narrowed and got very fast. He also knew that there was another good spring where they could get cool, delicious drinking water. While they could, of course, boil water that they could later drink, it was never the same. River water always tasted of sediment and clay. Although the clay sections of the river were small, they sometimes colored the water's appearance and almost always colored the flavor.

The walk along the river was beautiful. The trail was a vibrant explosion of greens. The canopy of branches restricted the amount of the summer light that sneaked through—but it was just enough to allow the fabric and textures of branch and bark to play off each other. The fragrance of cedar and spruce would have been overpowering if it were a less pleasant smell. Instead, it had an elixir-like quality—pungent, robust, and rich.

The trail ended abruptly and the smell of the woods was replaced by the smell of the river. The sound of buzzing insects and distant chickadees was also replaced—by the light sound of riffles and the deep, barely noticeable sound of a rolling, liquid current on its inexorable move to the sea a hundred miles away in Penobscot Bay.

The magic was short-lived. As the tribe stepped from the cool, moist, environment on the trail, the heat of the summer sun was striking. Butch had imagined a fun, relaxing afternoon of fishing the big pool. Instead, he had brought the tribe out of the woods and into a beach-like scenario—hot and steamy.

Quickly, backpacks came off and everyone stripped down to the barest of essentials. The men quickly took off their shirts. The women, jealous of that freedom, continued to sweat in their T-shirts and shorts. It was not until Ellen sat down and folded her arms that it dawned on her that she had never put her bra back on after gracefully removing it in the tent. For a second, she was mortified. She could not, perhaps since fifth grade, ever remember having been in mixed company without wearing a bra. She immediately turned toward O'Casey, who sat nearby, looking to him for a clue as to what to do or whether he had noticed.

While he had noticed—many times, in fact,—he'd chosen fleeting glances and never when Ellen or the others might catch him looking. He was now sitting close enough to signal that she was important to him and just far enough away to show a level of modesty and shyness that he knew Ellen appreciated. For someone who had a tremendous sense of self-confidence as an educational leader, as a man considering a relationship for the first time in years, he was a fumbling sixth grader, too afraid to act and too excited not to do so.

Ellen wanted to reach out and grab his hand. He wanted to do the same, yet neither dared. Ellen quickly forgot about her sans-bra attire. When she reflected on it again, and thought about all they had been through already, including her own near-death experience, going without a bra now seemed ludicrous and irrelevant.

As with the others in the tribe, the challenges they had faced and had yet to face were teaching them more than they ever would have guessed about what was and was not important in life. Redefining the concept and value of modesty was only one of the smaller lessons yet to be learned.

Butch had hoped there would be rising trout and an opportunity to give the women some fly casting lessons. Now, the heat was almost oppressive. It would be hours before the trout would rise again, perhaps not until late in the day or early evening. Still, the Chief could not resist doing a bit of fishing. He tied on a #12 bead-headed stone nymph and then a stinger #16 pheasant tail nymph behind it with an eight-foot, three-pound-test leader. Although the dropper rig could be a hassle sometimes, Butch found it to be ideal when the fish were down. He figured it would be the only chance he might have to stir up some action in the midday sun.

Actually, more than anything, he just wanted to do some casting. If the truth were to be known, this was his stage. Up to this point, he had not really had a chance to strut his stuff as a fisherman. Butch loved the big pool. It gave him an opportunity to make some extremely long, beautiful casts. For both the Chief and O'Casey, casting was at least half the magic. Both men had seen and critiqued the movie, *A River Runs Through It*. While they had laughed at the concept of "shadow casting," they had immediately gone out and tried it themselves in private with varying degrees of success.

Today, Butch knew that he would not be doing any shadow casting. Even on a calm day, trying to cast a nymph with a stinger fly was anything but easy. Although he was, to some degree, also showing off for the ladies, if he had *really* wanted to show off, he would have tied a #18 or even a #20 midge on with a hair-like two-pound-test leader. With a slight back wind, the Chief and O'Casey could both make casts approaching 100 feet. But even with the awkward dropper rip, Butch made some stellar casts. He then would adjust the line slightly, trying to keep the more rapidly moving surface line even with the slower moving nymph.

O'Casey was dying to join Butch. The big pool was such a great place to cast. There was plenty of back-cast room. The high ridges also blocked the afternoon breeze, which was nonexistent now anyway.

Butch made several deep-bellied false casts. His timing was impeccable. Just at ten o'clock, he would lock his whole forearm. It seemed glued to the butt section of his Sage 5-weight graphite as an inseparable extension of the rod. Then a quick pull backward on his forearm. No bend in the wrist. No sag in the line. It was just one beautiful sweeping arc backward. In the sunlight, the chartreuse weight-forward line looked like a giant loop in the canyon sky. The backlight further accentuated the beauty of the cast. Once again, at the perfect moment, just as the line straightened out, Butch moved his forearm from two o'clock back toward the ten o'clock position. Ten, two. Ten, two. Ten, two, cast. Just as O'Casey's grandfather had taught him. Butch was a master. In fact he was *the* master, perhaps one of the best fly fishermen and guides in all of northern New England. Orvis had even named a rod after him. While O'Casey was dying to grab the other rod and do some parallel play, this was the Chief's show. This was the unspoken *mime's soliloquy*, Granville Chapman's hour to strut the stage.

The tribe sat mesmerized. Even Jason, though he kept annoying Tiffany with an effort to squeeze her thigh, watched the Chief in relative silence. In a strange way, it was similar to the musical magic of the night before, as Angelo and Maria had shared their souls, note by note. The elegance was in the form, not the function. The light was perfect. It accentuated the rolling loops of golden-green fly line sparkling in the sun as the water flicked off its surface on the back cast. At the precise moment the line straightened out parallel to the water, the Chief snapped it forward as though conducting an invisible orchestra on a natural stage. His concentration in following the line along the pool was unswerving. At the tiniest, most imperceptible forward pull of the line, Butch snapped his right wrist back and the battle was engaged.

"Fish on." O'Casey whispered to the others.

There was no archetypal battle between man and nature as there had been with the monster square-tail O'Casey had hooked at the base of the dam. The fish that Butch hooked into—five in five consecutive casts—were all modest-sized brook trout in the twelve- to sixteen-inch range. Still, they were scrappy in their fights and beautiful to behold. Several completely cleared the water in their efforts to throw the hook. The morning air seemed to explode with golden drops of water as the backlighting of the sun and the dark cliff across from the Chief emphasized the contrast of sparkling water and golden line against the imposing granite wall on the back side of the pool.

Just as quickly as the proliferation of fish, one after the other, had come ashore, it ended. Cast after beautiful, magical, golden-green cast.

Loop after loop of line and back cast sparkling in the sun. No fish. And then, one last hit and one last fish. It was clearly bigger than the rest, and though not a monster, fought a brave and determined battle. It charged right at Butch's feet, trying to build up slack line before its incredible leap. The crimson, green, and silver colors of its thick, muscular body twisted and contorted in an effort to throw the fly. Skillfully, Butch pulled in the slack while the fish was in midair. He applied just the right leverage… and then it was over. The fish was large enough that he could *tail it* like a large salmon—grabbing it by the tail rather than the gills. He hoisted it for the tribe to see, as the nearly exhausted fish wiggled slightly in an effort to free itself for the cool, deep waters just below the fisherman's feet.

Led by the Chief's informal protégé, first O'Casey and then Ellen and the rest of the tribe stood and applauded for the encore performance. It was as though after going five for five, the Chief, like Angelo and Maria the night before, understood the demand for an encore. The squirming three-pound brookie, with its deep crimson male color and pronounced hooked jaw was the Chief's encore. In all his years as a guide, he'd never had such a responsive and respectful audience for his craft. He smiled broadly and took a bow.

Early on in his casting performance, he could see the tribe watching his every move. Butch loved to put on a show. It was part of who he was. However, he would have made the same magnificent sweeping casts and studied retrieves if he'd had the giant pool all to himself. For a somewhat crude, inartistic person, Butch knew a ballet when he saw one, and this morning with the sun backlighting his casts, the ballet was on.

The tribe continued to clap. "Bravo! Bravo!" they cheered, just as they had done for Angelo and Maria. This was all about one's personal best being showcased, as it had been the night before.

The Chief turned with a smile and bowed again briefly before his adoring fans. They were more than his fans now. They were a tightly connected family who had supported each other and even saved one another's lives. They were the tribe, *his* tribe…and he was proud to be their chief. He grinned his trademark grin, and then, as gently as he could, he lowered the fish back into the water. He quickly saw that the fish was too exhausted even to wriggle in the upside-down position. While he had no qualms about keeping any of the other fish, which would become their supper, this was one he wanted to release. Like the monster that O'Casey had hooked and lost, Butch almost never kept trophy trout. While the three-pounder was hardly what he would consider a trophy, in another two years, it would be. Butch pushed it forward, then pulled it backward, all the while holding its tail. Gradually, these moves helped pull water through the gills of the exhausted fish. *The joy of the moment will be lost completely if this fish dies*, Butch thought.

Convinced that the large male was not responding enough, he changed strategies quickly. He ran the fish up to the headwaters of the pool where there was a strong riffle and more oxygen in the water. Finding the bubbliest section, Butch repeated the process over and over. First there was little response. In fact, the trout started to turn on its side, the first sign of a dying fish. If that happened, it would soon be floating upside down and awaiting the claws of a passing eagle, or, worse yet, die a bloated and decomposing mess on the banks of Granite Lake. If it was within his power, Butch would not allow that to happen.

Slowly, ever so slowly, Butch could see the trout begin to work its gills, struggling to get desperately needed oxygen into its muscle tissue. The rhythm began to increase. The gills moved faster and stronger. First, Butch could feel head shakes and then the tail shakes. Finally, he could no longer hold its strong and reinvigorated tail. With one last powerful tail thrust, the squaretail shook itself free of the Chief and his supporting fans, surged up through the shallow riffles, and disappeared into the cool headwaters above.

Butch had won and the fish had won. *What a day!* he thought.

O'Casey, in particular, was very proud of the Chief's efforts. While the tribe could certainly use another fish for supper, it was too big and beautiful a fish to kill.

"I want to catch a fish like that today, Butch," Jason called out. He had been biting his usually loose tongue for longer than he could stand. Early on in the Chief's casting display, he had started to talk. To shut him up, Tiffany had held his hand. While it was more the gesture of a mother holding the hand of a three-year-old in church to keep him from talking, Jason naturally interpreted it as Tiffany's being smitten with his indefatigable charm.

Butch had no idea how to respond to Jason's request. The chance of Jason making a fifty-foot cast and placing it six feet above the ledge where the trout were hiding was about a million to one. It had taken Butch years to do that. Casting a tandem nymph set as he had done just then was the most difficult of all casting techniques. It would be like Jason trying to finish a slalom run on one ski. Then, for Jason to bring in a three-pound trout on a two-pound fluorocarbon leader lowered the probability of success by a factor of ten.

Still, Butch, the ever-gracious guide, said, "Uh…yeah. Sure, Jason, sure."

After what seemed like hours of coaching but was perhaps only twenty minutes, Jason gave up his one and only attempt at fly fishing. The Chief's prompting of, "Relax. Be gentle with the rod. It's not a hockey stick," fell on deaf ears. The ten, two…ten, two mantra all fly fishermen learn looked more like nine, three…eight, five. Soon, Jason was wearing more line than he was casting. Shortly after that, and mercifully, the pain of watching Jason fly-fish for lunker trout was over.

Silently, almost imperceptibly, O'Casey winked at Butch as Jason handed the fly rod back to him, and the Chief returned the wink. It's amazing how effective nonverbal communication can be between friends…or lovers. Ellen saw the wink and flashed one of her own to O'Casey. Hers meant something altogether different, and O'Casey returned the wink and a grin.

Because they still needed about five more fish for an adequate supper of trout, Butch still needed fishing volunteers, and all three women stepped up for the cause. Butch had purposely brought several spinning rigs along with his fly rod. He knew that with the heat of midday, the brook trout he was after would find the deepest, coolest water. That's why he had fished a bead-headed nymph and dropper. He had actually caught the big trout on the tiny #18 dropper nymph, which is why he had fought the fish so gently. With such a tiny fly and ultralight leader it would have been easy for all but the best of fishermen to have lost that fish. While he and O'Casey never "drowned worms" themselves, he knew that was probably the only chance for the women to catch fish on such a hot day. However, the fish were much more finicky with the hot weather, and particularly with the sun almost vertically overhead now.

While Tiffany and Maria worked under the Chief's tutelage drowning worms, O'Casey had other ideas. Butch happily agreed to let him borrow his favorite Sage rod. The Chief was tickled by what his good friend Paddy had in mind. "Ellen, would you like to learn to fly fish?" O'Casey said.

"Just try me!" she responded with her best flirting smile, and when she realized her somewhat Freudian slip, she added, "I mean, I'd love to."

O'Casey quickly removed the tandem flies that Butch had tied. While they were exactly the right ones to catch a fish in a deep hole at midday, they were also the hardest to cast. That was one reason Jason had had such difficulty. However, Butch had purposely not changed the flies for Jason. Making a cocky, arrogant son of a bitch look stupid is not always a bad thing, and it was the perfect thing that morning. O'Casey knew that a #10 caddis full-hackle parachute design might not take fish, but it would be easy to cast and be pretty on the water. He wanted this to be an emotional experience, not a shopping trip for supper.

First, O'Casey did just a tiny bit of showing off himself. If the Chief were conducting an orchestra on a grand scale for the tribe, O'Casey's performance was more akin to the mating ritual of a male loon in front of his female counterpart. It was a "Honey, watch this" display of casting prowess. "Now it's your turn," he told Ellen. "Just remember, your wrist and hand are an extension of your forearm. Keep it all together in one motion. Start with just a little line. It's better to have short smooth casts than long sloppy ones. Think ten, two. Ten o'clock is when your back cast stops and the rod starts forward. Two o'clock is when the forward motion stops and you either bring the rod back for another cast or let the rod tip drop as you finish your cast. Now you try it."

Fly fishing, like snowboarding, looks much easier than it is. With snowboarding, you usually just end up on your ass, feeling stupid. With fly fishing, you just *feel like* you've landed on your ass. Initially, Ellen looked and felt somewhat like Jason Foxworthy—silly and totally uncoordinated. Line was everywhere.

Jason laughed at her lack of coordination. "See? See? It's not easy, is it?" he shouted out, thrilled that Ellen had validated the difficulty of the skill. Daniel Boone now felt exonerated from his own ineptitude. *I knew she couldn't do it,* he thought to himself. At one point, Ellen just shook her head as she wore both line and fly. "At least, I caught something...me," she said with her usual good humor. O'Casey couldn't help noticing her green eyes sparkling in the noonday sun and the magical confusion of her curly chestnut brown hair. He also couldn't help noticing her small but well formed breasts outlined by her braless North Face T-shirt.

"Wow!" O'Casey exclaimed amid a tangle of fly line that now circled his head and arms as he waded in next to Ellen. "You've got me hooked," he said with a wink and a grin. Ellen returned the smile, thoroughly pleased with the metaphor. "Here, try this. You're wrist is too loose and you're casting at three and six. Watch!" O'Casey made one quick demonstration cast. He then slid in right next to Ellen, the way he had when he tried teaching his young son to cast the summer before he died. Only this time, he didn't have to get on his knees and help his little guy hold the tiny five-foot fly rod he had custom built for Matthew as a birthday present. For just a moment, O'Casey tensed up at the painful thought.

Ellen turned as if on cue. "I need some help."

"Here," Sean responded as he held the rod with her and snuggled in close. Ellen could smell his strong, masculine scent. It made her forget the task at hand. She looked up at his handsome scarred face. She looked past the slight indentation where even the best surgical team had been unable to completely reconstruct his severely fractured skull. She looked past the deep scarring along his hairline where his scalp had been reattached. All she saw were his gray-blond curls. *There is a bit of Robert Redford there*, she thought.

"Hey, pay attention! I don't want to wear that fly," O'Casey chided with a smile as the fly went whizzing past his ear. Slowly at first, instructor and student worked together. What began as an extension of the loons' mating dance quickly turned into more serious business. Ellen began to feel the rhythm. Though she had never been a great athlete, she was quite coordinated and had been a very good dancer. She could feel the ballet-like fluidity and grace that were needed. *It is all about smoothness, timing, and grace*, she thought. Long after she understood O'Casey's directions and even well after the rest of the tribe had taken several glances at the snuggling couple, Ellen reluctantly whispered to O'Casey, "Let me give it a try."

Her first few casts were still pretty sloppy. "Keep your wrist firm and at one with your forearm," O'Casey coached. "That's it. That's it."

Suddenly, Ellen had the feel, the flow, the rhythm. The caddis fly rolled smoothly onto the water ten feet away. Then fifteen. Then eighteen. Ooops, bad cast. Then another fifteen-footer...and then twenties, one after the other. Consistently now, Ellen and the rod were one. She could feel it, and it felt beautiful. And it looked beautiful. It was not Butch. It was not O'Casey. Ellen was making smooth flowing casts, some over twenty feet. Suddenly, the large caddis disappeared as an eager fourteen-inch brookie rose from the depths to slurp in the fly. In that second, Ellen was hooked, just like the fish. As the brookie ran in terror toward the upstream riffles, she could feel the adrenal surge that almost every fisherman remembers on first fooling a fish with a fly. She shrieked with delight like a little kid. The fish jumped and then jumped again.

"What do I do? What do I do?" she yelled as the fish ran first away from her then toward her. Fortunately, the fish was hooked well in the upper lip with the sharp #10 hook and heavier leader. Had this been the #18 nymph and the lighter leader, the fish would long since have been gone. Using the reel at this point would have been useless, since she had so much line out and was wearing much of it.

O'Casey showed her how to strip in the line quickly and play the fish with a stripping rather than a reeling technique. After a mighty, albeit somewhat clumsy, battle, Ellen stood with perhaps the broadest grin of her life. O'Casey hoisted the beautiful raspberry-and-gold-colored female up for her to inspect.

"You've got to kiss it now!" O'Casey announced with an authority that dictated no room for compromise.

"What? You're kidding, right?" Ellen blurted in disbelief.

"Those are the rules," Butch chimed in. "You always have to kiss the first fish you get on a fly...and the first of the season."

"Those are the rules," Sean confirmed.

As Ellen leaned over to kiss the fish, Maria snapped a picture with her little disposable camera. "I sure hope this comes out. It will be worth a million dollars one day when Ellen becomes a world-famous fisherman."

"Do I also get to kiss the fisherman?" Ellen asked with an even bigger grin as she looked at O'Casey. Before he could even think to say no, Ellen kissed him like a schoolgirl stealing a kiss on the playground. O'Casey was speechless.

"Bravo!" Tiffany cheered.

"Bravo!" Maria joined in. "It's about time! You two have been school kids on a field trip all morning, just dying to kiss and hold hands. Give her a kiss, Sean. Give her a kiss!"

In a flash, and still blushing from the attention, O'Casey leaned over and gave Ellen a peck on the cheek. It was confirmed officially now: they were an item. *Might as well take out a front page ad*, the Irishman thought to himself. *If Maria knows, the world will know. She'll be telling the eagles and the rabbits any minute.*

And then for a second there was marvelous stillness. Ellen and O'Casey exchanged the kind of smiles that a bride and groom might share after their first wedding kiss. It was official.

The rising water licked slowly at their feet and the noon sun announced to everyone that the moment of romance was over. It was hot. Damn hot.

Summer Time, and the Livin'...

"Who wants a cold be'ah?" Butch asked rhetorically, making sure his best Maine accent rolled smoothly from his lips. The beer wasn't exactly cold anymore, as the last of the ice was already gone and the last of the cold-pack chill was almost gone as well. Butch knew they had brought more beer than he ever wanted to see on a trip like this. Most of that came at Jason's insistence and most of it had already passed through his kidneys. Still, right now there was enough cool beer left that Butch wanted to dispose of, and he thought now was just the time to do so. It would be easy to sell beer of almost any temperature on a day like today. It was almost ninety degrees, most unusual in Maine for mid-June. The usual joke was that Maine had two seasons—winter and August. In fact, Maine had just one type of weather—unpredictable. Hot summer weather was relative. For some Mainers, anything over seventy was hot; and cold was defined as anything under twenty...below zero.

The sandwiches the women had made tasted great. The beer tasted even better. Fifty-degree beer might taste warm on a cool fall day, but today, it tasted heavenly. Once again, Butch had read their minds, especially Jason's. Beer was the ultimate elixir. On this day, everyone seemed to enjoy the beer. Butch had brought the last two six packs, mostly because he was tired of having its weight in the canoe and figured he'd be exchanging beer for the fish he hoped would replace it as important cargo. The tribe had eaten very well both on the first day of a trip and on the second, thanks in large part to the gifts from the buzz-off gods. They had hit the jackpot on this trip and still had some apples, potatoes, flour, and wine left from the buzz-off box.

Jason was well into his second beer when Butch gave him the word: everyone got two beers, no more, no less. The implication clearly was that Jason was not to beg beers from the women, a skill which he had carefully honed. Once the beer rules were established, the women, in particular, seemed to get the point that they were not only to *not* to share their grog, but also, they were expected to finish their own allocation as well. As the beer went down, the level of silliness went up. For the women, it did not take much. O'Casey and Ellen were the first targets. Ellen leaned next to O'Casey and gave his hand a squeeze.

"No smoochy-moochy, now," Jason chided.

Normally, everyone else might have found that obnoxious. Today, they found it hilarious. And so it went. The beer went down and the hilarity went up, especially among the women as they finished their allotment—which rendered all three just a bit in the bag.

"Who's for a swim?" Butch said out of the blue. "This is the best place on the whole river. It's where the current is the slowest and the water the deepest. It will be warm in the shallows and freezing about three feet down. Let's go!"

Butch jumped up from their sandbar lunch perch and dove in. Jason was fast behind him, and O'Casey was on his heels. The women were speechless. The men were in the river splashing and laughing. It was easy for them; they had only been wearing their shorts, so it took no effort for them to be up to their eyeballs in the cool, enticing water.

"Let's just go in our underwear," Maria said with the eagerness of a hippie at Woodstock. In another moment, the usually self-conscious Maria was down to her bra and panties. For Maria, it would never have been a privacy issue. As the only girl with five brothers, she had seen more male anatomy than some drill sergeants—and similar language, too. But as a woman who had thought of herself as *fat* for most of her life, sharing her near-naked body with five strangers would have been unthinkable just a few days ago. However, after all that had transpired, she looked at herself and her friends in an entirely different light. They were her brothers and sisters. She felt no shame or embarrassment. Having consumed two beers in ten minutes didn't hurt her sense of confidence, either. On a beerless afternoon, she would have still been watching the boys.

That being said, the others, both on the sandbar and in the water, were almost in shock at what stood before them. Maria had the largest breasts any of them had ever seen, and then some. Standing on the edge of the water getting ready to make the plunge, Maria exuded more than a sense of confidence. She was Amazon Woman, or, more appropriately, Earth Mother. Although no one was about to change her title from Superwoman to any other moniker, it was impossible for the rest of the tribe not to notice. Size matters.

Tiffany knew within seconds of Maria's decision that she, too, would be in the water. It was her second home. Though she was exceptionally modest in almost any other environment, the waterfront had a separate set of rules for her. She recalled that she was wearing a matched set of Victoria's Secret Ladies First midnight blue underwear that was perhaps less revealing than the bikini she had been swimming in the other day. Before Maria had waded in up to her knees, the splash beside her was a fluid and graceful Tiffany gliding through the water. A long ten seconds later, her head popped up from the far side of the stream. The trout had found their match in her underwater strength and speed.

Only Ellen remained on shore. "I just ate," she called out. "My mother always said that I should wait a half hour after lunch before swimming."

"How old are you?" Jason scoffed.

Ellen immediately blushed at the pathetic excuse. It was, as she would occasionally describe it later, "a palm-to-the-forehead, dumb-blonde move for a brunette who could create a stereotype all by herself."

"Come on, sister, we'll do it together," Maria smiled and held out her hand. Ellen was not about to remove her shirt as everyone else had. Without a bra, everyone could see her nipples already, and she was uncomfortable with that. This was the first day she had *ever* walked around without a bra. Unlike Maria, she had never seen her older brothers naked, and they had certainly never seen her. At least, not since she was a little girl. Reluctantly, she peeled off her walking shorts, though her shirt stayed on. Then, very slowly, she reached for Maria's extended hand. One minute the two women were dry, and the next minute they were wet—thoroughly, joyfully soaked.

The water fight that ensued was nothing short of spectacular. In seconds, six former strangers were splashing like eight-year-old best friends at a pool party. First, it was the boys against the girls, as one might expect of three very macho guys. Then it was everyone against the

Chief, then everyone against O'Casey, then everyone against everyone. There was a magic, childlike abandon that filled the very edges of the big pool and reverberated in the canyon. Even Jason, whose ability to transcend his own self-serving needs was virtually nonexistent, shared in the silliness. Because the water had risen on one side of the big pool to an area of clay and bog-like soil, it became very slippery. Once, as Jason ran to dive in, he slipped and fell on his butt. The tribe howled with laughter. Then O'Casey ran over and slid as though on an icy patch of the recess playground in midwinter. He slid the entire length of the clay area and into the water. Again and again the silliness was repeated, as every member of the group had to try the clay slide.

Suddenly, their attention turned to Butch, who was standing fifteen feet up on a ledge. "Are you really a member of the tribe?" he said, in a taunting voice reminiscent of a schoolyard truth-or-dare challenge. Then he yelled "Geronimo!" with the exuberance of the best cannonball specialist. A huge tower of water splashed up in the air and then down on the tribe. Within seconds, Jason was at the ledge and then O'Casey. "Geronimo! Geronimo!" went one and then the other. Butch high-fived them both as he waited on the edge of the eddy. The gauntlet had been thrown!

Although Tiffany had never been crazy about heights, she had been a superb three-meter low-board diver. She had already handled so many challenges on this trip that she was not about to stop. Slowly, she climbed up to the ledge. Fifteen feet seemed much, much higher than the three-meter board she had climbed onto so many times. *I can do it. I can do it*, she told herself. *Same dive; different day. Focus. Focus.* Then she bent her legs and pushed off with the elegance and grace of an Olympian. *Tuck your chin. Hands up. Point your toes. Now reach for the water. Reach!* Tiffany remembered it all. As she tumbled almost effortlessly in the steamy noon air, the others felt like they were watching the Olympic trials. Tiffany had completed a perfect one-and-a-half with a twist—her favorite dive. While she had literally done that dive a thousand times, it never seemed to have more meaning and...for the first time ever, it was fun.

"The Russian judge gives you a freakin' forty-seven on a ten-point scale! You da man! You da man!" Jason screamed as Tiffany's head came to the surface after the dive.

"Unbelievable! You are something!" O'Casey cheered. "That's about the most amazing thing I've ever seen."

While Ellen was lost for words at her friend's remarkable dive, she was almost hurt by O'Casey's enthusiastic praise. "Great job," Ellen said, in words that seemed to lack her normal level of enthusiasm and support.

"You are not only *in* the tribe, you are both Sacagawea and Pocahontas. Amazing," Butch smiled.

"That was really stupid on my part, Butch. I should have asked you before I dove just how deep it was. There's a big difference between a cannonball and a one-and-a-half. I only thought about that as my head broke the water. Not smart."

"Darlin'," Butch said affably. "I knew you were going to dive. It was obvious. I wouldn't have let you flex your muscles if I didn't think there was at least fifteen feet of clear water below you. Great job!"

"Well, sister, I don't know about you, but I can't dive like that," Maria said to Ellen, "but let's *jump* together!"

They were an odd pair in several ways. Maria was short and wide. Ellen was tall and thin. Maria's size 40D-cup bra, soggy to the point of barely holding her in, was creating shade for her feet. Ellen, with a 34AA, had her small, delicate breasts tightly sculpted by the wet T-shirt clinging to her body.

As she climbed the narrow path to the ledge, she quickly forgot just how revealing her T-shirt and wet bikini panties really were. *Maria is such a good friend*, Ellen thought as she gingerly walked up the granite trail to the ledge. She barely noticed the burning hot sharpness of the coarse granite under her feet. All she saw was the increasing distance between herself and the water. "Holy shit," she whispered with uncharacteristic frankness to Maria. She almost never swore, yet she had already used the F-word once that day and could feel another one about to erupt. "This is…it's…it's…fuckin' lunacy. I can't do it." She could feel a deep-seated fear begin to take over. She was very uncomfortable about the height and equally uncomfortable about her attire, or rather, the lack of it. She knew that top and bottom were in various stages of revelation.

"Come on, sister," Maria urged. "If there's one thing I've learned on this trip, it's that we can do *anything*. I'm Superwoman and so are you. If you think you are, you are! Give me your hand," she ordered, just as Ellen was getting ready to quit and head back down the trail. "We're doing this together. Me and you, sister. Me and you."

O'Casey was just about to tell Ellen that she didn't have to jump; he'd still love her. Then he bit his tongue. He didn't want to embarrass her, and though he felt it, he wasn't quite ready to share the L-word either in public or in private. Maybe he never would be.

"Geronimo! Geronimo!" the women shouted to one another. Maria almost launched Ellen off the ledge as she jumped a split second early. It's a good thing Ellen had decided to jump because, as Maria knew, she'd be going anyway. Still, she was proud to have jumped and not just been pulled off. She almost got another "Geronimo!" off before she had hit the water. Even though the height was terrifying, the actual jump was exhilarating.

Suddenly, Ellen had another problem. As she hit the water, her T-shirt filled with air, and because her arms were over her head, it came part way off. Coming to the surface, she was more concerned about getting it away from her face so that she could breathe. She surfaced and stood up both in triumph and in terror. She was half undressed. One breast was completely exposed as she had one arm in her T-shirt and one out.

However, not even O'Casey was looking at Ellen. As Maria came to the surface in triumph, her bra was *completely* gone. It had almost exploded upon impact with the water. Like Ellen, she had gone into the water with her hands above her head rather than down by her sides. It was not until she stood up in triumph and shouted the tribe's standard victory cheer, "Yee-hah!' that Maria realized she was completely naked from the waist up. It was almost as though she were at a women's liberation bra-burning in the sixties, cheering at her freedom from the constraints of the bra industry.

"Hey, guys, I need some help," Maria said with remarkable aplomb and her characteristic grin. "Can you help me find my holster?"

She didn't even try to hide her nakedness. She just stood there, scanning the pool, looking for anything large, white, and still floating. Ellen was so amazed and startled by what she saw that she forgot her own dishevelment—one arm in, one arm out, one breast exposed and one covered. For almost five minutes everyone searched for Maria's bra. Even Ellen scanned the water for thirty seconds before realizing her own situation.

And then something happened that none of the tribe would ever have predicted. Butch shouted with a huge grin, "Bathing suits are now *optional!*"

No one ever asked if he did this to support Maria's state of undress or because it was just part of the growing laissez faire spirit of the moment. Whatever the reason, it worked...sort of. The men immediately dropped their drawers right where they were. Even O'Casey, who could be modest about many things and enjoyed his personal space and privacy, quickly dropped his shorts and underpants. Maria, forever the good sport, was already half undressed and already had a massive wedgie from her jump. Her panties did little to hide a very large derriere. Apparently, it just seemed natural and plain fun for Maria to follow the chief's directive as well. Off came the undies. Maria stood naked, wearing only her inimitable smile from ear to ear.

Once again, Ellen found herself the last of two, with just a single sister helping her decide what to do. She had been the last to want to jump off the cliff. Only Maria's prompting kept her from being the odd person out. She looked at O'Casey, standing naked in the sun. He looked natural and wonderful in his nakedness—sexy yes, she thought, but just wonderful. "Come on, sister. I'm not doing this by myself," Ellen said to Tiffany. She had realized that the wet T-shirt was giving her almost no privacy anyway. *And just maybe,* she rationalized, *maybe when O'Casey gets a glimpse, he'll want to see it again.* She knew that was almost entrapment, but she really cared about Sean and wanted him in every respect. Once she made up her mind, the T-shirt was gone. The panties were a much more difficult decision, but soon they were gone, too. She couldn't believe what she had just done. She had never been skinny-dipping in her life. Nor could she have imagined it. Yet, there she was, standing naked in front of a group of people who a few days ago were just strangers. She felt the warm breeze caress her body ever so slightly and felt, more than anything else, very, very alive.

For a moment, Tiffany looked at the rest of the tribe, naked as babes. She had rarely seen other women naked, let alone a group of men. Even though she was a swimmer, most of the locker rooms where she swam had private dressing rooms. Even in college, most women did not remain undressed for more than a second or two as they quickly put on a towel or hopped from the shower to a bathrobe. Now, her best friends were totally naked waiting there for her to disrobe and join them.

It was Maria who started the cheer, like a college student during a drinking contest. "Tiff-a-ny! Tiff-a-ny! Tiff-a-ny! Tiff-a-ny!" They didn't want her to chug a beer. They wanted her to remove her bra and panties. This was crazy. She couldn't. She just couldn't, she thought.

And then she thought about her first day on the trip, when she'd rescued an otherwise drowned Jason. She had then stood trembling, exhausted, and cold as Maria and Ellen had stripped off her wet clothing, combed her hair, and dressed her. She had stood completely naked just inches from two relative strangers for perhaps five minutes. The guys had probably seen the whole thing. She knew that Angelo had. Yet she remembered Angelo's kind and supportive eyes. There was no shame that day. She had felt nurtured and cared for by these very same people.

What would my mother think? Tiffany reflected, as she always did when she had to make big decisions. That one thought then changed *everything*...and forever. "Screw it. She's not my boss anymore," Tiffany muttered under her breath. Her mother was no longer going to determine what she did and didn't do. *What the hell*, she thought. *Look at what's already happened to me.* After being attacked by an angry bear, what was a little nudity by comparison? She smiled to herself and then just did it. Quickly, she unsnapped her bra. Then she dropped her panties as though teasing a lover. It was almost like a gift she was giving freely, if somewhat shyly.

"Tiff-a-ny! Tiff-a-ny! Tiff-a-ny !" they cheered again. She was now officially one of them.

This crazy, lunatic bunch of friends then cheered her on as she made a naked plunge from the "big jump." What a great feeling! She had never felt so totally free in her life. *If my mother could only see me now!* Tiffany said to herself. She'd go out of her mind. *Good*, she thought. Her mother would never control her life again. This was how it should be. This was how it should feel. She could feel the warm breeze running across her body. Her nipples stood erect—not from anything erotic, although it was, just a bit. Rather, it was simply a tremendous adrenaline rush and a sense of total freedom that made her feel completely alive for the first time in her life.

She then looked over at Maria, who was howling with laughter. First one, then another of the men slid bare-bottomed across the clay slide they'd created and into the water. Tiffany just loved Maria, the most atypical friend she could ever have—a chubby, Latino Texas Catholic with size forty breasts, standing naked as a jaybird, hooting at equally naked men. Her mother would die from a heart attack. Tiffany smiled as she reveled in an unfettered freedom and joy she had not known in years. "What a day! What a nutty freakin' day!" she whispered to herself.

SORRY! EDEN IS NOW CLOSED

The tribe entertained themselves with various levels of swimming, splashing, and sliding. Aside from the occasional glimpses that all of them had made, the nudity quickly became a non-issue. For a brief period, the men were complete and utter juveniles. The more their slide area got wet, the slipperier it got. The more slippery it got, the more tricks they could do. The men filled empty beer cans with water to groom their slide to a perfect consistency. They were seventh graders all over again. O'Casey could slide for almost ten yards down the bank as though on a skateboard. At the last moment, he would do a flip and land feet first in the water. The women, all sitting nude and relaxed in the sun, cheered wildly for what were now young teenage boys showing off.

Butch was never one to be outdone, particularly when it involved an audience of nude women appreciative of almost any talent, however veiled it was. He stood at the top of the slide for a moment, calculating his next move. He had toyed with a handstand slide. While he was easily capable of the handstand, he figured he would quickly flip over and land with an unattractive flop on his back. That would garner minus five points from the Russian judge. He needed more water. O'Casey and Daniel Boone helped him groom the slide until it was just right.

Butch paced backward like a pole-vaulter, planning his every step. Suddenly, he dashed forward and leaped in the air, stomach toward the slide. The men gasped at the imminent impact and the pain that would ensue. At the last moment, Butch put his hands over his crotch, protecting the very significant anatomy that had already been the subject of the women's attention and secret giggles. Even Ellen, who was quite pleased with O'Casey's compelling endowment, couldn't help stealing glances at Butch. Remarkably, he protected himself perfectly, and slid the entire length of the slide with his arms tucked in the way a penguin might slide down an ice flow. He slid smoothly into the water and came to the surface pumping his fist like a diver who had just nailed his most difficult dive.

Spontaneously, the women jumped to their feet to cheer. Naked women jumping up and down. The men all but had to pinch themselves at their good fortune. *I am not worthy, I am not worthy,* Butch thought to himself at the sight. He considered bowing to the girls, but realized it would make them self-conscious of their nudity. That was the last thing any of the men would want to have happen, since they were all so very appreciative of the dress code. This was as much a first for them as it was for the women, and they were all struggling to keep their bodies from *showing* their appreciation.

Jason, however, began to lose that battle. His growing state of arousal at the sight of Tiffany's perfect body reflected more than his self-control could stand. He quickly dove back into the water to hide his growing enthusiasm. As he stood waist deep, waiting for the cold water to temper his male response to the nudity, he began to plan his next slide maneuver. Even more than the Chief, Jason Foxworthy could not stand to be shown up by anyone. He figured out what he wanted to do, then worked the slide to a level of what he hoped was sheer sliding perfection.

Jason was actually a fine, albeit out of shape, athlete. After several mental rehearsals, he rocked back and forth several times and then charged forward. Down toward the slide of slippery clay he ran, faster and faster. Then he jumped butt down and landed on the slope with an audible thud that was hardly attractive. Still, his forward motion was perfect. He zipped down the muddy slide as water splashed in every direction. He then turned his torso and slid backward toward the water. His arms were up and his fists were ready to pump in triumph. He grinned with the mental fantasy of a man about to get a forty-seven from the Russian judge and an enthusiastic hug from a wildly enthusiastic, naked cheerleader—Tiffany. He was just about to leave the muddy ledge and hit the water when his path altered slightly and sent him toward a small jagged rock on the edge of the slide.

He let out a howl of pain just as he hit the water. Rather than leaping out in triumph, a distraught and highly pained face broke the surface. "I just ripped my ass open!" Jason stammered, wincing as he tried to catch his breath. He turned to look as he waded toward the sandbar. As he did, the entire group could see a red, bleeding raspberry of abraded skin running the entire length of his right buttocks. "That freakin' kills," he wailed. "Butch! Butch! Where's your first aid kit?"

Everyone crowded around Jason to inspect the nasty-looking scrape. Silently, each was glad that it was not their butt suffering the indignity of being studied and repaired by the Chief.

All great ideas have their own shelf life. There is a tipping point that takes the kernel of an idea and moves it toward an almost universal action. Such action is also mitigated by circumstance and, occasionally, by perfect timing. By themselves, the factors of hot weather, cold beer, and tempting water would not have been enough to have caused this afternoon's actions. However, the combination of a lost bra and the Chief's "bathing suits optional" announcement became the tipping point factors that led otherwise straight-laced people to become temporary nudists.

Jason's road-rash fiasco just as quickly ended the tribe's brief entry into Eden. In the Book of Genesis, Adam and Eve noticed their nakedness within moments of being exiled from the Garden of Eden. Jason had single handedly just gotten them all kicked out. Their two-hour tour had ended. The bus was leaving. Tiffany was the first to notice that the magic that had prompted her to willfully, almost joyfully, remove her clothing was now completely gone. The innocence of the moment was gone. The silliness was gone. The levity and laissez faire attitude had vanished and would never come back. What had, for a brief period, been one of the most carefree and liberating events in her life, was now over.

Jason was kneeling on one knee as Butch dutifully put his first aid hat on and tried to clean up the shallow but very long raspberry and the golf ball-sized hematoma that now adorned his rear end. Tiffany and Ellen were commiserating quietly over Jason's plight when Tiffany realized that she was standing only four feet away as Jason knelt staring, eye level, at her crotch. Even though she had felt some attraction to Jason, his actions now made her skin crawl. This was no longer a magical moment with friends playing on a sunny day. She was a naked and vulnerable woman being ogled sexually by a man she barely knew and felt she might soon come to despise.

First Tiffany and then, somewhat reticently, Ellen sneaked off to the hastily thrown pile of clothing and dressed. While Ellen, too, began to feel vulnerable, she had thoroughly enjoyed the strange freedom she had felt being naked, particularly so close to an equally naked O'Casey. Now, as she dressed, she felt as though she was leaving a magical land she could never return to again. The sign could have read *Eden now closed. Thank you for coming.*

Suddenly, she heard what sounded like distant thunder...or an explosion. "Butch, what was that?"

As Butch listened, he could hear three more distant but distinct echoes rumble through the low valley.

"Sounds like thunder," Jason speculated from his indelicate position on his knees.

"Shit!" said Butch. "They're gunshots! Angelo's in trouble."

For a brief moment, as the Chief got ready to run for camp, he forgot that he was still naked. While this would not have stopped Butch in the least, he could certainly not run to help Angelo without his hiking boots for the rough terrain. As he hastily pulled on just his shorts and hurriedly grabbed his first aid kit, he turned to O'Casey, "You're in charge. Fill up the canteens at the double spring and meet me back at camp as soon as you can. 'Houston, we've got a problem.'"

"Hey, Chief, what about my ass? You've got the first aid kit," Jason shouted as Butch turned toward the trail. Butch shook his head in disgust and disbelief, quickly tossed a bandage to O'Casey, and dashed back up the trail toward camp.

Even though he was in reasonably good shape, Butch was amazed by how out of breath he got as he ran back toward camp. There's a big difference between needing short bursts of strength to traverse a section of white water and running almost a mile along a rocky trail that seemed to go almost straight up, though it was really just a steady incline. Several times he had to stop to catch his breath. The hot, steamy trail felt more like the Brazilian rainforest than the fir- and cedar-lined path that had always been his friend. Oxygen seemed like a lost element as Butch struggled for breath and could feel age and weight he had barely noticed before taking a toll on the speed of his mission.

Finally, he caught sight of Angelo on the far side of the camp, in a kneeling position. *Good,* he thought. *Angelo's safe.* He had feared that the sow bear had returned to what she thought was an empty camp and had surprised and perhaps attacked Angelo. As the Chief ran the last hundred yards, he kept yelling, "You OK? You OK, buddy?" Angelo looked up from his kneeling position. His appearance told Butch more than he wanted to know. Angelo was pale, almost a gray-white. The Chief had never seen anyone look so ill. While he had seen dead people at wakes and funerals, he had never seen a dead man, gray and lifeless, staring back at him. That was precisely how Angelo looked. Butch took his handkerchief out and wiped the corners of Angelo's mouth, which still dripped with pale green vomit. His shirt and jeans were all but awash in the same repulsive slime.

"Let's get you cleaned up, buddy," the Chief said gently as he tried to get Angelo to his feet.

"I'm OK, Butch, Angelo gasped. "Just give me a minute to catch my breath. I just threw up again. I can't seem to stop."

"Yeah, I could use a breather, too," Butch responded sympathetically. His chest was still heaving from the forced run. As he struggled to get his breathing under control, he scanned the campground. Nothing seemed amiss. No bears. No tipped-over coolers or torn tents. "What happened, Angelo? I heard the gunshots, and I knew you were in trouble. I heard four shots. I told you to fire three if you were in trouble and figured when I heard the fourth that the bear had returned with a vengeance."

"I'd rather be mauled by a bear than feel the way I feel right now. At least the bear would put me out of my misery. I feel like I'm going to die."

"I won't let that happen. I promise. Honest Injun," Butch said with a forced smile as he crossed his heart like a kid. "So what the hell happened to you?"

"I think I screwed up big-time. I think I got into some bad water."

"What do you mean? You had a great big bottle of water. That was good water, the same water that we all drank. It came from 'bubble up,' the mineral spring we used the other day."

"That's not the water I drank. My hand was really killing me, so I decided to take some more aspirin. I put the big water bottle down when I went to my pack to get the aspirin. I must have knocked the freakin' thing over. When I came back, the last of the good water was running down the hill. I really wanted and needed some water, Butch. It was awfully hot here. My hand was killing me. The fire was out and I couldn't find any matches to try to boil water. So I decided to go looking for some safe water to drink. I figured with all the runoff I shouldn't use the river water. I found a small stream running into the river about a quarter of a mile from here. Butch, it looked like clean water. It really did. I thought that I would be OK. It was very clean-looking water, really. But about a half hour after I drank it, I started to feel sick. It just seemed to run right through me. I started to shit my brains out."

Angelo caught himself and apologized. "Sorry, Butch. As you know, I don't usually talk like that, but that's how it felt. Then everything headed in the other direction. I stopped going to the bathroom and started throwing up. About a half hour ago, I thought I was going to pass out. That's when I used the pistol to dial 911."

Butch had to laugh. Four gunshots was not exactly a phone call, but he was glad that his emergency plan had worked. He knew his friend was in serious trouble. At least he was here now and could help. Slowly the Chief guided Angelo away from the vomit and closer to the tent..

"Butch, this is stuff you don't want to touch. This is stuff nobody can touch. Universal precautions, Butch, remember?"

"Screw the universal precautions. You're sick. I don't give a shit about a little vomit on your shirt. You're my best friend, Angelo. You and O'Casey are like family to me. If I had children or if I were still married, I'd do it for my kid or my wife. I'd certainly do it for you."

"You can't, Butch. You can't. Please, Butch, please!"

"Let's get this shirt off, buddy," Butch said, ignoring Angelo's protests.

"Stop, Butch! Stop!" Angelo said, almost shouting. "You can't touch this stuff. It's contaminated!'

"A little barf doesn't scare me," Butch replied as he tried to unbutton the sleeve of Angelo's vomit-laden shirt.

"Butch, stop!"

There was a long, painfully silent pause. Butch could hear himself still breathing heavily. As the wind shifted and his adrenaline level settled down, he moved from a fight-or-flight reaction to a more methodical triage mode. He was suddenly aware of the overpowering, nausea-inducing smell of vomit, and noticed that it almost covered his friend—his shoes, his pants, his shirt, and even his hair. This beautiful man who sang Verdi and Puccini with such delicacy that even Butch was moved to tears was now crying himself. Big tears rolled down his pallid face, slowly at first and then almost in torrents. For several minutes, Angelo just cried.

"Butch...Bu-Butch," Angelo struggled through quiet sobs, "I have AIDS! I've been HIV positive for several years. That's why I always insisted on your using universal precautions on my hand. That's why I never drank from the wine bottle when it was passed around. I've been so-o-o careful not to let anyone know...about *anything, ever.*" He stopped, took a breath, and looked up at his friend. "Butch, I'm gay...and I think I'm dying."

The two men stood quietly together for several minutes. Angelo continued to sob slowly, wiping his eyes occasionally with the sleeve that was not speckled with vomit. He also shook with a tiny tremor. Butch could not tell whether it had been induced by his tearful breakdown or by the chills that had accompanied the vomiting.

The Chief could still hear his own breathing, which had almost returned to normal. He took a few slow, deep breaths, purposely inhaling through his nose and exhaling through his mouth. O'Casey had taught him this technique as a way for him to deal with angry parents or students, as Butch had a tendency to respond with the same voice tone that had been delivered. O'Casey had admonished him once, "We always need to be the professionals. The more others lose it, the more we need to stay in control."

Again, Butch practiced his best deep breathing as he reflected on what he wanted to and needed to say to Angelo.

"First of all, Angelo, I don't care if you're gay. I always assumed that you were. That has no more impact on me than Maria's being chunky... or that she has the biggest, bounciest naked boobs I've ever seen." Butch was trying to inject some levity, and then realized that Angelo had not been there to see Maria's bra explode. When Angelo looked puzzled, the Chief corrected himself. "I'll explain the boob thing later. Just follow me here. I love Maria for being who she is. I don't care that she's short, heavy, a bit homely, and grew up in the barrios of West Texas. I don't care that O'Casey sulks on the edge of camp sometimes, drinking Irish whiskey to forget his dead wife. I still love them.

"And most importantly, Angelo, I could give a rat's ass whether you are gay or straight. I don't care if you have HIV or STP. I don't care. I love *you!* You are one of my very best friends. You were the best music teacher I've ever seen. Your students loved you at Welton Academy, and now that you're a principal, it's the same thing. Your students worship you. Your colleagues respect you. The parents love you. That's not going to change even if you'd just had a 'coming out' party."

Angelo almost laughed through his tears. "I'm not a debutante, Butch. It's not a coming out party. The expression is 'coming out of the closet,' Butch…and I guess I just did."

"I don't care if you come out of the closet, or come out of the teachers' room. I will defend you and your job to the death. I have before and I'd do it again. You are one of the best educators I've ever met and one of the best friends I have.

"I don't mind taking those universal precautions, now. That's fine, if it will make you feel better. But I'm going to take care of you and get you through this. Let's start by getting you cleaned up."

Butch then put on his latex gloves, stripped Angelo down to his shorts, and showed the same tenderness in caring for him as the women had shown in ministering to Tiffany after her rescue of Jason. Butch hurried to complete his work and bag up Angelo's clothing, knowing that Angelo would be mortified if the others saw him covered in vomit and completely disheveled. Angelo took great pride in his personal grooming and was the only one of the four men who had shaved and washed his hair with lake water each morning.

Butch did a last once-over on Angelo to make sure he was comfortable and clean before the rest of the tribe came back. His main concern then was about Jason Foxworthy's potential reaction to Angelo. The Chief figured that Jason would be moaning all the way down the trail, complaining about his sore ass. *I'll give him a sore ass…and a black freakin' eye, particularly if he ever gives Angelo any shit*, Butch thought to himself. He knew of Jason's contempt for both gay men *and* gay women, and wished he had never allowed Jason to invite himself on the trip.

As Butch thought about Jason wincing and complaining as the tribe trekked back to camp, he took some solace in the fact that Jason, the one and only pain in the ass on this otherwise great trip, now literally *had* a pain in his ass. What poetic justice! It proved once and for all to Butch that God still had a sense of humor.

Little Lamb, Who Made Thee?

As O'Casey packed up the group and followed the Chief's hasty retreat toward camp, for some reason, he could not get William Blake's poem out of his head:

> *Tiger, tiger burning bright*
> *In the forests of the night,*
> *What immortal hand or eye*
> *Could frame thy fearful symmetry?*

It just kept rolling around in his head, which was an odd thing, even for an English teacher. O'Casey mused that he should at least be thinking about Maine black bears rather than William Blake's tigers. "Plenty of bears here, but no tigers," he muttered to himself. Sometimes daydreams just can't be explained. Sometimes night dreams can't be explained, either.

O'Casey had had a terrible dream the night before about Angelo, so awful that he'd squirmed and accidentally woke Ellen, who had snuggled in beside him to enjoy his body warmth in the cool Maine night. Ellen had assumed the worst—that he'd had a nightmare about the accident and the death of his wife and child. Instead, though he could not remember the details, it had been about Angelo's death. He had no idea where the dream had come from or why the poem would not leave his head.

Like Butch, O'Casey was worried about Angelo's hand. He had dreamed that the bear had come back, but this time, for Angelo's hand. *But where did the tiger come into the picture?* O'Casey wondered as he put the tribe in quick-march back to the campsite.

Back at camp Butch quickly realized that Angelo's condition was far more complicated and beyond Butch's basic first aid skill level. Not only was his hand worse than ever, but this water-borne illness, which was probably giardia, put him in a potentially much more serious situation, especially now that he understood more about the state of Angelo's compromised immune system.

Butch was glad when O'Casey arrived at the camp, albeit with Jason in tow. With Angelo settled into his tent and feeling somewhat better, the two leaders reviewed potential first aid and rescue options. O'Casey, who had a strong knowledge of health and medicine, was concerned about Angelo's electrolyte balance and his becoming dehydrated. His first task was to brew some herbal tea, a mixture of peppermint, ginger, and alfalfa that he thought would help. He added some honey for both taste and badly needed glucose. Fortunately, Angelo was able to keep it down and appeared to be resting comfortably.

Butch and O'Casey then formulated their rescue plan. "You and I will need to go for help in the morning," the Chief began. "Angelo is too weak for us to get him out of here. He can barely stand, let alone walk. He certainly can't hold a paddle. I'm afraid that he would literally fall over in the canoe and the water is really too wild not to have someone handling the bow. Even a minimal bow stroke is still a necessity in this kind of water. I'm pretty good, but I don't think I could get us through the big rapids by myself. You and I can make it down the last part of the river in two hours, and then we've got a three-hour canoe ride. If we leave just before daybreak, we can be at the Granite Lake landing by noon—maybe earlier, if we can flag down a boat. We could have a hospital chopper dropping a basket on the beach here to pick up Angelo by midafternoon, four o'clock at the latest."

"Don't you want me here, holding the fort and taking care of Angelo?" O'Casey asked. "You could have Tiffany run bow for you. Jason is freakin' useless, but Tiffany could do it."

"I thought about that, Paddy, but we're going to be facing some *brutal* water—probably class three and four and maybe some fives thrown in if we miss a portage. Have you noticed how high the water is right now? They must have all the gates open back at the dam. It's still rising. In two days, even this beach will be underwater. There would be no place to drop a basket then. The beach at Big Pool was disappearing right before our eyes, and this beach is twice its size. We'll be hitting some nasty water; we just can't afford to dump. We're Angelo's only hope, I'm afraid. If we lose the canoe, we'll probably lose Angelo. Also, we're going to have to portage the big falls. My understanding is that that portage is nasty—very steep. I'm just not sure if Tiffany could help me pull the canoe up and over the ridge. Even if she could, we'd then have a very tough paddle the length of Granite Lake. That's twelve to fifteen miles depending on our route, but if it's into an east wind, it will feel like forty. Sean, I need you…and what's more, Angelo will need you helping me. You can't do much to help Angelo here. The ladies can feed him your magic elixir, which does seem to be helping, by the way. How does that sound?"

"Sounds like a plan, Chief." O'Casey smiled, and then stuck out his hand. Butch reciprocated. The strange, almost formal handshake was O'Casey's way of saying, "We're going to do this. It will be hard and dangerous, but we're going to get it done. We have to if we're going to save Angelo's life."

There was much to do and to plan if all this was going to happen. Even though it was late afternoon, the Chief inspected everything, planning what he wanted to take and what he didn't. He was glad they had brought a good bit of rope to help with the portages. He took a third of the rope and lashed it to the canoe. He was also glad that he, like O'Casey, had brought his best high-neck life jackets. Since they would be doing some class three or four rapids at least as bad as the Cut, he would want his best equipment. They had all seen the consequences of poor equipment. Jason's ancient, hand-me-down lifejacket had almost cost him his life—so much for nostalgia.

While the Chief prepared the canoe and got things ready for supper, O'Casey's thoughts turned to Angelo, who was still sleeping. Even though it was still dreadfully hot, O'Casey could tell from the gray and white mares' tails in the upper atmosphere that the weather would soon be changing for the worse. He had long ago learned that when warm and cold fronts collided, particularly in this part of Maine, both the ocean and the mountains could have a significant impact on those fronts and the resulting weather. The June heat often created late-afternoon thunderstorms in the mountain areas near where they were. It was obvious from the rapidly rising water that the upper valley above the dam must have experienced severe thunderstorms the night before. Bangor Hydro apparently had the dam gates nearly wide open now. While the tribe had heard and seen the storms to the north, they had received only one period of heavy rain last night. The distant rumbles of thunder told O'Casey that all that was about to change.

Like all successful principals, O'Casey was good at seeing potential problems and thinking through creative solutions. The Chief had told him about Angelo's severe vomiting and diarrhea. Sean could imagine poor Angelo sitting in the imminent rain, shivering and trying to deal with his illness in the primitive facilities of the camp. While the Chief worked on dinner plans and the rest of the tribe enjoyed the late-afternoon sun, O'Casey created a new version of the Half-Moon Hilton, this time with Angelo in mind so that he could have both privacy and protection from the rain.

With his folding saw, he cut down some tall streamside alders, the forest equivalent of a weed he didn't mind thinning out. He used his cruising axe to trim the poles and fashion them into a teepee-like frame to support a large blue plastic tarp they had found by the buzz-off box. Then he lashed two extra canoe paddles onto a frame made from three-foot alder stakes he'd driven into the ground with a rock. He then dug a small slit trench with the collapsible WWII trenching shovel he had from his early Boy Scout days and always took on camping trips. In less than an hour, he had constructed not only a crude but effective raised toilet seat, but also a somewhat weather resistant shelter to help keep Angelo dry. The tribe quickly dubbed O'Casey's primitive bathroom the New Blue Hilton.

For the first time since they'd started the trip, Butch did not announce dinner with the normal fanfare, nor were there the usual fancy appetizers. However, dinner was still exceptional. Since Butch knew that they would be ending the trip early, and since the cook would be leaving on the rescue mission in the morning, it served no purpose to stretch out the perishable goods. So Butch served brook trout almandine with fried potatoes, onions, and bacon. The vegetable was sautéed fiddleheads, a small fern-like bank side green that, to the uneducated tongue, tasted quite similar to Swiss chard or kale.

Butch knew this would be their last fun night together, and he wanted to keep it as light as possible. Though he was not in the mood to do his foolish British or Italian accents, he wanted the meal to be as positive and enjoyable as possible. Luckily, there were still two bottles of chardonnay left, courtesy of the buzz-off box, and that certainly would help.

However, the dinner conversation became far more subdued than at any other meal they'd shared. Everyone knew about Angelo—at least that he was sick and trying to get some sleep. At one point, Angelo became very self-conscious about the obvious sotto voce chit-chat in the campsite and called out to the tribe, "Hey, guys, I'm just resting. You can talk. I'm not dead yet. This isn't my funeral, you know."

With that, Maria piped in, "Angelo, they'll just have to take a rain check on our rendition of *Carmen*."

From the tent came Angelo's gentle reply as he tried to be his affable self: "You can count on that. Maria, I've never had a better singing partner."

His voice was so different, so weak-sounding that she didn't try to respond again. She and the others didn't want Angelo to speak; they wanted him to save his strength and get some sleep.

The silence at that moment was almost deafening, as each person struggled with the fact of Angelo's declining health and how to break the tension that had descended on the tribe. Tiffany made a remark about the J. Lohr Chardonnay being an excellent match for the fish. Jason made a few of his usual stupid comments. Having already been influenced by three glasses of wine, he asked Butch where he'd found the weeds that were pretending to be vegetables. Because no one even bothered to respond, dinner ended as a nourishing if slightly sad event.

O'Casey checked in on Angelo and found that he was fast asleep, though still looking very gray. Butch then went over the rescue plan with the tribe. Though he did not share Angelo's HIV/AIDS status, he did tell everyone that they needed to use universal precautions when helping him. He explained that Angelo's immune system had been compromised, in part by the infection in his hand and that his situation was quite serious.

"What does that mean, Butch, *compromised*? He doesn't have fuckin' AIDS or anything, does he?" Jason said, then whispered, "I always knew he was a fag."

O'Casey was up in a second, heading straight for Jason. Fortunately, the fireplace separated the two, as well as women on either side of him.

Both Ellen and Tiffany stood up as well. They sensed a fight in the making and wanted to intervene, if only to keep from waking Angelo up. "You watch your mouth, Foxworthy," Sean hissed with a look that surprised even Ellen. Sean's eyes were wild and distant. The women turned to Butch, whose face was even angrier than O'Casey's—uncharacteristically blood red. His dark brown eyes seemed to bulge from his face. The sweat from the evening heat and his newfound rage dripped from his thick, furrowed brow.

Butch said, "If you ever say that again, I'll get my Smith and Wesson and run your sorry ass right out of this camp and into the woods. Then you can take your chances with the freakin' black bear who wanted you for supper. I wish I had saved the bullets and let you keep dancing with that sow last night. It would have served you right."

No one said a word. The three men glared back and forth, none willing to back down. The only question was who would take the first swing, and at whom.

Finally, Tiffany broke the stalemate. She grabbed Jason's arm and pulled him away from the tribe and down to the far end of the campsite. She did so not because she cared about Jason anymore, but rather because, as a well-trained educator, she knew the best way to break up a fight—separate the combatants as quickly as possible. Because both Butch and O'Casey wanted to beat the crap out of Jason Foxworthy, she knew that it was Jason who needed to move away.

Distant thunder interrupted the silence. Jason's stupid comments were soon lost in the campers' concern about the impending storm. First one and then another flash of lightning stretched the length of the near horizon. The booms were immediate. Another flash. Butch counted, "One thousand one. One thousand two. One thousand—" Boom! Boom! "Whew! It's close. Super close! Maybe only a half mile away. We're going to get soaked. Let's batten down everything. *Now!* If you want it dry, put it in your tent. It's going to be a wet night and a long day tomorrow for everyone," Butch warned. "Hurry!"

Within minutes, the rain started. First it was just a few heavy drops—*thunk, thunk, thunk* against the tents. Then the skies opened up. The tribe still had much to do that couldn't wait for the rain, and the camp swung into chaos mode. The Chief barked orders as the heavy winds blew cooking gear about and campers ran to gather up the wet shorts, shirts, and underwear that had adorned the bushes. Butch had been concentrating so much on his rescue plan, he'd failed to hear or see the approaching storm till it was too late. *Another mistake*, he admitted ruefully to himself.

But the tribe functioned as a well-oiled machine on overdrive, running from one directive to another. O'Casey, with Ellen's help, put rocks down to weight the edges of the New Blue Hilton and keep it from blowing away. Tie-downs were reinforced on all the tents. Storm flaps were closed and secured. Even Jason, who had become an instant pariah, saw work to do and did it. At the last minute, Butch remembered to pull the canoes and kayak much further up the sandbar. Had he not done so, the rushing waters from the evening rain would have washed the boats down the river, and with them any hope for Angelo's rescue.

The rain became a steady drumroll on the taught nylon of the tents. There was no time to do the dishes. The fry pan looked as though it were boiling over as the rainwater danced in the greasy bottom of the pan. Remnants of fried trout and potatoes floated in the slick of oil and water and eventually washed off and into the soil below. The fire hissed in protest as the rain spoiled its plans for lighting and heating the evening guests. The dry kai Butch had stacked nearby got saturated and would be useless in the morning to dry out and warm seven shivering bodies.

What might have become an erotic evening for some of the tribe became anything but. The thoroughly drenched semi-couples retired to their respective tents, where the first order of business for everyone was to get dry—or as dry as might be possible. Little did anyone know this would be their last opportunity to be dry or comfortable.

A day earlier, the tent-mates had found various ways to deal with the privacy issues. Tonight it was amazing what several near-death experiences and a day of skinny-dipping had done to their modesty thresholds. O'Casey was one of the last to enter his tent. When he did, Ellen was completely undressed and looking for dry clothing in her knapsack. The rainwater had done little to mitigate O'Casey's anger or his wish to hurt Jason Foxworthy. However, as he knelt at the inside edge of the tent and saw Ellen's delicate, naked features, he froze. "Come in and dry off. You're soaked," Ellen said with the gentle authority of a wife watching her farmer husband coming in from a rainy day in the fields.

With no regard for her own needs, she slid over to Sean and pulled his dripping-wet shirt off. She folded it carefully and put it on top of her own wet clothing in the far corner of the tent. Then, with a skill that had been totally absent the night before, she deftly unbuckled his cargo pants and pulled them off. Finally, she pulled down his boxer shorts.. She was full of love and admiration for this man she had hardly known a week before. Although she wanted to bury her face in his chest and kiss him passionately, she took a moment to study his tired, wet forehead, dirty cheeks, and curly brown hair graying at the temples. She grabbed the towel she had planned to use on her own wet body. Silently and ever so gently, she toweled off first the water from his face and hair, and then moved down to his chest and beyond. Her heart began to pound harder than she could ever remember, and she could feel her small nipples stand out straight and firm.

O'Casey pulled the towel from her hands and threw it in the corner. The rain beat ferociously against the tent and water clanked on the plates and dishes a few feet away. Neither Ellen nor Sean noticed. Through the failing light of dusk they pulled their dripping bodies into each other and kissed, slowly at first and then with the same passion as the pounding summer storm. They dropped from their kneeling position to the soft and warm down sleeping bag below them. "I never thought I could feel this way again," O'Casey smiled. "You look so beautiful right now." As he pulled Ellen toward him he grinned, kissed her softly on the lips, and said, "Thank you!"

Suddenly, from what seemed like right within their tent, O'Casey was rocked to his senses. "Paddy, I need you! I need you *now!*"

WELCOME TO THE HILTON!

O'Casey knew from the sound of the Chief's voice that there was trouble. "I'm so sorry," he said, kissing Ellen on the forehead. He took one brief glance at the beauty and the nakedness he had never before dreamed of exploring. Then he pulled on his still sopping-wet cargo pants and was gone.

The strobe-like flashes of lightning lent a phantasmagorical quality to what had quickly become a grave situation. The ground seemed to tremble in terror. It shivered with the relentless pounding of the summer storm.

O'Casey ran for the New Blue Hilton. It was worse than he could have imagined. Angelo looked like a little old man sitting on a grotesque throne in some Fellini-esque carnival. His pants were at his ankles as he half-sat, half-leaned against the makeshift toilet seat. Gray-brown watery diarrhea poured from his beleaguered body. The pale, almost white knuckles of his left hand seemed glued to the Chief's arm as he tried to steady himself against the onslaught.

Angelo retched again and again. Patiently, Butch held a dented aluminum cooking pot before Angelo's face as he vomited almost constantly. Then dry heave after dry heave. "I'm sorry. I'm so sorry," Angelo whispered hoarsely. The beautiful tenor was now in a ghoulish masquerade, his voice nothing more than dry toast. His eyes were bloodshot and bulging. He stared into an emptiness beyond O'Casey that only he could see. As bizarre as he looked, there was also a profound sadness in his eyes—the sadness of a man who knew what his fate would be, even as his friends tried to alter its course. His hair, now greasy and matted, was a contradiction of the meticulous man who even ironed his underwear and socks.

Green stringy vomit and mucus hung from his chin and littered his sleeves and pants. Butch gently tried to brush it away from Angelo's face with a wet handkerchief. Suddenly, O'Casey noticed the Chief's hands. He was wearing his latex gloves—"universal precautions," as Angelo had so correctly insisted. While it was clearly the appropriate decision from a health standpoint, the opaque white latex seemed, like Angelo's face, a ghoulish charade being perpetrated on an almost saintly, suffering man. *Why do bad things happen to good people?* O'Casey wondered. Maybe that was why he could not get Blake's poem out of his mind. The Little Lamb stood before him, shivering and gray. O'Casey had pondered the contradiction between the Tiger and the Lamb many times. Where was God tonight he thought? He had asked that question far too often in the days following the car accident; he had railed against God more than once as he sought that answer.

"We need your help, Paddy," Butch pleaded, as he sought to get his friend refocused. "We *really* need your help. Can you get Angelo some clean dry clothes, and can you fix the Hilton?"

"It's getting a little drafty and damp," Angelo said with the ghost of a grin as he tried bravely to find some humor in his plight. Water was running down into his face from the top of the teepee and the buffeting wind was finding its way in through the door flap.

O'Casey took a few seconds to size up the needs and tasks. Angelo was soaking wet and shivering uncontrollably. The bandage on his hand was a tattered tail of bloody gauze. It looked like a red and white snake uncoiling slowly and slithering in a mystical dance from Angelo's left hand. The door flap of the Blue Hilton fluttered madly in the storm's fury.

As quickly as he had arrived, O'Casey was gone, scurrying to get what he needed. He dashed back into Ellen's tent and methodically grabbed first one then another item, this time in total ignorance or nonacknowledgment of her exquisite nakedness. "Angelo's dreadfully sick. I've got to run. Bye…Sweetie," O'Casey whispered as he exited the tent.

Although she was terribly sad about Angelo's current situation, Ellen's thoughts kept returning to the rough, handsome man who had just left to help a friend in his time of trial. She whispered the word again and again: "Sweetie. Sweetie." The most wonderful word she thought she had ever heard. Although she'd had many boyfriends, during her forty-two years of life, including several brief "live-ins," she had never had the kind of long-term relationship where anyone ever used a term of endearment like *Sweetie*. Her eyes landed on Sean's favorite fishing shirt in the corner of the tent, still dripping wet from the downpour. She hugged it against her naked breast. It smelled of O'Casey, a strong, masculine smell that Ellen had quickly grown to know and enjoy. She sniffed the shirt again and hugged it. "Bye, Sweetie!" she said to herself. Her heart pounded with the new emotions that she had never expected to find in the dark, foreboding woods of Maine.

From Ellen's tent, O'Casey dashed for Angelo's tent to get more clothes. "Knock, knock," he said before opening the tent flap. As he entered, about it occurred to him how incredibly juvenile that must have sounded, but he didn't want to just barge in on Maria. As he entered, he saw her sitting in the middle of the tent, big tears rolling down her cheeks. *That's odd*, O'Casey noted. *Maria never seems sad*. She routinely had a broad smile on her face, and almost literally a song in her heart. It was impossible not to like her. She could have been a poster child for the Dale Carnegie philosophy—never criticize, condemn, or complain.

Yet, here sat this happy, positive, chubby-faced woman with tears welling in her eyes and spilling over. The sadness in her eyes was exacerbated by her appearance. Her wet hair was gnarled and wind-blown. She had stripped off her wet clothes and thrown on a T-shirt, panties, and nothing more.

She was so distraught over Angelo's condition that she seemed totally oblivious to her appearance. Even though she would never be described as highly attractive, Maria still took great pride in how she looked. Such concerns were nonexistent now. She had quickly sensed from the Chief's shouts and the loud, almost palpable dry heaves occurring only a few yards away, that Angelo was deathly ill. The fact that she was barely dressed and tearful was unimportant to both O'Casey and Maria.

"I need some dry clothes for Angelo."

"Can I help? What can I do?" Maria pressed.

O'Casey smiled grimly. "What you can do, if it's at all possible, will be to try and get some sleep. I know that's hard, but you have to. It's going to be a *long* night and an even *longer* day tomorrow. We're really going to need your help and leadership tomorrow. You can't be sharp it you don't get some sleep. We're going to need your A-game." Then he grabbed what he needed without further words and ran back to the Hilton.

"Gloves, Paddy," the Chief whispered as O'Casey got ready to take Angelo's shirt off and clean up his face.

If anything, Angelo seemed even worse now. He could barely stay erect. His shivering had gotten much worse. The cold, wet clothing seemed to be melting off his gray skin. His white knuckles were small snow-capped peaks clinging to the ridges of the Chief's shoulder. Angelo was trying to hang on, to stay awake and stay focused, yet he was clearly fading. Like a woman after thirty hours of hard labor who tries to catnap between contractions, he desperately tried to grab a few seconds of sleep between the painful retching stomach contractions and dry heaves.

Much as Maria and Ellen had ministered to Tiffany, Angelo's friends now ministered to him. It seemed ironic that the man who had watched that delicate dance of friends helping friends only a few days ago was now on the receiving end of that tenderness and support.

O'Casey and Butch worked like well-trained EMTs, knowing both what to do and how to do it. First, the hand was bandaged. The coiling red-and-white gauze snake weeping clots of blood and yellow pus was cut away with surgical dexterity and thrown to the ground. O'Casey tried hard not to show his shock at seeing the hot, throbbing red line running from Angelo's hand to a point well above his elbow. *Christ Almighty!* he thought to himself when he saw the gaping raw wound in the center of Angelo's palm. *He'll be dead in a day if we don't get him out of here.*

O'Casey could see his own mask of calmness on the Chief's face as well. Both men knew that panic on an EMT's face would set off panic in the patient. "Don't worry, Angelo. You still have all your fingers. You'll be playing the piano again by the first day of school."

Angelo struggled bravely to force a grin for his friends. Even as his health was failing, the music man showed the class and courage that had always been his hallmark. "Not exactly a GQ moment, is it, Chief?" Angelo said.

The Chief tried to think of something funny to say. Quick wit was *his* hallmark, yet nothing came to his lips. The absence of a humorous retort instead became a glaring silence, even amid the pounding rain and wind against the blue tarp. The silence also told Angelo what he already knew.

Instead of words, Angelo's friends spoke with a voice of skill and caring, slowly and gently undressing and then dressing him in dry clothing. They knew that the vomit-laden clothing would be difficult and uncomfortable to remove in the normal way. So O'Casey took his bent-blade Swiss Zep surgical scissors and cut away the soaking-wet river shirt and University of Maine T-shirt.

Butch and Sean also knew that the shivering was causing Angelo to tire to the point where shock could soon become a real possibility. Sean unpacked his favorite Bean goose-down vest from the small backpack of essentials he'd just grabbed on his forage from tent to tent. "Here you go, buddy. Let's get you warm." O'Casey smiled as he helped Angelo put first one arm through and then the other. "Buddy" had been his favorite nickname for his son, Matthew. When they were together, whether fishing at the little waterfalls near town or just riding on the tractor, they were buddies.

"Thanks, Paddy," Angelo said, purposely using O'Casey's nickname to convey his profound appreciation and affection. He had thought to protest, knowing that O'Casey had just given him one of his favorite articles of clothing.

Like his tan Orvis fishing shirt, O'Casey loved that dark blue vest. His wife had given it to him as a Christmas present, supposedly from Matthew, when Mattie was still a baby. Years later, Mattie would say, "Daddy, you're wearing my vest." Even though it had a big rip-stop patch on the back, O'Casey wore it with a mixture of pride and sadness. It made him feel close to Mattie, and yet it was a constant reminder of a little guy who'd meant more than anything in the world, a little guy who was gone from his life forever.

While Angelo did not know those details, he did know that O'Casey loved the vest. Now it might soon become covered in vomit or worse. He wanted to protest O'Casey's generosity, but he was just too sick.

With Angelo dry and dressed from the waist up, O'Casey took a slow deep breath and mustered a soft, slowly spreading grin. "Hey, Chief," he said.

"What, Paddy?" Butch responded as though part of a bizarre comedy team doing black humor at an inquest hearing.

"Angelo looks good in blue. I think that's him. When we get home, I'm going to buy him one of these. I'd give him this one, but it's my lucky fishing vest. I think there still may be a few old worms in the pocket," O'Casey said with a grin.

"You promised those to me, Paddy. I didn't have much for supper. Those worms sound pretty yummy to a chowhound like me, given how little supper I've had."

For just a few minutes it appeared that things were beginning to turn a major corner. The wind had slowed, the rain had diminished, and the New Blue Hilton was relatively dry. Angelo took a slow deep breath and smiled briefly at his friends.

Ask Not for Whom . . .

Parallel battles ran on throughout the night. At times, the storm seemed to abate. The flapping of the Blue Hilton plastic was the visual and auditory barometer for the camp. The pockets of pale blue plastic seemed to pucker in slowly and then pop out, making a rhythmic, if laborious sound, as though exhaling the thick, damp night air. During these lulls in the storm, Angelo closed his eyes, trembled almost imperceptibly, and sought refuge in an elusive sleep, much as a mother-to-be might seek in the transition state of labor—total and utter exhaustion punctuated by near chaotic, terrifying pain and an almost palpable sense of panic and dread. His friends had hoped to get him into his bunk, but as long as the explosions of nausea and diarrhea were coming about ten minutes apart, Angelo wanted to stay upright, and he found a bizarre comfort in the New Blue Hilton surrounded by his best friends.

During the lulls, O'Casey and Butch communicated silently, mouthing phrases or short thoughts to each other over the inhale and exhale of the plastic. The Hilton had become a weird blue cocoon protecting the shriveled and ever-changing figure that had first entered its portal. The metamorphosis, however, was dreadful. No butterfly would ever emerge. Angelo's once cherubic face, usually so full of life, was now gaunt. His sky-blue eyes were now a vacant, sad, near colorless gray. During the lulls in Angelo's personal storm, his eyes became distant, drifting, and melancholic. When the attacks of vomiting or diarrhea returned in a rage to savage his body, his eyes bulged wide in disbelief.

As the plastic slowly puffed and pulled, Butch turned to O'Casey and mouthed the words, "He's dying. He'll never make it through another night."

"I know. We'll have to leave at first light...or even before."

These brief exchanges often moved from silent mouthed syllables to barely audible phrases. Occasionally, Angelo opened his eyes, as though in the fog of anesthesia, not able to discern what was being said but aware that it was about him. Angelo knew how bad things were. He could feel the life slipping from his body. He was not afraid of dying. He could sense it, much like an aging cancer patient lying quietly, almost eagerly, awaiting an end to the agony. Angelo's fear was not death, but rather that he would infect one of his beloved friends. They were his family, his only family now that his mother had died. His father, long since dead, had abandoned him emotionally well before he abandoned the family physically. The biggest loss for Angelo had been his brother, who had moved to Tennessee and "gotten religion." In a born-again fit of homophobic sanctimony, he had told Angelo, "You are dead in my eyes and in God's eyes until you renounce your lustful, deviant lifestyle."

The torture of those words from Marco still rang in his ears. That pronouncement was worse than what he was suffering now, thought Angelo as his mind slid in and out of consciousness. He drifted through the fog of dreams, muffled rescue plans, and the relentless pucker of the tattered Blue Hilton, sucking his life in and out with it. "Oh no, here it comes again," he moaned.

His muscles tensed. His face contorted. His colorless fingers and knuckles danced a dance of death along the Chief's shoulder once again as they sought a place for leverage. Angelo bent forward and vomited a thin green foamy slime into the dented cooking pot O'Casey held up to his friend's weary face. Again and again, Angelo struggled to make something—anything—come up. The violent, unproductive dry heaves had come back. The diarrhea had fortunately all but stopped except for an occasional trickle down his bare legs.

The plastic gloves O'Casey and the Chief wore were no longer the sterile, hauntingly white universal protection barrier that Angelo had insisted on. They were now thoroughly mottled, almost caked with a pathetic rainbow of the night's activities. They told a sad, graphic tale of suffering and kindness.

In the other tents, various members of the tribe drifted, like Angelo, in and out of their dreams and fears. Ellen, though asleep for much of the short night, continued to clutch O'Casey's still damp T-shirt. "Hi, Sweetie," she would say softly to the wet mass of tan cotton when she woke up. She strained her ears during one of the lulls in the storm, listening for sounds of Sean Padraig O'Casey over the pulsating, rhythmic breathing of the Blue Hilton and the thunderstorm's fading wrath. She strained to sort through the muffled voices, groans, and incessant flapping plastic. Slowly, she squeezed the damp reminder of her tired Irishman and closed her eyes again to seek better dreams and a better time.

Maria took O'Casey's advice seriously. She knew that she would need all her strength to deal with the morning soon to come. Several times she had been awakened by Angelo's dry heaves. More often, it was from a crash of nearby thunder or the driving rain that shook the storm flap of the tent to a point where she was certain it would be blown away. Her real terror was in the white flashes that preceded the thunder. She remembered from a science lesson she'd taught many years before that lightning produces an impact temperature of 5,000 degrees...or was it 50,000 volts? Or was it 5,000,000 volts? She struggled to remember. Then she decided it would not make any difference—she would be dead, and dead is dead.

Maria knew this was just a deep-seated phobia she'd always had. Ironically, she was not afraid of snakes or scorpions, both of which had been abundant in West Texas where she grew up. But the severe summer thunderstorm, which was attacking them now with an all too familiar ferocity, reminded her of similar storms during those painful, occasionally terrifying, days outside Waco. In spite of the taunts of her brothers, Maria's only solace during those storms was to kneel and pray with her head in her mother's lap. She could remember the gentle touch of her mother's thick hands and tender chubby fingers as she stroked Maria's hair and rubbed the back of her neck. That magical, almost mystical touch became her focus now. Maria kept her thoughts on the soft, gentle strokes from her mother's hands and drifted fitfully back to sleep.

In the tent furthest from the Hilton and the chaos of the night, Tiffany was thankful that Jason had finally passed out. What had started out a positive, almost sweet exchange had ended up with Tiffany getting ready to scream for help or flee in panic from the tent. Jason had insisted that, for privacy reasons, they locate their tent at the far end of the sandbar.

Tiffany had been reluctant. Although she initially had found Jason very attractive, she had quickly discovered that some of his behavior was annoying to the point of near repulsion. She knew that she'd always been attractive to the bad-boy types, in spite of her mother's protestations. This breakthrough had come during a counseling session with her therapist, Allitara, who used no last name. Tiffany had concluded, after persistent, almost ruthless questioning from Allitara, that she liked bad-boy types because it pissed off her mother. She went to Allitara only briefly, and grew to hate the sessions— and even hated her therapist's name, which was actually Martha Cheeseman. Much like her own mother, Allitara was all pretense and show. That pretense finally came to the surface when Tiffany lost it at the end of their last session.

When she could not longer take the phony concern and the usual "and how does that make you feel?" psychobabble, Tiffany had the only meltdown of her life. "This sucks. It's really stupid, and I'm not doing this anymore. My mother is the one who needs to be here. Not me. I'm outta here," she smiled.

"But you can't leave," Allitara protested. "You've just had your first real breakthrough.."

"Screw your breakthrough," Tiffany shot back with a level of candor rare for someone who had learned to deal with her mother's incessant bullying by restrain her feelings and frustrations. "Allitara, I don't like you. I don't like your name. I don't like your phony concern. I don't like your questions...and your nail polish job sucks. Did you get that done at K-Mart?"

She couldn't believe she had said those things, but it felt so good that just maybe all those sessions had been worthwhile after all.

"You spoiled little bitch!" Allitara exploded. "You and your snobby fucking mother can shit up a rope. She is a piss-poor tipper. She wouldn't even give me a reference to join the Club. She just hates me because I'm not a size four like all her rich-bitch friends."

"No," Tiffany had retorted calmly, "my mother hates everyone. She's an equal opportunity hater. I hate you because you are an asshole and a pretentious fraud...just like Mother. There! I said it! I had my breakthrough, just like you wanted. And you did, too. Now we're even. I think I'm done now."

Tiffany had grabbed her sweater and left, knowing that she had, in fact, had a breakthrough: her mother was a pretentious asshole, an even bigger one than her pathetic, now-speechless therapist, the Allitara the Great.

Now Tiffany was paying a price for always wanting to piss her mother off. She turned toward Jason's sleeping hulk. The empty bottle of Yukon Jack was neatly tucked under his shoulder. His slow, staccato snores and labored breathing were a counterpoint to the sometimes pressing, sometimes distant thunder, none of which seemed to startle Jason in the least.

It is amazing how circumstance and level of sobriety can alter perspective. Men often share an old obnoxious adage: "What's the difference between a fox and a dog? About four beers." While Jason was neither, he had looked very attractive to Tiffany when they'd first entered the tent. He had a remarkable ability to get women inebriated without their knowing it, and Tiffany had finished several glasses of wine with dinner. When the rains came, Jason had grabbed the bottle of Yukon Jack as they dashed for the tent. Like everyone else, they were both dripping wet as they ran for cover. Tiffany had turned away from Jason to get out of her wet clothing and into her dry, warm sweats.

Although her modesty coefficient had changed since the skinny-dipping episode, she was still not comfortable being nude in front of Jason. She felt that it gave an impression she did not want to convey. While they *were* tent-mates, they were *not* roommates "with privileges."

As she'd started to button her sweatsuit top, she'd felt a surprisingly fluffy towel on her head. Jason began to towel off her wet, somewhat stringy hair and still-damp shoulders. She was startled by what appeared to be a very tender and comforting side of Jason she had never seen or expected. She began to relax and let Jason continue with his clumsy but apparently sincere efforts. Before she knew it, they were both were tossing down shots of Yukon Jack and laughing about how he'd rescued her from the bear. Even through the haze of liquor, Jason's version somehow did not fit Tiffany's recollections.

Still, he was very funny, masterfully so. It was his one endearing attribute, when that fun was not at other people's expense. He growled as though he was the bear. Tiffany was in the grip of a bad boy again. He knew it and she knew it. Everyone has a personal side they are not proud of—everyone. In this case, Tiffany knew that she should see if O'Casey and the Chief needed help. She knew that she should check in on her friends Ellen and Maria. Instead, she drank shots of Jack and grinned as the entertaining bad boy distorted the truth and plied her with just enough liquid gold to do what he had planned all along.

"Tiffy," Jason pandered in an effort to be cute and sweet. "You missed a couple of buttons." Her moist breasts were slightly exposed and very inviting to Jason's watchful eyes. As Tiffany reached down to button up, he put his hand on hers.

"I have an idea," grinned Jason. "How about we play a couple of quick hands of poker? If you win, you get to button up. If I win, I get to *un*button."

"No way! No way!" Tiffany protested, half seriously and half as a schoolgirl playing truth or dare.

"Aw, come on. It'll be fun. When was the last time you played strip poker?"

"Never," Tiffany giggled as she racked her brains to recall a time when that had ever happened or could happen. Girls in Tiffany's crowd might play high-stakes bridge or go to a casino for blackjack. But no, she was sure that she had never played strip poker. The thought of playing such a game would never have crossed her mind.

"Here are the rules," Jason stated formally, dealing cards that had almost miraculously appeared in his hands. "The winner keeps the deal. The loser takes a shot—for courage—and then takes off an article of clothing. We're playing five-card straight draw. Deuces are wild."

Before she could protest further, she was picking up her hand. She already had two jacks and a deuce. She would win the first hand for certain. Jason laughed at her great skills in poker as first his T-shirt and then his pants came off. Tiffany had always been impressed with Jason's torso. He had great pecs and biceps. The six-pack abs that he'd had in college were long gone thanks to multiple six-packs of another variety. And though his beer gut was now *potentially* apparent, Jason was working as hard as he could to suck in his stomach and accentuate the positive.

"Hey, how come you didn't take your socks off yet? Tiffany queried.

"Loser's choice," Jason smiled as he tossed down the required shot of Jack he had so masterfully earned after intentionally throwing away three kings in his last hand.

He was a skilled card player. Still, he thought, this was just child's play as he lost the first four hands and then made Tiffany lose the next two. "Hey, you forgot your shots," he grinned as he poured three inches of Yukon Jack into a cup for her. "Down the hatch!" he insisted.

Tiffany struggled to get the burning yellow liquid down. Jason tipped the glass up and up as she tried to swallow. She gagged, and some of the liquor dripped down her chin and onto her J. Crew sweats.

As she wrestled with her second sock, the warmth and uncertain glow of the Jack began to take its toll. Her mind began to swim. Everything seemed distant, including the storm and even the ongoing catastrophe in the Blue Hilton. Jason appeared almost larger than life. His arms and chest were rugged and hairy. His stomach, once gone, now seemed large as well. In spite of her lightheadedness, she could see the bulge in Jason's white Fruit of the Loom briefs and knew what that meant. Though she was not yet drunk, she realized she was losing control. She absolutely did not like that feeling—ever.

"Jason, let's stop. I'm getting a little dizzy."

Jason's grin disappeared. He looked unsettled. "One more hand. Let's be fair. You've only lost twice. I've lost four times. Just one more hand. Pleeease?" Jason begged, bringing out his well-mastered, thoroughly plastic, charming and disarming smile.

"Well...just one more. Last one. Promise?"

"I promise. Cross my heart and hope to..." Jason said with a smirk as he dealt the last hand.

Tiffany grinned with enthusiasm as she saw her three kings. She grinned even more when her two discards were replaced by two queens. "Kings over ladies," Tiffany announced with pride, remembering a term that sounded cool: "Kings over ladies."

"I win!" Tiffany beamed. "Beat that!"

Jason's face was glowing with a cockiness that was almost frightening. *How ironic*, he thought. Kings over ladies. *That's just what I'm planning—this king over that lady.*

With the steady hand of a veteran big-pot poker player, which he was, Jason laid down first one and then another spade in sequence. "Eight, nine, ten, jack, queen. Last time I checked, a straight flush beats a full house. You lose!"

Tiffany looked incredulously at her hand and at Jason's. How did he do that? she thought to herself. She did not want to have another drink of Yukon Jack. Worse than that, she realized that her top would need to come off. Until this point, the game had seemed fun...and even a little erotic, she admitted to herself. But now...

"Come on, Tiff. Off it comes. Off it comes." Jason was now almost leering with anticipation.

The Yukon Jack seemed to be commanding her to take her top off. Yet somehow, she also knew it was wrong, almost unclean. But seconds later, Tiffany sat naked from the waist up. *This does not feel erotic anymore*, she thought. Although her nipples were standing very erect, it had nothing to do with any sense of eroticism. Instead, every muscle in her body began to tense up.

"One more shot," Jason pressed, leaning toward her with another three-inch glass of Jack. "Up, up, up!" he insisted as he literally tried to pour the triple shot into her mouth.

Instead, she jerked her head to one side and the sticky yellow liquid ran down her chin and onto her chest. Tiffany looked in shock at the mess and recoiled at what had happened. Jason grabbed the towel he had used with such tenderness to dry her hair, and tried to wipe the Yukon Jack off her chin. Then he leaned over and began to lick the wet, sticky remains from her breast.

Tiffany drew back in disgust. "Are you crazy? Stop it! Stop it! This game is over. I'm done. Stop!"

Jason had heard the word *stop* many times in his life. This was just one more. He knew what stop meant. Stop meant he was almost there. Stop meant she really wanted it. Stop meant that after a couple of good licks, her nipple would be hard again and so would he. Jason stopped licking Tiffany's breast and began to run his tongue slowly up her chest and toward her beautiful, plump, and pouty lips. He'd give her something to pout about, Jason grinned.

"For Christ's sake, will you stop? If you touch me again, I'm going to grab your crotch and squeeze so hard your eyeballs will pop out. Leave me alone, damn it!" Tiffany shouted so loud that the loons could have heard her all the way down on Granite Lake. Unfortunately, the driving rain and earth-shaking thunder seemed to absorb her protests. On another evening, her shouts would have brought the cavalry and an end to what was now an assault.

Tiffany glared at Jason. Even in the dim light of the battery lantern, she could see an evil, driven man—not just a "bad boy," as she had been led to believe, but the self-centered sadist who did not mind hurting grown women and middle school girls (or once, even a helpless bear cub) when it served his purpose.

"You bitch," Jason scowled. "You want it. You want me and you know it. I'm the best you'll ever have. Before this trip is over, you'll be begging me for it." He grabbed his crotch as though it were a showpiece, smiled, and then proceeded to drink the remaining third of a bottle of Yukon Jack in one disgusting swallow. As Tiffany got up to leave, he rolled over and closed his eyes. Within seconds he was snoring.

Tiffany waited for the surge in the storm to end. Then she sneaked quietly out of the tent and joined Ellen.

As she opened the tent flap and entered, Ellen awoke. "Hi, Sweetie!" she mumbled with a smile, certain that it was O'Casey coming back to get a few hours of sleep.

"Nope. Not your sweetie. Just me. It's a black day over in Bedrock Canyon. Do you mind if I bunk in? That is, until your sweetie comes back. I'll explain it all in the morning," Tiffany said.

Soon both women were sound asleep. The Yukon Jack had overtaken Tiffany, and some badly needed company helped Ellen to return to her dreams and a tightly held fishing shirt, still smelling of O'Casey.

POINT OF NO RETURN

The warm night air hung thick with moisture. Occasional mosquitoes and the tiny, dreaded midges with their burning bite began to make their presence known. All three men had found just enough comfort in their semi-seated, semi-standing positions to have dozed off, but now all were awake again.

Angelo whispered, "I think I'm OK for now. It's been a little while. Let's give it a try. I am so tired."

They immediately carried their friend like a wounded comrade into his tent. They worked to get him as cleaned-up as possible and then tucked him in. Butch pulled the sleeping bag and extra blanket up to Angelo's chin; O'Casey patted him on the head as he had often done with Matthew and said, "Good night, buddy. Sleep tight. The cooking pot is right by your side if you feel you're going to get sick. Call us or wake Maria if you need anything."

It was now approaching daylight. There was still much to do and precious little time. O'Casey and the Chief knew they had to work quickly and efficiently. Their friend's life hung in the balance. They also knew the rescue mission would be perilous to their own safety. The water had risen almost a foot during the storm. Their large sandbar campsite had been reduced from a spacious peninsular to a small sand hill at the edge of the forest. Butch was thankful that he'd had the foresight to pull the canoes up next to the tent sites, fifty feet from the water's edge. Had he not done so, the canoes would have disappeared downriver and any chance of rescuing Angelo would have been gone for good. It would have taken a full day to hike back through the woods and out to the dam where they had portaged several days before. Even then, there was no guarantee that the land line at the dam would be working, and cell phone service was so unpredictable that they might have had to walk another three hours to the car and drive for an hour before reaching a logging camp for a land line. Angelo never would have made it.

Their current strategy was to push off just before daylight. Neither Butch nor O'Casey had ever fished beyond the sandbar. They knew the group was within an hour's canoe ride from the lake—maybe even closer. They also knew there was a huge, very dangerous falls they would have to portage at the base of the lake. From there it would be a hard twelve-mile canoe trip to the end of the lake, to the Jeep and, hopefully, cell phone service. They calculated that if they could then get a medevac helicopter to the campsite, Angelo could be in a hospital by early evening.

It was Angelo's only chance. He was terribly weak—almost in shock. He had two exceptionally serious yet separate problems compromising his health and safety. The giardia had left him completely dehydrated. The vomiting and diarrhea had drained him of badly needed electrolytes and fluids. If only they could give him an IV....And he could also use a very aggressive broad-spectrum antibiotic to stop the infection that announced itself as a thick red line creeping upward above his elbow and toward his shoulder. The giardia was the last thing that a person with a severe infection needed. Both problems were further compounded by Angelo's advanced HIV situation. Without immediate intervention to the contrary, he would die within forty-eight hours, and possibly within twenty-four. Butch knew it. O'Casey knew it. Most sadly, Angelo knew it.

This created a palpable sense of immediacy in the actions and activities at camp. O'Casey and Butch worked as a team, readying their own canoe and planning the needs and strategies for the rest of the tribe. Finally, it was time.

Butch crept quietly into his tent and woke Maria. While he had great faith in Ellen's steadiness and Tiffany's outstanding physical strength and skills, he knew that there could be only one leader to support the remainder of the tribe. Maria had tremendous inner strength. More importantly, he knew that she could be a surprisingly tough leader. She ran a large middle school with great skill. This short, chubby Latino woman could make the toughest fourteen-year-old gang member cringe. When she got angry, even veteran teachers said "Yes, ma'am!"

"Maria," Butch whispered. "It's light enough for us to see the big rocks. We should make it to the lake in an hour, maybe sooner, depending on how long it takes to portage the big falls. It should take us another three to four hours to get to the landing and the cars, depending on the wind and waves. Then we should have an opportunity to reach a 911 operator by then. I know there is cell tower by the landing. Hopefully, I'll be on a medevac helicopter hovering over this campsite between noon and two at the latest. We're purposely leaving as early as possible. Angelo doesn't have a lot of time—probably no more than two days, and maybe much less. If anything happens to us, it will happen in the next hour or so. The river is roaring. If we're not back today, we're not coming back."

Shivering slightly, still dressed in just her T-shirt and underpants, Maria tried to protest. "Butch, you're the Chief. You can do anything."

"Listen to me, Maria!" Butch interrupted. "You're in charge. Don't take any shit from anyone, especially Jason. What you say goes. If we aren't hovering over this sandbar by two at the latest, something has gone seriously wrong and you'll need to get everyone out. Right now, the river is roaring. If the water level drops, and it may by late afternoon, you might be able to canoe about half the distance to the lake, but don't count on it. You'll have to portage the last mile or two because there's a big falls at the base of the lake. I've heard that the portage trails along the river are pretty good, but tough. Once you get below the falls, put everyone into the canoes. I'd put Angelo in the kayak and tow it. Just take what you need for food and water. Shit-can the rest. It will slow you down. We all have just one job now—to save Angelo. Right? I've left more than half the rope for you. You'll need it for the portage. Good luck."

Then Butch did something he could never have imagined and Maria could never have even dreamed of happening. He kissed her squarely on the mouth. It was not a passionate kiss in any way. However, it was a kiss. It was intentional. It was meant to say, "I trust you. I admire you. I like you." Maria was literally speechless. Butch, never a sentimental or romantic person, then turned away to get his life jacket on and secured. "Butch," Maria called softly through the morning mist and growing dawn, "I won't let you down. And you'd better be here by noon or I'm coming after you!"

Butch smiled broadly and then finished his last-minute preparations and mental checklist.

O'Casey was finishing his own whispered conversation with Ellen in the next tent. He stroked Ellen's hair, much as he had once stroked Catherine's. He never thought another woman would be in his life. Yet, here he was, looking at Ellen's soft green eyes and curly auburn hair. Even in her discombobulated state, Ellen's soft features and delicate voice gave O'Casey even more of an incentive to survive the rescue mission. "Everything will be fine," he told her. "We'll be back. I *have* to be back. I need you. You have no idea how much I need you…Sweetie." O'Casey had let that word slip out once again. It had been his favorite term of endearment for Catherine. He could never have imagined using it again—not for any reason or for any other person.

Still, it had come out. Ellen slid out of her sleeping bag and motioned O'Casey out of the tent. She did not care that Butch was within eye-shot and earshot. She did not care that she, like Maria, was wearing only a thin white T-shirt and pink cotton panties. She needed to kiss this man and hold him as long as she could. This was not a passionate kiss. It was the kiss of a new bride at the train station, watching her G.I. go off to war, not knowing whether she would ever see the man—a man she was now in love with—ever again. She pressed her slender frame against O'Casey's muscular torso. With his khaki shirt, cargo pants, and long hunting knife at his side, O'Casey looked like a warrior going off to battle.

"Come on, Romeo," Butch called in a way that only a best friend could pull off.

"Good-bye, my Sweetie," Ellen whispered to the morning air and to the tall figure now adjusting his life jacket in the bow of the canoe.

"Glad I brought the good ones," Butch said quietly. He didn't want to wake camp, and he also didn't want to worry either Maria or Ellen, who were now standing next to each other, arm in arm, watching their men go off to war.

Butch knew that the next hour would be extremely dangerous. The two kelly-green Class 5 PFDs were L.L. Bean's very best personal flotation devices. Their high-necked collars were hot and irritating on a long summer lake paddle, but they could keep even an unconscious paddler's head out of the water in the event of an accident; it sometimes meant the difference between life and death. A cheap, worn-out life jacket had almost cost Jason his life. It had been a huge mistake to let a drunken Jason paddle the Cut, and the Chief didn't want to make another mistake that might cost Angelo or even O'Casey his life. Butch had a strange kind of invincible attitude when it came to his own life, though. He could not imagine a situation that he could not personally handle.

As he had done so many times before, Butch slid the bow out into the current as O'Casey stabilized the forward motion. The Chief slipped gracefully into his stern thwart seat. They were off. Each man turned upstream and saw a woman with tears in her eyes. Neither man could ever have expected this, nor had they necessarily even wanted it to happen. But for both it did happen. Sometimes, good things do happen to good people…and sometimes bad things also, as O'Casey knew all too well.

Within seconds, their canoe was around the first bend. Even the smell of the weak campfire the Chief had built was a mere wisp of curling gray smoke mingling with the morning fog. It danced slowly on the thermal blanket of warming summer air and slid into the oblivion of memories, tears, and time.

Some men dread battle. Others long for it. So it was for Granville Butch Chapman. This was his "smell of napalm in the morning." This was what he lived for and prepared for every year. Those who believe that we all live multiple lives in other times and places would certainly have found an ally in Granville Chapman. At that moment, he was Meriwether Lewis leading an uncertain, often terrified company through wild, uncharted white water … or perhaps an Iroquois chief carrying a message to his tribe that an impending Huron war party would soon be arriving. He was keenly aware that Angelo's life would hang in the balance of their success or failure. He would not let Angelo down. He would not let the tribe down.

O'Casey, like Butch, was an expert in a canoe. He knew when to power stroke, when to back paddle, and when to compensate, even when the Chief made a rare error in steerage or when the current was even stronger than the Chief had anticipated.

O'Casey was the perfect bow stroke. Unlike Jason, who had the potential strength and skill to handle the bow, Sean Padraig O'Casey knew there could only be one leader. It was the Chief's job to call out the strokes. Often, he didn't have to, since O'Casey could anticipate almost every situation. However, he willingly took his friend's direction. There could be no ego in the bow stroke. Whatever the call, O'Casey responded. "Left, hard left!" Butch would shout. "Drive. Drive. Big one! Big one!"

O'Casey knew what each directive meant.

This singing out of calls and directives was the Chief's opera, the opera of the Allagash—*whitewater opera* at its purest level. His shouts, though often non-melodic grunts and barks, gave him the same level of satisfaction that Angelo found in his arias. It was transcendent vocalization—strangely spiritual, like the wilderness church O'Casey felt he attended when casting for trout.

On this morning, however, there was little that was peaceful or still. Although the runoff from the thunderstorms had long since stopped and the river was beginning to recede, it was still some of the roughest white water either paddler had ever encountered. The duo had entered spring races on the Kenduskeg and the Dead River on several occasions, and always finished in the top ten. Racing was a fun, though often very cold, Saturday event. Even wearing a torso wetsuit jacket, spring white-water paddling could be a bitterly cold and sometimes hazardous event. Even on this June morning, the water was cold enough to cause hypothermia in ten to fifteen minutes without a wetsuit, which neither had brought. Drifting with an overturned canoe, even with the mixture of warm summer rain, could still result in numbing hands within a few minutes and death within a few hours.

There was no time for either man to think of such things. Every bend, every section of the river brought a new challenge. The near-empty canoe responded quickly to the solid bow strokes and deft stern ruddering. Butch had lashed two water bottles and a day bag on the midship brace. The bag contained a small first aid kit, emergency whistle, and two apples to help the paddlers with their blood sugar. He had also lashed a smaller, collapsible paddle, along with a hundred feet of three-eighths-inch Dacron portage line to the forward brace. There was no need for more equipment. This would be enough for them to make it to the end of Granite Lake—that is, if they could just survive the next set of rapids and the next.

"Jesus!" Butch yelled as the bow dipped completely underwater for a second and then shot back into the air. "I didn't see that drop!"

What had appeared to be just a small dip was in fact a mini falls, not unlike Black Powder Pitch, though smaller. The dim light was making it difficult for Butch and O'Casey to see the drops. The Chief had surmised that with the storm having moved to the east, a clearing wind would have brought with it a fresh westerly breeze and brighter skies. Instead, the summer low had apparently stalled offshore, and a surprisingly stiff morning breeze and heavy drizzle were keeping the cloud deck low and the light dim.

It had been another small misjudgment. Still, Butch was glad they were on the water and moving their rescue effort forward. It would soon be full daylight and much easier for them to pick up drops like the one they'd missed. Overall, though, they were doing remarkably well, Butch thought. An hour's paddle took half that, given the incredible speed of the current and the passion both men brought to their task. Every stroke was a second closer to help and to saving Angelo. The green canoe flew downstream, grazing some boulders and just missing others as the duo fought for control.

Even though both men were wearing their favorite hats—Butch with his crushed red velvet classic Bean hat, with a leather band where he tucked a favorite fly for window dressing, and O'Casey with his sacred Red Sox hat—the rain and mist continually ran into their eyes and distracted them from their looks downstream. Had it been a sunny day with little or no distraction, they might have seen the most important sign on the Allagash Waterway: YOU MUST PORTAGE NOW! This sign, erected and repainted annually by the Boy Scouts, announced to the boys, and, more importantly, to the Scoutmasters, that Grand Pitch was less than a half mile away. While this was not a point of no return for Scouts doing the river in the dog days of late July or early August, it *WAS* the point of no return for the rescue team. Working the left side of the river because of its deeper water and absence of large boulders, both O'Casey and Butch strained their eyes downstream to see the next stack of white water and calculate the best navigation route. In doing so, they zipped quickly past the toppled green sign that would have saved them from a disaster neither could imagine. It was already too late.

"Hard left! Power, power!" the Chief yelled. As commanded, O'Casey skillfully dug his paddle deep into the churning gray water. Even with his strong and determined strokes, the canoe bounced off a massive granite boulder protecting the sluice ahead.

"Shit! Shit! I thought we were going to make it!" O'Casey shouted as the canoe shook and then slid down into another, even more aggressive dip. Once again, the bow went under and the canoe took on more water.

Both men could feel the canoe become sluggish. Things were getting to a critical point, and they both knew it.

"Let's get over on the right side, bail her out, and catch our breath. We must be coming up on the falls pretty soon," Butch yelled over the roar of the water that was now building into haystacks as high as the top of O'Casey's head.

"What?" yelled O'Casey as he struggled to hear over the deafening noise.

"Right! Hard right!"

Butch had made another mistake. He had not calculated the speed of the river or just how quickly they would arrive at Grand Pitch. They were much, much closer than he had anticipated. The second falls and the four-foot drop they had just gone over was Chicken Pitch, and he had not expected to reach that for another ten minutes at least. *Had the map been wrong? No*, Butch thought. He had screwed up again.

He screamed at O'Casey now. "Right! right! Give me everything you have!"

The canoe was now almost a third full of water. Though O'Casey and Butch were driving with all their might, the canoe was slow to respond. The current was pulling them downstream two feet for every one foot they moved toward shore. As the canoe came within twenty feet of the approaching bank, the Chief's face turned white with dread. The forest of fir, pine, and cedar had been replaced by a wall of solid granite. There was no soft banking or gravel eddy to slide into, nothing to protect them or help them slow their terrifying downward momentum.

Butch had always felt invincible, always in control. His marriage had failed, his ex-wife had told him, because he could never let anyone else lead; he could never relinquish control.

Now he had lost control completely. The river had them both…and for good. It would not let go. They were on the edge of a vertical granite wall, but it was too steep to pull over. The sheer ledge was first four feet high, then ten, then twenty as they hurtled downriver. His mind racing for solutions, the Chief looked downstream. Fifty feet ahead was a small dead cedar tree leaning out over the river. It was stuck in a crevice in the rock. In the low water of summer, the branch would have been well above the river, but now it hung within reach.

"Grab the branch! Grab the branch!" Butch screamed.

Bracing his legs on either side of the unstable canoe, Sean prepared for the impact. His shoulders and face collided with the dead cedar limb. The canoe pivoted as the momentum of the stern swung the canoe into a backward, downstream position. Sean dug his hands into the cracked gray arm of the cedar, reaching out like a dead man trying to rescue the living. The sheer weight and force of the water almost yanked O'Casey from the bow. He had purposely wedged a leg under the bow thwart, which helped keep him from flipping completely out of the boat.

The five-inch cedar limb ripped across the side of his face, knocking his beloved Red Sox cap into the wild gray water surging along the canyon wall. It tore through the skin along his temple and opened a gash across his forehead. The cut was not unlike the one he'd received in the dreadful crash that had killed his wife and child. Now his life was in peril again, this time with his best friend. Adrenaline surged through his body. Though his hands had been torn and bloodied as they slid over the jagged nubs of the cedar limb, he found just enough of a branch jutting out from the limb that his wrists and fingers could gain some leverage.

For an instant, it appeared that there was hope. The canoe was now parallel to the canyon wall and only inches away. O'Casey strengthened his grip on the branch as the blood ran down his forearms. He tried to shake his head to chase away the blood that was dripping into his eyes. Through increasingly blurred vision, he looked to the branch and to the granite crevice for a solution. The canoe bobbed up and down in the wild water. In the distance, both men could hear the roar of the falls. The terror of their circumstance was now palpable. There was no room for ego or blame. There was no room for anything. There was no time. All O'Casey could do was hang on and keep the shifting water from changing his balance and overturning the canoe.

The Chief was trying to paddle the canoe upstream, but even he was no match for the wild water surging under them.

O'Casey took another look at the crevice of granite that had trapped the cedar branch, which was now their lifeline. Pulling on the branch, he was able to move the canoe forward several feet. At one point, he could feel the bow start to swing out into the current. "Right paddle! Right paddle!" he screamed to the Chief.

With incredibly powerful strokes the Chief was able to bring the bow back to the left. In the process, O'Casey was able to grab another six inches forward onto a better part of the branch.

Butch was now almost even with the crevice. "I can't hang on much longer," O'Casey shouted, as his bloodied fingers began to cramp up against the tremendous pressure and torque of the water against the flooded canoe. "Jam the mini-paddle into the crevice and tie it off!"

In an instant, Butch saw the wisdom of O'Casey's plan. The head of the paddle could function like a carabineer clip for a mountain climber. A rope could then be lashed to it to stabilize the canoe, and maybe, just maybe, they could use the crack as a way to climb the face of the cliff to safety.

O'Casey, who had always prided himself on being a McIver-type character able to fix almost anything with duct tape, had sized up the situation well. Gingerly, Butch slid forward. At one point, the bow almost dipped below the surging water again, which would have immediately flooded the bow, capsized the canoe, and resulted in almost certain death for the two friends. Reaching out more cautiously now, the Chief untied the yellow-bladed paddle and extended its telescoping handle. He grabbed the Dacron anchor line and tied a quick clove hitch around the paddle. *No time for a bow line now*, Butch thought. He then studied the crevice for what seemed like minutes to O'Casey but were well-spent seconds to the Chief. He turned the paddle sideways and carefully slid and twisted the paddle until the handle caught in the crevice.

"It's holding. It's holding, Paddy!" the Chief shouted with a brief smile. He lashed the loose end of the line to the thwart at his feet. Much of the water in the bow now ran toward the stern as the hydrodynamics of the canoe changed.

"Put your foot on the paddle and climb up the crevice!" O'Casey yelled. "I'll follow you."

"You go first!" Butch shot back, afraid that if he slipped in the crevice he would take O'Casey to his death with him.

"If I let go now, we'll flip. Just climb the fuckin' cliff, will ya!" He could feel how precarious his footing in the canoe was and knew that he couldn't hold on much longer. He also doubted that he would be able to climb the cliff anyway with his hands so weak and tattered.

Butch responded to his friend's pleading and moved slowly forward. Just as he raised his foot toward the paddle handle, the water from the stern surged forward again. That put additional weight on the point right where the rope was tied and onto the handle. The black plastic exploded immediately. The Chief fell forward as the water surged toward the bow, which dipped immediately downward. The cedar branch ripped from O'Casey's hands, and the bow swung precariously into the current.

The canoe was now almost completely flooded. Even as the team struggled to get the bow headed downstream and into a point of control, it was a useless effort. They immediately slammed into a large granite slab which had, years ago broken from the face of the cliff. It smashed the canoe at the midship point. It would have cut almost any other canoe in half. Still, it was enough to capsize the canoe completely. Both men struggled briefly to the surface and looked across the wild white chaos seeking a last glimpse of each other. Then the roaring foam blinded them and they were lost to each other's sight and a forty-foot descent into the maelstrom.

Biting Flies and Little Else

As the morning dragged and turned toward noon, the drizzle and easterly winds had ceased but the heat and humidity had not. The temperature rose with every hour. The air was thick with moisture... and with black flies, the most dreaded pest in the Maine outdoors. The Chief had seen it ruin many a fishing trip. Grown men would all but cry, begging the Chief just to bring them home and away from the biting onslaught. Deer and moose would occasionally go insane from the incessant attacks, running for so long that they would literally die from the fatigue and panic brought on by the black fly hoards.

Ellen knew from the tales her brother and father had told her that only a smudge fire and lots of Old Woodsman's bug dope could repel their bloodthirsty attacks. Ellen stirred the fire with a long stick as the black flies nipped at the area behind her ears, along her thin, delicate neck, and around her ankles. She had tried to put the Old Woodsman's on, as had Tiffany, but they were both so repulsed by the putrid smell that they concluded they'd rather be eaten alive by ants than put another drop of the brown slimy liquid anywhere near their bodies. The Chief could just as easily have selected Cutters, a modern-day miracle of insect protection. But, not surprisingly, Butch found Old Woodsman's to be a magical concoction for the soul; the earthy, manure-like sweetness was just a part of the macho ambiance that he loved. That Cutters worked much better was irrelevant. The Chief considered these ozone-destroying elixirs, full of DEET and repulsive perfumes, just another New Age insult to the woods, the culture, and the mystique that is Maine.

With almost no wind reaching into the canyon, the gray smudge from the wet pine and fir boughs hung at the edges of a thermal blanket. It slid along the tops of the trees like a thick lazy python curled at the water's edge waiting for an easy meal. It drifted with the river's flow down, down, down toward the massive falls where the constant updraft of spray mixed with the smoke and fell back slowly to the water. A pair of turkey vultures, with their majestic wingspans and repulsive curled red beaks, drifted over the rising thermal updrafts at the falls. With vision rivaling that of the bald eagles and fish hawks they competed with for free meals of dead or dying fish, the vultures scanned the slack water at the head of Granite Lake and just below the boiling water at the base of the falls. Sorting meal from non-meal images, the vultures paused momentarily over the barely spinning blue hat with the faded red *B* on the cap. The once coveted possession drifted slowly with the current and then washed ashore, just as it was about to sink to the bottom of the river. The clunking thud of the overturned green canoe against the granite boulders brought the vultures back for another look before they turned their wings slightly and headed east along the thermals in search of food.

Tiffany joined Ellen by the fire. While the low heat of the smoldering fire seemed almost torturous on an increasingly warm morning, it provided some relief from the incessant buzzing and biting. Both women strained their ears over the occasional snapping of burning pine boughs and the constant, low-frequency buzz of the black flies. Unlike mosquitoes, whose buzz is high and directive, black flies make a lower, deeper, more elusive sound. One can't just hear and hit. More often, it's a question of reaching back and touching one's neck or ear to find a bloody mass of bites or still biting flies. And for some, these bites can infect and cause serious reactions. For Ellen and for Tiffany they simply brought misery and heightened their impatience.

Again, Ellen struggled to sort sound from sound, buzz from snap. It was a manmade sound she hoped she'd hear. O'Casey could pick up the sound of an incoming chopper that was still miles away. That instinct had saved his life on several occasions in Vietnam. Even though only a boy of eighteen, he could tell every chopper type by sound, and claimed he could tell pilot from pilot by their approach patterns and how low or high they flew into an LZ. But his skills were of no help to Ellen now, though she thought of nothing else and no one else. *Sweetie* was the only word in her vocabulary at present. She wanted to hear only one noise now—the deep, slow *whup-whup-whup* of distant helicopter blades.

In spite of the sweat running down her face and a T-shirt drenched with perspiration, Maria didn't even try to mop her brow or wipe away the tears rolling down her cheeks. Angelo was having his third convulsion since daybreak. He was in a near coma-like state. Sometimes he'd wake up and whisper to Maria. Sometimes, he'd look at the gray bucket. He was too sick even to raise his head to vomit. Though the nausea and diarrhea were almost gone, occasional dry heaves might produce a tiny amount of the thin green slime so present the night before. Maria wiped his chin and occasionally his bottom the way she would her child, had she ever been given that blessing.

She dabbed a moist cloth along Angelo's forehead. She hated the latex-glove barrier between her and Angelo. The impersonal shield robbed her of any sensory closeness. She couldn't imagine those comforting touches from her mother done through a shield of latex. No wonder men hated condoms she thought. The latex gloves robbed her now of a healing touch she wanted to share with Angelo to let him know she was there to comfort him and to care. All the while, her ears strained, like Ellen's, for a sound she begged God she would hear, as she had begged God to keep the Chief safe and Angelo alive. She wondered if God had heard her. She listened and prayed. All she could hear was Angelo's slow, labored breathing and the deep annoying buzz of the black flies that bit the backs of her ears with relentless precision.

In spite of the heat, the bugs, the tension, and the fear that filled the camp that morning, Jason Foxworthy continued to sleep. At times he even snored. It was nothing for him to drink the best part of a fifth of scotch or gin. Last night's draining of almost a full bottle of Yukon Jack was hardly his best performance. However, the most frequent consequence of such episodes was near paralytic sleep. Only the Chief could get away with rousing Jason from such an unconscious stupor, and then only because Jason knew the Chief could still kick his ass. In fact, those had been Butch's exact words at times. On this steamy summer morning, although Butch could have safely roused Jason from his stupor, that would not and could not happen. Today, Granville Butch Chapman's near- lifeless body bobbed slowly against a fallen fir tree hanging precariously at the water's edge just below the raging falls.

Ellen mindlessly poked the fire, much as a ten-year-old Scout might do at his first camporee. In the distance, her now-focused ears picked up a sound, not of bugs, or water, or birds, or fire. It was an engine, distant and droning…and it was coming toward them.

The Cessna L185 floatplane emerged slowly from the distant valley fog, a mystical haze that would be there one minute and gone in another as the easterly breeze moved indecisively in counterclockwise bursts. Skippy Chapman, ironically a distant cousin of the Chief's, though neither was aware of that, chatted away as he flew his newbies—first time travelers—toward their Chamberlain Lake destination. Skippy loved to play with the minds, and sometimes the wallets, of his customers. Most were wealthy businessmen who were there to get away from their jobs, their wives, their mistresses, whatever. Some would be drunk before they landed. Skippy didn't care about that, as long as they didn't barf in the plane. When they did, they paid. It was that simple. "Christ's sake!" Skippy would yell. "I'll never get that smell out!" And when the bill came, sure enough, there would be a charge for $100 and an asterisk with the line item *Cleanup and Sanitation.* No businessman wanted to explain a more detailed message to their company comptroller …or to their wife. The bills were quickly paid. Skippy did not fool around.

Today, as the plane buzzed slowly along the river valley, Skippy strained his eyes to look for moose or black bear. A good sighting would give him an opportunity to make up a tale about a charging moose or a bear attack. There was nothing Skippy enjoyed quite so much as scaring the shit out of a Westchester businessman who wouldn't know a black bear from a grizzly or a moose from a cow. "They get wicked mean this time of year. It's the black flies that do it. They'll charge just about anything or anyone," Skippy would swear with all sincerity.

As the plane headed west along the valley ridge, Ellen and Tiffany were frantic. While they soon realized it was not the rescue helicopter they'd hoped for, they thought perhaps it was a rescue plane that might drop supplies, or at least acknowledge in some magical way that help would be arriving. Ellen and Tiffany ran to the edge of the river, where they would be most visible. They waved their arms and jumped around, hoping to be spotted. "Help! Help! We need help!" they screamed. Ellen in particular was in full panic mode now. She had long since envisioned the worst for the Chief and her sweetie. "Please help us! Angelo's hurt! Angelo's hurt!" she screamed again and again.

As the Cessna continued its westward flight, Ellen's eagerness turned to despair. Tears rolled down her cheeks and onto her chin. She strained her ears and eyes for any change in the plane's direction, maybe doubling back for a second look at the camp and at the panicked campers. But the plane kept to its course and disappeared. Ellen cried quietly so as not to disturb Angelo.

Maria had wanted to run out of the tent when she heard the plane, but did not want to risk waking Angelo, whose head was in her lap now. She stroked his hair and soothed his brow with the damp gray cloth she had just remoistened.

Tiffany walked slowly over to Ellen's side, gave her a gentle hug and kissed her on her tear-laden cheek. "It's going to be OK. We're going to find your sweetie ... and Butch. I promise. And we're going to get help for Angelo."

"Thanks," Ellen smiled. She squeezed her friend's hand in gratitude as they sat by the smoldering fire. "I know you're right," Ellen continued. "I'm just worried to death. The morning's already gone. I really think that if everything had worked out, even planes like that floatplane we just saw would be looking for us. I know Butch and O'Casey. They make things happen. It's not that windy today. They'd have done that twelve-mile paddle in half the time anyone else could. They'd be back here by now. All this waiting is killing me."

Then she and Tiffany began to concoct a rescue plan of their own.

Little did Ellen know that the waiting was killing the Chief as well. His near-lifeless body floated like a large piece of driftwood in the big pool below the falls. The cold water was putting his body into a state of hypothermia, which, among other things, slowed his peripheral circulation as his body struggled to maintain what little life was left. The Chief's head rocked awkwardly in the high-necked life jacket that had saved his life so far. The tightly fitting floatation system was also helping to insulate his body core from the cold Maine water. In his semiconscious state, Butch could not feel the numbing cold or his fractured skull.

His good friend Angelo was also now is a semiconscious state. Unlike Butch, Angelo would, on occasion, wake up enough to smile at Maria, squeeze her fingers through the cold filter of latex, and try to mutter words of thanks. Somehow, Maria found it almost more comforting to have Angelo keep his eyes closed. When he would struggle to stay awake, she could see the sadness and the sickness in his eyes. It was not the look of a man afraid of death, but rather embarrassed that his friends had to witness the pain and the unpleasantness of his dying. Angelo was perhaps the most unselfish person Maria had ever met. His thoughts were never of himself. Even as he lay there dying, he still somehow smiled and squeezed her hand in appreciation.

Suddenly, the tent flap opened and Tiffany whispered an invitation for Maria to come outside to join her and Ellen in their discussion. Maria made Angelo as comfortable as possible, kissed his forehead tenderly, and exited the tent.

"Here's what we think," Tiffany explained. "If Butch and O'Casey were OK, someone would be here by now. Waiting isn't going to help anyone. In the event that they had some minor problems and a helicopter or plane comes, we'll probably all hear it. In that case, you can all meet Ellen and me at the foot of the lake. We're not going to try to canoe down the river. We're not that good. Butch said that a trail runs along the river all the way to the lake. We're going to follow the river until we find the guys. If we don't, one or both of us will be back well before dark. You take care of Angelo. Don't worry about 'jerk face' over there," Tiffany said, pointing to her tent. "He's useless. He'll probably stay passed out much of the day. He tried pretty hard to get into my pants last night. There's no way I can stay alone here with him and Angelo. If there's a problem, I'll come back running. I'm pretty fast…for a principal."

And just like that, they were gone. Maria watched as the two women she had barely known a week ago quickly blended in with the green, gray, and brown of the forest. Tiffany's neon blue L.L. Bean daypack, loaded with rope, a first aid kit and a few supplies, stood out for a moment or two against the more somber forest tones. There it was. There it was again. Then it was gone. They were gone. Both her new friends, two of the most special people she had ever met in her life, were now gone.

Thin wisps of gray smoke from the fading fire and the bite from a knot of black flies congregating at the nape of her neck, reminded her of where she was. Then came the saddest of all noises for Maria—the deep, almost morbid staccato that meant only one thing—Angelo's dry heaves had returned. Maria trudged slowly back to her pale and quivering friend.

SHATTERED CANOE. SHATTERED DREAMS

Although Tiffany did not have the same level of passionate purpose that Ellen had as they embarked on their rescue mission, she had grown to love *all* her new friends. Love was certainly not the word when it came to Jason, but these other new friendships had become almost organic, palpable, and fundamentally refreshing for her. To this point, much of her life, her family and her friends had been all about *show*. All about the superficial—European double hugs, "kiss-kiss," and "ciao." Tiffany was amazed, as she dashed headlong down a dark and foreboding path with a woman she had hardly known a week ago, that she and her new "sister" were now rushing to rescue her new "brothers," Butch and O'Casey. They all felt like family in a way she had never experienced in her life.

As the pace picked up along the trail by the river, Tiffany moved with purpose and precision—the lives of her new family members depended on it. Both women understood that another mistake could cost even more lives. They walked quickly, but were careful to warn each other to watch out for this rock and that root. "Be careful. It's slippery here," one or the other would caution as the trail meandered through the woods above the wild, churning river.

After about a half hour of *quick march*, Ellen stopped and raised her hand much as she had seen Marine veteran O'Casey do while walking point a few days before. "What's that?"

"What's what? Tiffany responded.

"Listen…. Oh my God!" Ellen exclaimed in panic as she veered off the path and directly toward the river. She ran so fast through the underbrush that as the forest suddenly ended, she almost stepped from the edge of the thicket and into the white water ten feet below. She stood breathlessly on the lip of a thin white granite crag, almost at the same point where Butch and O'Casey had first heard the roar of the falls for themselves and noticed too late the steep, inaccessible bank on the south side of the river.

"Oh my God," Ellen repeated aloud as Tiffany came up behind her. "That must be the falls Butch was talking about. I heard him tell Sean it was nicknamed *Killer Falls* because that's what it would do to you if you went over it. Maybe they pulled over when they first heard the roar."

"They didn't if they were on this side. I've been watching for their tracks along the path. They haven't been here today. No one has but us. The rain washed the trail clean."

"Let's go. Let's go!" Ellen shouted as she again took the lead. The caution was gone. There was no time to remind each other about slippery spots. Even though Tiffany was the far better athlete, she was surprised by Ellen's speed, coordination, and stamina. They were almost in a full run now—at least as much as the trail would allow, particularly now that much of it was uphill. At one point, as they drew near to the falls and the sound was almost deafening, Ellen slipped and fell on the steep, muddy trail. She slid headfirst ten feet down the trail.

"Are you OK, Ellen? Are you hurt anywhere?"

As Tiffany helped Ellen to her feet, she noticed blood running down Ellen's leg from cuts on her kneecap and shin. Ellen wiped the mud from her face and then wiped her filthy hands on the new white GAP jersey she had thrown on that morning. Her fall down the rock-strewn trail had thoroughly destroyed the shirt and put a three-cornered tear in the front pocket, exposing her favorite pink bra. She didn't notice or even care. Those days were over. Today, she had only one thought on her mind. She ran in terror up the hill and toward the roar of the falls. *Please, God, no! Please, God, no!* she chanted to herself.

As they reached the crest of a small jagged cliff at the edge of the falls, the women looked down in horror at the white madness below them. It was as if they were peering over Niagara Falls after a friend had just gone over it in a barrel. Though hardly of that magnitude, Grand Pitch—aka Killer Falls—was still a death trap with the churning storm runoff. The river had narrowed into a terrifying funnel with no point of escape. As

Butch and O'Casey had discovered too late, the high water had obscured the warning sign that offered a last chance for canoeists to flee the grip of the river. The water at the base of the falls was a giant sucking vortex. Though it was deep enough for someone to survive the initial fall and brutal impact, the swirling maelstrom made the likelihood that one could emerge without drowning seem an impossibility.

Through the mist from the crashing water below them, Tiffany and Ellen searched the shoreline for signs of life or signs that either of the men they cared about had survived the falls. The farther they were from the falls, the easier it was to scan the shore, since it was less shrouded in mist. They soon focused on the end of the first big pool where the white water subsided and the river broke hard to the right.

"There! Oh no! Oh no!" shouted Tiffany, pointing to the edge of the chaos. Ellen followed Tiffany's arm to the area at the end of the near shoreline where the river narrowed briefly and then disappeared around the bend. The horror in her voice reflected what she saw—the distinctive forest-green Kevlar Bean canoe, overturned and bobbing in the foam within the gnarly grasp of a cedar tree downed by the recent storm. Both women cried as their eyes frantically searched first the distant shore by the canoe and then worked through the mist toward the shore below their feet.

"There! Butch's paddle…and there's Paddy's!" Ellen yelled over the roar of the falls. Ellen had loved it when Butch used O'Casey's nickname. Now, all she could find of her sweetie was his varnished paddle, trapped in a dark eddy almost side-by-side with his friend's. *How ironic*, she might have thought were she not in such a panic—the paddles appeared as inseparable as the friends whose hands had held them.

Not surprisingly, each man had his own favorite paddle, and each debated and defended his personal choice. Butch liked the look and feel of the newer carbon fiber broad-blade racing design, while O'Casey loved the look and feel of his traditional Old Town varnished ash paddle. Besides, it was a paddle his grandfather had given him on his sixteenth birthday, and, like his Orvis fly rod, was one of his truly favorite possessions. As they watched O'Casey's classic paddle brush back and forth against the rocks next to the Chief's black and gold one, the women saw no evidence that anything else of the men had survived.

Tiffany quickly found the steep portage trail, which got them down off the precipice and closer to the water's edge. Now, they were farther away from the blinding mist, and, to some degree, away from the terror of the falls. The women surveyed every inch of the near shore. Suddenly, Tiffany screamed, "There he is! There he is!"

In an eddy just below the falls, and almost directly under where they had been standing, she spotted Butch. It was a terrifying, gruesome sight. Until now, the Chief had seemed indestructible. He not only conveyed that air of invincibility, he carefully cultivated that perception, and had grown to believe it himself. In fact, it had become one of the few things he seemed almost arrogant about—that he was so in tune with and so knowledgeable about the woods and water that he could meet any of their challenges...and win. On this day, his ashen face and closed eyes contrasted sharply with his green life jacket. Granville Butch Chapman looked more like a drowned newbie than a Master Maine Guide. This was a battle he had never anticipated losing. Was he alive? Was he dead? They couldn't tell but desperately needed and wanted to know.

The women soon realized there would be no simple way for them to reach their beloved Chief. Although he was in a backwater below the falls, there was no easy access point for them to get to him. It was obvious that the only way was by water. The overturned canoe was a hundred yards downstream, trapped by the cedar blowdown, but it would not help them now with its badly cracked hull and a bow that was split in two.

"I'm going after him," Tiffany stated firmly. "It would take too long to get the canoe, and we'd probably get pounded by the whirlpool and sucked back into the falls anyway. Besides, I think it's ruined."

She seemed to know instinctively what to do, as she had in rescuing Jason. Her lifeguard training would pay off once again. "These jeans will just pull me down," she said as she quickly unbuttoned and removed her favorite Levi 504s. "Let's get the rope out of the backpack and tie one end around that tree. I'm going to tie the other end around myself, just in case I get caught in the current," she continued, with the same kind of self-assurance Butch or O'Casey might have shown in the same situation.

Although Tiffany had confidently worked out a fine plan, she fumbled hopelessly with one end of the rope as Ellen uncoiled the rest of it. She had no idea how to tie a good knot. By contrast, Ellen had played many "rescue games" with her brothers, who had taught her how to tie different boating and camping knots when they weren't tying *her* up or giving her a hard time.

"You need a bowline. It's the strongest knot," Ellen said, half to herself. "Now the rabbit goes up the hole, around the tree, and back down the hole…I think," she said almost mechanically. "Yeah, that's right," she said. Often, when her brothers and dad would leave her for a fishing trip, Ellen would sulk in the garage, tying knots and mumbling, "I'll show them. I'll show them." And in a way, she just had, as she tied a perfect bowline around Tiffany's waist. Tiffany smiled and was in the water even before Ellen could tie off her end of the line on a nearby tree. Quickly, she threw a couple of wraps around her own slender waist and paid out line as Tiffany swam toward the Chief.

Tiffany worked carefully and deliberately, trying both to hug the steep rocky shore and avoid tangling her legs in the pale gray-green lifeline trailing behind her. Meanwhile, Ellen looked for something, anything to anchor her end of the rope. She tried to back up slowly toward the solitary cedar tree that stood on the edge of the pool. It had somehow managed to survive on the steep granite shore with just enough earth to support its tentative root system, struggling to hang on to the soil much as Ellen was struggling to hang onto the rope, which had nearly reached its end.

As Tiffany got within ten feet of the Chief, she gave several hard frog kicks to drive herself closer. She wasn't moving. She turned in fear and concern, only to realize she had run out of rope. Ellen would not be able to use the cedar tree as a tie-off. "I need more rope!" Tiffany yelled. "Give me some slack!"

Ellen had felt the rope pulling on her thin waist and quickly realized what her friend, too, had surmised: if they were to rescue the Chief, Ellen would have to become the tree. She moved cautiously along the ridge above her friends. The three yards she was able to safely move toward the falls freed up just enough slack to allow Tiffany to reach the Chief.

"Butch! Wake up! Wake up,!" Tiffany screamed over the roar of the falls, which was now only ten yards away. When he didn't respond, she grasped him from behind and turned him around. His gray face and pale blue lips were within inches of Tiffany's. His deathlike appearance and the jagged tear in his forehead were horrifying. "Jesus, no! No! Butch, wake up! Please!" she shrieked again.

Tiffany, so cool and calm only seconds before, was quickly losing control at the sight of her friend. The icy-cold water was starting to exact a toll on her as well. *Don't panic. Don't panic!* a voice screamed in her head. Years of lifeguard training did battle with her subconscious to bring her back from the edge. She turned her head as she'd been trained to do and put her ear within an inch of the Chief's face. She could feel a tiny rhythmic breath against her cheek and hear a weak, gurgling, throaty sound.

"He's alive! He's alive!" Tiffany screamed with joy. "Pull us in. Hurry, Ellen!"

As Ellen yanked on the rope, Tiffany lost her grip on Butch's life jacket. "He's stuck!" she yelled. "I think his foot is stuck!"

Ellen looked down to pay out more rope and avoid tangling her feet in the small coil she'd created as she'd moved closer to her friends. When she looked back, Tiffany was gone. Butch floated awkwardly in the water, his head wobbling above his shoulders like a bobble-head dog on a dashboard. Ellen stared in terror, searching for any sign of her friend.

Suddenly, the Chief's head lurched backward, then forward, then backward again. His body shot away from the granite boulders where it had been trapped and out toward the current. Almost simultaneously, Tiffany's head broke the surface of the water. "Ahhh! Ahhh!" Tiffany shouted as she struggled to catch her breath after having been under water for over thirty seconds. She'd had to untie Butch's boot and free his foot from it because it was jammed hopelessly in the rocks. While the boot had saved his life by becoming an anchor against the current, it had also almost cost both him and Tiffany their lives. The Long Island beauty was now a nearly frozen mess of straggly wet hair just struggling to fill her lungs with air. But she had done it! *Butch is free and alive!* she thought, turning toward where he had been.

"Tiff!" Ellen hollered, pointing. "It's Butch! Butch! Hurry!"

As Tiffany turned around and saw that the force of her efforts to set the Chief free has actually pushed him away from the safety of the eddy and out into the main current. His chin was down against his life jacket and his body now bobbed in a lifeless dance with the current. Again, Tiffany's lifeguard training, practice, and a dozen rescues took over. In a few short seconds, she was by his side and heading downstream in the rescue position with her arm firmly, though awkwardly, around his chest. Although the jacket had saved his life, Tiffany found her numb hands struggling to get a good grip around his thick torso and the bulky life jacket. Finally, she was able to grasp an adjustment strap. She quickly wrapped it around her wrist and began to swim toward shore.

The pull of the current was powerful, and she realized almost at once that even her exceptionally strong kick was no match for its force and the 220-pound man she was trying to rescue. She was cold, exhausted, and barely able to hang on. She struggled to catch quick breaths of air in the white, churning foam.

"Pull, Ellen! Pull!" Tiffany screamed. It was the first time she had ever been in a water rescue and not been in complete control. She knew for certain that she needed Ellen's help to save Butch, and just maybe her own life as well. "Pull! Pull!" she shouted again with an uncharacteristic panic starting to settle into her voice.

If the two people in the water were in a life-threatening situation, Ellen was in a similar predicament. She was now standing precariously on a rocky ledge ten feet above the river and being pulled ever closer to the edge. In order to get the slack she had needed to help Tiffany with the rescue, she'd had to move along the narrow ledge and away from the small cedar tree she'd hoped would be her tie-off. Now, as her friends moved downstream with the current, she was trying to keep pace along the ledge and back toward the safety of the banking and the tie-off tree twenty feet away.

The pull of the pair drifting downstream was immense, as the forces of physics worked against all three friends. It was not just a question of holding on. The line around Ellen's waist was trying to cut her in half. More dangerous yet, she was being pulled toward the edge of the cliff more quickly than she could move downstream. Suddenly, her feet almost slipped out from under her. Loose granite chips kicked out and fell over the edge to the churning water below. Panting in absolute terror like she had never felt before, she struggled to regain her footing and leaned back against the line. She slipped again and crashed down against the granite ledge. Her already cut kneecaps and shins took the brunt of the force. Desperately, she scrambled to her feet to keep from being dragged off the ledge to a certain death.

As she looked in panic over the ledge at the jagged granite spikes in the water below, she realized her only chance was to *run* along the thin ledge to the cedar. She had to move faster than the speed of the current.

In doing so, she was able to get some slack and move off the ledge toward the cedar. Unfortunately, the slack meant that her friends slid further into the river's brutal grip.

"Ellen!" Tiffany screamed. "Ellen!"

As Ellen looked up, she saw Tiffany's face getting that same pale gray-blue look she'd had after rescuing Jason. Not only the current, but also the cold had a death grip on her as well. Her bare legs, though not weighed down by heavy denim jeans, were numb and almost useless. Ellen dashed to the cedar tree and readied her body for a last, desperate stand. She had no time to untie the rope, which had slipped down to her hips, and retie it on the tree. She sat down with her feet against the scraggly cedar, barely three inches in diameter, and braced herself for the inevitable shock as the slack in the rope began to straighten out.

Rizz. Rizz. Rizzzzzz! The line seemed to scream out a warning as it tightened and ran along the bank downstream. The moment came as Ellen's eyes briefly met her friend's. They eyed each other one last time with a mixture of love and desperation. Both knew this was it. This was the decisive moment that would determine their life or death.

The line straightened like a thin, ominous steel cable cutting into the very fabric of Ellen's being. It ripped against her body and tightened so much she could barely breathe. It slid from her hips up to her upper abdomen. As she twisted her body to free herself from the pain, the line rose up even further. It grabbed her just below the rib cage at the solar plexus and diaphragm. With her stomach muscles compromised, her lungs could not fill up. She fought for each breath.

The torque caused by the snap of the line might have caused Tiffany and Butch to be whipped off into the current, but Ellen's well tied bowline held firm on Tiffany's waist and her wrist and hand, wrapped around the strap of Butch's life jacket, kept the two of them bound together in the cold, wild water.

From a physics standpoint, that left Ellen as the anchor—a five-foot three-inch anchor weighing 118 pounds trying to stop a combined 340 pounds in a raging current. At the instant that ten feet of slack turned into a steel cable, something had to give. Ellen was yanked from her sitting position and launched into the tree. Her whole body shuddered at the crash of her legs, torso, and head against the trunk of the tree.

Had it been a larger tree or a rock that she hit face first, she might have been killed. Instead, the slender cedar tree bent with the force. It functioned like a fishing rod, which by design is really a long, flexible shock absorber that allows a fisherman to catch a thousand-pound shark on a line barely thicker than five strands of hair wound together. Like the angler's rod, the thin cedar bent but did not break.

Ellen and the thin red cedar were in parallel battles for survival. The lone cedar had struggled for years to survive in the strange and hostile granite crag that had been its home. It roots annually sought a better hold in the scant clay soil and decomposing leaves or moss that worked their way into and out of what was more ledge than forest or banking. Somehow the roots held on as the tree bent parallel to the ledge, but did not uproot.

Somehow, too, Ellen bent but did not break as well. The line tightened on her rib cage. She fought for every breath. It felt like she was suffocating. In an effort to change the angle of the rope, she shifted her weight with drastic consequences. Her body twisted and she whipped completely around the tree. She was no longer straddling the cedar with her face in the branches. Instead, she was face down and being pulled toward the river. Only her fingers clutching at the thin cedar trunk kept her and her friends from being dragged to their death. The rough bark and old broken branch stubs tore at her hands and face. Her bleeding fingers kept slipping and sliding further down the trunk. The upper limbs were thinner, and, though easier on her hands, were wet with spray from the falls. Ellen screamed and screamed. She knew it was just a matter of seconds. Her torn, aching fingers could hold no longer.

The cedar branches, so slippery now, slid finally from her grasp. The incessant, downward pull of the rope dragged Ellen feet first toward the raging river. Her face and torso bounced along the granite ledge. Her hands clawed at the rocks looking for anything to hang on to—anything! Like a climber about to fall to her death, her fingers worked instinctively to find a handhold. Then her frantic hands found a small fissure in the gray granite ledge just wide enough for her thin, bleeding fingers. One nail had already been almost totally ripped off. However, pain was not a factor now. The adrenaline surged through Ellen's body. A fight-or-flight instinct deep within her brain took over. It was not about Tiffany or Butch now. It was simply about surviving for another second to keep her body from being torn in half by the rope, to keep her lungs full of air, to keep herself alive...for just one more second.

Her legs and feet began to work now, too. Her feet found a crack in the granite big enough to wedge the toes of her hiking boots into and then push back against the constant pressure of the line. "Help! Help me!" she screamed again and again. Amid the roar of the falls and the sounds of her own screams and heavy breathing, she could hear Tiffany screaming back, "Hang on! Hang on!"

Even amid the chaos, she could hear another sound, distant and confusing. It was an odd yet familiar sound of anguish that seemed to hurt her more than the rope. Had she been able to turn her head and look toward the downstream trail, she would have seen a large dark figure emerging slowly from the path. It was a figure she would only have recognized by the Chippewa boots. His face was covered in blood. One arm dragged uselessly at his side beneath a sweatshirt almost torn in half. This caricature of a man dragged himself up the path one screaming inch at a time. His right leg, like his right arm was useless. The broken femur protruded from his tattered cargo pants and blood oozed with every movement of his body.

It was Sean Padraig O'Casey...or what was left of him. As he had gone over the edge of the falls and into the abyss below, he instinctively tried to protect his head. Although he had landed in over ten feet of water, it was still not enough of a cushion to protect him from the forty-foot drop to the whirlpools and rocks below the walls. His right leg hit an underwater ledge first, immediately breaking his femur. The bottom end of the bone then broke through the skin at mid thigh. Unlike the Chief, who'd received a severe concussion on impact, O'Casey's arms had protected his head. However, his left shoulder had dislocated when his elbow, bent at a right angle to his chest, collided with the upper portion of the ledge. Had he fallen two feet closer to the falls, he would have been impaled on the broken trunk of an old oak tree waiting silently to destroy all in its path. Had he fallen four feet to the left, he would have been sucked into a vortex and drowned within seconds.

Almost miraculously, he had managed to survive the fall and the severe injuries. The current had taken him around the bend and eventually toward slower water two hundred yards below the falls. Though in nearly unbearable pain, O'Casey thought only of his friend. When he broke the surface and took the first deep lifesaving breath of air, he screamed and swore at the pain. He knew immediately as he struggled in the current that one arm and one leg were useless. He fought his brain's attempt to move both arms and legs in a normal swimming action. The pain in moving them, particularly his leg, was indescribable. He had looked upstream briefly, in the hope that Butch could somehow help him. What he saw terrified him—Butch's apparently lifeless body bobbing in the eddy.

"Butch! Butch!" O'Casey had screamed again and again as he drifted around the river's bend and out of sight of his best friend.

As soon as he had found a place to come ashore, he had struggled to get out of the water and to help his friend, but it became an impossible task. He was in excruciating pain. Every movement on the left side of his body caused white, blinding pain. Still, he knew he had to get out of the water, both for the Chief's survival and his own. He was already shivering uncontrollably. He knew all too well that hypothermia was already setting in. As he looked first upstream and then downstream for a solution, he saw a stout seven-foot oak limb, which had once been part of a beaver dam. One end had been gnawed to a point, as had all the branches. The limb would become his rescue staff. Little did he know how valuable that crude staff would prove to be.

Slowly and arduously, O'Casey had dragged his broken body, racked with pain, up the banking and toward the falls. He would move the staff forward six inches, lean into it with both his good arm and leg and painfully drag the left side of his body toward the staff. It was hardly a walk. It was more like a macabre dance. The pointed stick would lead. His body would follow. His eyes welled up with tears, not just for the pain that he felt, but for the friend he knew was either dying or dead. He could not let that happen. He wouldn't.

As O'Casey got within a hundred feet of the chaos, he heard a familiar sound above the vicious roar of the falls that he and Butch had heard too late to save themselves. It was a sound of women's voices, of voices he knew and loved. The dance steps quickened. *Stab forward. Lean in. Pull with the right arm. Drag your leg. Scream.* "Ahhh! Ahhh!" He had this horribly painful dance step memorized. His focus now was on picking up the pace to get to the voices. One of them was Ellen's. He could tell now for certain. But it sounded like she, too, was screaming…and that she was in pain or worse. "Ellen!" he tried to yell back, but the words somehow seemed faint in his ears. "Ellen!"

As he tried to rush forward, his dance step quickened. But the cumbersome cadence could not be hurried. He fell forward, lost his grip on the beaver staff, and landed leg first on his broken thigh. His shriek of pain was the sound Ellen had first heard, a bizarre sort of high-pitched wail above the roar of the falls.

She screamed as well, but not in response. What she'd heard was unrecognizable noise above the roar of the falls, and above her own pleas for help and those of Tiffany in the river. This was not the ghostlike harmony of loon to loon in the distant night. True, it was an eerie wail, an echoing series of calls in the wilderness. These, however, were the pathetic last calls of friends whose lives were fading and ebbing before them. For Tiffany, who could barely move in the freezing chop of white foam, and for Ellen, just barely hanging on with her battered face squeezed against the cold wet granite, these were their last calls of desperation.

O'Casey heard and felt that desperation. Now, however, he could no longer even get on his knees. He had tried to pull himself up on his staff, but he was too exhausted. All he could do was slide on his back along the trail, using his one good leg to push his body forward. Like a grotesque, mangled caterpillar, he arched his back, pushed with his good leg and slid along six inches at a time. *Arch. Push. Slide. Scream. Arch. Push. Slide. Scream.* The tattered caterpillar moved his torn and bleeding carcass toward the falls.

Ellen could no longer hang on. *This is it*, she thought. She would be dragged the remaining six feet into the maelstrom and to her own watery grave along with Butch and Tiffany. In those last seconds, her fingers were almost literally being ripped from the granite crevice. Suddenly, she heard a gruesome, bone-chilling scream. She knew that voice. A heavy, wet body—a giant, gruesome caterpillar—crashed on top of hers. Suddenly, the weight on top of her body seemed to take all the pressure off the rope. There was a new anchor helping her body to hold on. A strong, familiar arm wrapped about her waist.

"Kick, Tiffany, kick!" O'Casey bellowed over the roar of the falls. "Kick!"

Using his one good leg, he wrapped his foot around the line as it played out just below Ellen's legs. He pulled with all his might. As he tried to use the leverage of his one good leg to help move the line parallel to the shore, the pain exploded again as the broken femur in his other leg pushed even further through his skin. He screamed in agony with every movement of the good leg. But the extra force was just enough to help swing Tiffany and the Chief out of the middle of the river, where they'd been stuck in the hydrodynamics of the current.

The line moved slightly parallel to the granite shelf where Ellen and O'Casey struggled to hold on. Tiffany, now completely numb and almost catatonic with the cold, suddenly felt a new reason to struggle and expend the last bit of available energy. Her frog kicks, though no longer strong, were strong enough. The new anchor of Ellen and O'Casey held. Like a trout bobber finally drifting free from the pull of the current, the lifeline tether, which had almost become a death line, swung free from the grip of the raging white water and into the shallow edge of the eddy. Tiffany could feel the exquisite joy of shore beneath her feet as she pushed her shaking body toward land and toward life.

"SHOULDERING" MORE RESPONSIBILITY

For just a moment, Tiffany and Ellen lay almost motionless on the shoreline with their eyes closed, inhaling deeply and purposefully just trying to catch their breath. Each was celebrating a narrow brush with death. Their momentary joy in the rescue was quickly offset by the chaos and suffering on the shoreline. Tiffany's shivering brought her quickly back to her senses. "Help, Ellen. Help!" she said through chattering teeth. "We need to get the Chief out of the water."

With the delicacy and caution of a parent moving from the bed of a slumbering toddler after story time, Ellen rolled gently away from O'Casey. His anchoring weight had saved not only her life, but that of Tiffany and the Chief as well.

O'Casey was too exhausted and in too much pain to move his damaged body. As he looked down at the river's edge, he was appalled by what he saw. The Chief looked dead. His motionless body lay against the banking. This big powerful, confident man was now a lump of wet, cold, blue-gray flesh. His face was barely recognizable. A gash ran from his forehead to his ear, exposing bone and raw flesh as blood oozed slowly down his face. Only Tiffany's encouraging words that he was still breathing led O'Casey to believe that his friend was not a corpse.

Neither Tiffany nor Ellen looked much better. Tiffany's lips had the same bluish pallor from the cold water, but her face lacked the grayish-white coloring that shock brings to the body, particularly when one is near death. Several days earlier, O'Casey had actually laughed to himself when he'd seen Tiffany arrive at their rendezvous point for the start of the trip. She looked like she had just stepped out of a GAP fashion shoot.

This "rich brat," as O'Casey had so wrongly assessed her, had just saved his best friend's life. Her South Hampton image was literally in tatters. Her long blonde hair was a mass of filthy knots. Her Abercrombie & Fitch T-shirt hung like old wet skin, wrinkled and faded. Her pink lace panties provided a near useless cover-up of her femininity. Modesty was no longer a word or a virtue. It was the least significant casualty of the war they had been through. This once modest paragon of image consciousness shivered uncontrollably as she focused on just one thing— getting the Chief out of the water and onto dry land.

Though Ellen was the only one of the group not hypothermic, her body, too, bore the marks of battle. Her knees, which had originally been gashed when she fell on the trail, had been made worse by her slide along the granite. She had severe friction burns on her back and sides where the rescue line had slid beneath her jersey and carved its outline into her skin. The lacerations on her face from being dragged along the ridge and into the cedar branches were more annoying than serious. The blood slowly wept into her right eye and caused her vision to blur. She had to use a corner of her tattered jersey to wipe it constantly from her forehead.

Still, it was the fingernail almost torn from her ring finger that caused the most pain. Two thirds of the nail dangled from her finger and caught on everything as she worked with Tiffany to haul Butch out of the water and onto the shore. Finally, in a moment of desperate frustration, Ellen ripped the dangling fingernail completely off. Although the initial pain of the frantic gesture made her scream, the loose nail was there no longer to catch on everything it touched. Ellen would have loved to have had the time to throw at least a Band-Aid on for comfort, but she and Tiffany were in survival mode now, first ministering to the needs of the Chief and only then attending to O'Casey. Once they succeeded in dragging their friend out of the water and up onto the bank, they lay briefly on their backs together to catch their breath.

From his vantage point a few yards away, O'Casey realized that, although he could not physically help, he could direct the rescue. "We need to get him as warm as we can. We *all* need to get warm. Tiffany, start gathering some wood. The movement will keep you from becoming more hypothermic. Most everything is wet, so look for small dead branches still hanging on the pine and spruce trees. Get the smallest, thinnest stuff first. No thicker than your pinky, and smaller if you can.

"Ellen, there's a small first aid kit that should still be tied into the canoe. It's in a waterproof bag that I lashed in early this morning. Hopefully, it's still there. We'll need everything in it...and then some. Be careful. It's in a slack water area, but it could still be deep there. Stay out of the current. That's an order...Sweetie!"

Somehow, through all the chaos and pain, he still found a way to maintain his sense of humor and that of the tribe. That was his way. It was a learned and practiced skill. He found it much easier and safer to disarm a student using humor than with force. Now O'Casey used his humor because he had to keep himself and everyone else from panicking.

He knew, or at least assumed, that Butch had a fractured skull and was in a shock- or injury-induced coma. There was nothing they could do for the injury, but if Butch was to survive, they had to get him warm as quickly as possible. O'Casey knew that he, too, was in trouble, but that would have to wait.

Fortunately, Ellen was able to salvage the first aid kit, but she was now thoroughly soaked like the rest of them. Tiffany arrived with enough twigs for O'Casey to get a fire going. Then she and Ellen moved the Chief gently toward a dry bank-side area where they could make him as comfortable as possible.

Pushing with his good arm and leg, O'Casey was able to slide on his back to a point where he could build the fire and begin to assess the Chief's needs. Even though it was still a fairly warm afternoon, the damp, drizzly air around the falls made for moist, uncomfortable conditions with the heavy easterly breeze. Given that Butch had been in the water for over half an hour, O'Casey knew that his core temperature was dangerously low, even for a June day. Getting him warm and dry was imperative for his survival. O'Casey's meticulous efforts with the pine and fir twigs soon yielded a safe, steady heat source to warm Butch and help raise his core temperature.

Tiffany was still shivering almost uncontrollably, and once again, Ellen came to the rescue. She had thrown a fleece jacket into the small backpack she brought, along with several water bottles. Tiffany needed little prompting to put on dry clothes, including the jacket. With no thought about modesty, she stripped off her wet panties and pulled on the dry jeans she had wisely removed before jumping in to rescue Butch. She had not had time to do so in her rescue of Jason, and she had learned the hard way just how difficult it was to swim in jeans and sneakers. She could never have survived the Chief's rescue with that additional weight pulling her down, though she might have been warmer as she drowned. With O'Casey's now roaring blaze, soon Tiffany, too, was warm as well as dry—though she was amazed at how long it took for the shivering to stop.

It was not until both Butch and Tiffany had been made as comfortable as possible that Ellen really noticed O'Casey's condition. Although the bleeding around the protruding bone had slowed, the compound fracture itself looked ghastly. Even O'Casey tried not to look. But he knew what had happened and what needed to happen next. Ellen took a bandanna from her backpack, moistened it with water, and delicately began to clean up O'Casey's still-bloody, completely filthy face and head.

"Not now," he said. "There's something I want you and Tiffany to do first. It's not going to be fun, especially for me, but it needs to be done. My shoulder is dislocated and needs to be put back in. It's an old rugby injury. I've had to do this before, but it's never been this bad. Once it's in, my arm's going to feel a whole lot better."

O'Casey then directed the women in the gruesome task. It was difficult to tell who least wanted to have this happen. Ellen desperately wanted to help this man she had quickly grown to love, but the thought of causing him pain was almost too much for her to bear. Tiffany had once thought about medical school but switched majors to education after fainting during a cat dissection. O'Casey, more than the others, knew how bad the pain would be. Still, he knew it needed to be done and done soon.

Using the rescue rope, he fashioned a large double loop that he slipped over his head and placed just under his left armpit and torso. "Ellen, I saw how strong you were as the anchor for the rescue line. You're going to be my anchor. You're going to keep my body from moving. When I say 'Ready,' I want you to put your foot against my right hip and then lean back against this loop. It's going to hurt an awful lot anyway, but I can't have my hips move. If my hips move, my left leg will move and that fracture will get even worse. You can't bail out on me, Honey. No matter what name I may call you for doing it."

He then turned to Tiffany. "You saved Jason's life, though I wish now you'd let the son of a bitch drown. You saved the Chief's life, and if I live to be a hundred, I'll never be able to repay you for that. Now, you've got to help me. When I say 'Go!' I want you to grab my hand and not let go until I say 'Stop.' You need to pull hard—to lean back. When it's in the right position, it will snap back in on its own. I may pee in my pants from the pain, but you *can't let go.*"

"I can't do it, Sean. I can't."

"Bullshit. You can do it. You've paddled through class three rapids better than almost any *guy* I know. You saved two grown men in the river. A bear attacked you. You've already qualified for a Congressional freakin' Medal of Honor. You can do anything. You've got to!"

He turned again to Ellen. "Let me borrow that huge freakin' handkerchief. I've got lots of plans for this bad boy in just a minute." He adjusted the rope and went over the directions once more, first with Ellen and then with Tiffany. "Now remember, Tiffany, I can't just reach up and give you my hand. I can't raise it at all right now. You've got to grab it when I say 'go' and pull until I say 'stop.'"

Sean Padraig O'Casey knew the moment had arrived. Sweat was already running down his face, not from the nearby fire or the throbbing pain in his leg, but simply in anticipation of the next few moments. Calmly, also softly, he looked at Ellen and said with a tiny smile, "Ready?" She nodded in terror, her green eyes dilating as adrenaline once again poured into her system. Following his meticulous directions, she placed her boot against his right pelvic area, just at the hipbone, and leaned back. Immediately, his left side rolled upward and slightly off the ground. The broken femur pressed upward as well, poking further through the skin.

Just as he uttered "Go!" he grabbed the kerchief and jammed a portion into his mouth and bit down.

Tiffany grabbed his hand and leaned south while Ellen leaned north. O'Casey's entire body shuddered at the pain. His screams, though muffled by the gag, did little to mask the horror of the moment. The first pull appeared to do nothing. A muffled scream of "Stop!" brought thankful relief for both women, but little for O'Casey.

He took first one deep slow breath and then another to clear his head and dissipate the pain. "This time, Tiffany, I want you to pull with more of a sharp yank upward than a steady pull," he said with the focus of a surgeon watching med students work over a cadaver.

The women waited for their commands. It was a painful drill they already had down. At "Ready," Ellen placed her foot as gently as possible against O'Casey's hipbone and leaned on the rescue line. Again, he shoved the kerchief into his mouth and a muffled "Go" brought an immediate contortion in pain. This time, Tiffany yanked sharply out, up and forward. The snap was audible to everyone, and O'Casey slumped over in the exhaustion that comes from an end to excruciating pain.

Though still shivering with the pain and cold, he could now move his elbow upward and across his chest. "And now, if one of you ER docs would be so kind as to take this saliva-drenched kerchief and make a sling out of it for my arm, that would be great. I just need a moment to catch my breath."

After Ellen fixed his sling, O'Casey slumped against the rock next to his buddy, the Chief, and closed his eyes briefly to rest. When he awoke, he was surprised to realize that he had slept for over an hour. He turned toward his friend and was pleased to see a healthier color in his face. His lips were no longer bluish in color, nor did his face have the gray-white cast of someone in shock. Although his regular breathing and improved color were positive signs, Butch was still unconscious. The women had cleaned and dressed his head wound. At least now, his appearance had lost the ghastly Halloween pallor of a death mask.

As O'Casey gradually came fully awake, he turned toward the women and was surprised that they had cleaned up quite nicely—and had just finished making their own plans for rescue, much as he and the Chief had done the night before.

WEEDS AND FLOWERS

Tiffany gave one last look at the Chief's bandaged head and slumping shoulders. She could never have imagined him looking like that. He was their *Chief*, their protector. He was the Master Maine Guide who had taught them how to handle wild white-water haystacks. He had fired his pistol calmly and coolly over the head of a raging bear. *He shouldn't look like this*, Tiffany thought to herself as she turned to Ellen and O'Casey, who were cuddled awkwardly next to each other.

O'Casey, too, looked like a caricature of himself. Like Butch, he had a bandaged head. Although the falls had been kinder to O'Casey's forehead, he had still received a severe, though non-life-threatening gash. His injuries were simply more visible and all to the left side of his body where the primary impact had occurred. His left arm and dislocated shoulder, now back in place, was tucked comfortably into a blue-checked kerchief that had become the perfect improvised sling.

Next had come the "walking cast," as he had dubbed it, which was really a crude but effective splint. On his instructions, Ellen had found several broken boards amid the washed-up wood on the banking near where the canoe had overturned. O'Casey then had her cut up a portion of the backup life jacket he had lashed to the canoe. The ribbed jacket became the first layer of the splint, and the two boards helped to support the jacket and keep his leg straight. While it looked like *who-done-it-and-ran*, it was exceptionally effective in keeping O'Casey's leg as stable and comfortable as possible.

Tiffany gave Ellen a quick hug, tapped O'Casey gently and affectionately on the cheek, and said with feigned self-confidence, "I'm off. You take care of this big lug. And when the Chief comes to, you tell him this is one hell of a way for him to get a free canoe ride home."

Then she was off. At the top of the hill, she glanced back and waved to her friends looking up through the mist and roar of the falls. As she turned to head down the trail, she slipped on the wet moss near the falls and almost slid over the edge. Her heart pounded as she picked herself up, wiped her hands on her once again filthy pants, and looked back. Fortunately, Ellen and O'Casey were looking at each other and had not seen the blunder. *What a way to begin*, she thought. *How would you like to put your rescue hopes into the hands of a clumsy oaf?* She shook her head and watched much more carefully as she headed away from the water and down the trail.

Soon she could feel herself picking up the pace. But she knew that was precisely why Ellen had fallen. They had been in a near sprint when they heard the roar of the falls. The moss-laden path was narrow and primitive. It hardly lent itself to rapid transit. Still, Tiffany had several reasons to hurry. As she thought of all the people who were depending on her now, she struggled to keep her pace safe and manageable. Yet, her instinct was to sprint, to run in a panic-driven dash headlong down the trail. No, the tribe could not afford to have a fourth member down. She wished that Ellen could have joined her rescue team of one, but Ellen was needed at the falls.

Even though O'Casey had tried to convince them otherwise, the women knew that he could not go down the trail and fetch the firewood that would be needed to keep both men warm. And while he put on a brave face, he was still seriously hurt himself. He had not even told the women of his broken ribs or the spleen he suspected he'd bruised, if not ruptured. He knew there was nothing that could be done for broken ribs other than taping them up a bit. He'd had broken ribs before. They hurt like hell any time he had to take a deep breath. When he flinched in pain, Ellen assumed it was just the result of his shoulder or broken thighbone. For O'Casey, it was just another source of pain he struggled with silently. He had also learned from his devastating car crash that physical pain is almost a welcome distraction from the constant torturous pain that grief can bring. His days and years of grief were now mitigated for the first time by green eyes and brown curls. He hoped and actually prayed silently that Catherine would understand. *It was time*, he thought. *It was time.* As the afternoon light began to wane and the thickening clouds returned, he leaned into Ellen's warm and comforting body and smiled again. *Yes, it was time.*

Tiffany began to jog now. The trail was wide enough and flat enough that she felt comfortable picking up the pace. She, too, could feel the change in the weather once again as cool damp air ran down the valley. "If it rains," she thought out loud, "this would really suck." She rarely swore and didn't even use words like *suck* very often. However, as she mentally worked her way through the rescue plan, she could readily imagine what it would be like to break camp and do a three-mile portage in the rain. "Yes, it would suck," she said again.

Suddenly, out of the corner of her eye, she caught something that sent a shiver right down her spine. Long, pale yellow streaks ran down the entire length of a hemlock trunk at the edge of the trail. Had she not been listening to Butch's trailside chat with Jason and Ellen, she would never have known what the marks were—but she did know. They were rake marks. They started perhaps eight or nine feet up on the tree; they were very wide and deep. Tiffany could easily imagine a bear, larger than the one that had chased her, standing at that very spot. Her imagination painted a vivid picture of a black bear standing on his hind legs and raking the hemlock in a show of power and anger. She could feel the anger. She could see the massive black head, the long yellow fangs and three-inch claws raking the bark. Sap oozed like fresh blood from the mortally wounded tree. Adrenaline surged through Tiffany's legs and arms as she broke into a full run. She didn't care if she fell. She had to get back to camp and away from the rake marks. She just had to—and *now*!

Her powerful, well-measured strides seemed to shrink the distance to mere seconds now, when it had felt like hours before. As she smelled the pungent, oddly sweet smell of wood smoke in the distance, she began to slow down a bit. She knew she would be safe now. Besides, she thought, she did not want to burst into camp in full stride with tales of a bear on the trail. That would be no way to start a rescue mission.

As she neared the camp, she once again went over the details of their plan. They would break camp and take only the essentials. O'Casey had told them about how wild the river had been and how impossible it was to escape the current because of the steep banks and nonexistent exit areas. It was just too dangerous to risk a river rescue. They would have to portage everything—and most importantly, Angelo.

Each of them would have to drag a canoe or a kayak. The hope was that Angelo could be made comfortable and safe in the kayak and that Jason could make a drag to pull him, at least to the big hill near the falls. That plan, of course, was contingent upon Jason...and as Tiffany discovered when she arrived at camp, the plan was in trouble right from the start. Jason was in no mood, and hardly in any condition, to pull anything or anyone.

The Yukon Jack had only partially numbed Tiffany's senses the night before. Jason, however, was coping with a severe hangover. Even though he was capable of drinking a great deal—and often did—he was now paying for having consumed almost an entire bottle. While Tiffany had perhaps had four or five shots, Jason had finished everything else. As most serious drinkers know, it is the sweet drinks that produce the worst hangovers.

Once Jason had awakened, later in the morning, he had suffered, but not in silence. Jason was anything but a martyr. He had cursed everything and everyone. He cursed the New Blue Hilton, which smelled of vomit. He cursed the lack of breakfast and the lack of lunch. He cursed the lack of firewood and the abundance of black flies. He cursed O'Casey for his Orvis fishing shirt, and even Butch for laughing at his Sears life jacket.

All morning long, Maria listened to his repulsive mumbling and ranting. While the curses were more for his own benefit, they were intentionally loud enough to create a show for Maria, the way a child's temper tantrums were meant to garner attention and sympathy from a parent. But there was no such sympathy from Maria, who had grown up with bullies like Jason. She had worn enough of these invectives as a young Latino girl in a primarily Anglo school. People like Jason did not scare or intimidate Maria. They disgusted her.

Had she not been afraid to wake Angelo, she would have told Jason where he could put his curses. Although she rarely swore, even when angry, she had learned to defend herself verbally and physically. After all, she had five brothers. She had heard, and on rare occasion used, almost every word her brothers knew. She would have loved to use such language now, but it would probably awaken Angelo, and if it did, he would certainly be upset to hear and feel her anger. "Let sleeping dogs lie," her mother used to say. *Seems like good advice now*, she thought, despite her wish to do otherwise.

As Maria dabbed at Angelo's brow and tried to keep him comfortable, she was struck by the contrast between the two men. Jason was one of the least sensitive men she had ever met. Angelo was easily the *most* sensitive. He was a kind, almost a *flowerlike* man—soft, fragile, delicate, and beautiful. Jason, on the other hand, was a weed, Maria mused. *Like poison ivy with its red-green slick and shiny leaves, it looks pretty and attractive, but its poisons cause suffering to all who come near.* As she dabbed at Angelo's forehead, the contrast between the withering flower and the toxic weed became almost intolerable.

Unfortunately, the toxicity was about to get worse.

The Slug and the Butterfly

Although it was officially almost summer, the cold easterly breeze that came rolling in from the Gulf of Maine pushed both additional moisture and remarkably cool damp air to the campground. The hot morning air pushed north and the cold, damp air rolled up the valley. As Tiffany slowed her breathing and began to explain the rescue plan to Maria, she shivered almost constantly. Her shirt and bra had never dried out from the afternoon rescue, and her run through the damp forest had only added moisture to the clammy cotton top.

The breeze strengthened as it blew its way through the canyon. Under different circumstances, the cool air might have been refreshing after the oppressive heat of the day before and the early morning. Typical Maine weather—wait a minute and it will change … and it quickly did.

Tiffany was about to pause her rescue narrative long enough to change into dry clothes. The breeze blowing on the back of her neck and against her damp cotton jersey sent repeated chills down her spine. Then she thought about Jason Foxworthy still grumbling and cursing in the tent where her dry clothes lay waiting. The chill she received from that image made the breeze seem gentle and kind by contrast. How could she have allowed herself to believe Jason Foxworthy was anything but a letch? And to think that she had not only allowed him to see her naked both at the swimming hole and in the tent was almost more than she could bear. "Maria, would you mind getting my backpack out of the tent? I just can't go in there. He was all over me last night like a high school wrestler at an all-night drive-in. But I need to change. I'm soaked and freezing."

"Honey, I'm glad to. I've got to get that clown out of his bunk to help us break camp anyway."

Not surprisingly, when she quickly entered the tent, every one of her pleadings and directives was met with epithets and complaints. The last straw came when Jason suggested that they just leave Angelo behind with a jug of water and let a rescue team come for him in the morning.

"Look, you son of a bitch," Maria exploded, "if you want, we can just leave *you* here! That big bear is still out there somewhere and she's looking for your ass. I'm *happy* to leave you here. Just sit by the fire and wait for the bear...because I'm sure she'd just love to have you for supper!"

"Up yours, bitch," Jason snarled. Still, the thought of being left alone with that bear gave him a shiver of his own. Ordinarily, he might even have given Maria a backhand, as she had fully expected. Jason, like all bullies and batterers, had that move down to a science. However, both the image of a raging black bear in camp and the raging headache throbbing in his skull diminished his anger. Slowly and clumsily, he began to stuff his backpack with his clothing, which was strewn about the tent. Maria grabbed what she needed for her friend and left.

Tiffany ducked into the large dome tent where Angelo was sleeping to change into dry clothing and continue sharing the rescue planning with Maria. Once again, there was no time for modesty. Tiffany quickly stripped down and began to put on warm clothing. She was not sure if Angelo was still asleep, but she undressed anyway. She loved Angelo and Maria. They were her brother and sister now. Naked or not, she did not care what they saw. She was who she was for the first time in her life. She was among real friends for perhaps the first time ever. They didn't care about the labels on her clothes or whether things matched. They didn't care who she knew or even *what* she knew. They just cared about *her*— and it felt good.

At Maria's directive, Tiffany "gloved up" as they began to get Angelo changed and warm for the rescue effort. Maria spoke to him gently about what they were going to do. From his somewhat fetal position, she turned him onto his back and Tiffany saw his face for the first time since he'd become really ill. What she saw was appalling, almost nauseating. In spite of her best efforts to keep him clean, Angelo still had a thin stream of green-brown vomit crusting on his chin. The trail of liquid had run down onto his neck and chest below the now filthy down sleeping bag. At that moment, Tiffany almost screamed at the sight of her friend. Though she had never seen a dead person before, other than her grandfather at his funeral, she assumed that Angelo was near death. His face was gaunt and gray. His eyes, though closed, seemed to be gray hollow caverns set deep in his skull. He appeared to be a person she hardly knew. This once handsome man, meticulously dressed, always cheerful, was now a pathetic old man, limp and decrepit.

Much as she had risen to the occasion in rescuing both Jason and Butch, she took a deep breath and kept saying to herself, *I can do this. Please, God. I can do this.* The task of readying Angelo for the portage was made all the more awkward and gruesome because of the latex gloves they were wearing. At one point, Tiffany pulled one of her gloves off and was getting ready to remove the other. "I hate these things! I can't hold onto anything. These things are disgusting."

"Stop it, Tiffany! Look at your hands, which were still weeping blood. You have to wear them. No choice. Universal precautions. Remember, that's what Angelo would want."

Tiffany looked down at her hands. They were all cuts and rope burns—lots of open tissue. Maria was right. It was just hard to work, particularly moving Angelo around while wearing the slippery white gloves. Tiffany, the woman who had dropped out of pre-med after fainting at the sight of a dead cat in formaldehyde, somehow managed to help clean up and dress a man still covered in vomit and diarrhea. It was surprisingly easy, working side by side with Maria. At one point, as they were buttoning up his shirt, he opened his eyes. They no longer had that dark-blue glow that had always given Angelo his handsome, almost angelic look.

Angelo struggled to keep his eyes open, to stay conscious, and to take in where he was and what was happening. It was almost too much for him to sustain. As he looked up at Maria and Tiffany, he smiled faintly and whispered, "Thank you." He then closed his eyes and drifted back into the deep, almost coma-like state of a man too exhausted and frail to hang onto the last vestiges of consciousness.

Jason was in a totally *different* state of consciousness. Coordinating a rescue plan with an arrogant and toxic man still wallowing in the self-pity of a ruthless hangover proved more challenging than the task itself. There were both physical and interpersonal challenges to overcome. Jason was nearly useless as Tiffany and Maria broke camp and determined what would be portaged and what would be left behind. O'Casey had been very explicit about leaving everything but the drinking water, dehydrated food, a large, lightweight blue tarp, the cruiser axe, and a few other survival items. Jason wanted to take everything—at least everything that was *his*.

The real problem for Maria and Tiffany was in creating harnesses with which to drag the canoes and the kayaks. They had strategized correctly that it would be way too dangerous to canoe even a portion of the river, and impractical to carry the canoes one at a time. It would be dark in a few hours. Trying to portage through the winding and dark trail would be difficult, dangerous and, in all honesty, terrifying at times. Tiffany didn't dare tell Maria about the rake marks. And had she ever known how large the big male bear was, perhaps the biggest boar in the Allagash, they would never have walked that trail at all, even in the daylight hours.

Tiffany had a new reason to be even more terrified. She had peed in the woods just before they headed out, only to discover that her period had just arrived. For Tiffany, this was far more than an inconvenience. She had cringed when Butch had told them they'd be safe from bears … as long as none of the women had their periods. Now that was all Tiffany could think about as she and Maria first tied and then retied loops and knots. After the Chief's comments, Tiffany remembered counting days, trying to figure whether her period would arrive while they were camping. It had. She tried to concentrate on the knots, on the ropes, on anything but the rake marks and her earlier brush with the angry bear by the Half-Moon Hilton.

Fortunately, Maria interrupted her mental anguish. "I think we're all set. Let's put Angelo in the kayak, and then we're ready to roll." She had purposely waited until the last moment to load Angelo. She knew this would be a contentious moment, and it was. "Jason. We *really* need your help," Maria said in the kindest, most ingratiating voice she could muster. She didn't mind this effort to suck up to Jason. Even though he was a complete slime-bucket, she was willing to beg if necessary to help Angelo. They couldn't make it to the big falls and the rest of the tribe before nightfall without Jason's help. She asked again.

"I still think we should leave him," Jason replied.

Although she just wanted to bang his egotistical head against a rock, she chose to avoid a confrontation she would otherwise have relished.

She took a deep breath and used the skills she had honed as a principal with some of the toughest students she had ever faced.

"Here's the deal, Jason. We can't do this without your help. You're twice as strong as either of us and you're in much better shape. We can't and won't leave Angelo here. The kayak is lighter than the canoes and easier for us to strap Angelo into. You're the only one strong enough to pull him. We can't, but you can. Please! It's starting to rain. It will be dark before we know it. It's your choice. You can either stay here or you can come with us. Please!"

The strategy worked. Maria had appealed to Jason's masculine vanity and had assumed a subservient, weak submissive female role—just what Jason liked. She had also reminded him of looming nightfall and with it, thoughts of a lurking bear. Most importantly, she had given him a choice. She had not ordered or directed. She had begged, or at least made it appear that way to Jason. He agreed.

Although he was almost loath to help put Angelo into the kayak, he did just enough and the women quickly tucked him in as comfortably as they could. The kayak functioned as a cocoon of sorts. They used the sleeping bags as cushioning for his body and head. Again, as he was being tucked in, Angelo opened his eyes slowly, stared directly at Maria and smiled softly. This time his smile was more than enough to say the thank-you that he had whispered earlier.

"Let's get this show on the road," Jason announced with the indifference of a man forced on a mission he had no interest in completing. And he didn't. His only interest was in getting away from the campground and away from the bear he knew would surely be coming…for him.

This was just one more chapter in Jason's life story of using people for self-indulgent purposes. He knew Maria was right about the bears. With all the gear and food still lying around the campground, he knew that the site would become bear heaven. He also knew that his chances of being accosted by a bear would only be one in five as long as he stayed with the group. And after all, he grinned to himself, how fast could Angelo run? As he pondered that thought, he slipped into the harness and smiled down at Angelo. "Gr-r-r," he growled with another grin. "Can't run too fast now, can you, partner?"

"Yup. Still Alive."

The rain, which had started as a light drizzle, had become a driving shower. Unlike the summer thunderstorm that had brought the lightning, thunder, and torrential rains the night before, this weather had come out of the east rather than the southwest. Southwesterly showers are often the early-summer byproduct of the first Bermuda highs. The air is warm, sometimes hot, and occasionally stifling; the rain, however, always seems warm, almost monsoon-like. By contrast, summer nor'easters, as they are known in Maine, bring cold air from the still-frigid Down East waters, strong winds, and moisture from across the Gulf of Maine. Such conditions can make a June evening feel like March in Chicago. As the rain began to drive through the overhanging fir and cedar, the trail conditions worsened, as did the amount of light reaching the trail.

Virtually everyone had underestimated the ordeal before them. Each member of the rescue team strained under a load they were beginning to curse. Maria, though perhaps the most determined, had by far the most difficult challenge. Her physique was antithetical to that of Tiffany, the tall, lean athlete. Maria had never been athletic. In fact, her brothers used to tease her when they played baseball, their favorite game. "Hey, Maria. Come join us for a baseball game," they had once said in jest. She remembered that painful moment all too well as she strained against her canoe harness. She vividly recalled that day as a nine-year-old girl. Being invited to play baseball with her five brothers was a rare event—particularly when her brothers' friends were with them. While one or two of her brothers might, on occasions, ask her to join them to play catch, they never, ever asked her to join them when their friends were present. Never! Her heart jumped at the thought that she might actually be joining them to play baseball with *the gang*. Her hopes had been quickly dashed by a cruel hoax. "Yeah, Maria, we needed someone to play second base, and we thought you would make the *perfect base!* You're soft and well stuffed!"

As she strained against the weight of her increasingly heavy load, Maria could still recall the much greater pain those words had brought her. It had been one of the saddest days of her life. Being called a *base*, a sack over which people ran, was exactly how she felt as her brothers and their friends laughed at her expense. This was one time when she just could not laugh while being laughed at—not this time. Carlos, the youngest of her brothers, had looked back and seen the tears streaming down Maria's face, then looked away. Later that day, when no one else was around to hear his words, he had apologized in a very heartfelt and humble way. Although Maria had greatly appreciated Carlos's kind words, no balm could ever really soothe that pain. It told Maria that she was a short, fat little girl who could never and would never be a baseball player. Then and there she had resigned herself to her body type and to her lack of athletic prowess.

Maria escaped the pain of that day and many other days in the solace of her books. And in her prowess for reading, Maria found more than solace. She found wisdom, knowledge, and courage. Sacagawea, Nancy Drew, Rosa Parks, Madam Curie, all became her heroines and good friends. They became her idols and role models. Although she loved her mother for her kindness and inner strength, Maria was determined to escape the barrio life her mother had inherited as a nineteen-year-old bride and twenty-four-year old mother of three…then five, then six. No, Maria had set a goal to overcome her short, stocky stature and Latino heritage, and had become a highly respected school administrator in the final stages of a Ph.D. program.

But Maria hardly felt like a soon-to-be *Dr. Maria Gonzalez y Ramirez* now. Her short, stout, unathletic frame was hardly a match for a fourteen-foot aluminum canoe laden with some of the gear they would need to survive. Tiffany and Maria had tried several sling-type configurations. Although the final design seemed to be working, the rope was already creating a friction burn on her shoulder. Maria had tried to keep switching shoulders, but her right knee was already bleeding from a fall she'd taken early in their portage. Since she was using her left leg to drive forward, that forced her to keep the sling over her right shoulder.

She had developed a purposeful and steady cadence, much as O'Casey had done with his walking stick. In this case, Maria would drive with her left leg, lean forward with her right shoulder, and move the canoe about a foot. Then she'd pull her painful right leg forward, picking up the slack she'd gained, and prepare herself for the next effort. It became, as O'Casey had learned earlier that day, a dance of pain. *Sore right shoulder forward. Sore right leg forward. Left leg push.* On and on she danced along the increasingly slippery trail.

In some ways, Tiffany had the most difficult job. She knew that Maria would have a hard time with such a physically demanding task. She had seen Maria straining to the point of exhaustion just on their brief four-mile paddle from the landing to the dam and then later across Wilson Lake. Tiffany had deliberately taken O'Casey's heavy fiberglass cruising canoe and most of the gear. She was outraged by Jason's insistence on bringing his entire backpack, replete with God knew how much alcohol already packed inside. Tiffany had also packed all the water bottles, knowing how important that would be for everyone. Even for Tiffany, who was always in excellent condition, pulling a fully loaded canoe along a narrow rocky trail became a grueling experience. Like Maria, she soon developed chafe points that grew into friction burns, and eventually into bleeding sores. Each step became more painful than the one before, particularly as the driving rain began to turn the trail into a dangerous quagmire.

While Maria had wisely remembered to bring a hooded sweatshirt, which protected her somewhat from the driving rain and the deepest cuts from her harness, Tiffany had misjudged the Maine weather. Her light-blue Abercrombie & Fitch sweat suit top did little to cushion her shoulder or keep the rain from running down the back of her neck. It soon became a saturated mass clinging to her skin. Once again she was wet, cold, and shivering.

She also found herself surprisingly exhausted. Her rescue of the Chief in the cold roiling water coupled with her run back to camp had taken far more out of her than she had thought. Equally important, she had not eaten all day, and she knew that low blood sugar was also contributing to her fatigue.

Tiffany was also keenly aware of the impact her period tended to have on her energy level. She again thought about the poor timing of her monthly biology, especially as it related to the rake marks and the massive growling black terror that might be lurking on the edge of the trail…waiting just for her. Wisely, she asked everyone to stop for a water break and a badly needed handful of gorp—the mixture of peanuts, raisins, and chocolate bits that hikers count on for an energy revival like the one Tiffany herself so desperately needed.

Jason grumbled incessantly. He guzzled water so quickly that it ran recklessly down his stubbled chin. He threw handful after handful of gorp carelessly at his face rather than into his mouth. He seemed more like a madman oblivious to the rest of the tribe than a colleague on a rescue mission. For Jason, it was all about self-preservation and self-indulgence. In fact, he was even more concerned about the bear than Tiffany was. As he played back the mental tape of the bear attack, he knew that he had recognized the sow as Yellow Flank, the same bear whose cub he'd killed and hung on his bathroom wall. *Stupid freakin' cub!* If it hadn't bitten him he would not have had to kill it. *Could that sow actually know I was the one?* Jason had continually pondered the question after the attack back at the lake. The thought of being left at camp honestly terrified him. Maria's strategy was on the mark. Jason's fear of the angry sow was the only thing keeping him on the trail with the women. He didn't care at all about Angelo. He would just as soon have used Angelo as bear bait. But if dragging Angelo helped to keep him with the women and improve his odds if the bear returned, he would do it…for now.

All three members of the now fractured rescue team were immersed in their own thoughts during the break. Each one, exhausted and in pain, dealt privately with his or her own level of fatigue. Jason's vanity and masculine pride had given him some initial impetus to show the women that he could haul *three* canoes if he needed to. But after several hundred yards of pulling Angelo and the kayak with the bravado and drive of hitting a football sled, he had to admit—at least to himself—that he was no longer in football shape. In fact, he was in no shape at all. He could feel the ache of lactic acid already building up in his thigh muscles, and an old Achilles tendon injury began to rear its ugly head.

Maria took a few quick sips of water, tossed down a small handful of gorp, and then turned her attention to Angelo. Even with all the bumping along the trail and a driving rain soaking his gaunt face, Angelo remained in a deep, profoundly disturbing sleep. Maria knelt by his side to again minister to her friend's needs. She seemed oblivious to the puddle of cold rainwater and mud seeping into the baggy sweats she had jumped into hours before.

Maria reached into her already saturated pocket and pulled out a handkerchief to dab some of the moisture from Angelo's face. The action had little purpose or value. The already wet handkerchief could do little to stop the onslaught of the driving rain, which was now stronger than ever. Still, Maria worked delicately and methodically. She wiped the beading water from Angelo's eyes, his cheeks, and even his brow along the edges of his black curly hair. Her touch somehow seemed to reach deeply into Angelo's semiconscious state. His eyes opened ever so slightly. He was too weak to smile or even to open his eyes fully. For Maria, however, this was still a gesture of love. Angelo knew she was there. That was the message she wanted to give, and that was the message she needed to receive.

The break was over. First one, then another person looked down at their watch and then down the trail, trying to calculate whether or not they could make it to the falls before dark. The two-minute break for a sip of water had turned into twenty minutes, and it was now almost six o'clock. They had traveled less than a mile. The portage had been infinitely more tiring than anyone had imagined. They had all thought it would be hard. Instead, it was brutally difficult, tediously slow, and more painful than expected. Jason swore epithets about the weather, O'Casey, Angelo, and even Butch as he slid the slippery loop of mud-laden Dacron line over his shoulder and leaned forward. Mile two of their trek began.

Maria looped the rope over her shoulder, as well, and once again began the awkward dance she had reluctantly mastered. Left leg push. Right shoulder lean. Drag up the slack with the sore right leg. Unfortunately, as the slow dance continued, she added new elements. Pause for a minute. Two deep breaths. Adjust the line tearing into her shoulder. Then pull up the muddy sweat pants that were literally falling down. She was so focused on helping Angelo and on the rescue mission that she had never thought to change, to put on a pair of jeans…with a belt. She would give anything for a belt now. Her sweats were saturated as well as muddy, and the extra weight of the saggy, soggy sweats added to her fatigue and made her feel even heavy and dumpier than she had ever felt. *Where did Superwoman go,* she wondered.

The light levels dropped quickly as the sun slid lower in the western sky. A high granite ridge well to their right blocked most of the indirect brightness filtering through the moisture-laden sky. The canopy of blue spruce and fir seemed to grab the little light that was left. Although there were still almost two hours to sundown, it was already dusk to those on the trail. It became more difficult to spot the rocks, roots, and branches that waited to insult a face, knee, or shin.

Maria was the most frequent casualty. She had based her footwear choice, like her apparel, on the quickest items she could find. Now she was paying dearly for her focus on Angelo's needs rather than her own. The three-year-old cheap running shoes had long since lost their traction grooves, which made walking on the wet trail difficult, if not dangerous. Pulling a fourteen-foot canoe had become a dangerous adventure with every step. First one knee and then the other wore the damages of her falls. As she felt the blood trickle slowly down her aching shinbones and into her muddy socks, Maria prayed.

Only occasionally did Maria pray for herself. Growing up in a devoutly Catholic home, she had learned about a suffering Christ, carrying a cross to his death. She now felt this was her own humbling walk toward Golgotha. She, too, was suffering for a purpose, she reminded herself. She prayed first for Angelo, this wonderful, sweet soul she had come to love like a brother. With every step, she prayed, "Please God, if it is your will, let Angelo live. Please God, if it is your will, let Angelo live." She then prayed for Butch and O'Casey. She had learned from Tiffany that they were alive, but that Butch might die at any moment. She still marveled at the kiss she had received from him, and struggled to interpret its meaning, not wanting to hope too much that it could mean more than it was. Yet, she could dream. Kisses for Maria were a rare wine to be savored and remembered forever, knowing full well there might not be another. She mixed her dreams and prayers. The driving rain rolled down her forehead; it fogged her black-rimmed glasses. Maria focused on her dance—*left foot, right shoulder, pull then pray; left foot, right shoulder, pull then pray.*

Tiffany, too, continued to struggle. She had purposely chosen the heaviest canoe and the greatest load. She would have thrown out

Jason's thirty-pound backpack, but she didn't want to risk his physical and verbal rage. He was an essential part of the rescue mission. With each pull against her increasingly exhausting load, she kept her focus. Much as she had done in grueling practices for the swim team, she concentrated on the moment, on the next stroke, the next lap. *One hill at a time* became her mantra. Soon, however, it became *One step at a time*. Tiffany had run so fast after seeing the rake marks, she had forgotten the series of small steep hills. It was not yet mile twenty in the marathon. Heartbreak Hill had come early and often.

Each hill became more grueling than the last and required a new set of tactics. By the second hill, Jason could barely pull Angelo to the top. After falling on his face in the mud, the women thought they could hear Jason crying—sobbing in fact. Maria slipped out of her harness and ran to help him up. His face was filthy. The mud was caked on the stubble of his day-old beard. In spite of a feeble effort to wipe his face clean with his muddy shirtsleeve, tears still ran down his cheeks and onto the stubble. "What the hell are you looking at?" he sputtered, clearly embarrassed that Maria had witnessed his tears.

Once again, Maria was a master of psychology when it came to dealing with Jason or any other recalcitrant child. "You've got the heaviest load," she said with a sympathetic smile, knowing full well it was not true. "Why don't you swap with Tiffany for a while and give yourself a break?"

"I can do it. I'm fine. I just slipped, that's all. This hill is really steep and muddy," Jason rationalized as he struggled to defend his bruised ego. Without even asking for his consent, Maria and Tiffany grabbed the stern of the kayak as Jason slipped into his harness and pulled from the bow. The footing got worse by the moment. As they neared the top, Tiffany suddenly fell on her face, just missing a jagged piece of granite jutting up from the edge of the trail. Jason, oblivious to or unconcerned with Tiffany's near brush with disfigurement, turned, and like a spoiled child exclaimed, "See. I told you it was slippery."

Now vindicated by Tiffany's fall, Jason Foxworthy enjoyed the downhill slope. He grinned to himself as he and the kayak picked up speed going down the hill. The trail turned slightly at the bottom and Jason strode quickly to the right now that he had ample slack. The kayak and its precious cargo did not follow. It lurched headlong into a tree at the bottom of the hill.

The women missed the collision between kayak and tree, having just returned to the bottom of the hill to begin the process of hauling Maria's canoe up the slope. Jason had turned just prior to the impact, amazed at how free he had felt from the burden of the load against his shoulder. Now he stood with his mouth agape, not moving, just watching as though staring at an imminent car wreck, enthusiastic about watching the outcome. If Maria had not insisted at the last minute that they strap Angelo in, he would surely have been launched into the woods and might have died on impact. Instead, the sleeping bags had helped to cushion the forces of the collision. The tie-in strap Maria had so crudely fashioned had, in effect, saved Angelo's life. *Ouch! That must have hurt,* Jason said to himself after witnessing the kayak's collision with the tree. He peered over the kayak and assessed Angelo's state. He was still breathing. He was not bleeding. *Yup. Still OK.*

Had either woman witnessed Jason's callous assessment, they might have flown into a complete and utter rage. Instead, they were busy pulling and pushing the reluctant aluminum canoe. The tandem effort seemed to make good sense on the hills, they had decided. Neither was surprised that Jason did not offer to help. Instead, he was enjoying what he saw as a well-deserved rest at the bottom of the path. Unlike Jason, who could not have imagined the forces of physics working as they did on the kayak, Tiffany and Maria anticipated what would happen to the unchecked slide of the canoes. Each helped the other on the downhill run. The women had wrongly assumed that Jason had done the same with his responsibility.

The new tactic had been established. The women helped Jason up the hills and walked back down to get their canoes. Jason would grin and watch one collision after another, as the kayak would hit something or other on the downhill run. It seemed funny to Jason. "Yup. Still alive," he would mumble to himself. He had such contempt for gay men that he somehow saw Angelo's plight as punishment from God. Although he no longer believed in God, he had been raised by two Southern Baptists who were proud of their heritage and instilled that pride in Jason. His parents had, on a number of occasions, announced to Jason, to his friends, and to anyone who would listen during their beer-induced dinner or nighttime ramblings that AIDS was simply God's way of teaching "the fags" a lesson for *their sinful ways.*

As Jason inhaled slowly and tried to catch his breath on this cold, rainy evening, he found a macabre satisfaction in the painful trudge up the hills and the inevitable secret collisions as the kayak careened out of control downhill toward a tree or rock. The private refrain continued unabated and just out of earshot of the women.

"Ouch! I bet that hurt...."

"Yup. Still alive."

Yoknapatawpha Women

Thick gray coils of smoke wrapped around the frail cedar at the base of the falls like an anxious serpent waiting for its prey to exhaust itself before lunging. The cedar leaned even more precariously over the granite ledge now that Ellen had almost ripped its tenacious roots from their hold in the sparse soil. Ellen, like the cedar, bore the scars of the afternoon battle. Her hands, ripped open as she had slipped along the razor-sharp granite ridge, continued to weep blood into the crude gauze bandages O'Casey had tried to fashion for her. The Band-Aid that he had put on her ring finger with just one hand provided a modicum of relief for a fingernail torn off almost to the cuticle. While his gentle first aid skills provided great emotional comfort for his "Sweetie," they could do little to ease the constant pain that pulsated in her hands.

Each time Ellen carried back another bunch of branches or thicker dry kai, it seemed the sharpest branch spur could find its way into the most sensitive spot in her palm. The wet granite ledge and mossy paths she trudged all day long in an effort to keep the fires going generated a further source of pain. Slip after painful slip seemed to provide ongoing opportunities for her torn shinbones and kneecaps to compete with her palms and fingernail for painful attention. Still, Ellen felt she had little choice. It seemed obvious to her that the rescue party would not come back that evening. She now had a singular focus. It seemed more important than any job she had ever been given. She would find a way to keep these two men whom she cared so deeply about *alive*…not just tonight, but until they were all rescued. That was her mission. She would not quit. She *could* not quit. *Alive*. That was the job. *Alive*. It was that simple.

What might otherwise have been the easy task of keeping a fire going proved a full-time and arduous chore in the alternating drizzle and pouring rain. With some quiet coaching from O'Casey, Ellen had learned the best and worst sources of firewood for such conditions. The pine and fir branches from dead but still standing trees or leaning trees were the best. Branches on the ground were easier to gather but were often soaking wet, or worse, rotten. To Ellen's surprise, the branches on the trees, particularly the dead standing variety or those newly fallen, were remarkably dry, even with all the rain. However, snapping them off meant excruciating pain. She trembled from head to toe as she leaned her body into the trunk of the tree and snapped downward. The thin, pinky-size branches proved the easiest to snap but burned with a quick fury. Often, she would leave her prize fire as a bright, crackling blaze she knew would warm her charges, only to return ten minutes later to find a humble, smoldering glow that needed immediate attention. She did not have the strength or the skill to use the cruising axe to cut up the bigger branches that would have lasted longer.

Ellen was also concerned that O'Casey appeared to be getting even more exhausted and somewhat listless. For brief periods when they huddled together in the warmth of a new blaze, she closed her eyes and imagined that she and her Sweetie were on a honeymoon in the wilderness, enjoying the solace and tranquility that lovers can find in a fire and a streamside evening. Then he would shift his weight slightly to find a less painful position and Ellen would feel him shudder in silent, white-hot pain.

The protruding bone screamed a message of pain that O'Casey was only now beginning to understand. The icy waters had slowed his senses. The cold had, in many ways, quite literally numbed the pain. Still, even four Advil tablets were not nearly enough to block his pain receptors. Although he could take an additional dose now, he was trying to measure out his consumption, since there were not many tablets left. He had a full bottle of aspirin, but suspected that he probably had internal injuries, possibly including a ruptured spleen. From his rescue training, he knew that aspirin would increase the likelihood that he would hemorrhage internally. He shivered through the surges of pain. He wanted to live so that he could be with the ones he loved—Angelo, the Chief, and this woman he could not stop looking at, even through the miasma of pain and exhaustion.

As O'Casey's spirits and enthusiastic chats dwindled to dry whispers, Ellen strained her ears. Her eyes, like his were heavy with fatigue. She closed her eyes slowly even as her ears continued to work. She listened for what seemed like hours through the smoky haze and failing light of the fire. *What was that? Is it them?* She heard, or thought she heard, a twig snap in the distance. Was that Tiffany coming down the hill?

Or was that...? Her ever-drowsy thoughts turned to the bear, its jagged yellow teeth bared and terrible. The massive black form was as much phantom as real for her. The tape in her mind could not shut off. It was here now in camp! Its vicious teeth were just inches away! She reached into the depths of her lungs to scream out—to warn her treasured O'Casey. She screamed and screamed. Yet, the bear did not move. Nor did O'Casey wake.

The bear was in a rage now. It seemed to tower over everything. It was a wild uncontrollable massive blackness with claws raking at the very air before their faces. The putrid smell of death still lingered on the spike-like claws. *This is it,* Ellen thought. Her screams no longer made noise. They were a blast of useless air. Nothing more. They seemed like fog coming from her mouth, like a cold mist now hiding the face of the bear, making him disappear. As Ellen screamed and screamed, the noiseless mist enveloped the bear, the camp, even O'Casey....

Little Ellen reached out and felt a hand whose touch gave her instant comfort. "Honey, it's OK," her mother said in the soft, almost fragile voice that even time could not alter. "You're safe with me. It's just an old bear in a cage. He can't hurt anyone. It's time to go home, anyway." Ellen's mother squeezed her hand with the delicate reassurance only a mother can provide and led her along a glowing stream of light, away from the bear, away from the zoo, and away from her frequent childhood nightmare.

Ellen suddenly woke up in a startle from the troubled sleep that had come with sheer exhaustion. The fire was barely alive and her two close friends lay in varying states of injury and danger.

There was, of course, no bear in camp, as she had dreamed...but what she did not know was that there was an enormous bear less than a mile away and on the prowl, looking for its first good meal in many days. Several days ago, it had given up on the scent of the twin fawns and instead changed directions to follow the scent of campers, food, and, perhaps, an easy meal.

The rescue mission, further up the path, was an ongoing nightmare of mud, exhaustion, and grotesque contrasts. The macabre dance continued up and down the short hills of the trail just before the falls. Tiffany and Maria dropped their slings and heavy loads to help Jason pull Angelo and the kayak up one slippery hill after another. Jason would then adamantly refuse to help them in return, saying he needed to stay with Angelo or feigning some injury or another. Somehow, the two women continued with their struggle. They were the toilers—the women in William Faulkner's Yoknapatawpha County. Some women not only endured, as Faulkner maintained. They *prevailed*. They were the heart and soul of life.

Up and down the hills the two women trudged and prevailed. Tiffany would grab the harness and drag from the bow. Maria would put her shoulder into the stern of the canoe and push. Her stout body and thick legs made her the logical choice for this role; she was the tugboat that got to push from the stern. It was always the least glamorous job, but the role someone had to assume. That seemed her role in life, she thought. Pushing, nudging, encouraging. Even as a leader, she somehow seemed to work from behind the scenes rather than out front as the lead tugboat.

And now, as she dug first one leg and then the other into the muddy hillside, she smiled. *I think I can. I think I can.* Maybe that's why it was always my favorite book, Maria thought. *I'm* The Little Engine that Could. It truly was her favorite book as a child. Now as an adult, she loved the story and the metaphor. Often, while working late into the night on her doctoral projects or waking to a cruel alarm clock after only three or four hours of sleep, she found herself grinning and saying, "I think I can. I think I can."

It was that attitude and that smile which Tiffany and the rest of the tribe found so special about Maria. Even as her legs seemed to go numb from exhaustion, she somehow found ways to smile or encourage Tiffany. At one point, as Maria drove both legs forward as they approached the top of the hill, her feet went out from under her. She did a full face-plant in the muddy hillside. Wet moss clung from the edge of her thick glasses and her wiry hair was an electric afro of matted, muddy curls. Her forehead and chin bore the brunt of the mud and slime, as did one lens of her glasses.

"Hey, Tiffany!" she called out. "What time is the prom?" Maria grinned through the slime, the rain, and the pain. Sometimes you just had to laugh at things, if only to stay sane. And that's just what Tiffany did. She looked down and just lost it. How could she not love this woman? How could anyone not want her as a best friend? In the midst of chaos, pain, and ignominy, somehow Maria could turn despair into triumph.

Tiffany was no longer thinking of her own painfully bruised knee. Gone for the moment was the revulsion she felt for Jason, his near rape the night before, and his cowardly avoidance of helping them now. As she smiled back at Maria, she could feel solid footing beneath her and drove with her legs to purchase the last few feet of real estate she needed. She and the canoe had reached the crest of the hill.

Strangely, the laughter she'd heard on one side of the hill was now matched by laughter on the other side—a bizarre male echo to the feminine laughter coming from Maria. For some reason, Jason was roaring with laughter…and Tiffany could not figure out why. He couldn't see Maria; she was still down the hill. And he wasn't looking at *her*.

Tiffany strained her ears. *What's he saying?* she wondered.

"That had to hurt," Jason kept saying in between bursts of laughter.

Who's he talking to? Then she realized it was Angelo. Jason was laughing at Angelo. The kayak was resting in a near vertical position, jammed into the branches of a thick fir tree at the bottom of the hill. It was as though the bent fir tree had it arms around the kayak, holding it from falling backward to the ground.

Tiffany was horrified as she realized that the vessel had slid out of control and skidded or sailed into the tree. And there stood Jason like a primitive savage grinning at some pagan ritual he had just completed at Angelo's expense.

"You bastard!" Tiffany screamed as she ran down the hill. She shoved Jason in the chest with enough force that he almost fell over. Immediately, she went to the kayak to rescue it and keep Angelo from falling backward off the fir tree and into a steep ravine that led to the wild water below. "You asshole!" Tiffany screamed again, as she wiped the mud and rain from Angelo's ashen face.

Jason shrugged. "He's still alive. No different. I keep checking. He's still breathing…I think. At least he was on the *last* hill."

"No thanks to you. You imbecile. What the hell were you thinking? What the hell were you doing?"

"I was just fooling around. He's OK. These kayaks are tough. They can take a little impact now and again."

Tiffany was in complete disbelief that Jason Foxworthy could enjoy playing a game with a person's life—watching a dying man crash into a tree and then talk about the event as though he were selling kayaks. "Get out of here! Leave! We'll do this ourselves. I saw the bear's rake marks a little while ago. That means we're near the falls, and I heard the roar of the water on the last hill. Go get Ellen. She'll help us. We don't need your help, and we sure as shit don't need *you!*"

"Up yours, bitch!" Jason shot back. His face turned an ugly crimson. In the rapidly failing light, Tiffany saw a face more terrifying and cruel in some ways than that of the bear that had been protecting its cub.

"You useless waste! We don't want you here and we don't need you hurting Angelo or anyone else ever again."

As he walked by Tiffany on his way up the hill to retrieve his loaded knapsack from the canoe, he gave her a last leering glance. "I would have been the best you ever had," he sneered. "You're just lucky I had too much Yukon Jack. I would have shown you stuff you never dreamed of…bitch!" And as he walked by her on the way back down, he gave her an elbow to the chest that was meant for her right breast but caught her on the bicep and clavicle. The pain brought more than shock and tears. Tiffany was wild with rage. She wanted to humiliate Jason in a way that would hurt him the way he had hurt Angelo and had just hurt her.

As he started up the next hill, Tiffany tried to think of something to do or say. As if in a schoolyard insult contest, she shouted, "Hey, Jason! Don't flatter yourself. I'm amazed that you ever went skinny-dipping with us. You have the smallest dick I've ever seen!" Suddenly, the words were out and she couldn't take them back. She wanted to hurt Jason, but could never have imagined the impact a few words could have.

"You bitch!" he screamed. In a second, he was down the hill. His backhand to her face sent Tiffany tumbling, knocking her over the kayak and almost into the ravine. Jason had mastered the forehand slap from his mother and the backhand smash from his father. He had seen his father adroitly use it as well on his mother whenever she "got too big for her britches."

"You're lucky I'm not in the mood now or I'd show you just how big I can get...and I'd let your fat-ass, curly-haired friend watch for free." Jason glared down at Tiffany and then looked up briefly at Maria, who had just come over the hill.

Even though Tiffany was still smarting from the backhand and the elbow to her chest, she looked up in loathing at the monster of a man leering from above. "I hope that bear who chased you at the lake has you for breakfast. I saw those rake marks just a little ways back. Let's see how tough you are with the bears!" Tiffany shot back as she wiped away the blood that was tricking down her chin.

"Let 'em try me. I've got Butch's gun now. I'll blow that son of a bitch back to the Stone Age. If you or Fatso up there give me any more shit, maybe that's what I'll do with you, too."

And with that, Jason turned and disappeared down the trail. His dark form drifted into the night, and he was gone. As Tiffany scowled and peered into the darkness, she knew in her heart and soul that it would be just fine if she never saw him again.

ET TU, BRUTE?

Although the easterly wind and the rain had slowed somewhat, the drizzle still seemed to find its way onto the back of Ellen's neck. Her shivering continued in spite of the modest fire that crackled before her. She was afraid to move now. She had snuggled in next to *her Irishman* both to keep him warm and, selfishly, to provide a measure of emotional comfort for herself. Physically, she was miserable. Her hands continued to burn with the severe lacerations and scratches. Occasionally, she noticed trickles of blood seeping from the tattered bandages. The last time she had moved to get more firewood, it had briefly awakened O'Casey, who screamed in pain as the protruding thighbone reminded him of its gruesome presence.

Ellen's bladder was about to explode. Though she'd had little to drink, and nothing to eat for hours, she had not had a chance to take care of any of her personal needs. As she was trying to ever so gently move her arm and slowly disengage herself from her cuddle position with O'Casey so she could sneak off to pee, she heard a distinctive noise even over the dull roar of the falls. Something or someone was coming down the trail. She was fully awake now; she could feel the adrenaline rushing through her system. She knew this was no dream. There was clearly something on the trail, but she couldn't see. Her back was to the trail, and she was facing the river. She was afraid to leap up for fear of jostling "her Paddy" and causing him even more pain. Just as her heart was about to explode with fear and dread of a real bear attack, she heard a very familiar voice. It was Tiffany!

"Ellen," she whispered at seeing O'Casey still asleep, "are you OK?

How's O'Casey? How's Butch? We need your help," she continued without waiting for answers. She was all but babbling now. "Jason was being a complete asshole. He let Angelo's kayak crash into a tree. Angelo's alive, but just barely. Jason left us. He's gone. He bailed out on us, the bastard. I didn't see him on the trail. He must have gone the other way at the fork, but he's gone. He took most of the water and food…and the gun."

"We really need your help," she rambled. "We've got the two canoes and Angelo in the kayak. He's just barely alive. Sometimes, I'm not even sure about that. It's hard to tell now that it's almost dark. When it was still just barely light, I could see that his chest was moving and thought I could hear him breathing, but I don't know. Now that it's dark, I could barely stay on the path. I was terrified that I'd get lost, but I could hear the falls and my eyes seemed to adapt after a little while. It would be a whole lot better if there was a moon rather than all this drizzle."

"We're OK here, Ellen. *They* need your help," O'Casey whispered in the darkness. He smiled weakly.

"Hi, Sweetie," Ellen smiled back. It was amazing that in such a short time she had already grown to love and admire this man she'd hardly known a week ago. This adventure—or misadventure—in Maine, Ellen thought, had changed her life forever. In fact, it had changed all of their lives forever. Her real fear was that it might cost at least one life, and quite possibly more. Conceivably, she knew, it could cost *all* their lives if their rescue failed completely or the bear returned.

"You're going to need a light," Sean continued. "In the little green bag you got from the canoe when you got the first aid kit, there's a headlamp. You can hold it or you can wear it, but you're going to need it to get back to Maria. There are a couple of energy bars in there as well. I'm not hungry. You guys are going to want all the energy you can get. Go. Get out of here. And while you're at it, bring Butch and me a large mushroom and pepperoni pizza and a couple of cold beers. Now go!"

And just a suddenly as Tiffany had arrived, she was gone, but this time with Ellen. O'Casey had been so forceful and insistent in his directions, that Ellen had not even rebuilt the fire before leaving. O'Casey could feel his core temperature dropping. He also knew that for Butch to survive, he had to be kept from going into shock. O'Casey slid himself closer to the fire and with one hand, poked and prodded the coals and partially burned sticks and logs until the fire was burning robustly again. It would be a long enough night anyway, O'Casey thought, but it would be a much longer and perhaps deadly night without a fire. As he settled himself back into what was a tenuous semblance of comfort, he wondered about his good friends, Angelo and the Chief. He wondered if either would survive this ordeal. As his thoughts turned to favorite memories with his two friends, O'Casey drifted back into an exhausted sleep that even searing pain could not delay.

Though bone-weary from what seemed like days rather than hours portaging the canoes, Tiffany confidently took the lead now that she had a flashlight to help guide her. It was also a fairly quick though slippery trip on the mostly downhill trail heading back toward Angelo and Maria. Although she tried not to give it much thought, she knew these downhill portions would soon become an uphill nightmare of mud, pain, and exhaustion. At the end of a long flat stretch, Tiffany noticed the bend in the trail where it forked either toward the river or toward the deep woods. *Jason must have taken that trail,* she thought, *either by mistake or on purpose.* He had not gone by way of the falls, or if he had, he had chosen not to stop. Tiffany did not know... and given Jason's brutal actions and more brutal words, she did not care.

The headlamp she was holding made the portage trail appear even more sinister than it had seemed in the dark. Somehow, she had been less afraid in the dark as she had struggled to stay on the path. Maybe it was because she'd had to use every sense just to survive, to keep from getting lost, to once again be the key person in a rescue. *There was no room to fail,* Tiffany kept saying to herself. It was not unlike the conversation that Maria had been having with herself.

"You can do this," Tiffany kept repeating under her breath as she struggled to stay on the trail, to keep her footing under her, and to keep the river close. At some points, it seemed like she was almost on the edge of the riverbank, particularly by the falls, but she knew from their daylight trek, when they'd found the Chief and O'Casey, that the portage trail ran painfully close to the river.

Still, it was better to stay close to the river, even at times when she was not sure she was on the trail. She figured that as long as she didn't fall in, she was safer than if she lost the sound of the river. That would be a death sentence for her and for Ellen, and Tiffany knew it.

Unfortunately for Jason, it was a painful lesson he would learn too late. He was already hopelessly lost, having mistakenly taken the freeze-out road into the woods rather than the portage trail. The freeze-out was actually a larger trail that had been used years before as a logging road. Over time, however, it had become little more than another access trail that had fallen into disrepair. While a skilled hiker could use it as a way to find a main logging road and eventually safety, Jason was anything but a skilled hiker.

He was fighting the first strong bouts of panic, though they would be nothing compared with what he would soon experience. The large black bear that would eventually smell Jason's fear and blood was still a half mile away, sniffing the air and looking for an easy meal. This powerful bear, which had almost found the twin fawns several days ago, had once been the alpha male in the region. It had fathered all of Yellow Flank's cubs, including the one Jason had killed and skinned. It had even fathered the cub that was on the edge of camp with her mother by the Half-Moon Hilton. It was, in fact, the biggest bear in T6 R7, the nameless region on the map hunters often just called "the wilderness." T6 R7 was part of "the big woods," an area half the size of Rhode Island and lacking a single blacktop road, shopping mall, or hospital. While a hospital might still be helpful for Butch, O'Casey, and possibly even Angelo, it would soon be of little help for Jason Foxworthy.

The bear that Jason would get to know only too well was the oldest and largest bear most hunters would ever see. This bear, now very much on the prowl, was even larger than the one Jason had so bravely shot at almost point-blank range from his pickup truck at the Grand Lake Stream dump many years before, the same mammoth bear that O'Casey had seen from his tiny Honda Civic. The massive bruin now sniffing the air and working his way down the trail and toward the women; it limped awkwardly as it walked.

As it wandered through the big woods in search of food, its limited mobility made the chances of chasing down even a spring fawn or moose calf an unlikely event. While it had made the large rake marks on the portage trail earlier in the day, Brute could not really sustain a territorial battle with another male. Even a boar sixty percent his size would be a threat. Though Brute was easily the largest bear in the county, his days of domination were over. Now, as the big beast limped along the trail, it was struggling just to survive. It needed an easy meal—ideally, a large incapacitated animal it could feed on for several days. It was very hungry, a hunger that occasional beechnuts, alder shoots, and grubs or carpenter ants could not satisfy. It needed meat and needed it soon.

Tiffany was the first to notice the new rake marks. They were not the set she had seen earlier in the day on her run to the camp. Those looked recent but not fresh; these looked brand-new. Her flashlight had reflected off the long white marks on an otherwise dark tree. She studied the young fir tree briefly with her light and could see the sap oozing from it. They had to be fresh, she surmised, shuddering at the thought of another bear encounter. Once again she remembered the Chief's half-jovial, cautionary tale about bear attacks and women's periods. She imagined it as the Chief had comically described it—a "Soups On" message for every bear that had a nose. She didn't tell Ellen of her inner terror or her biological plight. However, she quickly picked up the pace; they all but sprinted the last two hundred yards to where Maria sat resting next to Angelo.

While Tiffany was gone, Maria had sat on the kayak next to Angelo. She stroked his head and occasionally cleaned his face with a neckerchief she had been wearing. Maria had also been praying—in Spanish. Although she rarely used her Spanish anymore unless she was with her family, she had learned all her prayers in Spanish years before she learned them in English. "Padre nuestro que estás en el Cielo…" she began.

Brute sniffed the air. He stood up on his hind legs, favoring his left side. The gunshot had altered not only his mobility, but his diet, as well, making him much more dependent upon carrion already picked over by coyotes and ravens. To compensate for his decreased ability to hunt on foot, his sense of smell had sharpened. In the moist night air and swirling easterly breeze, he could pick up human smells, smells he had grown to loathe from his distant memory of the hunting camp. He also smelled blood, in fact an amalgam of several blood smells and from several different locations that confused his primitive instincts. His thinner but still massive frame stretched well over seven feet into the night air to sniff out a clear direction. He headed down the long beech ridge toward where the portage trail met the freeze-out road. Enjoying all these new smells, Brute grunted in satisfaction. Yellow foaming saliva began to drip in anticipation from his thick black jowls. His limping gait picked up in speed. A meal was in the offing.

THE ROAD NOT TAKEN

The women made Angelo as comfortable as they could. He was now clearly unconscious. He could no longer open his eyes, smile weakly, or show in any way that he was still alive. None of the women spoke of Angelo's condition. It was apparent to all of them that without immediate medical intervention, he would not survive. The only questions were how long he could hold on, and how long it would take to get him to a place of rescue.

If that was not motivation enough, thoughts of the Chief, also in a coma, and O'Casey with a shattered leg and dislocated shoulder, added haste to their efforts, particularly for Ellen. She had seen and heard Sean suffering through his afflictions. As she slipped the kayak harness over her shoulder and assumed the role that Jason had briefly played in the rescue mission, she knew that in order for O'Casey to survive, she would have to help them *all* survive. She did not look at this as a necessary evil, but rather what she would gladly have done for any member of the tribe, any member except Jason Foxworthy.

Jason was dealing with his own self-inflicted suffering. He had hoped to hike for an hour or so and then make camp. He was angry from his confrontation with Tiffany, and wanted to spite her by putting some distance between himself and the tribe. He had taken the only copy of the map in the Chief's tent. He'd also grabbed most of the food and of course the one bottle of liquor left in camp—vodka the Chief had found in the buzz-off box and had planned to use to sterilize and cleanse Angelo's hand.

Jason had studied the map and intentionally took the freeze-out road because it looked like a more promising exit from the woods. He rationalized to himself that because he was the best athlete and the most fit person left in camp, it made sense for him to strike out on his own. He needed to get himself safely out of the woods. This was survival of the fittest, he told himself. Just like football. He was the fittest and needed to survive. That's what he'd learned growing up. "Take care of numero uno first," he'd been taught. "No one else is going to." That's what his dad had said…and had practiced. *Was he ever right,* Jason smiled.

That's all he was doing now—looking out for numero uno. Sure, he'd send a rescue party for Butch. After all, they were good friends. They'd find the others, too. Even though he only cared about Butch, he didn't want the rest of the group to die, even if some of them deserved it, he thought.

Unfortunately, he had underestimated how difficult it would be to stay on the trail. At one point, he realized he was no longer on the freeze-out road. Everything looked the same. He panicked. As the fear took over, he dashed headlong through the brush, first one way and then back the other way, struggling to find the trail he'd lost in the twilight. He reopened the gash in his forehead that he'd gotten from the bear attack, and also split his lip open. Breathing heavily, he sat down for a minute to catch his breath.

Calm down, big boy, he told himself. He took off his backpack, which had originally been filled with almost anything of value he could find at camp. It wasn't stealing; it was surviving, he rationalized. Just before leaving, he had remembered to throw in all the leftover cooked fish. It would make a nourishing nighttime meal or even a good breakfast, he figured. Unfortunately, in his recent mad dash and several stumbles in the darkness, much of what he'd literally thrown into the backpack was now strewn about the forest floor.

Slow down, Daniel Boone, he told himself. *Catch your breath. What would Butch do now?* He fought an almost overpowering urge to panic again. Then a far more pleasant, subliminal message jumped from his subconscious. *Relax. You need to do something to calm down. It's five o'clock somewhere, Bucko. Have a little drink to steady your nerves. Catch your breath,* his self-talk continued.

Jason smiled as he gratefully discovered that the bottle of vodka had not been one of the casualties of his panic. He looked with comfort at his friend. It never let him down. He leaned back and took a long slow swallow. The vodka burned his stomach in a way he had grown to love. It was a friendly burn, comforting actually. This would slow him down and make him relax. And besides, he knew that it would help keep him warm. After all, that's why rescue dogs carried brandy, right? Hell, alcohol was the primary ingredient in antifreeze. He almost laughed out loud. This was *his* antifreeze! He'd just snuggle into his sleeping bag, pull his hat down a bit to keep the drizzle out, and wait until first light. In the morning, he'd find the trail again, and then he would hike to the main road. No question: he'd be home having a steak and a cold beer by supper. *It'll be a good night after all*, he decided. The vodka, his good friend and companion, was doing what it needed to do. He was warm and happy. Numero uno was in good hands—his own, for a change.

Five hundred yards away, Brute had slowed his pace again. He was getting all kinds of smells now. Lots of human smells. Odd sweet smells. Strange bloody smells. Other smells, too. What was this? Fish? His favorite smell. Brute stretched again. Yes, fish. His thick black nostrils pulled in as many of the smells as he could manage. There was a strong odor of fear and adrenaline, too. An odd animal-like smell, a smell like that from the bait station just before the blinding flash and the searing pain. Brute's genetic instincts and limited memory tried to compete for dominance and provide him with a clear direction for pursuit...and dinner.

Less than a thousand feet away, the rescue party continued with their painful portage. Ellen was the newest member of the tribe to learn her grueling responsibility. When on the flat, each woman dragged her own load. Ellen, with the freshest legs, volunteered to take over Jason's spot dragging the kayak with Angelo strapped inside. Initially, she was pleased that it did not seem like a severe hardship. She was sadly mistaken. The slight downhill run and that on the flat were misleading indeed. As soon as the trail took the first inevitable uphill run, the harness tore into her shoulder. It was already sore from in the ordeal of trying to save Tiffany and Butch. That rope had cut so deeply into her torso that the rope burns were still painful. Very quickly, the harness had found the same raw and tender flesh. These abrasions soon were quickly seeping bright red blood down her chest, her knees, and her shins.

Even more painful than her shoulder, her hands screamed for her to stop. They were no longer just weeping a tiny stream of blood past her ripped-off fingernail and through the gauze bandages. Blood was now running down her hands, down her elbows, dripping onto her shirt and pants and occasionally onto the ground.

As the hills once again got steeper, the women had to help each other. The hill by the freeze-out road, though not the steepest, was one of the worst. The clay that had covered that portion of the trail was now a muddy slime. It was a challenge just to walk and stay upright, let alone haul the loaded boats up the slope. The women pushed and pulled, slipped and fell. They got up and just kept going, their herculean efforts often producing unhidden grunts of pain.

It was hardest for Ellen, not because she was the most sensitive, but because she had the most open cuts and sources for pain to escalate. Worst of all was the bleeding fingernail bed; every scrape, every pull seemed to find her finger. No wonder, Ellen thought, that placing bamboo splints under fingernails was such an excruciating and effective torture. She could barely endure the pain. Still, with her friends at her side, or behind her pushing from below, she somehow did endure, as first the kayak, with pale Angelo dying silently and patiently…then the green canoe … and finally Jason's ugly aluminum albatross crept up and over the hill by the freeze-out road.

The three friends paused at the top of the rise, not so much admiring their handiwork as simply holding each other up in total exhaustion—each one more filthy and exhausted than the others. Surprisingly, none of them spoke. They were too tired to do anything more than survive the moment.

They were getting close now, Tiffany thought. One more slow downhill run, a long straightaway next to the river, and then the steep hill by the falls. Then it would be over—at least for the night. "Last big push, *ladies!* Let's get Angelo to camp," Tiffany said, purposely using the same humorously sarcastic inflection Butch had mastered. "Let's go, ladies" was an already too-familiar chant, but in this case, the three women simply smiled and silently assumed their workstations for the final section of the portage.

Jason, by contrast, was smiling for another reason. In twenty minutes, he had consumed almost half the bottle of vodka. The pale yellow, lemon-flavored Stolichnaya had done its work. Jason was no longer in panic; he was in heaven. He loved the warm glow of vodka. It brought a special, predictable kind of happiness. It was his only *real* friend. He could count on it every time. Better than beer, which took its own good time, Stolly was a best friend. It gave Jason that cocky "I just scored a touchdown" feeling, or better yet, that "I just blew my load with a beautiful babe" feeling he could never get enough of, never. Unfortunately, those babe experiences were getting more and more difficult to find as his lecherous reputation spread.

He could no longer count on women for anything. But he could always rely on his liquid friend. Stolly gave him that feeling all the time, every time. He smiled with contentment as he sipped away. Deep in his old down sleeping bag, he had found just the right body position where he was warm, dry, and slightly upright with his back against a tree, the perfect position to be doing what he was doing. Quietly, happily, Jason was getting trashed. His backpack had slid down the hill below his feet, but he didn't notice, and he didn't care. He had all he needed. He figured he would fall asleep soon, then he'd wake up warm and happy. It would be morning, and he'd walk away from this shit-hole of a wilderness and all that went with it. He'd never do this again. It sucked. The tribe sucked. But the Stolly, now that was a true friend.

Brute continued to sniff now that he was on the portage trail. At the base of the hill by the freeze-out road, the smell of blood was so strong that saliva ran down his thick black lips and jaw. He put his tongue into the water collecting in a muddy pool at the bottom of the hill. Fresh blood. It tasted good. Instinctively, the old bruin hastened up the hill. He would be eating soon. This would be an easier kill than a moose with a broken hindquarter or even a full-grown deer, injured in a coyote attack. Brute gained the hill quickly and sniffed the air. He hesitated in confusion. Two different sets of smells. Both said *food* to his primitive brain. Different smells. Different foods. The portage path toward the falls told him lots of food, lots of blood, but also strange sweet scents Brute had rarely smelled before. And smoke. He hated smoke. It was not good.

The freeze-out road—now that was fish for sure, blood, and fear— hopefully, a wounded animal, his primitive brain computed. He knew those smells. He liked those smells. Brute veered from the portage trail, away from the river, and away from the women. Instead, he followed the both the acrid scent of panic and fear ...and strangely, of cooked fish. Down the freeze-out road he limped. Brute sniffed the air greedily, grunting and growling in anticipation as he went.

BRUTE FORCE

The women were oblivious to the massive black bear scarcely three hundred yards away and now fortunately headed in another direction. Brute's decision to follow the pungent trail of fish, sweat, and blood dripping from a cut forehead had saved their lives and sealed the fate of Jason Foxworthy. Karma was alive and well in the thick, damp wilderness of Maine. One life to be taken, others to be spared...all because of several cooked trout selfishly thrown into a knapsack.

The trout now littered the trail scarcely a hundred yards from where Jason drifted in and out of a Stolly-vodka high. Almost unconsciously, he snuggled further into his sleeping bag and pulled the bottle of vodka close to his side. It was an odd kind of snuggling. He patted the bottle like a child with his teddy bear. He took another swig "for medicinal purposes" and prepared for a good night's slumber.

Brute's nose was now working hard. The thick black nostrils swelled open, sucking ever-larger quantities of moist forest air. The brief sweet smell of Ellen's hastily dabbed perfume was gone. However, the acrid smell of sweat, bread, and fish worked through his massive nose and into his fist-sized brain. The primitive neuron structures and pathways in the bruin's cranium tried to translate the data. Favorite dump foods? Good garbage or a camp raid at night? Cooked brook trout, bread, bacon, for certain. Even as Brute's nose worked along the ground sniffing for his first prizes, the hair on his neck went up as well. Thick sweaty smells, fear, and even panic from Jason's discovery of being lost, all mixed in with the food. Those human smells, like the ones deep in the recesses of his brain from the night he was shot nine months before, sent messages of fear, caution, and rage into the small primitive computer and genetic storehouse that guided Brute's actions. He was too hungry to be cautious. The trout was very near.

Had Jason been awake and sober, he could easily have heard the occasional grunts, rustling leaves, broken twigs, even the clacking of his teeth and jaws together in anticipation of a meal. When Brute was feeding, he was a reckless machine, ripping open trash bags with a single sweep of his razor-sharp claws. As he gobbled up the first twelve-inch brook trout, head and all, he smacked his lips greedily. Saliva oozed freely from his broken yellow molars. His fang-like incisors protruded almost two inches down from his upper jaw. More food. He could smell more food. This was just a little appetizer for an animal that could eat the entire hind-quarter of a young moose in three hours. Brute's nose was working again. Another fish on the trail and then bread. Brute loved bread. It was a favorite especially when coated with the grease Possum George had used at the bait station where Brute had been shot. Then bacon. Jason had taken the last of the bacon from one of the coolers and wrapped it in a red cloth napkin he found in the cooler outside the Chief's tent.

Brute slurped down first one, then another piece of raw bacon. The warm greasy strips hung briefly like the long tongue of a hairy black serpent licking at the night sky. The wet napkin, replete with beech leaves and green moss from the forest floor, hung ironically as well from a corner of Brute's jaw. When he had gnawed on it sufficiently to realize it was not food and had no more value, Brute ripped it from his face, shedding it as it flew in tattered red strips to the ground. Part of the shredded napkin still clung to his front claw as Brute stood erect now. He was very close to something large and worth fearing. Even the smell of candy bars and apples along the trail nearby were less dominant than the stench of sweat and blood that led up the small rise to where Jason Foxworthy lay sleeping. Occasionally, Brute in his favorite nocturnal foraging trips, would find a deer wounded in a recent coyote attack, lying in a thicket licking its wounds and just trying to survive. This was Brute's favorite meal. He could dispatch the deer in a quick pounce, slicing its throat open with a single swipe of its paw. He could then dine on it at his leisure, often coming back several times to snack further if the coyotes did not find it first.

Brute ignored the candy bars and gobbled a fast bite of a granny smith apple just twenty yards from the slumbering drunk. He was on a mission now. Weeks of waiting for a real meal were about to end. He had come so close to so many kills—mice, rabbits, spring fawns. His limp had cost him his ability to chase all but severely wounded pray. Now, however, he had surprised a large wounded animal. His badly needed meal was at hand. He could smell the blood still weeping from the camper's forehead. Jason snored in blissful ignorance. These thick, sharp grumbling snores and snorts of stupor and contentment rumbled from the camper's nose and mouth.

Brute seemed both puzzled and angered by the noise. It appeared to be some sort of masculine challenge, almost the kind of snort a young boar makes before a charge when bears are competing for territory or for a sow. Brute was no longer cautious. He was in a full charge now. He was up the hill in seconds, even with his limping gait. He pounced on Jason with the same wild anger the sow bear had displayed back at camp. This time, 600 pounds of black fury landed on the green sleeping bag and tore both it and Jason Foxworthy open in a single swipe. Even before Jason could come to his senses, he was screaming in pain. His left thigh muscles were splayed open and tattered. Blood sprayed the now crimson feathers and green clothing suddenly littering the hillside. Brute pounced again and quickly had Jason's leg in his jaws and crushed the calf muscles just below the knee. Brute could taste both the blood and the panic. It would be over soon.

As sheer terror began to brush away the alcoholic daze, Jason tried to kick his attacker in the face with his other leg. For a moment Brute released his prey, the torn calf muscle now full exposed and dangling in a bloody mass through Jason's thoroughly shredded jeans. The terrified camper turned his back to the bear, screaming in agony and panic. He reached around for anything to use in his life and death struggle. His once precious Stolly bottle was now within reach. Grabbing its thick neck, Jason swung the bottle at the bruin, using it like a short club as the bear pounced again. Just as Brute drove for Jason's jugular vein, the terrified camper smashed the bottle across the bear's broad black nose. The bear roared in pain and anger, its terrifying jaws only inches from Jason's face. Brute recoiled, and tumbled backward as if shot. It had not expected a battle. Adrenaline surged through Brute's veins and triggered more than just an attack initiated by his hunger. This was an outrage, a challenge to Brute's dominance by another large male, albeit a human one.

The massive bear stood on his hind legs, growling with a fury and ferocity he rarely used or needed, even in killing a large wounded moose. As Brute steadied his damaged leg and prepared to pounce one last time, Jason half tumbled and half dove down the little slope where his backpack had fallen. He fumbled frantically for the Chief's pistol, knowing that the bear would be on him in an instant. The cold metal revolver was now in his grasp. As Jason turned to fire, Brute pounced on his back. It mashed Jason's face into the wet slime and leaves at the base of the hill. The bear drove his teeth deep into Jason's shoulder, just missing his neck muscles and jugular vein. As blood sprayed from the deep but not fatal wound, Jason screamed again in pain. He screamed for help. He screamed for Butch, for God, for anyone or anything to save him.

Now 600 pounds of rage and fury had him pinned to the ground and were crushing and gnawing at his shoulder. It made it impossible for Jason to face the bear and shoot. He swung the pistol around his body and fired blindly backward toward the bite and the massive jaws ripping his clavicle open. The shot roared through the night, echoing across the hills and all the way to the river. The bullet caught Brute just above his thick, flared nostrils, splitting the top of them open in a second. Had Jason been completely sober, in control of his coordination, and able to see the position of the bear's face, the shot would have been fatal, even for a small caliber pistol like the snub nose .38. Instead, the shot had angled upward slightly, across the top of his nose and just above Brute's right eye and skull. If his wrist had been angle downward even a bit, the slug would have gone straight through the bear's nose, through his skull, and directly into his brain. Jason would have had his third and most prized *trophy bear.*

Both camper and bear screamed in pain now. The top front of Brute's nose was split almost in half. Blood ran into the bear's left eye. The bullet gashed opened the top of his forehead. It grazed his skull, but did little real damage. Brute roared in rage and pain. He bared his fangs in a final gesture of dominance and ferocity. Jason screamed one last time in a long terrifying crescendo that seemed to awaken the entire valley. The camper rolled onto his now decimated shoulder only to face the bulging eyes, bloody shattered nose, and ferocious jaws. He fired again, this time at point blank range only inches from the bear's gaping mouth. The last sound Jason Foxworthy would ever remember was the terrifying cold dull *thud* of a misfire and an empty chamber.

He was out of bullets. Karma had come to visit. Jason would pay the ultimate price for having treated Angelo so badly while hauling him in the kayak. Angelo had fired three shots as Butch had suggested and then fired a fourth round as an emergency call for the Chief's help. Had he fired three shots, there would still be one last bullet. It would have gone directly into the bear's wide opened mouth, just inches from the panicked camper face and killed it immediately. As Brute dove for the exposed jugular vein, Jason struggled in the haze of a vodka stupor to understand the dull click that had sealed his fate. Within seconds it was over. Jason gurgled in disbelief and terror as the severed jugular vein and carotid artery sprayed the camper's crimson life and dreams onto Brute's jaws. It mingled with the blood from the bear's own badly damaged nose. Jason's legs and fingers twitched incessantly as his blood and consciousness disappeared into the now steaming Maine forest. Brute roared in victory and domination. He was still the alpha male of the valley. He was still a force to be reckoned with in the big woods. Brute grunted in satisfaction. He slowed his deep breathing and pawed over the slowly cooling body, eyeing his prize and smacking his lips.

Last Dance on Heartbreak Hill

Even over the roar of the approaching falls, the women heard the gunshot. Its sharp report spoke to them as the black noise of terror above the loud gray droning of the water. Tiffany, in particular, thought she heard something else as well—high wailing screams and shrieks of terror—though she wasn't sure. She was the only one standing partway up the last hill getting ready for the final big push. Ellen and Maria were attentive to Angelo, talking quietly to him, encouraging the nearly lifeless man to stay alive. "Just hang on," Maria whispered over and over.

"Did you hear that?" Tiffany looked down the hill, trying to get a confirmation of both sets of sounds she'd heard.

"That was a gunshot. Must have been Jason," Maria nodded.

"Did you hear the scream? I think I heard some screams as well, but I'm not sure. Did you guys hear it?"

"We were talking to Angelo, but I did hear the gunshot.... Why would Jason scream?"

"Why would he use the gun? Why would he scream? God, I hope it wasn't the bear. Those rake marks I saw down the trail were very fresh." Tiffany shivered at the thought of a massive bear lurking in the woods—or worse, attacking a member of the tribe. As despicable as Tiffany had found Jason, even he didn't deserve to die like that.

"Well, I'm not *sure* it was a scream. Maybe it was a coyote or something that Jason was shooting at." She struggled to downplay the situation and comfort both herself and her friends, who were now wide-eyed with fear.

Ellen spoke up forcefully. "Let's get the hell out of here. If it's Jason, we can't help him now. He's got the gun. We don't even know where he is.

Maybe we can look for him in the morning, or maybe he'll head to camp. He should have stayed with us!"

She was angry *and* scared. O'Casey would know what to do: they had to finish the portage. She wanted to see her Irishman. She needed to see him. What if the bear was now heading for camp? Sean and Butch were barely alive. They'd never be able to defend themselves.

"Let's go! Let's go!" Ellen implored as she grabbed the harness for the canoe. They had decided to bring the empty canoes up the long steep ridge first, since they were lighter than the kayak. Maria didn't want to leave Angelo's side. His breathing was more labored now and his lips were tinged with blue. They were afraid that he was going to die, and Maria could not bear the thought of letting him die alone without someone holding his hand as she was doing now.

Ellen and Tiffany were beyond exhaustion. Even the light aluminum canoe with its contents removed seemed like a heavy steel weight. As Ellen leaned into the hill, she focused on her thoughts of O'Casey. Her sweetie was just on the other side of the ridge. She wanted to smell his hair, squeeze his hand. Mostly, she wanted him safe and alive. When she had sat many months ago at the Black Rose drinking with the tribe and talking about a canoe trip in the Maine woods, she could never have imagined she'd be in a life-and-death struggle to save three men she had grown to care for, one of whom she had grown to love. Ellen leaned her bruised and bloody shoulder into the harness and pulled against the weight of the canoe.

Tiffany shivered with both exhaustion and cold. She had been soaking wet most of the day. Having had almost nothing to eat or drink all day, her body was finally being pushed past its limit. She had accepted the challenges, and despite her once cover-girl appearance, had proved to be the Chief's equal. She had rescued first Jason and then the Chief himself from the cold and unforgiving spring runoff. She had already run the portage trail twice that day, even after almost drowning with Butch in the rapids below the falls. She had purposely taken the heavier canoe because of her superb conditioning and a leadership instinct even she didn't know she had. Everyone had depended on her before, and they were still depending on her now.

The last ridge seemed like her personal Heartbreak Hill—the great demoralizer in the Boston Marathon she had watched but never run.

This was worse, she thought. Her body was shutting down, and she could actually, palpably, feel it happening. Even though the rain was now just a slow drizzle and the air temperature had risen to the high fifties, it felt like thirty degrees with the strong wet wind. Tiffany had asked her body to do too much and had put too little back. The single energy bar she had eaten and the several sips of water she had taken were no longer enough to sustain her physical output. Whether the first shivers started with Jason's scream or the incessant drizzle that ran down her neck and saturated her back, Tiffany now found herself shaking uncontrollably.

Even worse, her quad and hamstring muscles were beginning to cramp up. Were she to try a water rescue now, she would drown in a few minutes. Her electrolytes were totally depleted—and almost non-existent. They cramps were incessant as she leaned into her harness. She looked up the hill at Ellen, who was almost halfway to the ridge. She looked back to Maria who was stroking Angelo's cheek. Tiffany pushed off, first with her left foot and then with her right. She could do this dance one last time. As she leaned into the hill, the drizzle ran down her delicate features, now plastered with caked mud and dirty stringy hair. This was not Long Island. It was almost a different planet. But as she looked up and down the hill one more time, she knew what she had to do for her new family.

The roar of the falls shook the hillside and became a constant source of worry as the women danced their gruesome dance up the hill. Left foot, right foot, pull. Left foot, right foot, slip. Even amid the pain and exhaustion, the slips were somehow the worst. The bottom of the trail was only ten feet from a sheer cliff dropping into the raging river and certain death. The muddy hillside on the last section of the portage trail had at first seemed like just the last physical barrier in the rescue plan. Now, it was a constant source of total, abject terror. As first Ellen and then Tiffany got closer to the peak of the trail, the steepness of the hillside, the mud, and their exhaustion made every step a nightmare. Both women were bleeding from their hands and knees. The thin layer of soil continued to wash away, and every slip brought contact with slivers of granite or sharp-edged pieces of the ledge jutting through the trailside.

Just as Ellen was about to make her last push to the top, her right foot slid out from under her. Her knee slammed into a spike of granite ledge, and she screamed out in pain. She fought to find firm ground with her left foot, but it slipped from under her as well. Although she had the lighter of the canoes, its weight and the steepness of the hillside caused both woman and canoe to slide backward. She dug and clawed at the ridge, trying to find at least a good handhold to stop her slide back into Tiffany, an unthinkable event that might drag both of them to the bottom of the trail and over the ledge to the eagerly waiting falls.

The instinctive scramble of hands and feet paid off just as it had when she was the human anchor earlier in the day. Once again, she was in survival mode, clawing and scratching the face of a granite cliff to avoid a plunge to near-certain death. Just as Ellen's canoe was about to slide into her friend and take them both down, the slide mercifully stopped.

"God, that was close!" Ellen gasped. "I thought we were goners."

"You and me both." Tiffany managed a tiny smile and grinned, "When we get all these guys safely home, they're going to pay. Now I know why they wanted us to come. They needed someone to do all the work and then save their ass."

Tiffany's words and attitude were like a magic elixir. It energized both women, and they conquered the last few yards together. They took a minute to celebrate their victory, and the quick hug they shared was more than just a victory gesture. It was a hug between sisters, two women with different backgrounds and different styles now united in a bond of love. They were family now, thrown together as the result of a cocktail party dare—a throwaway challenge: "You wouldn't *dare* join us for a week in the woods of Maine!" That was the gauntlet Butch had thrown down for them. And it was not what any of them had envisioned. Not in their wildest dreams! Not the women. Not the men. Certainly not a cold and lifeless Jason Foxworthy.

But now, as Ellen and Tiffany waved at Maria in triumph, both knew that peril and hardship had turned the six remaining educators who hardly knew each other into a new family, a tribe that even the Chief could not have crafted alone.

Ellen's thoughts quickly turned to O'Casey. She dashed the remaining ten yards so that she could peer over the ridge and down onto the campground. "Sweetie!" she hollered, now completely unabashed about her feelings for O'Casey. He couldn't hear her over the roar of the falls, but Ellen could see him by the light of the fire and knew that he was safe. The fire was still going, and O'Casey had a stick in his hand working the embers. Ellen controlled her desire to run down the hill and give him a hug. The women had promised each other that they wouldn't go down to the camp until Angelo was safely with them. With great reluctance, Ellen left the view she had longed to see and trudged down the dark, slippery hill with Tiffany.

"He's just barely hanging on," Maria told them. "His lips are getting blue. We've got to get him down by the fireside and get him warm and dry."

Neither Ellen nor Tiffany had complained when their friend had stayed with Angelo and had not helped them with the canoes. Not only was Maria exhausted, she was not in good shape and had already given more physically than the other women could have imagined. She may have had the body of a penguin, but Maria had the heart of a lion.

After wiping Angelo's face one last time, the women readied the kayak for the final assault on the hill. Ellen had taken charge of the lines. The others were amazed at her skills. She first insisted, given the steepness of the hill, that Angelo be re-strapped into the kayak with an even more effective system than Maria had created. "If the kayak rolls on its side as we get into the steepest part, I don't want to risk his falling out," she said as she tied Angelo in a complex crisscross harness. Ellen was glad now that her brothers had tied her up so many times and had taught her all their Boy Scout knots.

Tiffany would take the lead with the longest bow harness. Ellen had fashioned a shorter harness, which she tied off at the middle of the kayak, so that she could pull up the safer right side of the hill. It was too dangerous to ask anyone to pull from the riverbank side. Maria would push from the rear—be the "stern tugboat," as she described it. She didn't mind the analogy and actually shared it with her friends. "You're the best," Ellen grinned. "If you're a tugboat, then you're the prettiest and nicest tugboat in the fleet."

Even with all of them sharing the load, the task was still daunting. The usable part of the trail was little more than three feet wide and comprised of either slick, muddy clay or loose granite chips. Thickets crowded the right side of the path and the cliff was close on the river side. Footing was poor and dangerous. In the best of conditions, a three-mile hike was a workout for Maria, but today's treacherous portage had been the most excruciating experience of her life. Her cheap K-Mart sneakers had hardly been a match for the demands of the day. As she leaned into the stern of the kayak, she focused on keeping her footing and making her contribution to this last assault on the trail.

Ellen, too, was suffering, as mud and grit attacked the fragile flesh where her fingernail had once clung. The raw flesh was a magnet for every twig or piece of gravel. Each pull on the rope brought a shudder of pain. Only her thoughts of O'Casey, just fifty yards away, kept her from crying out in agony.

As Tiffany pulled from the bow, she could feel the leg cramp coming. Her state of dehydration made the cramping almost inevitable. Nothing short of a hot tub, a meal, and a few hours of rest could keep the cramp at bay. Further compounding her condition was the incessant shivering—she just couldn't stop it. She had little body fat to burn, and the calories from the energy bar she had shared with Maria had been long since expended.

Now, as she eyed the final five yards of steep trail, she felt the cramp building like an avalanche that would soon wash her right off the cliff. First her upper thigh, then her quad, and finally her calf began to quiver and contract. "Cramp!" she yelled. She squeezed hard on the rope and rolled onto her left side as her right leg collapsed in a contortion of knotted muscle tissue.

Maria tried to dig in and brace herself for the onslaught to come. She found solid footing and prepared her shoulder for impact. As she tried to stop the kayak's downward path, it slid over her wet sweatshirt, riding up and over, onto her shoulder blade. She was literally being run over by the kayak as it picked up momentum on its backward slide toward the river. The weight of the kayak mashed her face into the rocky, muddy trail. Yet even as the kayak slid over her, Maria kept reaching backward, trying to grab something, anything to stop the kayak—save her beloved Angelo.

Only Ellen was left standing, but that was quick to change. Like a mountain climber tethered into a safety line but linked to the climbers above and below her, Ellen was almost immediately swept off her feet. Tiffany's line, which she tenaciously held onto, caught Ellen's legs and dumped her headfirst along the edge of the trail. The kayak with Angelo strapped into it continued its downhill descent toward the ledge and the river below it.

After the kayak had run over her body, Maria stared down the hill in helpless horror as the kayak careened out of control. Neither Tiffany nor Ellen could get up on their feet. Yet neither would let go. They slid face-first down the hill as the momentum of the kayak dragged them along. The only thing that saved them was that they were on the right side of the trail, away from the river. Instinctively, they spread their legs and dug their feet in, trying to find anything to slow their descent.

Although Angelo had lost a lot of weight in recent months and especially in the last twenty-four hours, his stocky frame and the weight of the kayak sliding on the slick side of the trail pulled both women through the edge of a thicket and into the middle of the trail—and that much closer to the ledge. Maria screamed in anticipation of the inevitable.

At that instant, the bigger danger for Ellen was a large fir tree she was headed toward, almost face-first. She twisted her battered body just enough that she slid by to the forest side of the tree, narrowly avoiding a catastrophic collision. Tiffany, sliding just behind Ellen, but with the longer harness, stopped her slide six feet behind Ellen's battered legs. The fir tree, with Ellen's midship rope tight around its uphill side, had saved their lives

For one stunning moment, all was quiet except for the roar of the falls. "Don't let go! Don't let go!" Maria screamed as Tiffany and Ellen tried to recover from their brutal slide. Like a climbing team caught in an avalanche, the women tried to collect their senses and see which limbs were moving and which were not. "Don't let go!" Maria screamed again, as she half ran, half slid down the trail. She was barely recognizable. Her face was bleeding. Her glasses were broken and barely on her face. Mud and dirt were everywhere on her body. Yet, the little engine that could was making a life-and-death dash to rescue her three friends.

Even through the cracked and muddy lenses of her broken glasses, what Maria saw as she looked down the hill terrified her. On one side of the fir tree were two battered and bruised women staring up at her, desperately clinging to their harnesses. Wisely, Ellen had insisted that they make harness loops rather than simply pull on straight lines. Each woman was hanging onto a loop of rope that had become her lifeline. As Ellen and Tiffany looked toward the river side of the trail, they understood why Maria had implored them to hang on. While they were no longer in personal peril, Angelo was. The kayak hung in an almost vertical position, much of it already over the ledge. Had Ellen not insisted in strapping Angelo in, his body would have been launched from the kayak and into the raging river just above the falls, and death would have been almost instantaneous.

One of Angelo's arms flopped uselessly from the kayak, and Ellen realized that only the harness line she had hastily tied was keeping Angelo alive. *Please, God. Don't let that knot slip*, she thought as she mentally appraised the situation.

When Maria arrived, the other women tried to find footing underneath them to help pull the kayak away from the ledge, but even with Maria's help, the kayak wouldn't budge. As Maria strained with Tiffany on the longer harness, she noticed that the line was tied to the small handle line that kayakers used to pull their kayaks to shore or to secure a line for a car-top carrier. It was just lightweight nylon line and hardly meant to bear this kind of force. If it broke, the kayak, or at least Angelo, would be gone in an instant. Even if Ellen's line held, a broken bowline would probably flip the kayak over and toss Angelo into the raging river.

Pulling harder was too dangerous a solution. They could not risk ripping out the tiny handle line the long harness was tied to in the bow. Maria peered through the twilight to study the problem. If only O'Casey or Butch were here, they'd know what to do. Holding the harness line for safety, Maria crept along the ledge and closer to the kayak. She could see the problem. The bow was wedged into a crack in the last bit of ledge. Pulling from their present angle was only pulling the bow further into the crack. There had to be some way to get the angle of the line higher to get over those first few inches of ledge. They had to find a solution, and quickly.

"We've got to find something to change the angle to get the line up higher."

Ellen responded. "I've got an idea, Maria. You've got to take my spot. You're...you're heavy...you're *heavier*," she blurted out with an embarrassed look.

"I know. I make a better anchor," Maria agreed. Then she slipped into the loop and braced herself as Ellen slipped out and disappeared into the darkness.

After an eternity of thirty seconds, Ellen appeared from the trail, even filthier and wrestling with the broken portion of a log a foot in diameter and about six feet long. She could barely drag it over to the ledge, but clearly seemed to know what she was doing. Gingerly, Ellen used the bow harness, as Maria had previously done to help herself get further out on the ledge and closer to the kayak. The tricky part was sliding the log out with her. Ellen scooched along on her rear end with the log tucked evenly under her knees. She planned to use the log as a wedge under the line, if all went well.

Ellen felt herself shaking with fear. She had always been afraid of heights. Now, as she watched the wild water surging below the ledge, she was almost frozen with terror. She couldn't believe she was doing this. Ellen could feel herself beginning to hyperventilate, something she had always done when she was in high places. *Slow down*, she said to herself. *Deep breath! Deep breath!* That was her mother talking, almost literally. She could sense her mother's presence. It was her mother who had helped her to overcome her fear of heights by taking her to every high place she could find. Ellen had learned to love those trips with her mother. It was the one and only "girl thing" she had loved to do with her mom. "Deep breath," they would say together....

When she got the log in position beneath the line and several feet from the edge of the outcropping, Ellen lifted up her legs and the log rolled down the ledge and looked like it would fall into the water and be gone forever. At the last minute, it caught the rope two feet before the kayak. Ellen had judged it perfectly, and the log was almost exactly centered under the line.

"Hold on now. Don't let go!" Ellen begged as she slid within just a few feet of the ledge. Holding onto the rope, which was now directly overhead, Ellen used her legs to drive the log wedge even closer to the kayak. Although her last set of kicks almost upset the weight balance and pulled everyone over the ledge, the simple physics principle worked. The wedge raised the angle of the bow above the portion of the ledge that had been gripping the kayak.

"Easy now. Easy," Ellen coaxed as they began to pull the kayak up and over the log and away from the ledge. "We're almost there. Easy, ladies."

"Where the hell do you see ladies?" Maria grinned, as the kayak slid the last few feet to safety. "We may be a lot of things now, but we're surer than shit not ladies anymore. Do I look like a lady to you?"

She was right. With her shattered glasses and mud-caked face, Maria and the other tired and tattered women were anything but ladies. They were anything but principals walking the halls of their schools. They had changed forever.

Though horribly pale, Angelo had come through the disaster otherwise unscathed. As Maria did her usual brush of his curly black locks and kiss of his forehead, his eyes opened ever so slightly. He tried to speak, but couldn't. At the corner of his mouth, though, the "ladies" could see the tiniest of smiles. He was still alive. Still fighting. "Hang in there," Maria whispered. "We're almost home."

Last Stand, Hand in Hand

The welcoming fire blazed brightly as the rescue team finally arrived at camp. Even through severe pain, O'Casey had managed to keep the fire alive. At one point, he had even dragged himself down the trail to find more wood to keep the Chief as warm and comfortable as possible.

Despite the dire conditions of all three men, there was almost a festive atmosphere as the women carefully dragged the kayak the final few yards down the trail and toward the fire. Ellen's embrace of O'Casey was that of a lover for her mate upon his return from a combat tour. Ellen's passion and enthusiasm caused O'Casey to shudder visibly from the pain caused by her embrace. "Oh, Sweetie, I'm so sorry! I keep forgetting about your leg and shoulder."

Unfortunately, there was still very serious business to be attended to at camp. Otherwise, Tiffany and Maria would have had fun with the "Oh, Sweetie" remark. Actually, they were thrilled that Ellen and O'Casey had found each other. Both were kind, loving, and yet lonely people suffering in private with their own past losses.

As Tiffany and Maria attended to Angelo to get him warm and dry, Ellen foraged for firewood. Even though she was within eyeshot of the fire and camp, as she ventured into the thickets and fir blowdowns to drag out wood, every dark form appeared to be a lurking bear. She had never forgotten that terrifying childhood experience of having a caged bear at the Bronx Zoo stand on his hind legs within a few feet of where she was leaning against the fence. It did not matter that the bear was old, rather friendly, and behind a tall protective barrier. All she could remember was this massive black demon. Until her dream while asleep next to O'Casey, she had hidden that memory, though not the fear, deep in the recesses of her subconscious. Even with all the bravery she had exhibited thus far on the trip, Ellen had to dig deep within herself to continue her work. Only thoughts of her sweetie and her friends back at camp, wet and shivering in the cool Maine air, kept her focused. "You're safe with me," Ellen kept repeating to herself. Those had been her mother's words as she led her away from the zoo. "You're safe with me."

Those words were more than just comfort. As Ellen tugged large sticks from the thicket to drag back to camp, she could almost hear the soft, smooth tone of her mother's voice and feel the touch of her warm, thin fingers squeezing her tiny hands tight. Ellen squeezed back instinctively. The reality of a lost fingernail and puncture marks and slivers in both hands brought her back to a painful reality. Yet, as she trudged slowly back to camp, limping in pain from the cuts on her knees and shins, the thought of her mother's comforting touch and supportive words made a forty-something woman feel, just for a moment, like a little girl who was now safe and heading home. "You're safe with me," she whispered.

The scene that greeted her back at camp was like a scene from a Matthew Brady Civil War photograph—three battered soldiers propped against a granite ledge facing the fire. It was difficult to tell who was dead and who was alive. Clearly, Angelo already appeared dead. The firelight made his gaunt, lifeless face look as though he were wearing a ghoulish Halloween mask. He had lost so much fluid from the vomiting and diarrhea that his skin looked like it had been hastily glued onto a bony frame. The once handsome man now leaned motionless against the one person he would love to have had as a soul mate.

The Chief, who had always been unaware of Angelo's deep affection for him, was now even unaware of his presence. The women had ministered to the Chief as well, putting him in a dry shirt and smoothing out his hair—or what was still visible over the bandage across his forehead. The slightly bloody bandage gave Butch the appearance of Henry Fleming, Crane's bloodied protagonist in *The Red Badge of Courage*. In spite of his injuries, the Chief looked otherwise in much better shape than when Tiffany and Ellen had dragged him from the rapids below the falls. Color had returned to his face, and the blue pallor on his lips and fingers had disappeared. He looked like a sleeping warrior. Ironically, this former history teacher, who still regaled students with narratives of the 20th

Maine and their bayonet charge that had saved the Union in the Battle of Gettysburg, often pictured himself in that same battle. Now, as he rested in the deepest of slumbers with a severe concussion and fractured skull, perhaps the Chief was dreaming of being that wounded warrior, suffering in silence with his comrades-in-arms, having courageously earned a true red badge of courage in a failed rescue mission.

The women did what needed to be done around the camp. Ellen knew that it would be a cool evening. The rain was gone now, and although the stars were out, the mist from the falls made everyone and everything damp. Per O'Casey's directive, they had brought only what they needed to survive. They had purposely left the tents and had brought only a few sleeping bags. Fortunately, they had decided to tie one large cooking pot into the aluminum canoe. That quick decision would perhaps help to save their lives. Jason had taken much of the good equipment, including a portable reverse-osmosis water pump that could make fresh water from a mud puddle if necessary. Given what had happened to Angelo, none of the campers would dare to drink the water at the base of the falls without boiling it first. Out of sight of the campers on the far bank lay the carcass of a dead deer, washed downstream after an attack by a pack of coyotes earlier in the week. It lay decomposing and awash in the backwater. Had the campers been able to see it, they would have been less anxious to test the rice and beans now cooking in the water Ellen had hauled up from the river. But that same pot would soon be boiling the water they would need to drink on their last leg of the trip.

Ellen made no attempt at creating any dinnertime panache as she served the beans and rice. How could she? This was a survival meal. Still, the four members of the tribe awake and able to eat, gobbled down the simple food with as much gusto as any of the magnificent meals O'Casey and the Chief had labored to prepare. Ellen had made a double batch, enough for eight, and every grain of rice, every single bean disappeared. They would need every calorie in the morning.

The few sleeping bags were completely unzipped and then spread out. Six campers faced the fire and their own thoughts and maladies. Angelo and the Chief leaned into each other in humble silence, unaware of their plight or those who had ministered to them. The Chief breathed in slowly, deeply, and regularly. Angelo's breathing, now shallow and barely noticeable, highlighted their respective conditions, as did his pallor, which was now completely ashen.

Maria had positioned herself next to the tenor she had harmonized with only a few nights before. How life had changed for all of them, she thought. She closed her eyes and dreamed of that moment by the fire singing her favorite arias with Angelo. She smiled to herself as she remembered the loons, as if in response to their human harmonies, singing to the dark Maine sky in a timeless eerie harmony of their own.

Ellen snuggled in next to O'Casey. She was more cautious now of his injuries, choosing to lean gently into his right side rather than into his dislocated shoulder and shattered leg. He wanted and needed Ellen with him—the large, lonely man sandwiched between his best friend, now resting silently in a coma, and a woman who made him feel alive again. He knew she could never replace his beloved Catherine. Still, as Ellen ever-so-gently squeezed his hand and snuggled in beside him, he felt a special warmth he never thought he would feel again. As he closed his eyes and listened to the pop and snap of the softwood fire, it felt good to be needed again. It felt good to be alive. He opened his eyes briefly and found Ellen staring at him.

She looked past the old scars on his face and the new cuts and gashes from the accident today. All she saw was a kind and good man whose face seemed to sparkle in the light of the fire. She loved what she saw. O'Casey smiled back and then fell into a deep sleep that only the pain of dawn could awaken.

Maria was the first to fall asleep and the first to wake up. In spite of trying to sleep sitting up against a granite ledge and squeezed between friends, everyone had slept soundly. Exhaustion and shock will do that. Only Ellen had gotten up during the night, and that was simply to keep the fire going. The fire was her job. That's what she told herself. And besides, she thought, if these people she cared so much about were to survive, it was the least she could do. Still, and in spite of her best efforts, there was only a smoldering hint of fire as Maria opened her eyes. In the cold predawn light, a thin grey serpent of smoke slithered from the smoldering embers. The weak light cast an eerie pall over the campsite.

Maria instinctively stretched to work the kinks out of her body. She touched something cold, yet all too familiar. She gave it a squeeze and no warmth came back. In silent horror, she turned toward Angelo. He was gone. Although his head was still leaning against the Chief's, she could tell from his cold, lifeless hand that he was dead. Hoping against hope, she leaned over and listened for breath. There was none. Not a trace. She looked down at his chest. There was no labored breathing as there had been when they tucked him in at night. There was no movement, no breathing at all. It was over. As tears rolled down from Maria's broad cheeks, she knew that Angelo had lost the battle she'd begged him to win. "Hang in there," she'd whispered to him in between her prayers.

She had no way of knowing that in a manner of speaking *his* prayers had been answered. Angelo had been praying, too. He could no longer bear the humiliation of having his friends hold him up and witness the storms of illness that ravaged his body. As he felt his life ebbing, he had prayed silently and continuously, not that he would live, but that he would die with dignity next to his friends.

As Maria leaned past Angelo's chest and looked down, she saw something amazing, something that showed her Angelo's prayers had been answered.

He and Butch were holding hands. She could not tell who had found the other, who had awakened ever so briefly. She could only imagine. Tears rolled off her cheeks and onto the hands now held fast and tight as Maria looked back at Angelo. There was a look of peace on his face. Though it carried the gray mask of death, it was no longer contorted, as it had been previously. He had gone quietly in the night, with dignity and surrounded by friends. Maria leaned back against the granite, sobbing as quietly as she could.

Gradually, the campers woke, one by one. Maria whispered the news and each in their own way had time to grieve, first Ellen, then Tiffany, and finally O'Casey. Sean Padraig O'Casey was devastated by the loss of his good friend. Unlike the women, he had known Angelo for years, almost as long as he had known the Chief. Before Matthew was born, O'Casey would often have Angelo accompany him to listen to Catherine's performances. While O'Casey loved opera only because that was what Catherine sang, the music spoke directly to Angelo's soul. Often, when O'Casey would look over during a complex and challenging aria, he would see Angelo weeping at the beauty, preciousness, and delicacy of the moment.

As O'Casey wept now, his thoughts turned to those moments, to Angelo and to Catherine. This was a loss on many levels. And somehow, too, O'Casey felt a personal responsibility for Angelo's death. What if he had not drunk the contaminated water? What if they had not missed the portage spot and had not gone over the falls? What if...? O'Casey wept without shame at a loss he could not begin to describe.

A Tough Good-bye

Tenderly, they lowered Angelo back into the kayak, much as he had been positioned on the portage. Ellen gently strapped his cold and stiffening body in with the same makeshift harness that had kept his body from falling from the ledge. She even made a soft pillow from a chamois shirt she plumped up and delicately slid beneath his coal-black curls. They now stood out in sharp relief against his white-gray skin. It was as though she was preparing his coffin.

As the tribe readied for their departure, each said his or her own personal good-bye. Even O'Casey, before hobbling with Ellen's assistance into the lead canoe, whispered a good-bye to his dear friend. "Ciao, buddy. Enjoy Venice. Say hi to Catherine and Matthew for me." The tears flowed softly down his face, past the scars both facial and emotional that he wore without shame.

Tiffany poured a last few potfuls of water onto the remains of the fire, which hissed angrily back at her. The steam and gradually disappearing smoke marked the last campfire the tribe would have as they pushed off from shore and headed for home. O'Casey sat partially propped up in the stern of the lead canoe. Although he could not paddle due to his dislocated shoulder, he had instructed Ellen to tie his paddle against the gunnel of the boat. This allowed him to be a modified stern man. While he could not paddle, he could at least be the rudder. It allowed Ellen to concentrate just on paddling. He couldn't stand the thought of being a useless lump. He had to do something, to be part of the rescue in some way.

The second canoe rode much lower in the water. Unfortunately, the tribe was forced to use Jason Foxworthy's clunky aluminum canoe, as the Chief's prized L.L. Bean canoe had not survived the falls. In most situations, it would certainly have been a preferable to the aluminum canoe. However, Foxworthy's boat was wider and longer than O'Casey's canoe—qualities the rescue team now needed. The women had pulled the canoe almost into the camp, lowered the Chief into the bottom of it, and then gently slid it down the slight grade and into the water. Maria took the bow and Tiffany took the stern. This would not be an easy trip for either woman. They were not only going to have to paddle a poorly designed canoe twelve miles down Granite Lake with a two-hundred-pound man resting in the bottom, they were also going to be dragging the kayak as well.

O'Casey had begged the women to leave Angelo at camp. "We'll have a rescue party get him later today. That's what he would want. He wouldn't want you to risk your lives for him."

But the women would hear none of it. They refused even to consider it. Each had a different reason. Maria, the caretaker, couldn't imagine leaving this beautiful, kind man alone in death, any more than she would have left his side when he was ill. Ellen thought of Sean and how she'd feel if he had died and the tribe wanted to leave him. *Never!* she thought to herself. All Tiffany could think of was Jason and the bear. She knew deep in her heart that she had heard a scream along with the gunshot. All she could imagine was a bear—or a pack of coyotes—coming for Angelo's body. The thought of his body being savaged by animals was more than she could tolerate.

As Tiffany stepped into the canoe, she felt the heft of the large sheath knife O'Casey had asked her to wear. It felt awkward, cold, and primitive. It was something she would never have imagined as part of her attire—it was the antithesis of a debutante's accessorizing. Still, with thoughts of the bear fresh in her mind and the tremendous respect she had for O'Casey, she moved the knife further back onto her hip and shoved off.

The tribe paddled carefully through a single set of small rapids and then into the slow-moving current where the river opened into the lake.

Tiffany cautiously turned her head to see how the kayak was tracking behind her and noticed something disturbing. There were a number of significant cracks in the kayak just at the waterline. She couldn't see any holes and didn't remember seeing any when she was hauling the kayak through the twilight of the portage path. But she didn't know about all the times that Jason had allowed the kayak to crash into trees with Angelo still on board.

She also didn't know about the serious, potentially fatal damage to the kayak that was making its presence felt just *below* the waterline. The cracks in the lower hull began to seep with water—not big leaks, but a small and steady stream that would soon have dire consequences for the tribe.

In the lead canoe, O'Casey struggled to find a comfortable position to use his free right hand to work the makeshift rudder. Ellen, though a good athlete and a willing paddler, struggled to handle the significant task before her. She needed to place one power stroke after another to keep the canoe moving forward against the slight morning breeze and the modest chop on the lake.

While the weather was infinitely better than it had been the day before, it did not lend itself well to a rescue. Thick morning fog draped itself along the shoreline. O'Casey was not certain if it extended completely across the lake, but he couldn't take the chance.

He had decided they would follow the long shoreline and head toward the East Branch dam where the Chief and Jason had parked their vehicles. It would be a long, mean paddle. Sean had hoped that a fisherman out trolling the lake would find them and go for help, or perhaps an early summer resident might be at one of the few cottages on this side of the lake. Since there was no landlines and phone service on this, the less popular and populated size of the lake, he did not hold out much hope in that regard, nor was there a cell tower. He was also not very optimistic about meeting a fisherman. The fog was thick enough this early in the morning that a fisherman would have to be trolling within a hundred yards of the tribe to see or hear them. No, O'Casey concluded, they would probably have to rescue themselves.

Ellen leaned into every stroke, knowing that the sooner they arrived at the landing, the more likely the Chief might live. She was also very concerned about her big Irishman. He was beginning to develop a pale, somewhat gaunt look to his face, much as Angelo had shortly after he got sick. She was also very concerned about his injuries. She had managed to fashion a better sling for his dislocated shoulder. Although he almost never complained about the pain, she could tell, as she worked on the sling, that it hurt even more this morning than it had the day before. She also noticed how swollen and bruised his entire shoulder now looked.

His leg was even worse and far more painful. Ellen was surprised that she could even work to dress the wound, given her aversion to such gruesome sights. The femur protruding from O'Casey's thigh made her cringe. She wanted to turn away but knew she couldn't. This was her *sweetie*. Taking one deep breath after another, she gently wiped away the small amount of blood and tiny bits of bone and debris that still littered the wound. She talked quietly to O'Casey to distract him. Each time Ellen thought of the wound's grisly appearance and the graying tone of O'Casey's face, she leaned harder into her strokes.

For the women, the slow cadence of canoe strokes was much like the slow dance on the portage trail, replete with pain. Now, unfortunately, it was a different kind of pain—a brutal, steady pain. Ellen suffered the most, with an array of friction burns, lacerations, and, of course, the exposed bed of her missing fingernail. Somehow, though, she managed a smile as she turned back toward O'Casey.

The single wink he returned filled her heart with a joy she had not known in years. Here was a man dealing with life-threatening injuries, yet somehow finding the will to send a wink and a smile through his pain.

O'Casey ruddered the canoe remarkably well with his right hand high on the top of his jury-rigged paddle. When he needed the bow to move to port or starboard, he deftly pulled or pushed on the paddle. Sooner or later the bow would come around, not because of, but almost in spite of Ellen's paddling efforts. What she lacked in skill, she was making up for in a steady and determined cadence.

The aluminum canoe did not fare nearly as well, in spite of the two paddlers. The one advantage the boat had was that it was wide enough and long enough that the Chief could rest comfortably in the bottom and still leave room for Maria in the bow and Tiffany in the stern. Unfortunately, it had no keel whatsoever. It tracked badly. In spite of Tiffany's best efforts to J-stroke from the stern, the canoe moved in a continual snaking pattern. Because Maria was so short, she could not get much of the paddle into the water, nor could she exert any leverage on her strokes. And as she got tired, her paddling got worse. The more tired she got, the more frequently her fingers and paddle banged against the gunnels. The clanking was beginning to annoy Tiffany, as each stroke became like a set of fingernails on a chalkboard.

Had Tiffany not been a superbly conditioned athlete, the entire rescue would have been a pointless exercise. Ellen and Maria could never have done the work alone, in spite of their staunch character and determination. However, as with the portage, Tiffany could feel herself reaching a point of exhaustion as she fought the S-curve swings of the canoe, which seemed to be getting worse.

The processional slowed and stopped far more frequently than O'Casey would have wished. However, it was he who usually ordered the pauses. While he could rarely turn enough to see Tiffany's canoe, he could quickly tell when she was getting too far behind. He knew how imperative it was that they stick together. They had lost several of the life jackets in the crash and in the portage, and one had been cut up to serve as his leg splint. The women had insisted that Sean and the Chief, given their conditions, wear two of the remaining jackets. That left both Ellen and Tiffany without jackets in the event of a capsize. O'Casey could not let that happen. While it would have been quicker to canoe directly toward the landing, it would mean going well out into the lake and through the fog. His good compass had been lost when they went over the falls, and he couldn't risk guessing at the direct route if the fog held. So they followed the shore in a slow and painful parade that was getting slower by the minute.

Tiffany had hoped to J stroke most of the time—stroking primarily from her right side and her dominant arm. With the snaking movement of the canoe getting worse, due to the pull of the kayak they towed, Tiffany had to alternate strokes in a dance of two strokes to the right and one to the left. The large hunting knife on her left hip had initially been a serious and painful annoyance. With every stroke to the left, the sheath would dig into her thigh. After a while, however, Tiffany not only got used to its presence, it became a badge of honor. The knife became a symbol for her, a symbol of who she was, of who she had become. It was a mantle of the wilderness, a mantle of leadership that O'Casey had bestowed on her.

"Keep this close. Don't lose it. Don't drop it overboard!" O'Casey had warned, though she was not sure why. He didn't even tell her why she might want the knife. Still, she wore it on her hip with a strange sense of pride she had not anticipated. She was no longer some "freakin' debutante princess," as she had once been called by a boy she had broken up with in her freshman year. She had understood and resented the remark but sadly felt it was true.

And now, as she sat exhausted in the stern of a cheap Sears Roebuck canoe, with filthy stringy hair, a ripped shirt, and teeth that had not been brushed in God knows how long, she looked down at an old sheath knife and squeezed its thick deer antler handle. She had never even seen what the blade looked like, nor did she much care. She was the person five other adults were counting on to be their rescuer. Not because of her father's money or her mother's pushy influence. Not because of her college diploma or the building there that bore her grandfather's name. It was because she had saved two lives already. It was because she could canoe almost as well as the Chief. It was because O'Casey had believed in her and given her the knife and because she had two friends now in Ellen and Maria that she could not and would not let down.

O'Casey could sense that he and Ellen were pulling too far ahead of the other canoe. He figured it would be a good time to circle back and check on everyone face to face. He was increasingly uncomfortable about trying to lead a group he could barely hear and could not see. For a moment, everything seemed to stand still. The morning fog had suddenly gotten thicker, temporarily separating the two canoes. Tiffany had been deep in her own thoughts of her past. Maria, head down, was just trying to survive each paddle stroke, determined not to smash her knuckles one more time against the hull. Ellen, too, was almost in a trance, suffering in silence, listening to a distant loon, and drifting back to thoughts of her mother and her comforting words.

For one brief moment, the two canoes seemed miles apart rather than a few hundred yards. The mysterious thing about fog is that it distorts both sound and light. Suddenly, everyone seemed to be yelling at once. And everyone had a different suggestion about where to paddle.

Only O'Casey's instincts prevented a disaster. "Left paddle! Left paddle!" he yelled. It seemed like minutes, though it was only seconds, before their canoe was headed back toward the shouts and the sound of the aluminum canoe. It was Maria's paddle clunking against the hull that helped O'Casey the most. "Paddle! Paddle!" O'Casey commanded, not minding that he was being bossy. They had to link up with the rest of the tribe...now.

Just as quickly as they were lost, they were found. Maria's clunking paddle had proved a far better bell buoy than all the shouts dissipating in the fog. There they were—first Maria waving her paddle with enthusiasm at seeing Ellen. Then Tiffany waved and gestured, "Whew!" as she wiped her forehead in mock terror and relief. The tribe reunited in joy momentarily, each person talking faster than the next. It was as if they had disappeared for days rather than seconds.

Suddenly, O'Casey screamed, "The kayak! What's wrong with the kayak? Ellen, paddle! Hurry! Hurry! Paddle!" He was screaming now, barking orders as though they were in the middle of a class five rapids. They were getting closer to the aluminum canoe, passing on its left side and heading back toward the kayak. As everyone turned in response to the shouts, they could quickly see why he was panicked. The kayak was about to sink. Although Ellen and O'Casey's canoe was only twenty feet from the kayak and closing, Sean knew that it and his good friend were doomed. The kayak's bow was already under water and the cockpit was flooding fast. The underwater leaks in the bow had silently and slowly filled the kayak to a point of no return.

"Cut the rope! Cut the rope, Tiffany! Cut the fucking rope!" O'Casey screamed in uncharacteristic fury. It was all Tiffany could hear and all she could react to as she grabbed at the hunting knife dangling from her hip. Clumsily, she sawed at the rope. She could feel the increased tension on the line as she sawed and sawed. It was not cutting fast enough. Her hand, already cramped from paddling was now trying to perform a task it did not seem to understand. She renewed her grip on the knife with both hands and sawed frantically.

"Hurry, Tiffany! Hurry!" Ellen yelled as she paddled with all her might toward the sinking kayak. She understood O'Casey's fear, since she was the one closest to the kayak. If it went down with the lines still attached, it would also capsize the canoe, and with it, Maria, Tiffany, and a helpless Chief. All three might die, particularly now that they had strayed from a shore that was completely out of sight in the fog. Ellen reached out for the kayak. For just a second, she grabbed at the slippery hull but there was nothing to hold onto—nothing to stop its momentum.

It was not a high-end kayak with lots of bow flotation. Ellen had bought it at a yard sale with a caveat from the owner that it was a strictly calm-water kayak. "Be careful," the owner had said. Now Ellen knew why. As the kayak, now completely filled with water, began its slow descent to the bottom of the lake, Ellen quickly searched for Angelo. As Tiffany sawed through the last fibers of the bow line, the kayak slid faster and faster below the water. For just a moment, O'Casey, too, could see the cockpit and the face of his dead comrade, strapped into the boat and rapidly being covered with water.

In that moment, O'Casey stared in disbelief at the gaunt white face and curly black locks as they slid beneath the water... and then Angelo was gone.

The severed bow line slithered briefly across the surface, and then it, too, was sucked into the small vortex to join Angelo, sliding silently and peacefully to the bottom of Granite Lake.

Thank God for Beautiful Days and Noisy Motors

No one moved. Nothing moved. Even the slight morning breeze seemed to pause to reflect on Angelo's passage. Tiffany, in particular, stared fixedly at the hole in the water where the kayak had been. Distant loons, as if on cue, seemed to bemoan the loss of the opera singer. Slowly, deeply, they shared their ancient harmony across the lake, one deep, slow wail to another.

Then a soft sweet series of hoots and warbles glided smoothly through the fog. Along with the new sound slid the beautiful black head and deep red eyes of a female loon proudly swimming with her new chick riding high on her back for a first tour of the lake. The tribe, so shaken by the loss of Angelo, sat motionless and weeping silently in their grief, reflection, and respect. The mother loon, unshaken by the sight of two canoes emerging from the fog, changed her song slightly, along with her direction. As she glided silently within thirty feet of the tribe, she paused for a moment with her chick still proudly riding in the hollow between her thick folded wings. The loon stopped as though to inspect the tribe and count the heads of those present and those missing. She called out to her mate in a long purposeful warble, and slid like an apparition back into the thick white blanket of mist.

Like Angelo, she was gone in an instant, but the memory of that moment would last forever.

Even with the tragic loss of a friend, the beauty of the wilderness and magnificence of the moment broke the tension and helped uplift the spirits of the tribe. "It's time to go. Let's take the Chief home," O'Casey whispered.

Following his gentle directive, Ellen took the first hard stroke of her paddle to head the tribe east along the shore.

Tiffany's hands were still shaking from having cut the bow line of the kayak free. The bulging mass of knots she had clumsily tied when the tribe first set off in the morning stared back at her like a green snake as it twisted around the thwart of the canoe refusing to budge. The frayed line below the knot dangled pointlessly over the side. Tiffany picked up the stag-handled knife that had saved their lives, wiped it off on her tattered jeans, and shoved it in the tired leather sheath. As she did so, she gave it a friendly little pat as if to say, "Thanks. O'Casey knew you'd come in handy."

Lost in their individual grief, no one talked. The silence allowed even the faintest, distant sounds to loom large. The rattle of chain saws sang their metallic song, buzzing and whining in the deep woods as loggers slowly began their day's work. Occasionally, the tribe could hear the chug of kickers—the small trolling motors Maine guides preferred as they worked the far side of the lake looking for salmon.

Mostly, however, the tribe listened to their own sounds. Sounds of deep breathing as each sought to calm down from the sorrow they'd experiences as they watched the most special of friends disappear slowly, almost mystically, beneath the waves. With the kayak no longer a drag on their efforts, Tiffany and Maria slid stroke for stroke alongside Ellen's canoe. No one wanted to be alone. Tiffany, especially, did not want to risk getting lost in the fog again—not for a second.

With that additional weight off their canoe, Maria no longer felt the tremendous strain to put one power stroke after another into her emotionally driven effort to save Angelo. Now, she began to relax and concentrate on, rather than fight, each stroke. The silence of the morning made it even more imperative that she stop the constant scrape and bang of her paddle along the metal gunnel. It not only hurt her knuckles, it hurt her pride even more. She felt as though each scrape or clank announced her clumsiness, not just to the tribe, but to the Maine wilderness: "Here comes that fat Mexican girl who can't even paddle a canoe."

Although she feigned confidence with her ever-present smile and kind demeanor, her self-deprecating humor belied her true opinion of herself. The silence was too precious, she felt, to ruin it with each clunking stroke. She focused and practiced. *I can learn this*, she said to herself. *Focus. Don't let your elbow touch your body. If it can't touch your body, the paddle can't scrape the hull*, she reminded herself. First one, then two, then three silent, skillful strokes. Maria was getting it! Four, five, six strokes, then a little scrape. Focus! she commanded herself again as the success of perfect stroke after perfect stroke began to build. She could now hear not just her own breathing, but also the Chief breathing behind her. She could hear the water chortling under the hull and the swish of her paddle as it finished a stroke. She could even hear the other paddle strokes and sounds that had been hidden from her before.

Even with the loss of her sweet friend Angelo, Maria began to feel a quiet peace in what the Irish call a "soft morning." The cool mist of the fog now felt good, clean, and very calming on her smooth round cheeks.

The canoes rounded a long point of land and were now at what O'Casey surmised was the halfway point. "Just two or three more hours and we'll be done," he announced.   Maria gripped down on her paddle. *I think I can. I think I can*, the little engine said to herself as a delicate morning breeze began to blow softly into her smiling face.

Suddenly, she felt a strange vibration near her chest. *What was that?* Was she having a heart attack? She felt it again. What *was* that? Her brain raced to detect whether it was something happening within her body, or possibly a new threat to their survival. "Oh my God. It's my phone!" she shouted to herself.

"What? What did you say?" Tiffany looked up at her in amazement.

"It's my cell phone. We must have tower. I turned it back on when I got into the canoe just in case we ever got a signal. It vibrates like this when I have messages. I don't know who called, and I don't care. It means that we can call out!"

Within seconds she had dialed and reached a 911 operator. "We need help! Angelo's dead. Jason may be dead, also. We think he was killed by a bear. The Chief is in a coma. O'Casey's leg is broken. We need help. We need help....

"Yes, I'm serious! We need help. He's dying.... He may be dying." Maria choked back the tears and panic as she began to lose her temper with the incredulous operator. "No, I don't know where we are. It's some big lake in the Maine woods. O'Casey, tell her where we are! Don't hang up, lady. Please don't hang up!" Maria pleaded.

Once Ellen could get the canoe alongside, O'Casey took the phone and quickly and confidently convinced the operator that they were in distress and that Granville Chapman, a high school principal at Welton Academy, age fifty-one, probably had a subdural hematoma and was in a coma. They were in T6 R7 on the south shore of Granite Lake, about halfway between the falls below Wilson Stream and the dam at the East Branch of the Pentocket River landing.

The operator assured O'Casey that medical help would be dispatched to the landing. She would also see if there was a game warden's or State Police boat anywhere near the area that could be launched at the landing.

"We're going to be just fine. Help is on the way!" O'Casey smiled with almost indescribable relief. "Hey, Chief!" he shouted. "You're going to be OK. We're taking you home."

As Maria turned to look into the bottom of the boat, she couldn't believe her eyes. The Chief first opened one eye and then the other. He smiled ever so slightly and raised the index finger on his right hand as if to say, "I heard you. I'm OK." He closed his eyes and went back to sleep.

"He's awake! He's OK. I just saw him smile. He's going to be OK," Maria repeated over and over. Then suddenly the tears began to roll down her cheeks—tears of joy, tears of relief, tears of sadness, tears of fatigue. She was smiling for all to see but the tears filled her face. They filled her very being. Her face was a rainbow of sorts in its natural contrasts. Like the juxtaposition of rain and sunshine, her smile was a perfect counterpoint to the tears rolling down her cheeks and chin. She laughed as she cried, knowing full well how silly she probably looked. She didn't care. Maria knew she was with her family now. They had fully accepted the short, fat Latina with the kinky hair and dark skin. She didn't need to leave the lake to be at home. Here she sat, crying in the bow of a canoe she had somehow finally learned how to conquer. She looked down at the Chief, up at Tiffany, and then over to Ellen and O'Casey. She loved her new family. She loved the tribe and was so very proud to be one of its members.

The warmth of the June sun and the light morning breeze blew the last remnants of the fog away from the shore. The surface of the water suddenly sparkled into a million crystal mirrors, each reflecting the gathering colors of the summer day. The tribe stared down the lake as the last vestige of the fog dissipated in the breeze. Less than two hundred yards away, a fisherman and his grandson were trolling in a classic Penn

Yan lapstrake runabout. The grandfather was glad his Minnetonka trolling motor was so quiet, but there were times when he wished for more noise to drown out his grandson's endless stream of chatter and questions.

"Hey, Grampy. There's some fat lady in a canoe waving at us. She must know you, 'cause she's waving like crazy. How come you know *everyone*, Grampy? How come? How come?"

And that is how they were rescued, this strange amalgam of warriors and wounded. After first loading Butch and O'Casey into the boat, the grandfather had to remind his grandson to stop asking questions and help the ladies into the boat. "These here fellas look pretty new ta campin'," the old man said with his classic Maine accent and sense of the obvious. "Next time, ah'd take 'em ta L.L. Bean. Heard they got a pretty good program for outta statahs learnin' how ta camp. You ladies done good. Finest kind, helpin' them menfolk out," the old man said as he looked again in disbelief at the two seriously injured men leaning in obvious pain against each other.

With that, he tied the canoes off in tandem from the stern, fired up the old Johnson 30 horsepower instead of the trolling motor, and they sped off.

By the time they arrived at the East Branch landing, the ambulance was already there. The EMTs immediately put the Chief on a backboard and had an IV in his arm even before they put him in the ambulance. They then worked on O'Casey, placing an air cast on his entire right leg. Soon he was on a stretcher himself. "You're going to be fine, Sweetie…I love you," Ellen whispered in his ear. *There, it's been said,* she smiled to herself.

As the EMTs began to wheel O'Casey toward the ambulance doors, Ellen caught the eye one last time of this special man who had so radically changed her life. He looked up, smiled, and mouthed the words, "I love you, too." Just as the EMTs were closing the doors, O'Casey turned to his ambulance mate and squeezed the Chief's hand.

In another second, there was a cloud of pale white dust as the ambulance drove away, lights flashing. The fisherman and his grandson climbed back in their boat and headed out to drown some more worms.

The dust settled, the drone of the outboard faded, and the women were alone.

* * *

After a prolonged, almost awkward silence, Tiffany asked quietly, "What the hell happened?"

"What do you mean?" Ellen asked with a puzzled look. "They're gone. Headed to the hospital."

"No, not them. Us. What happened to all of us? Less than a week ago we were leaving this parking lot just as the sun was coming up. You and I were dressed more for a college reunion than a week in the woods. There were seven of us here, loading gear, goofing around, getting to know each other. Now look at us—just three of us standing here. Two good friends are headed to the hospital. Another is dead. And Jason was probably breakfast for a bear. And look at us. *Us.* We're still standing, but we look like shit! We're tattered, torn, and…and…we're sisters," Tiffany smiled.

They turned and headed slowly toward the Chief's SUV, walking arm in arm across the dusty landing. Each marveled silently at some version of the same thing—who they had been just a week ago and who they had become.

Maria quietly hummed her favorite *Phantom* aria as she thought once more of Angelo. She turned and took a long last look at Granite Lake and thought about the images and sounds that would stay with her forever.

As they reached the parking area, a lone yellow jacket noisily buzzed its way into an empty Coors can in the bed of Jason's pickup. Less than a week ago, but what seemed like an eternity, Jason had tossed it away just as the sun was rising on the lake, and the group was heading off from the parking lot to begin their adventure. "Breakfast," he had smiled, nodding toward the just finished beer can still rattling against the truck bed. Then he had slid into the back seat right next to Tiffany. He had patted her on the thigh and announced with a cocky grin, "This is going to be a *great* trip."

Now, as they pulled away from the landing in the Chief's black Jeep, Tiffany glanced at the rear view mirror. A thin film of pale yellow dust had settled on Jason's rusty Ford pickup sitting alone at the edge of the woods.

In the distance, a happy grandfather turned his grandson's Red Sox cap sideways. He smiled and said a silent prayer for a beautiful day and a noisy motor.

EPILOGUE

Tiffany was not sure what to find or expect as she tiptoed into the hospital room. While hospitals were not her favorite places, she had learned that her tolerance for what was uncomfortable had changed forever. She had not seen all her friends together since the door had closed on the ambulance and O'Casey and the Chief roared off for Bangor General almost two weeks before. Now here she was, about to see them all for the first time since then. As she poked her head around the door, it seemed more like a fiesta than a recovery room.

Maria had bribed almost everyone with her smiles, her positivity... and her homemade enchiladas. Hanging from an empty IV stand was a large green and red burro piñata. She knew it was tacky. That was the whole point. Maria could not stand the thought of two men she loved being in a room that didn't shout out happiness and celebration.

The piñata and an oversized sombrero decorating the other side of the room stood in stark contrast to the medical paraphernalia elsewhere. O'Casey's leg seemed elevated in traction halfway to the ceiling, mostly due to his long legs and the remarkably complex traction apparatus. An IV hung from behind his bed and draped down into his right arm. His hand was in a near death grip...as Ellen squeezed it with all her might, as she had been doing all morning. Her radiant glow and broad smile told Tiffany more about the medical situation than all the charts in Bangor General. The guys were going to be fine. They were safe. They were home. So was she.

Tiffany glanced at the Chief. He seemed hooked up to almost every machine one could imagine—EKG and EEG monitors, other devices, lines, and cables—the works. His appearance was even more bizarre. He had two black eyes and bruising on the entire right side of his face. His head was almost completely wrapped in gauze. He looked more like a mummy in a monster movie than the confident and cocky Chief who had talked so enthusiastically about the Maine woods. Still, he was awake and smiling. How could he not be, with Maria at his side chatting away and stroking the back of his neck, which was about the only spot of uncovered skin?

"Yee-freakin'-hah! You're here! We've just been talking about you," Maria grinned with her usual energy and exuberance.

"I hope it's good. I know I almost failed *Cutting and Sawing the Rope One-oh-One.*"

"Funny you should mention that, Tiffany," O'Casey said with a wink. "We've actually been talking about you for the last *few* days. All of us thought you were going to be such a huge drag on the trip. We knew we were going to be stuck with Jason. We were glad when you said you were coming, just so you'd keep Jason occupied and not let him ruin our trip. When I saw you step out of his truck that morning, I thought, 'Oh great—Barbie and Ken in the Maine woods. We've got Little Miss Perfect, and she'll cry when she ruins her pedicure.'"

"Boy, were we wrong!" Ellen chimed in. "You saved our lives, all of us, one rescue after another. None of us would be here without you."

For a second, each member of the tribe recalled the incidents of Tiffany's bravery and determination, from the water rescues of Jason and the Chief, to the portage, and to cutting the kayak line at the last moment to save everyone in the canoe.

"And besides that," Maria said, trying to lighten the moment. "Besides that, I now have a new sister—two in fact." She turned and smiled at Ellen as well. "I think we could all pass for sisters, triplets maybe, don't you?"

O'Casey looked first at short dark Maria and then at tall blonde Tiffany, and began to roar with laughter. "More like *twins*, I think! You and Tiffany could pass as twins and you could just say that Ellen was adopted!" The harder he laughed, the more the traction apparatus shook and the more pain it caused. "Ouch! Ouch! Stop being so funny. It's killing me here."

And with that the tribe laughed even harder.

After a minute, Ellen spoke up. "Tiffany, we have a couple of presents for you. Bonwit Teller was closed for renovations so we had to improvise." She handed Tiffany a beautifully wrapped box with streaming strands of blue and white ribbon.

Tiffany opened the box gently, wanting to preserve the moment that much longer. She pulled out a Ralph Lauren sweater-sized box and took the cover off. As she delicately pushed back the tissue paper, she had to chuckle. There sat a large rubber hunting knife and plastic sheath, looking every bit like the one O'Casey had given her, which still sat in a corner of her closet. The rest of the tribe laughed with her.

"This is so you'll have your own knife," O'Casey said. "I want you to practice your cutting skills and thought this would be perfect. Also, if you wanted to come over and play Davy Crocket with us sometime, we thought it would help to accessorize your outfit."

Tiffany loved the present. She knew it was a metaphor on many levels, both teasing her for her fashion-conscious dumb-blonde image, and congratulating her for the bravery and leadership she had shown in her rescue of the tribe.

"Here!" Butch whispered. "There's one more present. This is my gift to you."

As Tiffany drew near, Maria held out her hand. Tiffany looked at Butch, whose eyes welled with tears. "You earned this," he said.

Tiffany reached forward and Maria dropped into her palm a small patch of green cloth with red embroidery. As she flipped the cloth over and saw what it was, her eyes, too, filled up with tears. The patch simply said *Master Maine Guide*. It was the Chief's patch. It was his favorite possession. It was who he was.

"You earned this, *Chief*," Butch repeated with his trademark grin.

The new Chief was speechless. This small, worn piece of cloth meant more to her than all the clothing, jewelry, and trips she had ever been given. More even than her college diploma or the new BMW convertible her grandfather had given her on graduation day. This little green patch had been given as a gift from the heart and not the wallet. It was who Tiffany had become and who she wanted to be. As she smiled through her tears, she looked at each of them and whispered, "I love you guys." And as an afterthought to lighten the moment, she grinned, "And this is the best tribe I've ever joined."

Every member of the tribe nodded in agreement. For each of them it had been a defining point in their lives. None of them would ever be the same person who had talked eagerly or skeptically of a trip to the Maine woods over a drink at the Black Rose Pub that night. The trip had just happened, mostly as the result of the Chief's passionate talk about trout, moose, and fireside serenades by the loons. Two of the seven who formed a tribe that night did not come out of the woods alive. Neither O'Casey nor the Chief would ever look quite the same way again. Each would sport new scars, both physical and emotional. They would never view the woods, the rivers, or the loons in quite the same way again, either.

However, it was the women who had *really* been changed by the trip. Ellen, a fragile, introspective woman, still grieving for a mother who had died many years before, had learned to let go of the past and to build on a confidence she had rarely displayed or knew that she had. More importantly, however, she had found a rare, deep love with a man too familiar with tragedy and death, and with whom she'd been mysteriously united by a moonlit campfire. He, too, had learned to leave the past behind and to celebrate a new life, a new world, and a new love.

Maria no longer needed self-deprecation to make friends. Her body, appearance, and ethnicity would not change. However, she would no longer need to make fun of who she was to find friendship. She had true friends now who not only accepted her but embraced her. Like the others, she had learned much about the woods and about herself. She could portage and paddle. She could build a fire or nurse an ill friend. Mostly, she had so loved her duets with Angelo that she would sing every day and celebrate memories that would endure forever.

As she looked down at Granville Butch Chapman, she had no idea whether she might have found her first true love or whether the woods, the streams, or even another woman would steal him away. She didn't know and at that point didn't care. She looked over at the piñata and thought of next year and just maybe a Cinco de Mayo spent together.

Tiffany held her patch reverently. She looked down at the funny rubber knife. The gifts were a metaphor of the person she had become. The tribe had been right. She had been a blonde debutante expecting a Ralph Lauren sweater in a Ralph Lauren box. While she might still wear such sweaters on occasion, she knew that everything else about her would change. Maybe she would become an Outward Bound instructor.

There was something about the woods and the wilderness that spoke to her in a voice she had never heard. It was not even so much about being outside. It was simply that people she had hardly known had trusted her with their lives and that she had saved not just one, but all of them. It was a sacred trust they had given to her. The girl who'd been voted "least likely to succeed" in the woods of Maine had not only succeeded, she had prevailed against incredible odds.

"Sorry to be the party pooper here, but there's something important we need to discuss," O'Casey announced. "Tiffany, our lost friend is back here with us." He gestured toward a simple blue urn sitting on the table behind Ellen. "The game wardens' dive team found the kayak and our good friend Angelo. Wardens also found a few bones and pieces of a shirt they believe were what's left of Jason ... but that's another story."

"Tiffany," Maria continued, "we'd like to spread some of Angelo's ashes in Tuscany, a place he had always wanted to visit, and...and...and along the shore of Wilson Lake where Angelo and I sang our duet. We think that's what he would want and where he'd be happiest."

"Will you join us? For both trips?" Ellen asked.

There was a long, long pause. Tiffany stroked the patch. She looked over at the blue marble urn and back at her friends.

"Sure," she smiled. "Sure."

Acknowledgements

The author wishes to thank John Archibald, the first teacher who encouraged me to write and to Professor Leo O'Connor for inspiring my interest in being an English teacher. Thanks to the sixth graders at Manchester Memorial School for bugging me to write chapter after chapter. I'm glad you liked the trout that got away. Genie Daily, thanks for your great edit work. You were right . . . and Rebecca, you were right about the bear. Finally, thanks to my wife Anne for listening to page after page of unedited work—that's loyalty.

Thank you, Nana and Pop for teaching me, "Never ever, ever underestimate the value of a single act of kindness."

Erin, Ryan, and Maggie, I love being your dad.